THE YEAR THE CLOUD FELL

THE YEAR THE CLOUD FELL

Kurt R. A. Giambastiani

A ROC BOOK

ROC
Published by New American Library, a division of
Penguin Putnam Inc., 375 Hudson Street,
New York, New York 10014, U.S.A.
Penguin Books Ltd, 27 Wrights Lane,
London W8 5TZ, England
Penguin Books Australia Ltd, Ringwood,
Victoria, Australia
Penguin Books Canada Ltd, 10 Alcorn Avenue,
Toronto, Ontario, Canada M4V 3B2
Penguin Books (N.Z.) Ltd, 182–190 Wairau Road,
Auckland 10, New Zealand

Penguin Books Ltd, Registered Offices:
Harmondsworth, Middlesex, England

First published by Roc, an imprint of New American Library,
a division of Penguin Putnam Inc.

The Year the Cloud Fell
ISBN 0-7394-1744-4

PUBLISHER'S NOTE
This is a work of fiction. Names, characters, places, and incidents either
are the product of the author's imagination or are used fictitiously,
and any resemblance to actual persons, living or dead, business
establishments, events, or locales is entirely coincidental.

To Ilene
Thanks for looking up.

ACKNOWLEDGMENTS

It is with great humility that I acknowledge the primary source of inspiration and power for this novel: the Cheyenne people. Their culture, laws, wisdom, spirituality, and continued perseverance in the face of genocidal actions of the United States government cannot fail but inspire any who learn of them. I have endeavored throughout the creation of this work to respect the traditions and wishes of the Cheyenne. As a result, I have incorporated none of the specifics of their sacred traditions and songs, except those that they themselves have seen fit to share with the outside world. The rest is theirs and theirs alone.

I would like to thank the linguists and scholars of the Cheyenne language who have made their work available to me. Their materials have provided a deeper insight into the Cheyenne people.

Thanks also go to my agent, Eleanor Wood, for her steadfast belief in my abilities, and to my family and friends who have given me great assurance and assistance with their ongoing support.

And finally, I would like to acknowledge the aid and encouragement of my wife, who suffered along with me during the time it took to bring this story to the page.

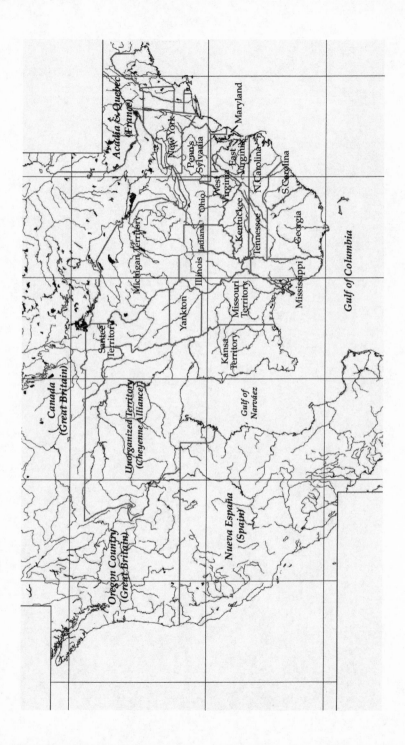

Canada
(Great Britain)

Santee Territory

Unorganized Territory
(Cheyenne Alliance)

Oregon Country
(Great Britain)

Michigan Territory

Yankton

Kansa Territory

Missouri Territory

Nueva España
(Spain)

Gulf of Narváez

Acadia & Quebec
(France)

New York

Penn's Sylvania

Maryland

West Virginia

East Virginia

Ohio

Indiana

Illinois

Kentuckee

Tennessee

N. Carolina

S. Carolina

Georgia

Mississippi

Gulf of Columbia

PROLOGUE

Moon When Ice Starts to Form
Forty-One Years After the Star Fell
Camp of Closed Windpipe Band, Red
Paint River

Outside the lodge, the crier's words carried through the chill evening air. "One Bear calls you. Everyone to One Bear's lodge. Speaks While Leaving is a woman today."

Speaks While Leaving could hear the people of the camp as they gathered. She heard the crunch and creak of their feet in the winter's first snow. She heard the smiles in their greetings and heard the tall pride in her father's answers to their questions. Inside, she felt the beat of her mother's drumskin like the pulse that lived beneath her flesh. She felt the heat of the fire before her and the cold of winter where it crept in under the lodge skins and touched her legs and back.

She stood naked before the fire as the elder women of her family prepared her. Her aunt combed her unbraided hair, still wet from her bath in the dark waters of the Red Paint River. Her grandmother mixed the red clay with which she would paint her granddaughter's entire body. Red, to swathe her in the color of warmth and home, the color of blood, to mark her in her first moon-time. The dusty smell of the paint mingled with the tang of smoke; earth and fire dancing in the air.

Her mother, Magpie Woman, sang as she thumped the taut circle of whistler hide against the heel of her hand. The drum rang. The song was a simple one, the melody rising up in anticipation and joy.

Behold her!
Behold the newest woman in the world.

On the bed, a finely quilled buffalo robe lay ready. At the central hearthpit, her other-mother—Magpie Woman's sister—pulled coals from the hot fire. Juniper and white sage lay close at hand, their scents sharp and ready. From beyond the pale skins of the lodge, she heard again her father's voice.

"Red Feather Woman, Little Sea Shell, Sits Above," he said, naming two widows and a man who had recently lost several whistlers in a raid by the Crow People. "A whistler to each I give you. In honor of my daughter's passage into womanhood." She heard the low murmurs of the people. *Three whistlers.*

Truly, it *was* an exorbitant display of generosity. Speaks While Leaving knew she should have felt something—pride, joy—at her father's honor to her, or at the prospect of womanhood, but she did not. All she felt was a deep encroaching fear.

"Ke'éehe, *náe'tótahe*," she said. Grandmother, I am afraid.

Healing Rock Woman looked up from her mixing, deep lines growing deeper in an ancient face.

"It's happening again," the girl said.

The old woman stood and came to her. She reached out. Speaks While Leaving felt her grandmother's touch like a burning ember against her young skin.

"You are ice."

"Ke'éehe." The lodge blurred as the vision fever swooped across her brain. "Make it stop."

At a gesture from the old woman, the drumbeat ceased and her aunt stopped her combing. "Go, my daughter," she said to Magpie Woman. "The *ma'heono* are coming upon her. Tell the men to move away. They will not want to be so near and have their power overwhelmed by hers."

Magpie Woman pushed aside the doorflap. She looked back for a moment and Speaks While Leaving caught a hazy glimpse of darkness and glowing faces beyond the door. Then her mother was outside and the flap fell closed.

Burning hands gripped the young girl's arms. She moaned as the white walls bled out across her sight. She was taken to a bed and a roll of trader's cloth was placed between her thighs. Fiery hands made her to lie down, touched her legs, her belly, her throat. Speaks While Leaving recognized her grandmother's healing touch, but it did nothing against the vision fever that blinded her eyes and sucked the warmth from her body.

"Ke'éehe, please, make it stop."

Hot fingers caressed her cheek. "If Ma'heo'o wants to talk to our little girl, who am I to say no?"

"But Ke'éehe—"

"Tsh-tsh-tsh. Let the vision come. If you fight it, you will only get sick. Then you will have the vision, and you will be sick, too. You remember the last time?"

Speaks While Leaving signed her agreement, already blind to the world around her.

"Good. Shut your eyes and do not be afraid."

"Will you stay with me?"

"Yes, Little Pot Belly," she said, calling her by her baby name. "We will all stay."

A skin of soft deer hide was laid over her, then the light touch of a blanket followed by the heavy weight of a buffalo robe. The soft fur with its musky, familiar smell comforted her. She shivered and curled up on her side. Someone entered the lodge.

"They are going," Magpie Woman said, meaning the people outside. "The men thank you for the warning."

The murmurs and footsteps outside grew distant and silent. Speaks While Leaving could only hear the snap of wood in the fire, the quiet words of her mothers and aunt, and the thrum of her heart in her breast.

Soon, even those sounds faded. Speaks While Leaving reached out through her silent white blindness and found her grandmother's hand. This vision is strong, she thought, and said so out loud, though she could not hear her own voice. She felt the hand that held hers give a squeeze of reassurance, and then she was alone, adrift in a pale sky.

She waited for the vision to come.

The world was white. She stood bathed in diffuse light. A wind lifted her unbraided hair and she smelled the wet dust scent of a coming storm.

The world around her dimmed. The light receded into little pools of brightness, becoming smaller as the sky darkened. Finally, the light became the rising sun and the morning star. The pale blue of dawn glowed between the heavy clouds and the dark prairie.

How funny, she thought. The thunder beings come from the west, not the east.

The sun rose quickly, out of time in the way of visions, and its light fell on the prairie.

Ahead and to either side she saw a line of men, each figure wrapped in strands of fine thread, head to toe. The strands shrouded them, making a cocoon of each one. From each figure's back stretched a single cord that shone in the sunlight like spun silver. She saw all the threads stretching back to a single point, and there she saw the Trickster, Vé'ho'e, the spider-being of legend, and she knew then that the men were *vé'hóe*, the whitemen of the Horse Nations.

The cocooned figures marched slowly toward her. Their shuffling feet crushed the tender shoots of spring grass. As they marched, their silver cords stretched, and Vé'ho'e spun more silk.

Then from the sky she heard thunder and saw two men, thunder beings, their skin all black and with lightning bolts on their arms. They dove down out of the sky like arrows heading to earth. They flew past the marching men and rumbling power filled the air. Bolts of fire struck the ground before the line of men, but they did not stop in their marching. The thunder beings flew back up into the sky, stopping at a big cloud, gray with pending rain.

The thunder beings took the cloud by the sides and brought it down toward the ground. Speaks While Leaving saw that on it rode one of the *vé'hóe*. As it came overhead, the thunder beings made the cloud disappear and the cocooned man tumbled from the sky. Speaks While Leaving reached out and cushioned his fall. She stripped him clean of the clinging webs, even the one that tied him to Vé'ho'e.

Then the thunder beings flew back up into the sky, arrows rising, while the whiteman stood beside Speaks While Leaving. The pair faced the east and the line of men split, making a clear space between them and the Trickster Vé'ho'e.

Into this clear space rode ten whooping warriors. Speaks While Leaving saw that each rider bore the shield of a band of the People, so that all ten bands were represented. The riders spread out and cut the webs that tied the cocooned men to Vé'ho'e. As each strand was broken, one of the marching men disappeared. The riders cut and cut until the prairie was empty once more. Then the riders rode around Vé'ho'e himself, making a sacred hoop in the ground around him. Vé'ho'e could not move from the circle, and the warriors rode off.

The sun set in the west, and the shadows of Speaks While Leaving and the man from the cloud stretched out toward where Vé'ho'e stood trapped in the sacred circle. When their shadows touched him, the Trickster disappeared into the darkness of night.

Speaks While Leaving opened her eyes. She was very tired.

"Ah. You have come back." Healing Rock Woman smiled. Speaks While Leaving felt the cool caress of a damp cloth across her forehead. Magpie Woman knelt at her bedside as well, and she could see her aunt and her other-mother watching from near the fire.

"I saw—"

"We heard the whole of it," Healing Rock Woman said.

"You told the whole story as you saw it." There was pride in Magpie Woman's voice, but also something else. Speaks While Leaving looked into her mother's face.

"Do not be afraid of me, Mother. Perhaps this was just a dream."

Her mother and grandmother exchanged glances.

"Little Pot Belly," her grandmother said. "Do you think it was only a dream?"

Speaks While Leaving looked up at the smokehole where the lodgepoles met. The power of the vision still ran through her body. She could remember vividly the shrouded men, the thunder beings, the man who rode the cloud. She knew she could not forget it.

She shook her head.

"Good," Healing Rock Woman said. "It is a bad thing to ignore a true vision."

"But what does it mean?"

"That is for you to say. Not for us. For now, though, we will tell the camp of this vision. Tomorrow, we will dance your vision from the other world into this one."

"No," Speaks While Leaving said, suddenly sure of one thing. "We must wait. We should dance in the spring, when the grass is green and tender."

The elder women all agreed, for it was important to dance the vision at the proper time.

"That is good," her grandmother said. "Now, you rest."

But Speaks While Leaving was already asleep.

CHAPTER 1

Wednesday, May 5, A.D. 1886
Fort Whitley, Kansa Territory

Captain George Armstrong Custer, Jr., looked back over his shoulder, toward the fort's main gate. The cold breeze of early morning smelled of the waters off the Gulf, only a few miles distant.

Fort Whitley's tiny barracks were two hundred yards away, and its timbered walls enclosed the largest yard of any fort in America. Nearby, a table and two rows of chairs stood untenanted, looking lonely and out of place in the midst of such spaciousness. The space was necessary for their work, though, as Fort Whitley was not a simple frontier fortification, not just a lonely link in a chain that stretched out into hostile territory. Fort Whitley, as George liked it put, was where they built the future.

"Still no sign of him," Elisha said.

"He'll be here," George replied. I hope, he added to himself. The knot in his stomach twisted a turn tighter and he turned back toward the yard.

The wind grabbed the doors to the oversized barn and pulled them against the blocks that held them open. Men in blue struggled against guy ropes that hung from the huge construction, then tramped through the barn's doorway and into the mud, pulling their prize out of the hangar and into the morning wind.

The breeze freshened and the soldiers dug their heels into the soggy turf. One man slipped on the dew-wet grass and slid forward on his rear. Derisive laughter was cut short by a bellowed command.

"Stand to, you bastards," Sergeant Tack shouted. "This is no time for games."

Elisha chuckled. "As if Tack ever allows that there *is* a time for games."

"Oh?" George said. "You forget poker."

Elisha's smile broadened. "Ah, but I didn't, sir. To Tack, poker is not a game, but a business."

The two officers shared a laugh and watched as the sergeant put his men back under control. The subject of their labors hung in the air above them. George looked up as its midsection emerged from the barn.

It was huge—taller than a house and over a hundred feet long. The cigar-shaped frame was made from steel and the new metal known as aluminum. The white fabric that stretched to cover it shone in the morning light, making the craft look like some odd, symmetrical cloud lassoed and brought to Earth. Beneath its bulk, attached like sucker-fish to the belly of an airborne whale, hung the cabin and engine cars. Cabling from the dirigible's sides helped support the cars and steering vanes, and it was these wires that sang in the damp morning wind.

George had fought hard for this contraption. He had pushed for its acceptance, had battled for its commission, and had overseen its construction. It was the child of his own work and that of his friend, Ferdinand, an obscure German count who had worked for the Union during the Civil War. Their discussions, with minor modifications and the application of American resources, had created the two things George had sought.

First, the craft would provide the Army with an edge in its "conflict" with the Cheyenne Alliance.

Second, it would provide George with a way to establish his name as his own, instead of simply being known as the son of his father.

"This is the future," George said as he stared up at the recalcitrant craft. "No more horses and sabers for the Army. From this day forward we will rely on men and machines to lead us to victory."

Elisha shrugged. He flipped up the collar of his blue wool topcoat and held it close against the chill breath of spring's memory. "If you say so, Captain. For myself, though, I just don't see the generals lining up for a ride in this behemoth, or turning in their fine stallions for one of those steam-driven carriages."

George tried to envision his father in one of the fanciful Benz carriages instead of on Vic or Dandy and smiled at the image. He took a deep lungful of air and released a frosty breath. "You are right. There's just something refined about sitting a horse that mechanical engines cannot replace. But horses are useless against the Cheyenne."

Elisha looked as though he might have argued that point as well, but the sound of voices from the direction of the gatehouse drew his attention.

A squad of soldiers on horseback rode in from beyond the gate into the yard. They were followed by four open carriages with high-seated drivers like in the days of Lincoln. The dignitaries—senators and a few representatives who had come to view the official launch—sat in the high seats and craned their necks for a better view of the huge aircraft. Behind the carriages were more riders, but not enlisted men. These were old men, most portly, all but one wearing the dress blues of the U.S. Army.

The one rider who was not in uniform wore a long topcoat of dark wool, buff-colored riding pants, and a high-collared shirt with a cravat of watered silk. From beneath his high statesman's hat flowed his trademark: locks of golden hair, now paling with age. It was George's father, the Boy General, Hero of the Civil and Mexican Wars, and the Savior of the Battle of Kansa Bay. Colonel George Armstrong Custer, Sr., President of the United States of America, laughed with the generals and congressmen as they rode into the yard beneath a clear, crisp morning sky.

Men ran across the yard from the barracks. They assembled near the barn with a great deal of cursing and clattering of equipment. Custer brushed at his mustaches and beard with a gloved hand as they rode toward the ranks. His eye glanced toward where George stood with Elisha, but he did not acknowledge his son. The clenched fist in George's stomach, rather than relenting at his father's arrival, only gripped him the more.

Colonel McCormack, commander of the remote outpost, stepped before the small detachment. He saluted his commander-in-chief and was rewarded with a tip of the presidential hat.

Custer dismounted, followed by the generals who did the same although with less agility. The statesmen all debarked. A few soldiers were dispatched to stable the horses and unhitch the teams. The guests moved to the empty chairs. They milled about, chatting with one another, but did not settle into the chairs provided them. McCormack stepped to the table, pulled a sheaf of paper from his coat pocket, and cleared his throat.

George heard Elisha groan. "Please," the young lieutenant said. "No speeches."

McCormack was preempted, however, when Custer walked up and shook the colonel's hand, engaging him in friendly exchange.

"God bless the president," Elisha said. George hid a smile.

At forty-six years of age, George's father made an imposing figure. With a confidence born of two decades of command, he walked slowly toward the dirigible as he conversed with the officers and senators.

"My lord, but it's big," George heard his father say as they strolled closer. "Bigger than I'd imagined."

George and Elisha raised hands to salute as the president and their colonel drew near. The colonel touched his brim, releasing them. The president squinted.

"Tell me again why these savages won't just shoot you down and feed you to their lizards?"

"Sir," George replied. "We will be too high for them to do any damage."

"I see." Custer was obviously unconvinced. He turned to the colonel. "And they've flown it successfully?"

McCormack straightened. "Absolutely, Mr. President. Several times, sir, and each time better than the last."

"So, they haven't crashed the thing in what? Four months?"

"Five, Mr. President." McCormack smiled with pride. George winced. He knew his father. While the colonel beamed at having exceeded the president's estimate, George knew that the question had been designed to point out the fact that there had been even a single crash.

"Colonel McCormack, let me put it thusly. Four months, five months, a year; it makes no difference. Anything less than perfection is substandard. Is that clear?"

The colonel's ruddy cheeks paled and blushed at the same time. "Yes, sir," he said.

George stepped forward. "Sir, I was in command of the ship when we ran into trouble. The fault for the mishap is mine."

The tall, lean Custer looked down at his son with the look of stern regard that George and his sisters had come to call "The Official Glare." It usually preceded what his father considered a *bon mot* of common sense.

"The fault may be yours, Captain, but the responsibility is still the colonel's."

"Yes, sir," George replied and stepped back.

"Mr. President," McCormack said, having regained his composure. "If you and the other gentlemen care to join me, we can review the plans for the dirigible and for its mission while the men prepare for its departure."

The president smiled and nodded, once more the Spirit of Geniality. The colonel led the way.

Elisha humphed. "How are you, Son? Good to see you, Son. You're looking well, Son."

"That will do, Lieutenant."

"I'm sorry sir. It just seemed that a little 'hello' wouldn't have done the old man in."

"I said, that will do." George took a deep breath. "Remember that he is here as the president, not as my father."

"Yes, sir."

"It's not a family reunion."

"No, sir."

"It's an historic military operation."

"As you say, sir."

George ground his teeth, not sure what infuriated him the more, Elisha's studied deference or his father's complete lack of parental warmth.

"Ah," George bristled. "To Hell with you both. Sergeant Tack!"

The men wrestled the dirigible to its mooring spire. George and Elisha—along with Private Lescault, who would act as their fireman—climbed up the ladder to the pilot car to begin their check and recheck of every operational aspect of the huge machine. Elisha and Lescault concentrated on the boiler and engine apparatus. George climbed up into the belly of the beast to inspect the superstructure from within.

The beam from his candle-lamp pushed up through the humid gloom. The danger of an open flame in a lighter-than-air craft had been greatly limited when George replaced the German count's design for hydrogen with American-supplied helium. Still, though, George took great care with the lamp. The internal bags were flammable, as was the fabric skin.

The ladder led up to the catwalk that ran the length of the aircraft like a spine. Gas-filled bags pressed up against the dirigible's internal skeleton of steel and priceless aluminum, holding the whole of it aloft. Sunlight struggled in through the fabrics of skin and balloons. It shot through the needle holes of the outer seams, filling the interior with odd linear constellations.

George paced slowly down the catwalk. The walkway rang like an ill-forged bell. His gaze sought evidence of a wrinkled bag or stretched seam. His fingers plucked the cables, searching for the string out of tune. He checked the water levels on the ballast tanks that lay underneath the catwalk. The air smelled of dust and grease and sooty welds, and now and again the whole structure would grumble and turn on its mooring pin as the wind settled into a new quarter.

Inwardly, he kept coming back to the spot rubbed raw by Elisha's words of reproof against his father. "The General," as his father was often called—though he'd only risen to the permanent rank of colonel— had always been a complicated man, and one not well-suited to fatherhood. George was of the opinion that he confused his father nearly as much as his father returned the favor. The situation was different with regards to Maria and Lydia. Upon one's daughters it was not unmanly to dote. With a boy, however, his father's parental instincts quarreled with codes of military and social conduct.

The clang of his boots on the catwalk reminded him of a day long ago when he had caught a glimpse behind the tough façade.

In his memory, a hammer rang on an anvil as the smith put the proper curl into a horse's shoe. George stood as a young boy in the smithy of an Osage outpost. The General stood next to him and explained the workings of bellow and forge to his son. George, still blinking in the sudden shade after the hard light of the Ozark summer, took a step closer to see better the breathing, fiery beast that inhabited the farthest darkness of the shop. Smoke, heat, and the volcanic smell of hot metal filled the air.

From his left came a sound. He turned. The horse's foot caught him in the chest and sent him through the air to crash against the wall amid tools and bar iron. The pain was sharp. The fear that washed over him was cold. His heart labored and his skin was too tight. Then his father was there—The General. Tears built in the boy's eyes as the realization of what had happened took shape. His father grabbed him by the shoulders and looked him up and down. The smith stood behind him, iron glowing in his tongs.

"Is he all right, sir?" the big man asked.

George's father swallowed and blinked. Then he untied the kerchief from around his neck and gave it to George.

"He's all right," Custer said. He stood and held out his hand.

George took the extended hand and was pulled upright. He sniffed and wiped at his face with the kerchief. Blood from his nose stained the blue cloth black.

"It takes more than a horse's kick to keep a Custer man down, eh, Junior?"

With a nod, George gave the only acceptable answer to such a question. Slowly, he accompanied his father back into the glare of the Missouri coast.

The hatch to the pilot car clanged open, bringing George back to the present. "Are you ready for a steering test?" Elisha called.

"Go ahead," George called from the rear. "Left side first. Then right."

"Your left?" Elisha said. "Or my left?"

"Aw, Hell," George said beneath his breath. The Army, in a prideful attempt to purge from this project any possible connection with the Navy, had decreed that all terms such as "port" and "starboard" were not under any circumstances to be used. As a result, George had lost count of the times he and Elisha had had this selfsame conversation.

"You know what I mean," George bellowed in mock exasperation.

"Aye-aye . . . I mean, yes, sir!" his lieutenant said. The long drive chains began to rattle as the boiler built up steam. George checked the connections down the length of the interior. Then he opened one of the observation doors in the dirigible's side and peered forward at the wide-bladed propeller turning slowly on its shaft. Behind, rudder and stabilizer panels moved through their range and back to a neutral position. George scuttled over to check the action of the opposite side. Everything was working as expected.

The belly of the aircraft began to fill with sound as the rotors picked up speed. The chatter of the chains grew into a smooth, deep-throated roar.

He checked the propellers again. The blades were now a whirling circle of translucence and the wind that they created made him squint. He shut the doors and made his way back to the pilot car.

"No problems," he said as he released his grip on the ladder. "It all looks good. How are things up here?"

Elisha finished his check of the instrumentation. "Looks fine." He turned toward the door to the engine car. "Lescault!" he shouted. "How is the engine behaving?"

"Good as gold, sir," came the reply. "Good as gold."

"We're ready, Captain."

George stood at the car window and looked down. The sergeants of the outpost again gathered the men into ranks near the mooring spire. The officers and senators emerged from the front door of the colonel's house and began to make their way across the boot-high grass.

"They're coming to see us off," he said.

"Well, sir, you'd best get down there."

"Don't want to disappoint, do I?"

Elisha smiled and George was glad they'd been able to melt some of the frostiness that their earlier words had created. He pushed open the car door and dogged it so it would not swing freely. Then he grabbed the railings along the jamb and swung himself out and onto the wooden rungs of the rope ladder. It was not a long descent—perhaps twenty-five feet—but it was precarious. He didn't want to slip and fall into the mud at the feet of the dignitaries. Therefore, he took a little longer than usual and stepped to the ground just as the guests arrived from across the yard.

At a bark from Tack, the ranks snapped to and stood tall. George gave salute once more to his colonel. "The United States Army Aircraft *Abraham Lincoln* is ready for active duty, sir!"

McCormack stepped forward and cleared his throat. George, fighting the urge to look up to the pilot car, stayed at attention. There was no rescue for them this time. Even his father would not be so rude as to step on this moment of commander's prerogative. McCormack faced the assembly.

"Today," he began, "is a day on which history shall be made. Today, the Union once again sets forth to claim the territories that are rightfully hers. For over one hundred years . . ."

The breeze freshened and the dirigible groaned on its mooring, echoing George's opinions. McCormack droned onward.

In time, it was done, and the colonel invited the president to address the troops. Custer stepped up beside the colonel. He stood straight, proud, supremely confident.

"I would like to extend my thanks to the commander, the officers, and the fine men of this outpost. What you have achieved, what you have created, is nothing less than remarkable." The senators applauded these words and the generals followed suit. "And to the men who will drive this amazing machine, remember that as you pass over and into the untamed lands of our great nation, our prayers go with you. Good luck, and Godspeed."

Again the guests applauded. Custer turned and walked over to George with a smile.

"Get a good look at them, Son. Find out where they are and how many they are so we can know where and how hard to hit them. The Frontier is too

big for us to run around looking for them. Understood?"

"Yes, sir."

The look in his father's eye softened a bit. "And
be careful, Son," he said, extending his hand. "Your
mother worries so."

And you do not, George thought. But when he
clasped his father's hand, he felt the thinness of the
bones within it. His father's cheeks were gaunt beneath eyes of cornflower blue, and his long hair was
nearer to white than blond. The office and the Union's
reconstruction after two terrible wars had taken their
toll on the Savior of the Battle of Kansa Bay.

"Tell her not to worry," George said. "I just wish
we'd had a few minutes to talk."

"Plenty of time for that. After the mission. I'll have
the band play 'Garry Owen' when you ride back
into camp."

George nodded, stepped back, and saluted a final
time. Custer returned it with a wink, and George
turned and grabbed the ladder. Climbing up, he
smelled the salt on the southwesterly breeze. Elisha
reached out from the car and helped him inside. They
pulled the ladder up and latched the door closed.

From the yard below, Tack's bellow echoed through
the yard as he ordered the men to clear out of the
way. George made sure the guests had all moved to
safety before he opened the first ballast tank. Water
streamed out from either side of the aircraft's midsection in a manner that was vaguely obscene.

"Thar she blows!" shouted one of the men from the
yard. Tack yelled for silence. George pushed the lever
shut, a mischievous smile on his lips.

There was no immediate sense of movement. Elisha
raised an eyebrow. "More?" he asked. George shook
his head.

"Wait."

Then, like a lumbering sea beast lifting itself off the
shingled strand, a ripple moved through the craft as
the nose began to slide up the spire.

"Forward thrust, one eighth," George said and Elisha turned the throttle lever to match the command. The pitch of the propellers changed and the blades bit the air. The craft shuddered once more and then slipped up and off the spire without another sound.

A cheer went up from the men below as the dirigible cleared its mooring. It floated upward. Inside, without any sense that it was they who were in motion, George felt the brief initial disorientation of balloon flight; the fleeting sense that it was the world that was dropping away and not the reverse. As the tip of the spire drifted below them, George gave the command for half speed. Elisha complied and George's brief vertigo disappeared under the craft's slow but perceptible acceleration.

He steered them to the north-northwest. "Give us some elevation, Lieutenant. Ten degrees."

Elisha manned the crank that controlled the pitch of the craft. As he turned the winch, cables ran up into the body and moved the counterweight that ran underneath the catwalk. The counterweight moved aft, and the nose of the craft lifted up into the sky.

George checked the bubbles in the attitude meters. "That's good," he said.

Now safely underway and climbing, he went to the open window. Below and behind them, the outpost was shrinking to a small square of mud and sedge amid the greater green of springtime. The men still in the yard were like lead soldiers, a tableau of wonderment watching the unlikely aircraft lift itself gracefully toward the clouds. George took off his cap. He waved out the window and the soldiers came to life, waving back. Behind the men in blue, he saw the dark figures of the statesmen, and the man with the long pale hair. He wanted the man to wave, too, but he knew he would not.

George squelched his own irrational annoyance and turned back to the task of guiding their course. The boiler let off a puff of excess pressure as they rose. "Tamp it down a bit, Private."

"Aye-aye, Cap'n," Lescault growled in answer. Elisha laughed, pointing at George's scowl of consternation.

"And after you worked so hard to make this an Army mission."

"I can see now that there's no point in continuing the struggle," George sighed. "All right. I admit it. It's a ship. Airship. Vessel. Whatever you like. Port. Starboard. Bow, and aft. It's a ship!"

"Huzzah!" shouted Elisha and Lescault together.

"I'll deny in public I said it, though," George told them. "And no one will ever believe the likes of you two."

They reached altitude and headed along the northeastern limit of the Gulf of Narváez. Shoals of fish flashed and spun in the warm, shallow waters below. Small, leather-winged cliff dragons sailed from the rocky breakwaters and dove for their silver-sided prey. George looked ahead. He and his small crew were flying toward a land full of things found nowhere else in the world: huge buffalo, giant lizards, and the American Indian.

On paper, the western border of the United States was a thousand miles distant, somewhere along the spine of a mountain range that only a handful of white men had ever seen. In reality, it was formed on the northwest by the Red, Sheyenne, and Missouri Rivers that limited the Santee Territory. In the south it was made by the Sand Hills and the coast of Kansa Territory along the Gulf of Narváez, that body of water that stretched up from the Gulf of Columbia into the heart of the North American continent. As the three men traveled north from Fort Whitley, they entered lands that had been purchased from the King of France two generations past, but which had never been explored, much less settled by their owners.

Long snakelike necks lifted out of the water as huge behemoths watched the passage of George's craft. The dirigible flew over long stretches of swamps and fens. The air smelled of salt and mud until they came to the dense forests of the Kansa coast. For miles the greenery of towering ferns hid the ground from their view, and George and Elisha could see only the sudden flights of birds that flashed in colors of pink and blue as the flocks took to the air.

As they left the forested rim of the Kansa coast behind them, George took a deep breath, anticipating the mission ahead of them.

"Welcome to the 'Unorganized Territory,' " he said.

Elisha looked up from his navigation charts. "It does look rather disheveled," he said jokingly.

To George's eyes, it was beautiful. A few miles inland and over the heads of the coastal hills, the land presented itself slowly. The low folds of the Sand Hills gave way to a vast prairie that stretched on forever. The horizon was flat and unmarred, but as George sailed the *A. Lincoln* onward, the land developed features. Rises— they were too subtle to be called hills—lifted and fell beneath the ship. Rivers laced the landscape with silver ribbons. Forests of cottonwood and box elder lifted green-feathered branches above fern-lined creekbeds. Beyond, ahead of them like a placid sea, lay league after league of prairie grass at least knee-high and pale green with springtime growth. The rivers and even the woods wound and twisted lazily until they blended into the low curve of the land, but the prairie itself continued onward, onward to the horizon, where the green of the grass met the blue of the sky in a turquoise melding of heaven and earth.

George marveled at the sheer expanse of land. He picked a metal wedge out of the rack and snugged it in place against the spokes of the pilot's wheel. He let down a window and leaned out on the sill. The air was still cool but no longer fresh from the sea. He took a slow chestful. This was *old* air. It smelled of sweet grass, a touch of rain, and miles and miles of land.

In the forest below he caught sight of movement.

The whole ship grumbled with the vibration from the boiler and pistons and chains, and the wind sighed through the wires and through the whirling propellers. Even above such noise, however, he heard the call of the animals that ran through the trees.

"Whistlers!"

"Where?" asked Elisha, crowding up along the sill. George pointed down to the forest edge.

On strong hind legs the large, lizard-like whistlers ran, fleeing the approaching noise and shadow of the airship. They ran from the trees and onto the freedom of the prairie. Tails held straight out behind them, front arms tucked in close, the whistlers ran with great speed. Their skin paled as George watched, shifting from shadowy gray to a brindled green that turned the running lizards into phantoms fleeing through the tall grass.

They ran away from the ship, outdistancing it easily with a mile-eating gait. He saw them roll an occasional eye backward to check on the threat. Their calls of warning trumpeted through the air, amplified by the long, bony crests that curved back from their heads and over their necks.

Then they disappeared. George and Elisha gaped.

"Where did they go?"

George went to the wheel, undogged it, and steered the ship in the direction they had last seen the flock. The ship turned and settled into its new course. He rejoined Elisha at the window.

As they neared the place where the flock had last been seen, George noticed something irregular in the grass far below.

"There," he said, pointing.

The flock, skin tone now a perfect match to the prairie grass, had stopped in their flight *en masse* and hunkered down to hide in plain sight. From above, the two men could see the slight splaying of grass, but from the ground they would have simply vanished.

"In all the world," George wondered aloud, "why do we only find these creatures here?"

Elisha bit off the end of a hard biscuit. "You only found horses in Europe," he said while he chewed. "Or in Asia. Weren't any horses here until the Spanish brought them."

"That's not what I asked," George said.

"No," Elisha agreed. "But no horses here. No giant lizards there. Answer one, and I bet you'll answer the other."

George shrugged. "Maybe," he said. "Maybe."

As the ship came over the beasts once more, turf flew as they bounded off. George let them go and returned the dirigible to its original course.

The door to the boiler room opened and Lescault entered the pilot car. He smelled of smoke and oil and sweat and was already sooty up to his elbows.

"You missed our first whistlers," Elisha said as the fireman opened the opposite window and leaned out into the cool breeze.

"Bah," said the private. He wiped his dirty face with a slightly less dirty kerchief. "I hate the beasts."

Elisha took a jug of water out of stores. "You've seen them before, then?" he asked, pouring a cup.

"Thank you, sir," Lescault said as he took the cup and drank it off. "And yes, sir. Seen 'em plenty. My grandfather was a trapper up north in Assiniboine territory. My mother and father ran a trading post of sorts just the far side of the Santee border. I've seen more than my fill of hardbacks and whistlers. Hardbacks can at least be put to a little use, but even they're a stupid, foul-smelling breed. Give me a good Penn's Sylvania dray anytime."

"And whistlers?" George asked, taking a drink himself.

"Worse than useless," Lescault answered. "Smart, to be sure. Too smart. And bad-tempered, too. Untrainable. Good for nothing, if you were to ask me. Not for eating. Not even for tanning their delicate hides."

"You've eaten whistler meat?" Elisha asked with a laugh of surprise.

Lescault nodded. "Once, sir. I was a boy and it was a terrible winter night. My pa heard one calling. Got separated from its flock in the storm, we figured. Stringiest, most rancid-tasting meat I've ever had." He took another drink. "No, I've seen enough of whistlers. Got to give the Indian credit, though, for getting any use out of them at all."

"Too much use," George said, looking back out the window. "My father used to say that, were it not for the whistlers and the walkers, he would have taken the territory in '76."

"Did you ever see a walker?" Elisha asked the private.

"No, sir, but I've seen what they can do. One night we woke up to a terrible racket coming from out in the barn. Pa went out with his rifle. We heard a howl and a shot and then Pa came back inside, wide-eyed and white as a new cotton sheet. Wouldn't let us open the door 'til morning. We lost a horse and the milk cow that night. A few weeks later we were heading for Penn's Sylvania. Pa never went back to the prairie."

"What about you, Captain? Ever seen a walker?"

"Once," he said, a bit surprised at the terse tone of his own reply. The men across the cabin remained expectantly silent but, "Just once," was all he offered them. He turned his gaze back out the window. The others replaced the water jug and returned to their duties.

"We've picked up a tail wind, Captain. We're making good time."

George turned but Elisha had anticipated his question. His calipers were already walking across the map.

"We should reach our first waypoint in about eighteen hours." The lieutenant looked up from his calculations. "If the information we have can be trusted, of course."

George nodded. "How long until we reach the edge of our charts?"

"Ten hours. Around dawn."

"Well, we couldn't have planned that better. We'll

have the whole day for charting. Let's take the speed down a notch. I don't want us to overshoot our maps before daylight."

"Yes, sir."

George pulled out the telescope. Feeling more like a privateer than an officer in the U.S. Army, he scanned the vista.

There was no sign of habitation. No homesteads, no Indian camps, not even a lone rider. They were alone on a hostile sea and sailing toward the limits of their knowledge. For four years, it had been the only subject of George's dreams.

The reality made him queasy.

Beyond the warm lamplight of the lanterns, the night was a void roofed with a million pinprick diamonds. The light of the waning moon lit the dark land like pale gossamer; a dream laid out beneath them.

The crew were to spell one another throughout the night. At such a lazy cruise and with the weather retaining its mild countenance, the *Abraham Lincoln* required little attention. Only the occasional shovel of coal or adjusting touch to the trim was needed. Elisha and Private Lescault got their rest. When George's turn to sleep came, he let it go. Uneventful though the evening had been, he knew that lying down to sleep would be a vain endeavor.

Instead, he watched the jeweled sky for shooting stars. He judged the ship's land speed by clocking the passage of ribbons of reflected starlight in the land below. He marked their progress on Elisha's maps. He nibbled on hard biscuits and dropped morsels out the window, watching them disappear into the depth of darkness like an ember into a nighttime pond. It was quiet and unexciting activity, but it kept him busy. Still, his heart leapt at the airship's every creak, and his breath grew light whenever he adjusted their course or checked the boiler, for it was at such moments that the magnitude of his responsibility was clearest: the first powered aircraft on its maiden voyage. His first real command.

As dawn approached, George became aware of an odd, recurrent sound. It would begin as a faint and infrequent groan—barely realized before it ceased—and he could not locate the source. Soon, however, the frequency increased and it grew into a consistent grumble of varying pitch. It was still faint, but it was definitely not his own tired imagination.

He nudged Elisha and Lescault awake and told them of the sound. "I'm going up to the bags," he said. "You poke around down here." He left them rubbing the sleep from their eyes and climbed the ladder up into the body of the craft.

The sound was less obvious up above. The chains rattled through their traces, the guys were all taut, and none of the gas bags showed any sign of damage. Even the ballast levels were consistent. All was as it should have been, and that did nothing but increase his trepidation.

"What else can it be?" he wondered aloud. If it was more pronounced in the cars, that would most likely indicate the boiler, but all the readings were fine when he had checked it.

He stepped down to the engine car. The sound was definitely louder here and, he believed, louder than it had been before. He walked forward to the pilot car and found Elisha and Lescault leaning against opposite walls, arms crossed, faces dour.

"What is it?" he asked them. "Do you know the cause of it?"

Elisha nodded. Lescault looked distraught.

"Well?"

"Over here," Elisha said. George moved closer as the lieutenant opened the window. The sound increased. It was coming from *outside* the car.

The day had dawned gray and cloudy. The sky—so clear at midnight—was a dark pall. Groans filled the air, even above the whir and chop of wind and propellers. He looked down.

And saw buffalo.

What he had thought was the lingering shadow of night was instead an immense herd of shaggy, hump-backed bison. They stood so thick in spots that he could not see the earth between them. The dirigible passed over them, creating a swath of panicked beasts, and it was their lowing that he had heard, even at such a height and above the sound of the engine. He had taken their calls of animal fear for a groan of mechanical doom.

George closed the window. He saw that the dour faces and even Lescault's teary eyes were not the signs of imminent disaster, but of laughter held in too long. With a shrug and the shake of his head, he released them. Their humor came out in gales.

"There," Elisha said, looking through the telescope.

George squinted into the gloom beyond the windows. The day had grown darker instead of brighter as the southwest wind brought heavy weather in on their rear quarter. This terrain was much different from the flat Kansa plain where they had tested their skills. Here it was a gray, folded landscape that hid its features from the unaccustomed eye. He could make no sense of it.

"Where?" he asked.

"There," Elisha said again and pointed. "The line of cottonwoods that runs out to the left. That must be where the White meets the Missouri."

George squinted again but his attention was taken by another gust that rocked the dirigible. He pulled the wheel to counter the wind and shook his head. "As you say, navigator. I'll just be glad to have our nose into this wind. We're scudding like a crab with it on our backside. Give me some speed, Lescault. We're going to head into it."

The private shouted his acknowledgment and the boiler roared as the firebox drafts clanged open. George pushed the throttle lever open to increase the pitch of the propellers. The ship shuddered again as another gust rolled around her girth.

The pilot's wheel was stiff, then loose, then stiff, all in a matter of seconds. George cursed as he pulled the wheel to port and reset the trim. The wind rippled across the grassland. Ahead, the line of cottonwood trees lashed and bent. Finally, he saw with his eyes what the lieutenant had been pointing to. In the middle of the forest was a band of foamy water. The White River rushed down out of the obscuring hills, its final run a rocky rush to confluence with the larger, wider, more stately Missouri.

The rolling of the ship eased off as the *A. Lincoln* put her nose into the wind. George relaxed his grip on the wheel. He checked the ground, some five hundred feet below. The trees slipped by beneath them, but in the wrong direction. The ship was pointing westward, but was traveling east, pushed back by the strong prairie wind.

"I need that speed," he shouted over his shoulder to the engine car.

"It's coming, Captain. Pressure is building now."

The tone of the engine changed, its regular thrum becoming more insistent, more urgent. The hiss and pop of the pistons merged into a long sibilant exhalation. The ship rang with the vibration. George felt it in his feet and through the wheel in his hands. Slowly, their backward progress reversed itself. The landscape crawled toward the rear and they were again underway, heading west above the White River.

The weather ahead of them did not look any friendlier. The sky was dark and low. Rain hung like veils from cloudy ramparts. Lightning winked and flashed across the belly of the storm.

"Damn," muttered George.

Elisha noticed, too. "What shall we do? We're barely making headway."

George did not like his options. It was a roll of the dice, no matter how he decided. Higher, lower, ahead, or back; there was no correct choice. He could only hope to give them the best odds.

"We surely can't get above it. If we anchor, we're a sitting duck for that lightning. The winds make it too dangerous to go any lower anyway. If we run before it, we'll be back in the States before we can turn around again. I say we ride through it from here, beneath the clouds but high enough to give us some breathing room."

"Very well, sir."

The men moved quickly to prepare the ship for rough weather. Loose items were stowed, cabinets were locked, and all doors and windows were secured. Then they were ready. Riding at full speed, the airship crept toward the onrushing stormfront.

The wind gusted. It wailed through the cabling and rattled the windows like a ghostly siren. Thunder rolled across the plain. Rivulets of water began to stream down the airship's sides. George looked at his gauges and saw them changing.

"Downdraft! Get to the winch. Pitch up, fifteen degrees. We've got to keep our altitude." He opened two toggles and pulled the ballast release. More water streamed downward as four petcocks opened in the ship's sides. The ship reacted slowly, but it did respond. He saw the nose lift. He held the ballast lever open a few seconds more and then pushed it shut.

Lightning blistered the air, and thunder shook their bones. The ship had started to regain some altitude, but not fast enough.

"Increase pitch to twenty degrees. Lescault, I need more power for the props."

Again the sky flared. The storm was atop them, battering down. Fat raindrops turned to hailstones the size of a man's fist.

Oh, Lord, George prayed. Help us. She wasn't designed for the likes of this.

They climbed up toward the belly of the clouds. George held the wheel against the gust. They rose quickly now. The ship groaned. He looked up the slope of their ascent.

The clouds above were streaking across their path. The ship was still sailing west, into the wind, but the clouds were moving to the south. The ship was climbing up into a broadside blast.

"Pitch down!"

"Captain?"

"Down! Now!" He slammed the steering vanes into a dive. "There's a crosswind above. If we hit it, we'll be torn apart."

The ship gave a second groan. This one ended in a sharp report and the whistle of a snapped cable.

"Oh, God," Elisha said as the floor slewed beneath their feet.

The forward half of the ship twisted as it was hit by the sudden air above. It rolled, and the floor now slanted to the rear and the left. Two more shots shook the airship. The nose deformed visibly as George watched, and the ship rolled another eighth-turn.

"Hold on!"

George grabbed the wheel. Elisha hung on to the winch pedestal. Lescault shouted blasphemy from the engine car and then the ship rolled some more. Metal wedges slipped from their coves and cracked the windows below. A cabinet door burst open and a water jug fell down and smashed against the portside wall. The windows looked down on the dark river and up into the darker clouds. To the fore, George saw the nose bend a third of the way down its length. The wind finally caught the tail and pushed the ship up on her head. The men cried out as everything twisted and pitched down to point at the ground. Lescault fell through the cabin, screaming. He burst headfirst through the windows and was silent as he fell in a squall of shattered glass down to the cold water nearly 500 feet below.

George gritted his teeth and held on all the tighter to the wheel.

Cannonshots sounded through the length of the interior; braces buckled all down the ship's spine. They were doomed now, he knew; a dead ship going down. Bags of helium burst with the hiss of mammoth snakes. As George lay sprawled across the pilot's wheel, he looked down. The ship had been blown back away from the river and now it was the ground that was accelerating toward them.

He said a prayer. He made it brief.

As the shadow of the ship came down to earth, Elisha and George shared a glance.

"Take care, Captain."

"You, too."

The nose of the airship hit the ground and crumpled. Crushed gas bags exploded and the skin of the ship blew outward with the escaping helium. Cables snapped and the engine car keened as it fell away from the ship, ripping out metal arms and chains like viscera. It crashed against the bottom of the pilot car, knocking George loose from his unstable perch. He hit the forward wall and grabbed on to the cabinet handles, the only thing within reach. Elisha had kept his hold on to the base of the winch. The body of the ship imploded as it drove into the ground. Bursting gas bags sent shards of metal flying. Glass shattered and the storm's thunder was transcended by the detonations.

George hid his head and curled into a ball around his feeble anchor. The pilot car was pulled away from the ship by the falling engine car. George's world turned upside down once more as both cars flipped over. The fore cables held a moment longer, slowing the descent, and then George saw the prairie grass come rushing upward.

It seemed an age, an aeon, between the time he tried to open his eyes and the time he actually did. When he finally succeeded, he saw a gray sky. He felt the light touch of drizzle on his cheeks. He felt the earth beneath him, and felt a hand beneath his head. He heard a voice, humming softly.

A face came into his view, and he saw a woman. Dark-haired and dark-eyed, she looked at him with concern knotted between her brows. It was she who was singing, ever so quietly. Her cheeks were broad and her skin the color of oak.

An Indian, he thought, and was afraid. The Cheyenne did not take prisoners. His briefing had been quite definite on that point. He struggled to rise, but she pushed him back down and shushed at him.

"Ecouté, ami," she said. Listen, my friend. "You are wounded. Keep still."

George's French was rusty, and his skull was ringing. He tried to focus on the woman's face, but could not. She became a dark blur against the pale sky. His fear reached back into his mind and tried to form the words that he hoped would save him by making him more valuable as a prisoner than as a corpse.

"Je suis . . . le fils de . . ." He could barely think of the words. I am the son of— He tried to think of the name the savages had given his father during his campaigns. Pieces of the word rattled around in his head, then came together.

"Tsêhe'êsta'ehe." Long Hair.

"I am the son of Long Hair."

CHAPTER 2

Ball Game Moon, Waning
Fifty-Three Years After the Star Fell
Where The White Water Meets The Big
Greasy

They had seen the column of smoke rise beneath the thunderhead. By the time Storm Arriving and the two other warriors of his patrol rode up to the site, the rain had passed. To one side, the thin line of smoke trailed upward. Everywhere else, white cloth flapped and fluttered in the steady wind. An acrid scent covered everything. Amid the torn cloth, Storm Arriving could see twisted branches of pale metal.

The smoke and flapping cloth made the whistlers jumpy. Storm Arriving slid off the back of his riding mount and staked its halter rope to the ground along with the rope from his war mount. Big Nose did likewise, but when Laughs like a Woman began to dismount, Storm Arriving spoke to him.

"I want you to come with us to inspect this thing. The whistlers are frightened, but I do not want any of us to stay with them."

True to his vow of contrariness, Laughs like a Woman retook his seat. "No. I will not stay with the whistlers."

Satisfied that his companion would keep an eye on the mounts, Storm Arriving turned and walked toward the wreckage. He was glad to have Laughs like a Woman on this patrol, but his friend was a *hoh-*

nóhka—a Contrary—and it was sometimes difficult to speak to a Contrary and get things done right.

He walked to where Big Nose was waiting.

Big Nose glanced toward Laughs like a Woman. "It will be a good day when the thunder beings relent," he said.

Storm Arriving looked back at the stern warrior kneeling astride his hump-backed beast.

"Yes," he said. "It would be good to laugh with him again as we did when we were boys." He turned back. *"Nóheto,"* he said. Let's go. "I want to see what this thing is that has left its bones on our land."

They walked toward the wreck, bows ready, watching for dangers. The thunderstorm had doused most of the fires; only the one section still burned. Storm Arriving leaned over and touched one of the scraps of metal. He picked it up. It was as long as his arm and about as thick.

"Big Nose. Feel this." He tossed the scrap to the tall warrior.

Big Nose raised his eyebrows in surprise as he caught the scrap. "It weighs nothing," he said. He slashed the grass with it. Wet stalks flew about him and he laughed. He put his knee to it and bent it. "Hunh," he said. "It would make a poor lance."

"Still, we should bring some of it back to the Council. It may have other uses and there is a lot of it here. We will bring some of the cloth, too."

They moved on and saw a body: a bluecoat *vé'ho'e,* a soldier. The man was obviously dead, his neck twisted at a ferocious angle. Storm Arriving tapped the man's head with the end of his bow but it was no coup.

"The coat on this one is still good," Big Nose said. "Do you want it?"

"You take it," Storm Arriving said. "I don't like *vé'ho'e* clothing."

"When have you tried white men's clothes?"

"Once," Storm Arriving said. "Up in Santee country before Long Hair took it. We stopped at a Santee trading house. The man there had some *vé'ho'e* clothes. I tried them on. The leggings pinched in a very uncomfortable place and the coat fought with me when I raised my arms. And that was only part of what a *vé'ho'e* wears every day. Even in the hottest weather."

Big Nose shrugged. "I don't know about that. All I know about this coat is that I can trade it well to the Little Star People."

Storm Arriving considered it. "You're right. Maybe there's another. I'll take the next one," he said.

Big Nose set to removing the dead man's coat while Storm Arriving continued onward.

He stepped around a pile of wreckage, looking for another body. He inspected the polished grain of a wooden door and the shiny curve of a yellow metal handle.

The things he makes, Storm Arriving said to himself. He thought of the rifles and carts the *vé'hó'e* used. He thought, too, of the tales of huge iron hardbacks that the *vé'ho'e* made to run on long iron roads.

And now the *vé'ho'e* makes things such as this. Storm Arriving scanned the long stretch of ruined metal.

Though not very well.

He saw the feet of a second body sticking out from behind a large plank of wood. As he stepped around it, the first thing he noticed was the bandage around the man's head. Then he saw the blue eyes—hooded, but aware. Then he saw the pistol in the man's hand.

The gun went off before he could back away, but the shot was wide and the recoil sent the pistol tumbling.

Whistlers cried and he heard Big Nose shout. Storm Arriving knocked the soldier in the head with his bow, and dove for the pistol. He stood up and pointed the pistol at the *vé'ho'e*. The man held his hands before his face and was saying something over and over. Storm Arriving tried to make out the words.

Big Nose ran up, arrow nocked and ready. He

aimed at the soldier, but Storm Arriving shoved his hand away.

"I was not going to ruin the coat," the big warrior said, perturbed.

"I do not care about the coat." He waved his arm to Laughs like a Woman to show that all was well and turned back to the wounded soldier. "Listen to what he is saying."

Big Nose leaned forward to listen.

"S'il vous plaît . . . Je suis le—"

"He speaks the Trader's tongue."

"Shh!" Storm Arriving said. "Listen. Listen to it all."

"Je suis . . . le fils de . . . Tsêhe'êsta'ehe."

"Long Hair?" Big Nose snorted. "He is a crazy *vé'ho'e.*"

Storm Arriving put his weapons on the ground and squatted down next to the muttering soldier. "I am not so sure," he said. He saw the seep of blood in the the cloth bandage that covered the soldier's brow and part of his left eye. Protruding from beneath the cloth was the kind of moss and herbs used by the People.

"Ecouté," he said to him in the Trader's tongue. "Listen. Long Hair is a bitter enemy of the People and our allies. It would give me great pleasure to cause Long Hair anguish by killing his son. But before I do that, I want to know what you bluecoats are doing here. How did you get here, *vé'ho'e?*"

The soldier looked at him. "I fell from the clouds."

Storm Arriving stood, shocked.

"Did he just say—"

"Yes," Storm Arriving said. "He said he fell from the clouds."

"Do you think he is the one that—"

"No. I do not." He grabbed the pistol and aimed it at the soldier's head. "I will kill him now," he said.

"No." Big Nose pulled at Storm Arriving's arm. "You do not know that you are right."

"Yes, I do. Look at his head and at that wound

binding. He did not do that for himself. That's a Tsétsêhéstâhese wound binding, but there is no hanging
moss here. Someone came here before us. Someone
helped him and they must have told him what to say."

The soldier lay there, arms raised in impotent protection. "I am the son of Long Hair. I fell from the
clouds. I am the son of . . ." The litany in broken
Trader's tongue and Tsétsêhéstâhese was repeated.

Storm Arriving aimed the pistol again. The bluecoat's words came faster, higher.

"You risk too much," Big Nose said. "Her visions
are not to be ignored. Look at the binding again. Who
do you think wrapped it?"

"You think it was she who tended this man?"

"Who else?"

"Then why did she leave him? Why is she not
here?"

"Because she is not a fool," Big Nose told him.
"She knew we were out here on patrol. She knew we
would find him. The smoke led us right to him."

"But why did she not stay with him?"

Big Nose looked Storm Arriving squarely in the
eyes. "Because she knew it was you who would find
him. You. She has not forgotten."

Storm Arriving stood silent for a moment, caught
in his own sudden doubt.

"Are you all dead?" came a call from beyond the
ruins.

Storm Arriving scowled, uneasy. "Yes," he called
back to the Contrary. "We are all dead. Come and
help us." He turned back to Big Nose. "You really
think it was Speaks While Leaving, then?"

"Yes," the big man said. "I do."

The *vé'ho'e* had stopped his prattling and now lay
shivering on the wet ground. Storm Arriving scowled
some more.

"You are a thin, weak, and cowardly little bluecoat," he said in the Trader's tongue. "And I would
kill you rather than listen to more of your womanly

begging. But my friend has persuaded me to let you live. Get up."

The *vé'ho'e* nodded, his sign for understanding. He tried to sit up but winced and fell back hard. He tried again and succeeded, but stopped, a hand to his forehead.

"And you think that *this* is the man from her vision? The man who rides clouds?" He reached down and grabbed the bluecoat's arm. Then he hauled the soldier up onto his own back like a sack of maize.

"Gather some of the soft metal and the cloth. We head to the Council at once."

George's vision swam and grew dark. Blue and red suns burst inside his head as the taller of the two Indians hefted him like so much cargo. The Indian wore leggings and tunic of some kind of supple animal hide. The right side of his head was shaved close along the temple and above the ear, and several long earrings dangled and chimed as he moved. His hair was long and braided, as was the other man's, and at the nape of his neck a white feather was tied with a red lace of leather. George was carried across the grassland in a jarring walk, and bit back a moan as his world spun again and the ground came up hard beneath him. He held his head in his hands as the Indians spoke in their native language of hisses and whispers. Behind him, he heard the movement of another. He remained still, not wanting to increase his troubles.

The sound of movement came closer. He heard a snuffle and then felt a warm breath on his neck. He turned his head slowly.

He scrambled backward with a shout. The large beast recoiled in alarm. The skin along its nose and brow changed from green to gray as George felt his own face pale.

The two Indians laughed at his fright. One reached out to soothe the frightened whistler. Ashy bars and splotches of pale green spread from its head back along its shoulders as the tall man spoke to it. Then he pointed to George, and the beast leaned forward again. George froze.

"Such a coward you are," said the man who had nearly killed him. "She is only curious. She has never seen a *vé'ho'e.*" He clucked his tongue and said something to the beast. "Give her your scent. She must know you if she is to carry you."

The animal was huge. It was close to fifteen feet long, though a sinuous neck and a long, whip-like tail accounted for most of it. The tail was held suspended behind it, a counterbalance to the head and neck on George's end.

The fulcrum on which the whole beast teetered was a pair of two long and powerfully muscled legs. The blunt, spade-like claws of its three-toed feet dug into the turf. Its forelegs were small and did not reach the ground. The digits were heavy, designed for digging and less like paws or feet than like animate tools. Just above its forepaw was a patterned wristband of woven leather and beads of many colors. The rest of the animal was incredibly bird-like, and it minded George of some monstrous, plucked goose except for the smooth skin and oddly shaped head.

The head came close again as the whistler extended its neck. The muzzle was shaped like that of a deer or elk: large nostrils over a smaller lower jaw, but the mouth was not soft; it was beaked, with upper and lower jaws coming together in a hard-edged mouth designed for cropping grass and stripping the leaves from fronds and twigs. It looked at him sideways, like a robin eyeing a worm, and George saw the huge crest that arched backward from the beast's brow. The crest was a long extension—not an antler, but a hollow length of skin-covered bone—as thick as a man's forearm and twice as long. A wattle of skin stretched between it and the whistler's neck. It smelled of grass and the soil, but also of something dry and spicy like cinnamon.

As it came close, the beast made a small grunt, a

wordless question that resounded from mouth and crest alike.

George did not move as it swung its nose near. The Indian stroked its long neck as its moist breath washed back and forth over George's hair, face, and chest like waves on a shoreline. It nudged him and grunted again.

"Your hands," the Indian said. "Show her your hands."

Gingerly, George offered his filthy hands, palms up. The whistler snuffled over them and then nosed them. Beyond the beak, its muzzle was warm to the touch and as soft as dressed calfskin.

"She will take you," his captor said. He patted the beast's neck and it bugled quietly, a sound that yodeled up through its bony crest. It withdrew from close inspection but did not move away. George decided the prudent course was to remain where he was.

His captor turned and spoke with a third man who sat astride another whistler. The rider was decorated in a fearsome fashion. A mask of black paint covered his eyes. Spots of white dotted his shoulders and upper torso. Yellow lightning bolts adorned his arms and calves. His hair was tied back, but loose. Like the others, he wore several earrings of shell and silver. In his left hand he carried a long, hooked lance with feathers tied along its length. From his arm hung a shield with arcane symbols upon it. He was agitated, and spoke to the first man with harsh words and gestures sent in George's direction. The tall man spoke calmly and with obvious patience. Suddenly, the painted man laughed, a high-pitched giggle, and all seemed well between the two of them. The glances he leveled at George, however, were still deadly. This, George thought, is a very dangerous man.

The second man—not as tall as the first but broad-shouldered and with a flat nose—returned from the dirigible. He carried several spars of aluminum wrapped in some of the airship's fabric skin. He also carried the coat from a lieutenant's uniform, and dangling from his belt was a gold pocket watch.

George's fear was overcome by rage. "You filthy scavenger. Those are Elisha's. You leave them with him!"

Whistlers trilled and the lead man interposed himself between George and the object of his wrath.

"Silence," he ordered in French. George realized that he had spoken in English and they did not understand his outburst. He tried to translate his words but his anger got in the way. He spoke in French and pointed. "That watch. That coat. They should be . . . buried . . . with my friend."

The Indian regarded George steadily for a full minute. Then he said something to the man with Elisha's belongings. They argued briefly. The other man weighed the two items in his hands and handed over the watch. The leader held it out to George.

"You may bury this with your friend."

"What about the coat?" George asked.

"Prix de guerre," the Indian said.

The *vé'ho'e* took the trinket of yellow metal. Storm Arriving unstaked the halter of his whistler.

"Follow," he told the soldier, and they began to walk back to the wreck.

Big Nose stepped up alongside. "Why are you doing this? We don't care for our enemy dead. We don't sing songs for the Crow People we kill."

"I am not doing this," Storm Arriving told him. "He is. I am simply allowing it. Besides, it is the first respectable thing this whining coward has done. I think that if we encourage him in such things he will not be such an embarrassment when we present him to the Council." He turned to the *vé'ho'e*. "You bury your dead in the ground, no?"

"Yes," the bluecoat said. "In the ground."

A shiver ran up Storm Arriving's back. "I cannot imagine the spirits are happy with that, but you may do it as you wish."

The *vé'ho'e* chose a spot away from the wreck and Storm Arriving directed the whistler to dig. The hen put her hands on the ground and tore at the dirt with her powerful rear claws. When the dark earth had been churned and broken up, he stopped her. He pointed at the bluecoat.

"Now you finish it."

The *vé'ho'e* looked momentarily affronted, then thought better of it. He picked up a bent length of the white metal and began the work of scooping out the grave. He stopped often for breath and to clear his head. Storm Arriving did not move to assist him. This was the bluecoat's right and duty to bury his dead. To help him would be to cheat him of the honor.

The *vé'ho'e* slung his comrade's corpse in a length of white cloth and dragged it into the grave. The man had been young, his face unlined and fresh. Pale in life, the dead man was even paler in death, his skin nearly blue like morning ashes. The bluecoat arranged his dead friend in the grave, setting his clothing to rights, putting his feet together, and placing his hands crossed on his chest. In the ashen hands the *vé'ho'e* placed the chain of the trinket. Then he closed the shroud over the body.

Storm Arriving watched all this and saw in his mind the burial of his father. It had been a bright winter day and the air had been sharp with cold and filled with the scent of pine trees and smoldering sage. The women had dressed the old man in his finest war clothes and wrapped him in a quilled robe to keep his spirit warm on the journey through the night sky to Séáno, the Place of the Dead. His other-fathers had lifted the body up onto the scaffold and arranged his hands and feet and hair with tender grief. Storm Arriving himself had placed his father's quiver and arrows beside him, much as the *vé'ho'e* had placed the tiny trinket.

"Perhaps they are not all savages," he said to Big Nose.

The warrior shrugged, noncommittal. "It only makes them more of a puzzle."

The bluecoat stood and stepped out of the shallow grave. He then made a mystic sign, touching head, chest, and shoulders. It was like a sign made to *Nevé-stanevóo'o*—the four sacred spirits—but all confused. Storm Arriving wondered how these men survived in the world at all.

The bluecoat stood silently for a moment, then said some quiet words in his own tongue. Storm Arriving did not understand the words, but he guessed their meaning and he kept silent. Then the *vé'ho'e* was done, and began to cover the body with dirt. This last Storm Arriving could not watch and he turned and stepped away.

"There was a third man with us," the *vé'ho'e* said as he stopped for breath. "Did you find another body anywhere?"

"No," Storm Arriving said, refusing to look at the grisly task.

The *vé'ho'e* was silent for a long moment, and then returned to his work.

After a time, it was done. Storm Arriving found the dark mound of earth oddly fitting next to the crumpled ruin of the bluecoat's fallen cloud. Neither of them belonged on the smooth blanket of the prairie; they were both things of the *vé'hóe,* unnatural and without connection to the land around them.

"Come," he said. "We are leaving this place."

Storm Arriving and Big Nose fashioned a travois out of two long pieces of the cloud-metal, strapping it behind Big Nose's riding whistler and wrapping the sharp ends with pieces of buffalo hide. The bluecoat looked worried as they tied down specimens from the wreckage: more pieces of the cloud metal, a bundle of the strong white cloth, sections of pounded iron and brass.

"What is wrong, *vé'ho'e*?" Storm Arriving asked him.

"Nothing," he said. "And my name is George."

Big Nose laughed. " 'Tshortsh,' " he said, trying to form the odd sounds. "That sounds funny. What does it mean?"

"I . . . I don't know," he said.

Big Nose laughed again. "Sounds funny and means nothing. We should call him Makes No Sense."

"No," Storm Arriving said. "That is not a good name either." He called to the Contrary in the language of the People. "What shall we name the *vé'ho'e*?"

Laughs like a Woman frowned in thought. "I think that Ame'haooestse is a bad name for him," he said.

Storm Arriving smiled, taking the Contrary's reversed meaning. "You are right, *Hohnóhka*." He turned to the bluecoat. "Your *vé'ho'e* name is hard for us to say and means nothing. My friend there has suggested we call you Ame'haooestse. It means One Who Flies. Do you accept this name?"

The bluecoat looked at them sheepishly. "Amehoo?"

Storm Arriving shook his head. "Listen carefully. Ame'haooestse. The last part is very quiet. Ame'-haooestse. Now you."

"Ame'haooestse."

"Good. That is good. You accept it?"

The soldier straightened, still serious. "I accept it."

"Good. In the Trader's tongue I am called Storm Arriving. This is Big Nose and that is Laughs like a Woman. Now prepare to ride. We are leaving. I do not wish to sleep in the shadow of this thing." To the others he turned. "Mount. We ride. Soon we will see our families."

George stood there as the Indians whooped in excitement. The mercurial nature of these men troubled him. In less than an hour they had gone from angry shouts to respectful silence to friendly banter and now cheerful song. He did not know which of these emotions—if any—was feigned, but he could not believe they were all genuine. Grown men did not behave that way, now boyish, now all in earnest.

And then there was the puzzle of their roles. The tall, lean man called Storm Arriving seemed to be the leader of the group, but he also did most of the work. The one called Big Nose seemed subordinate, but did less. And Laughs like a Woman, with whom the other two only argued, kept apart and did nothing. There was no order to it. The Indians were a complete cipher to him.

There were six whistlers with the Indians. Four would carry riders, one would drag the travois, and the last, belonging to Laughs like a Woman would be riderless. Storm Arriving and Big Nose strode to their beasts. At a command the whistlers crouched to the ground. The men climbed aboard, and at a second quiet word, the beasts stood. It looked simple enough but George remembered his first time bareback. Caution was called for.

Storm Arriving nudged the fourth beast, and it walked up next to George.

"Touch her back and say *Hámêstoo'êstse.*"

George did so and the whistler simply craned its head around to see who it was that disturbed it.

"Again," Storm Arriving said. "With less fear."

The beast's back was over George's head and it looked down upon him from a height of eight or nine feet. Trepidation seemed a logical reaction. Nevertheless, he touched the beast again and looking it squarely in the eye said, *"Hámêstoo'êstse."*

The whistler snorted.

"Hámêstoo'êstse."

With one eye staring straight at George, it crouched. Even with its belly on the ground, its head was level with George's own.

There was no saddle. None of them had one. There were only a few loops and lengths of rope decorated with disks of beaten silver and feathers wrapped with colored string. A folded pad of buffalo pelt was draped over the whistler's back.

"Now," Storm Arriving instructed him. "Lift yourself onto her back. Straddle her with your feet in the riding loops and the first rope over your knees."

George looked first at the bits of rope and then back at Storm Arriving to see how the Indian sat his mount. He did not so much sit as one would a horse; rather, he knelt, legs wide and shins fitting into natural depressions along the beast's back.

George put a hand on the spine of his beast. The leathery skin was soft and warm. He lifted himself onto its back. The "saddle" was simply a triangle of rope. The vertex of the triangle was attached to a loop that encircled the whistler's keel-like breast. The corners of the triangle's base lay on either side of the beast's spine and from each hung a loop. George folded his legs up underneath himself and slipped a foot into each loop. The pad of buffalo hide lay beneath his backside.

"Place the first rope over your knees," Storm Arriving said, pointing.

George grasped the two forward sides of the triangle. He lifted them up and slipped his knees underneath. Settling into place, the loops held his feet back and along the beast's side. The "first rope," as Storm Arriving called it, snugged his knees down. The position, combined with the plushness of the thick fur of the buffalo hide, made for a secure and relatively comfortable seat. He was not sure, however, that either condition would remain true once the beast was in motion. The whistler's back was much narrower than a horse's, so sliding off would not be as great a threat, but George was sure it could still happen.

There were no reins, there was no bit or bridle. There was only a halter around the beast's head, and the lead was tucked into the rope that went around the whistler's breast.

"You will direct her with a touch of your hand to her shoulder or with a kick of your heel against her side. She will turn toward your touch. Hold on to the first rope only in starting off or in need."

"How do I get her to stop?"

The corner of the Indian's mouth twitched in a tiny smile. "You ask her," he said. Then with the touch of two fingers, he turned his beast around. Big Nose and Laughs like a Woman signed to him their readiness.

"We go," Storm Arriving said. He whistled a three-tone command, and all the whistlers headed off.

George grabbed the rope across his knees more out of instinct than out of memory of his instructions. The whistler's long-legged walk was a slow rolling gait with a sideways sashay. Rocking along with the beast quickly nauseated him and caused his head to pound. By watching the others it became apparent that the best riding method was to keep one's head level and straight while the legs and hips moved with the beast. He found this effect, however, unsettling. The sensation was like his body had been disconnected somewhere between his hips and his navel.

The wind freshened in their faces, and as one, all six whistlers raised their heads to sniff the air. One of them whistled a quiet, questioning phrase. The others echoed it; George heard his beast's whistle reverberate through its bony crest.

Laughs like a Woman, riding apart from the group, spoke a few words. He gazed heavenward and the whites of his eyes were stark in the black of his painted mask. The other Indians looked to the sky, too.

"He says there is more rain coming," Storm Arriving explained. Then, as if in afterthought, he said, "Do not attempt to ride away or escape. If you run, you will be killed, One Who Flies. You understand me?"

George nodded. With his pounding head, the burial of Elisha, and the unusual experience of riding whistler-back, he had momentarily forgotten to be afraid. The Indian's words reminded him.

As they rode onward, westward, George looked back over his shoulder. The wreck of the *Abraham Lincoln* lay like the desiccated carcass of a huge monster on the windblown prairie. Aluminum ribs exposed and bent, fabric flapping like torn skin, it was a saddening sight. George thought of the shallow grave amid the metal spars, and said a quiet prayer. Then he thought of Lescault—floating down to the Missouri, unburied, unshrouded—and said another.

He wiped at angry tears. The magnitude of his failure was immense. Two men dead. An aircraft destroyed. Worst of all, his own behavior. He had traded on his father's fame to spare his own life. It was an act that was as pragmatic in its inception as it was humiliating in afterthought. That he had done it at all he found disgraceful, but he found greater guilt in the fact that he had done it without thinking. In his mind he heard his own whining pleas and he clenched teeth and fists at the memory.

He looked away from the wreck and faced the wind. A raindrop touched his cheek, then another. He rode on, head up, and let the heavens hide his tears.

From within the cool embrace of a stand of riverside alder, she had watched. She had watched as the warriors and the one they now called Ame'haooestse had discovered one another. Their voices had carried across the quiet prairie, and she had listened as the warriors bickered about what was to be done. And she had given thanks to the spirits when they had finally decided to spare him and take him to the Council. That was the most important thing of all. One Who Flies must meet the People. That his escort included Laughs like a Woman—a *hohnóhka* and therefore one of the chosen of the thunder beings—only increased her confidence in the vision.

Speaks While Leaving watched now as the men rode toward the glow of early evening. One Who Flies sat his whistler easily but not confidently.

Her hen snuffled where she lay in the undergrowth, keeping her skin dark and her voice silent. The whistler's face became blotched with white and crimson. She patted the beast's crest to soothe its agitation and impatience at their long immobility.

"I know," she whispered. "You want to follow. And we will follow. But later, Dear One. Agreed?"

The beast snuffled again and nudged her hand. Her spice filled the air beneath the trees. Speaks While Leaving caressed her hen's long nose until her colors quieted and darkened once more.

Branches snapped in the woods downstream. Speaks While Leaving motioned her whistler to silence. Bushes rustled and she froze in place. She saw a shadow in the forest gloom. A man crouched amid the brush and berry bushes of the river's edge. Through the leaves and advancing gloom of a cloudy evening she could not see who or even what sort of man he was. Only his furtive movements helped to identify him as an enemy.

The man crept out onto the prairie. He stayed low, limping badly and holding one arm. He glanced westward after the receding patrol, now well out of earshot in the freshening wind.

The sun dipped below the clouds on its way toward night, and the prairie was lit by a strong, copper light. The man squinted westward and shaded his eyes. Speaks While Leaving saw blue cloth and a wink of brass.

Vé'ho'e, she thought. And a bluecoat. A survivor!

"Eya," she whispered. "This is not good." She tried to think of what to do. The bluecoat limped onward toward the wreck.

Speaks While Leaving hid her pouch of medicines and her saddlebag beneath a bush. Then she looked around her, searching for a weapon. She found a long branch but it was rotten with age. The bluecoat disappeared behind the wreckage. The next branch she tried was still sound. Silently, she slipped onto her whistler's back and tucked her feet into the loops. With her tree limb at her side like a war club and one hand twined into the first rope, she spoke to her mount.

"Nóheto!" Let's go!

The whistler burst from cover like a rabbit. Speaks

While Leaving held on. With her heels she directed the beast to the right around the front of the fallen cloud so she could attack the bluecoat with the sun behind her. The whistler's neck and tail were straight out fore and back. Its short arms hung low to part the tall grass and make way for the long legs to push through. Speaks While Leaving touched the whistler's flank with her left heel and she leaned into the turn as the hen swung around the wreck.

The man was ahead of her, fumbling with a box. She shouted a war whoop as she rode down upon him. He looked up as she swung. The club hit him in the shoulder. Wood and bone snapped and the bluecoat howled in pain. She heeled in as she sped past.

"*Nóxa'e,*" she said, and her whistler slowed. She slid off to pick up a piece of metal to replace her broken club when there came a pistol shot and her whistler shrieked and pulled away.

She looked up.

The bluecoat had a gun, from where she did not know.

She leapt on her hen's back.

"*Nóheto!*" and the whistler's legs leapt up and sped them away. She heard a sharp crack and the hen crumpled. She leapt clear as they hit the ground. Her whistler thrashed in the grass. Speaks While Leaving got to her feet but a third shot snapped over her head and sent her back down.

A tearing howl slashed the air. Helpless against her whistler's agony, Speaks While Leaving could only grimace.

The bluecoat would come for them both, would shoot them both. At least that was what she would do were their places reversed. Thus she took no chances. She crept away through the tall grass, back toward the river.

As she reached the forest edge, the pistol fired once more and the whistler's painful calls were stopped. She wasted no time. She recovered her pouch and bag from the cache and ran to the river's edge. After a quick look back, she lifted the hem of her dress and stepped into the bite of the cold, knee-deep water. Wading upstream would be faster than fighting through the thick growth, and it would be quieter as well.

The pain of the cold water was quickly washed away by numbness. Looking back, she saw no pursuit. Halting, she could hear nothing but the whisper of the river, the sounds of chattering sparrows, and the patter of a rainshower on the growing leaves of the woods. The *vé'ho'e* was not pursuing her. She was safe, but now the problem was magnified. The patrol was riding off to the Council and the bluecoat would be running to tell his own chiefs of the disaster and more. She found herself between the two, alone, unarmed, and on foot; unable even to ride to catch up with Storm Arriving and One Who Flies. She could think of only one thing to do.

She would have to run through a night and a day to reach the place in time.

CHAPTER 3

Saturday, May 8, A.D. 1886
Somewhere in Unorganized Territory

George was miserable. It had been a day of mindless plodding, and with each beat of his heart and each bobbing step of the beast beneath him, the whole of his head would throb, shot through with pain from the wound across his brow. He shivered with the cold as the wind clamped an icy hand around his rain-wet shirt and coat. Even his stomach assailed him, nauseated by the combination of hunger and the rolling, twisting gait of his mount. To add insult to his injuries, his legs had fallen asleep again and now, having resettled himself in a slightly different position, everything from his knees down was coming back to life in a storm of electric agony.

It was a symphony of wretchedness against which he could do nothing more than hunch over, tuck his hands under his arms, and suffer.

His captors seemed immune to the effects of the weather. Even though Storm Arriving had been dampened by the same showers and chilled by the same wintry wind, the Indian, in only leggings and belted tunic of pale buckskin, rode tall through the gloom. Big Nose was dressed in a similar fashion but had draped Elisha's coat over his shoulders. After several sidelong glances from the broad man, however,

George believed the Indian wore it only to torment and not for any warmth it might impart.

As for the third man, Laughs like a Woman rode practically naked. His arms and upper body were exposed to the night as were his knees and calves. His breechclout and moccasins had been his only protection until an hour before when he had wrapped a buffalo hide around his waist. His only other apparel was a knife in a sewn-bark sheath, hung over his shoulder by a strip of leather.

The fortitude of the Indians only made George feel worse; yet another example of his own personal failures.

Storm Arriving was looking at him.

"What?" George asked, sullen.

"You should take off those clothes."

"What?" George asked again, incredulous this time.

"Your clothes. They are wet. You should take them off."

"And how is it different for you?"

"My clothes are not made of trader's cloth. Once trader's cloth gets wet, it stays wet. My clothing is not wet."

George frowned. "You expect me to ride through the night like him?" He hooked a thumb toward Laughs like a Woman.

Storm Arriving and Big Nose both laughed. "No," the tall man said. "He is a Contrary. I do not expect you to do *anything* that he does. Here." He detached a rolled pelt from behind him. "Use this instead."

George caught the hide and its sudden weight nearly pulled him off his whistler. It was a full-length buffalo robe, like one his father owned—a "souvenir" from one of The General's western campaigns—only this robe was soft and supple and clean where his father's had been old, stiff, and stained with . . .

George turned away from the memory only to see Big Nose inspecting the buttons on Elisha's coat. He saw the butt of his own revolver protruding from beneath Storm Arriving's belt. His memories of that old robe suddenly acquired a more sanguine hue.

"Souvenir," he muttered, and began to remove his wet coat and shirt.

The activity had to be done with care, lest he tumble from his unsteady perch, and the shock of his damp skin exposed to the night wind did not help. He tucked his coat under the first rope and draped the shirt behind him to dry. The heavy pelt he wrapped around his shoulders. Amazingly, he *was* warmer and almost immediately so.

He tucked the robe beneath his legs and pulled it close before him. His shivering began to subside, and with that, the maladies of his head and gut and legs seemed likewise reduced.

"Merci," he said to Storm Arriving. The Indian turned and gave a small nod.

To George's left, a sprinkling of stars dazzled in the gap between clearing clouds. He recognized the constellations and discovered that they were traveling more northerly than he had thought. The Michigan Territory would be to the east, across the Missouri and Santee rivers. He wondered if he could handle the whistler in a free run across the prairie.

He felt a touch at his side. He looked to find Laughs like a Woman beside him, touching his arm with the handle of his long knife. The painted warrior stared with his fearsome gaze, dark irises moon-rimmed in a mask of night.

"I see by your eye," he said in troubled French, "that you wish long here remain. Take gift, that you be without."

George could not make complete sense of the words, but the offer was unmistakable. The man's expression, however—jaw set, nostrils flared, gaze unwavering—was equally clear. His hand hesitated halfway to the offered knife.

"I would not suggest it," Storm Arriving said. "A Contrary's words do not reflect his meaning. He means that he sees you looking to the east. He sees you thinking of your home. He wants you to take his knife so that when you run, he can kill you with honor. It is not a coup to kill an unarmed man."

Slowly, George took his hand back within the folds of the buffalo robe. Laughs like a Woman prodded him again with the handle of the knife, but George shook his head. The Indian sneered and thrust the knife back into the sheath that hung from the strap over his shoulder. Then he guided his mount away, returning to his position apart from the others.

"You could have taken the knife," Storm Arriving said, riding close and speaking softly. "You could have taken it and not tried to escape."

"And then any excuse would have been reason enough."

Big Nose chuckled. "He is wiser than he looks, this *vé'ho'e.*"

"Why is he so contrary?" George asked.

"Laughs like a Woman? It is not the *way* he is. It is *what* he is," Storm Arriving said. "He *is* a Contrary."

"I don't understand."

"He is cursed," Big Nose explained, drawing nearer so that they rode three abreast. "It was long ago, when I was fourteen summers old, during the Moon When the Buffaloes Are Rutting. We were all three of us of the *Hoohtsetsé-taneo'o* then—the Tree People band— and we had known one another all our lives."

Big Nose's voice had assumed a quality that matched his gaze; distant, focused on the invisible horizon of long ago. Laughs like a Woman had ridden nearer, to share in the tale.

"Then the thunder beings, who live in the west, they sent down upon us a great storm. For three days it rained like it would never stop. For three days the people of the camp kept to their lodges. The children grew cranky and the parents became restless. The women played the seed game and the old men smoked their pipes. Still, it kept on raining.

"On the fourth day something happened. We heard a shouting in the center of the camp. We looked out of our lodges to see Strong Left Arm"—he pointed to Laughs like a Woman—"for that was his name in those years. He was standing out in the rain, in the clear space before the council lodge. He stood with his legs apart and he screamed up at the storm above us. 'Stop it now!' he shouted. 'That is enough! Go and bother some other camp!' "

The two Indians laughed at this memory, and George saw a smile touch the corner of the Contrary's otherwise terse mouth.

"Then," Big Nose continued, "the wind began to howl. Strong Left Arm jumped up and down and shook his fist at the stormclouds. The rain eased, but heavy hail began to fall, big as blackberries. Strong Left Arm shouted some more. Then he put an arrow to his bow and shot it up into the clouds.

"No one saw it come down. That was how high he shot it.

"It went up into the clouds where it must have struck one of the thunder beings because they threw down two bolts of lightning that hit the ground on either side of Strong Left Arm. The young warrior was knocked from his feet and he just lay there, shivering on the ground, as the thunder rolled over the camp and out onto the prairie."

There was a pause in the narrative, and George looked at the men one by one. Gone was any sign of mirth. They were each stern and silent. Finally, Big Nose took a breath and continued.

"The storm stopped then. The winds parted the clouds above the camp. But the thunder beings had sent down more than just lightning on the young warrior. They were angry at Strong Left Arm, and they sent down a terrible fear of their power upon him as a punishment. Over the years, he tried to fight this fear, but he could not. Finally, he accepted his fate. He took on a new name and took up one of the four Thunder Bows and became a Contrary. When the thunder beings relent and take this fear from him, he can return to the life of a man once more."

Storm Arriving made a low noise, approving the tale. The sky had cleared above them, as it had in the story, and starlight glinted from the Indian's earrings.

"But what does it mean?" George asked. "What is a Contrary?"

Storm Arriving answered him, saying, "A Contrary lives apart from all others. He does not marry. He has no band to call his own. He must speak and act in all ways contrary to the ways of normal men. In this way, he accepts the burden of the thunder being's attention. From such sacrifice, the Contrary gains some of the thunder being's power. The carrier of a Thunder Bow cannot be outmatched for bravery. Then, finally, when he has won the thunder beings' pity, they lift from him his fear of their thunder."

George chuckled and shook his head. "You can't be serious. One has nothing to do with the other. I just don't understand how—"

"You do not have to understand," Storm Arriving said with a sharpness that brought him up short. "Your understanding is not needed. Nor is your ridicule."

"I . . . I did not intend—"

"Enough." Storm Arriving said no more; with a whistle, he increased their pace. They rode through the night in silence beneath the growing field of stars.

The bowl of night had begun to pale near the eastern edge of the world when the smell of smoke lifted George from his stupor. He straightened awkwardly and nearly slipped from his seat. He had fallen asleep, somehow, while the whistler he rode walked onward. He rubbed his eyes and cleared the drool from his lower lip. Finally lifting his head, he looked about to see something he did not believe existed.

The Indians of the great interior plains had always been thought to be nomadic, following the immense herds of buffalo through their yearly migrations. Their villages, or camps as Big Nose himself had called them, were impermanent, raised up or torn down in a day. This was the way of all the tribes of the Alliance—the Cheyenne, Lakota, Dakota, and Arapaho—and all of the neighboring independent tribes like the Crow, the Blackfeet, and the Assiniboine, who lived to the north and west of the Alliance's territory.

This ever-moving culture had been the core of the Alliance's greatest weakness. Because of it, they had formed no industry but that which could be transported easily in a satchel tied to the back of a whistler, and relied on trade with the French and Spanish for more durable goods like iron and woven cloth. However, when combined with the Indian's fierce battle tactics and the Union horse's terror of the Alliance's lizard-like mounts, this migrant lifestyle created a formidable foe; one that did not succumb to the Union's standard methods of warfare.

That was what George had been taught at his father's knee, and what his military education and experience had reinforced. It was considered the way of things out west, beyond the frontier.

Thus it was with a fair amount of shock that George took in the sights around him.

To either side of the trail—for it was a true path now, worn down to the red earth, and not just an antelope track through an otherwise unmarred grassland—lay fields of crop plants. They were riding parallel to a river. To George's left, away from the river, were acres of maturing bean and berry plants. Ahead he saw the broad leaves and white flowers of tobacco. To his right, in the long, wide swath that lay between the path and the river, stood cornstalks already hiphigh. They were planted not in rows but in circles like green ripples in a living sea. Past all these he saw other crops, low-growing, perhaps melons or tubers; he could not tell for sure, so great was their distance from him.

The greatest marvel, however, lay not in the extent of the agriculture but in what lay dead ahead. Upstream, the river curled left and then right in a long serpentine that wrapped around the low bluff on the far bank. On the near side, in the river's ox-bow arms, lay what George could only describe as a town.

The homes were round, with conical roofs like simple huts, but they were neither small nor impermanent structures. These were impressive buildings, some of them forty or fifty feet in diameter and up to twenty feet in height. The walls were of timbers and earth or clay. The low-pitched roofs were of wood, earth, or thatch as the structure's size and use demanded. Smoke lifted silently from the hole in the center of nearly every roof.

The houses were laid out in clusters that followed the arc of the riverbank. Each group was composed of one large building surrounded by a few smaller houses. There was a huge building in the heart of the town—a meeting hall, George surmised—and he guessed that the whole of the town had over a hundred of the grouped clusters. There might have been as many as a thousand inhabitants in this one settlement, far more than the Union had guessed might exist in any one place.

"I had no idea," he said. Storm Arriving glanced over, a question on his face. "All this," George explained with a hand that took in the fields and the town alike. "We thought you were all nomads."

"*Qu'est-ce c'est* 'nomads'?"

"Ah, nomads. We did not know you built permanent homes. We thought you lived on the plains and followed the herds from place to place. Nomads: 'always-traveling-people.' "

Storm Arriving signed his comprehension. "The People—the Tsétsêhéstâhese—we are an always-traveling-people." He pointed to the town. "But this is a village of the Earth Lodge Builders, called the Ree or the Arikara. They live in lodges-that-stay."

"And they grow these crops."

"Yes. The People used to grow their own maize and beans, when we lived on the Big Water to the north, but we could not tend our crops and follow the buffalo, too. The Earth Lodge Builders—the Ree, the

Mandan, and others—they have always been here and they have always been good traders. The People allied with them during my great-grandfather's time, almost fifty years before the star fell. They raise the crops against the harsh winter moons. We protect the limits of the land and trade the buffalo for grain and tobacco. It is a good relationship."

"What do you mean," George asked, " 'before the star fell'?"

Storm Arriving looked at him as if he'd just asked where the sun rose. "Don't your people know of these things?" He sighed and looked forward once more. "There was a night, fifty-three years ago, during the Moon When Ice Starts to Form, when the sky was very clear. Often during that time of year you can look up and see stars move across the sky, but on this night there were so many it looked like the sky was on fire. Stars flew across the sky, more than a man can count, and the People came out to watch it. Some were afraid, but most just looked up in wonder.

"Then one star fell. It sizzled across the sky and hit the ground with a terrible noise. The next day, some people went to see the star that fell. My father was one of them. He told me that there was a place where the ground had been torn up in a big circle. In the center of the circle was a pit, and in the pit was a rock. It was dark and shiny and heavier than any other rock my father had ever seen. My father often wondered why if a star was so heavy, how did it stay up in the sky?"

Storm Arriving looked up at the last of the stars and did not speak for a few moments. "We call that year the Year the Star Fell, and we measure every year from that one. The time I was telling you of, when the People and the Earth Lodge Builders became friends, that was fifty years before the star fell."

George nodded in comprehension, and looked at the town they were about to enter.

The portico of each home was closed tightly against the night with buffalo-hide doorflaps. As they rode nearer, sleeping dogs and somnolent whistlers leapt up from their posts to bark or shrill their warnings. Other animals throughout the town picked up the call. He heard more dogs and many more whistlers in the cool, still air of morning. From beyond the buildings, he heard the grumbling of hardbacks. Then came the sound of voices and here and there a few of the townsfolk pulled aside their doorflaps for a look.

George spied a few naked children with short, blunt-cut hair peeking out from behind adult legs. They were snatched back by men with the same haircut and who wore little more than the children. He saw no women.

They followed the path into and through the town. No one came to greet them. There wasn't a soul in the street.

"What's wrong?" George asked. "You said you were allies. It is like they are afraid of us."

"They are," Storm Arriving said. "But of him." He pointed to the Contrary. "Not of us." That appeared to suffice as explanation, for the Indian said no more on it. George, last night's rebuke still fresh in his mind, kept quiet. "It does not matter," Storm Arriving continued. "We will not be meeting with them. We will be meeting with one of the People. He took a Ree woman for wife and lives here and keeps whistlers and hardbacks for trading."

Ahead, the river ended its left-hand curve and began the long right-hand sweep around the bluff. Here, the town ended and a series of corrals began.

The corrals were of upright branches with woven nets strung between them. Within the netting, flocks of whistlers craned their necks around one another to catch sight of the arrivals. Tassels made of dried corn husks, feathers, or tin bells had been tied to the netting. With the tiniest breath of breeze or when a whistler came too close, they moved and rustled and jingled. The tall bird-like lizards kept a tail-length between themselves and the fence. Calls flew up the scales from throaty to piercing as the flock hailed the newcomers.

George's mount answered, as did the others, with chuffs and whistles of their own. The whistlers inside the corral challenged the arrivals with flashes of red and white. George's mount and the others began to prance and color in return until Storm Arriving said something in his own language that calmed them all, corralled and mounted alike.

Down by the river there were other corrals; long ones that followed the river's edge. Within these were hardbacks; squat, stump-legged beasts. They had plates like tortoiseshell armoring their backs, and a club-like tail at the rear. The Eastern hardbacks—red-eared and blue-throated—had been hunted into oblivion by settlers hungry for meat and their armor plates. The Western varieties like these yellow-speckled hardbacks still thrived, and made passable beasts of burden, from all reports.

The hardbacks were penned in by the river on one side and short twigs stuck in the soft soil on three others. Any one of them could easily have thrashed the fence with a flick of its tail, but the thought obviously hadn't occurred to them. Instead, they stood by, peering dully through the line of hip-high twigs as through an impenetrable barrier.

At the end of the corrals was a small group of houses, and in front of these stood a man. His hair was not the blunt coif of the other townsfolk, nor was he dressed like them. His hair was long, shot through with gray and braided behind in a long rope that reached to his knees. He wore clout and leggings and shirt much like Storm Arriving and Big Nose. A long, dark feather stuck out from the braid at the nape of his neck, and his shirt was decorated with sewn beads and shells in geometric designs across his breast.

Storm Arriving raised a hand and spoke as they rode up and stopped. The old man returned the greeting.

"Hámêstoo'e," he said. All of the whistlers, including the ones unridden, crouched down at the old man's

word. The Indians dismounted and George followed suit, trying to shake some life into his deadened legs.

"Stay here," Storm Arriving said, and then followed the old man inside the house.

George lay the buffalo robe across his whistler's back and picked up his shirt. It was cold, but it had dried in the night air. He shrugged on the heavy twill and began buttoning. Just as he had finished tucking in his shirttails, Storm Arriving reappeared. The pistol that he had taken from George was now in the old man's belt.

Storm Arriving exchanged a few words with Big Nose. Then they began unharnessing their whistlers and removing their supplies. The travois was unhitched and laid on the ground. The old man had gone over to the corral. He took a coil of thin braided rope off one of the posts and entered. With gestures only, he separated six whistlers from the rest of the flock. He tied the rope in a noose and slipped it over the snout of the first. An arm-length down the rope, he twisted a loop in it and put it over the second whistler's snout. The six lizards stood silent and still as he roped them all together. Then, as calmly as lambs, they shuffled after him, out of the enclosure. Big Nose took charge of them and handed over the four whistlers that had originally belonged to him and Storm Arriving. Laughs like a Woman made no move to exchange either of his mounts.

Storm Arriving and Big Nose inspected the new whistlers, checking eyes, feet, and undertails. Satisfied, they then offered their hands, palms up to the beasts, Storm Arriving to four of them, Big Nose to the remaining pair. The whistlers colored green or blue down to the withers as they sniffed the hands of the men before them. George guessed that it was a good sign, for as soon as the last one had changed hue, Storm Arriving spoke to the old man. The gray-haired Indian handed over the wristbands from the original mounts and led the beasts into the corral with the rest of the flock.

The new whistlers were banded and harnessed in a matter of moments. George was introduced to the one he would ride. It sniffed him for a longer time than it had Storm Arriving, and seemed particularly interested in the wool of his coat.

Storm Arriving took two spars of aluminum and one small bundle of the white cloth. These he tied to the pack on the rump of his own beast while Big Nose dragged the rest down to the hardback corral. Then Storm Arriving mounted his whistler and motioned for all to do the same. There were now two whistlers for each rider. The spare mounts carried no burdens.

"*Nóheto,*" he said, and all the whistlers rose like piston lifts. They warbled and the flock behind the fence answered. George remembered to grab the first rope just as the beasts leapt into motion. Then they were flying down the river path, turning to the southwest, moving so fast that George felt like he was soaring across the prairie grass.

The whistlers changed color as they ran, matching the pale green of the sea of grass they traveled. Their necks were straight out ahead and their tails straight out behind. This was not the twisting plod of the previous night's trek. Unfettered by the travois, the whistlers now loped along in a fluid gait that barely jostled the rider as the ground sped past beneath. The effect was exhilarating. The air was fresh, the newly risen sun was on their backs, the sky was blue with puffs of brilliant white, and the rest of the world was a soft, rolling green that broadened the eye's horizons and brought a smile to George's lips. He thought it beautiful; beautiful in the way when all things are perfectly suited to their place. Such was this: the strange men around him, the limitless land, the improbable beasts they rode, all at home beneath the bright sun in a boundless sky. Everything was precisely where it belonged.

Everything except me, he reflected. I am the stranger here.

He tried to imagine horses on this landscape and

failed. Horses belonged in the glens and meadows, on the rutted roads and cobbled streets of the East. They were a civilized creature, a thoroughly husbanded animal, and while George could envision a scene in which they did battle here in a cavalry charge, his misty mind's eye could see neither the thin-limbed stallion nor the towering dray at home in this too, too-open land.

No, George thought to himself. This is a land of giant lizards and savage men. It is no place for a gentleman's sorrel.

A long line of trees lay ahead, stretching far to either side. From the lead, Big Nose spoke to Storm Arriving, who pointed at a place off to one side. Big Nose touched his whistler's neck, guiding it toward the spot indicated. The other mounts, George's included, turned to follow.

The edge of the wood drew near. George saw thick undergrowth between the slender boles, but he could not see through to the forest's far edge. They approached still at speed and were not—as best he could determine—slowing down at all.

"Do not guide her," Storm Arriving said over his shoulder. "There are whistler paths all over this land. They will find the way. Just keep your head low."

George only nodded and felt the roughness of the first rope in his grip.

Big Nose spoke to his beast. The whistler raised its head and yodeled a call that the others answered. Then it looked left and right at the approaching trees, and veered to one side. George held on as the others followed. Then they were in it.

Pale trunks flashed by and the scent of greenery was strong. The underbrush was less here and George realized that they were on a well-established track. To either side grew brambles and bushes. Saplings reached in close and low-hanging boughs cut at his head.

"Stay low," Storm Arriving commanded, and George obeyed, following the Indian's example and leaning down until his chest was atop his mount's withers.

The whistlers were dark green now as they sliced through the forest in a single sinuous line. Brindled patterns swam across their hides as they moved. George smelled the dark earth upturned by their passage. He heard the calls as the leader spoke to those behind. They twisted and veered along the narrow path until suddenly George heard water and they were splashing across a ford in a shallow stream. A mob of small fishing lizards scattered before them in a blur of legs and tails. Then it was upward, and back in among the trees on the other bank.

More trees and more careening turns. George could think of nothing but staying mounted. Hands in a cramping grip on the first rope, legs tight along the whistler's sides, he rode with his rear raised slightly above the bobbing spine and his face low to the beast's spice-scented skin. Each turn brought forth a grunt of pain and exertion as he fought to stay on. At last, he saw brighter light through the trees and in a rush they were out of the wood and once more on the open land.

George forced his hands to release the first rope. His breath was ragged and heavy. The whistlers left their single file and regrouped into a flock around him.

"Do we have to travel so fast?" he asked. "Won't the whistlers tire?"

The Indian snorted. "This is not fast, One Who Flies. This is a traveling speed. They will run like this for a day and a night without problem."

"Show him fast," Big Nose said. "Show One Who Flies what a whistler can do that the *vé'ho'e* warrior's domesticated elk cannot dream about."

Storm Arriving squinted in thought. Then he unhooked the halter rope of his spare whistler and handed it to Big Nose. He grabbed on to his first rope. *"Nóheto!"*

He was gone as if the others were standing still. His whistler's legs were a blur in the high grass, and he was a hundred yards distant in two breaths. Storm Arriving was crouched down along the beast's back, a quickly diminishing figure, and then was gone. George remembered the wild flock he'd seen from the deck of the *Abraham Lincoln* and searched for Storm Arriving hidden in the grass ahead. He did not find him, though, and they loped past the spot where he was sure the Indian disappeared.

Storm Arriving sped in upon their rear and tagged George with the end of his bow before George even knew he was there. The Indian let out a whoop of victory and smiled broadly showing white, even teeth. His whistler trumpeted a loud, long note. It snorted once, but was otherwise unaffected by its sprint. Storm Arriving brought it back in with the flock.

"That is only a small feat," Storm Arriving said, riding next to George.

"They are amazing animals," George replied calmly, but his thoughts were frantic. How could they hope to beat these people? The Union horses were no match against such abilities. Their mounts were faster, more agile, able to hide in open fields. The Army could not win a running war against these people. They would have to fight a different kind of war in order to take possession of this land; a patient war, a slow war, not the quick one for which his father wished. They would have to press their advantages in weaponry and technology and supplies. This was information critical to the strategies of the commanders back home. He only hoped he would have the chance to deliver it. Though unchained, he was still a prisoner. He resolved to keep that fact fresh in his mind.

"Where are you taking me?" George asked his captors.

Storm Arriving looked at him with a suspicious eye, as if sensing his shift in perspective. "We will join the People along the Red Paint River, in the shadow of the sacred mountains. From there I do not know. The chiefs will decide."

"How far is it to your encampment?"

Again the squinted eye and furrow in the Indian's brow. "Two days," he said, and that was all.

Two days, George thought. The smooth-running whistlers ran comfortably along as fast as a horse could gallop. Two days. Hundreds of miles, even if they stopped to rest. He would be deep in the heart of this vast unknown country; lost, alone, a hostage to be used as a bargaining chip. George felt a deep and sudden distress at his predicament and, just as suddenly, was sure that his next trip to Washington would be as a corpse.

He looked out across the land as they sped along. It went on and on, a million square miles of the unknown, and in it, one fairly frightened whiteman, hoping for a miracle.

She stood on the well-worn track, facing the river and the morning sun. She had arrived at the river before sundown and spent most of the night searching for the track. Now she waited for her quarry to emerge from their nesting thickets in the woods behind her and come down to the river for a morning drink. In her hand she held the long loop of rope she had woven from river rushes. The free end was tied securely to her wrist.

The morning air teased her, pushing stray hairs into her eyes and tickling her calves with the tips of rough-edged grass. She had removed her leggings after her long run. It was immodest to do so, but they were wet from wading across creeks and from coursing through the dew-sprung grass of dawn. Besides, she reasoned, there was no one near for miles and it let the breeze cool the sweat that glossed the back of her knees.

It is not as if I had taken off my rope, she reassured herself. She shifted her stance onto her right foot and felt the familiar caress of the thin rope that twined its way from her waist, around her thighs, and down to her knees. Every Tsétsêstâhese girl wore the rope as the symbol of her womanhood and of her chasteness.

Pity the man who touched it or what it guarded without the girl's permission. Men had been sent to Séáno for much, much less.

Conscience at rest, she stood with her leggings draped across her shoulder and waited. The sun inched upward in the paling sky and the breeze cooled her naked legs.

The grass behind her rustled and she froze, then forced herself to relax. She had allowed her attention to drift and it had nearly cost her the only chance she was likely to get. The breeze was full of their scent, a musk that in this season added the aromas of dark, fern-lined nests and fallen, crumbling wood to their familiar spice. She heard three, maybe four of them approaching behind her. She stood with her back to them to entice their curiosity. Slowly, she lifted her left hand up near her shoulder while, with her right, she tightened her grip on the stiff loops of the noose she had made.

The whistlers came closer, cautiously but not fearfully. The first one scooted around her, stepping off the familiar track and passing to her right. It was a mature hen, about eight summers old. Speaks While Leaving avoided her gaze as she passed; she did not want them to feel challenged.

A second one came up, this time on her left. Braver, it sniffed her upraised hand. She felt the warm breath briefly and then it, too, stepped off the path and around her. As it passed, she saw it was a juvenile male.

She could hear now that there were only three in this nesting group. This last one would be the adult male and the only one suited to her needs. The yearling was not strong enough and she would not take a nesting hen. She only hoped that the drake would be fooled by the uneventful meetings of the two before him.

He came up close and took a long draught of her scent. Slowly, she lifted her noose, keeping it low and hidden from the drake. Satisfied she was no threat, the drake took a step.

As he came forward, she threw the noose over his beak and back over his crest. He recoiled with a shriek. She let go of the noose but kept hold of the end tied to her wrist. The rope tightened as he pulled away, the noose cinched closed high around his neck. He shrieked again, wailing in distress, and paled to gray and green in a pattern designed to camouflage himself in the springtime grass. The juvenile fled through the grass toward the river. The hen stood in startled alarm but did not move to aid the drake. Her concern was for her nest; her mate would have to take care of himself.

The tall whistler gave up on defense. He flashed red and white in anger and kicked out at Speaks While Leaving with his rear feet. She kept the distance between them even—running forward when he tried to flee, dancing backward when he attacked—for she did not want to test the strength of her rope. She also kept the rope low and out of reach of his sharp-edged beak. His front claws, too, he used against her when he got close enough, though the buckskin of her right sleeve turned the worst of his bruising blows. In order to subdue him, however, she had to get close.

She held her leggings in her left hand. She had tied the fringes together to make a whole that was an arm's length wide and as long as her legs. The whistler gave up on pulling away, having learned that it only made the noose around his neck grow tighter. As he stood there panting, shivering, trying to think of what to do, she lunged, throwing the buckskin over his eyes. He flailed with his spaded fingers, trying to attack the blinding leather. Speaks While Leaving grabbed both ends of the leather before he could knock it free. Then she stepped in close and wrapped a loop of the rope around his snout to hold the buckskin in place. As she stepped away again, she looked down to see blood. A tear in her sleeve revealed two long scrapes on her upper arm. The scent of blood would not make her efforts with the drake any easier, but there was no time to do anything about it. The whistler stood away from her at the limit of the rope. He wove his neck from side to side trying to peer out from under the blind, and tore at the ground with his feet. Speaks While Leaving watched him closely as the darkness of the blinder began to calm him.

The hen showed a renewed interest. A well-aimed stone sent her running back down toward the river.

And so she was alone with her prize. All that was left to do was to convince the drake to carry her across hundreds of miles of prairie. She prayed to Ma'heo'o for strength.

Once she was sure that the hen and her yearling would not return, she removed the leather from the drake's eyes. He startled but did not bolt—a good sign. Still keeping from looking him in the eye, Speaks While Leaving took a casual step toward him. He pivoted and stepped away from her, keeping the full length of the tether between them. She took another step toward him; he took another step away. Within moments she had him walking at a steady pace, calmly, away from the nesting grounds.

They walked in a straight line for a while. Then Speaks While Leaving changed their direction slightly to make him accept her as the one-who-is-leading. Every boy and girl of the People learned the ways of whistlers. They were creatures of the flock and followed the ways of the flock: they took direction easily, and were not willful unless mistreated. The flock was one creature with a thousand eyes. When there was a need to move, one started to move and the rest would follow. After a hand's breadth of time he was walking with only an occasional glance in her direction, and at that point she stopped.

He stopped, too, but not because the tether had tightened. He stopped because she had. She turned her back on him and took a small step away.

He turned to follow. He took a step. She kept her shoulder to him until he was right behind her, until she could feel his breath on her neck. Then she completed her turn and touched him in the place-that-whistlers-love, the high place where the neck and back meet, where neither foot nor claw nor beak could reach. She scratched him there as would any other member of the flock, and the drake cooed in relaxed pleasure.

He was hers now. They were a pair, a flock of two. In a very short time, he would be carrying her toward home. There, she would add him to her own flock of whistlers, a drake for her hens.

"Two Cuts," she said, naming him. Then she moved her hand back along his spine.

The hotel at Candide was almost as cold and dark inside as it was outside. The sitting room smelled of wet wool and cigars. Several of the overstuffed chairs were occupied, and the room was full of the sounds of hushed conversation and rustled newspaper. Men stamped their feet on the outside stoop and hung their cloaks on pegs by the door.

President Custer sat near the small and ineffectual fire, covering his boredom and frustration by reading the week-old, four-page newspaper for a second time. The foul weather that had come off the water four days prior had kept him and the other dignitaries prisoner in this small frontier town near Fort Whitley. The storm remained out there still, a long procession of clouds and rain that turned fields into bogs and made roads impassable. Escape was out of the question.

Robert Matherly, the distinguished senator from the new State of Yankton sat down in a cloud of smoke. He pulled two more clouds from the butt of his cigar and spoke. "May I intrude so far as to wish you a good evening, Mr. President?"

"Not with that foul-smelling thing in your hand, no, you may not," Custer said without lowering his paper. "Douse it or I'll have you tossed."

The senator laughed—a trifle too high and much too long—but Custer heard the creak and crunch as the fat man leaned forward and stubbed out his cigar in the brass ashtray atop the walnut smoking valet.

"There, then. So, what's the news, Mr. President?"

Custer sighed and scanned the week-old print. "Oh, nothing much. There's to be a dance last Tuesday. And it says here that the president and his entourage are due here in the morning." He lowered the page and winked at the ruddy congressman. "Won't that be a thrill, Robert?"

"It will indeed, sir. I do not believe that I have ever been a part of an entourage."

They shared a weak chuckle. Matherly groomed his huge muttonchop whiskers with a nervous hand. "I was wondering, sir," he began.

Here it comes, Custer thought.

"—if I might prevail upon you to lend your support to a project of mine."

The Savior of Kansa Bay sighed inwardly and tried to look interested. It seemed that no one spoke to him anymore without it being to prevail, or beg, or entreat, or otherwise cajole him into doing some sort of favor. It was so tiresome. He didn't know how Lincoln had stood for it for twelve years, or how Grant had stomached it at all.

They were better men than I, he thought privately. I'll have to really think about it before I let myself get coerced into a second term.

As the Yanktonian senator continued outlining his plan for extending the railroad from the Rock Island bridge on into Washita, Custer considered his fate.

The leap from war-time commander to peace-time politician had been too severe. He ached for some activity that didn't involve sitting at a table and arguing. He'd had six years of talk, and was tired of it. He wanted action. That would have been reason enough to press the issues of Frontier Expansion, but he was thankful for anything else that helped his cause.

America had purchased the frontier territories two generations ago from a bankrupt king, handing over enough cash to bankroll Louis XIV through XVII. But the land still had to be won and now, after years of bloody conflict, they had taken most of it. No, *he* had. The new state of Yankton, and the territories of Missouri, Kansa, and Santee—also well on their own way toward statehood—these lands were theirs because of the campaigns he had commanded to victory. But the Unorganized Territory still lay out there, galling him with its emptiness.

But the American public didn't seem to care. The nation was bursting at the seams with its nearly fifty millions. Why, his home territory of Michigan had two million souls in it alone. One territory! They needed room, and room was one thing the Great Frontier still had in abundance. But the people—and the Congress—were against any further aggression to secure the territory.

It just made no sense. The Union owned it. The Union needed it. So damned be those who would deny it to the Union, and damned be the savages who would not admit defeat. He swore to see his grandchildren playing on the open prairie before he closed his eyes for the final time.

But such a plan needed more than just armies. It needed people. Regular people, and lots of them. Several pieces fell in place in his mind.

"Robert," he said, interrupting, "you've got a good idea there. A grand idea."

"I do?"

"Indeed you do, but your thinking is much too small."

"It is?"

"Of course," Custer said. "Don't you see? I mean, a rail line to Washita? Why stop there? Why not continue straight on through your whole territory and on, across the Missouri, and into the Frontier?"

"Well, why not, indeed!" Matherly warmed to the topic.

"Your territory could become the staging ground," Custer went on. "The jumping-off point for thousands—maybe even millions—who wanted to help tame the interior of North America."

"Ahh. I see what you mean. Like a . . . a western gateway."

"Precisely. A western gateway."

The senator sat forward in his chair, elbows on his knees. "Think of it," he said, and began enumerating on his fingertips. "Trains and ships and boats and carriages and coaches and wagons, all streaming in. Hotels to put them up in style or simplicity, according to their means. Restaurants and saloons to refresh them. Purveyors and grocers and stables and wheelwrights and blacksmiths to prepare them. And then, once they've gone, they'll still need products from the East. Steel, textiles, lumber. Oh, yes sir, Mr. President. I see it. I *see* it!"

"Good, good. Now you go back to Washita and work on it. That's the kind of plan that I need, Robert. Big and bold. You bring me a plan like that and I'll support it. You have my word on that."

The senator stood and bowed from the waist. "Thank you, sir. This has been a most enlightening conversation. Now, if you'll excuse me, there is much correspondence to which I must attend."

Custer nodded, dismissing the round man. He watched as the senator trundled off, calling for pen and paper to be sent to his rooms. The door to the sitting room closed after him.

"Go, Robert," Custer whispered, sending his thoughts after the retreating figure. "With you and with others like you, I'll flood the plains with people. Every homestead will be an outpost, every town a fort, every man a soldier prepared to defend and protect his land." He nodded, satisfied with the vision, and once again raised his paper.

From outside the window he heard the jingle and clop of an arriving horse. Quick steps and raised voices told of some urgency. Custer stood, folded the newspaper neatly, and placed it on the seat of his chair. He turned to face the sitting room door just as it opened.

It was Samuel, his personal attaché, and along with him were the two guards who "protected the presidential person"—a bit of the Lincoln legacy left over from a bad night at the theatre. Behind the trio stood a soldier—private or corporal, he could not see—soaked through and grim as death.

"Let him in," Custer said. "What is it?"

The young man came forth and saluted. He opened his mouth but did not speak, struck dumb by the legend before him.

"Spit it out, Corporal," he said, hoping to break through to the boy's military discipline with an officer's imperiousness. "That is an order."

The corporal saluted again, needlessly, but spoke. "Your pardon, sir, but there's news of the *Abraham Lincoln*. Bad news, sir."

"What is it? What has happened?"

Others around the room stood; two congressmen, a senator, the generals. They gathered closer to hear news of the great craft they saw sail off so gracefully a handful of days before.

"She's gone down, sir. A patrol picked up a survivor and brought him in. It's . . . Lescault, sir."

Custer did not flinch at the news, well aware that others were watching him. He maintained his composure.

"And the rest of the crew?" he asked in a calm voice.

"One dead, sir. The other wounded and captured by the Cheyenne. We don't know who."

The president stood, unmoving, eyes staring at the young soldier, through him, beyond him into the depths of infinity that stood at his back and threatened to roll forward and engulf Custer and all he knew.

One dead. One captured. For which should he hope?

"Get me a horse," he said.

"But sir," said Samuel. "The roads—"

"Get me a *horse*," he barked as his temper briefly gained the upper hand. Then, controlled once more, "If you please. I want to return to Fort Whitley immediately."

Samuel Prendergast, a thin, aged man who had served with Custer since his first days in Congress, stepped close and spoke softly. "Mr. President. We're already overdue in D.C. We must leave here as soon as possible."

"I can wait for the roads to clear just as easily at the fort as I can here in Candide. There's a survivor out at The Whit and I want to talk to him.

"Now get. Me. A horse."

Samuel nodded and stepped back.

"Yes, Mr. President."

CHAPTER 4

Hatchling Moon, Waxing
Fifty-Three Years After the Star Fell
Near Two-Kettles Creek on the Red
Paint River

The day had been clear and full of spring light. Now, with the sun asleep behind the distant mountains, the land gave back the warmth it had borrowed and the slivered moon lit their way.

They had ridden all day and into the night. And tonight was the first night of the Hatchling Moon, a time of family, of dancing, and the return of plenty. The camp of the People lay ahead, and the three warriors were anxious to be among them once more.

Storm Arriving looked forward to seeing his mother and younger sisters. He wondered if Standing Elk would send another proposal for Blue Shell Woman, his eldest sister, now that he would be home for a while. He hoped that she had not run off with the young Kit Fox soldier during his moon-long absence. Blue Shell Woman was a good girl, but Standing Elk was impetuous and impatient. Storm Arriving had not liked refusing his first proposal—that sometimes led to an elopement—but the young man had been too untried. He needed a few coup to count before he was worthy of a great chief's granddaughter like Blue Shell Woman.

He would know soon enough. Already he could smell the first threads of woodsmoke. There was a low ridgeline a few miles ahead and they had just passed

Two-Kettles Creek where, as a boy, his other-father Bull Cannot Get Up had lost the tip of his finger trying to capture a hatchling walker. The People would be camped in the plain just beyond the ridge.

The riders sped through the night, the moon their guide across the hills. Their whistlers were tired, but they smelled the closeness of home, too, and it made them stronger. Storm Arriving saw that his companions were likewise affected.

Big Nose sung a sweetheart song quietly to himself, thinking, Storm Arriving knew, of his wife and their young babe. Even Laughs like a Woman was affected. Though straight-backed and terse as usual, he kept an eye dead ahead and would occasionally lift his nose to test the air. Though the Contrary was bound to live apart and alone, it was better to be apart and alone and also near the circle of the People.

Only the *vé'ho'e* seemed unaware of their closeness to the camp. One Who Flies still sat hunched over like an old grandfather, his hand holding the first rope like an eagle's talon and his eyes seeing no farther than the crest on his whistler's head. Storm Arriving kept a close watch on him as they approached the dark line of the ridge.

The whistlers were panting hard now, but called out anyway in long whoops that ran from their bellies to the tops of their heads.

A man appeared, standing from his crouch down in the buffalo grass. He was of the People, but Storm Arriving could not see his face in the moonlight. Laughs like a Woman raised his Thunder Bow and let out a war whoop. The guard on the ridge recognized them and whooped in return. One Who Flies looked up suddenly, as a man awakening from a sleep.

He is blind with his eyes open, Storm Arriving thought with a shake of his head. I can smell the cooking meat and the whistler flocks, and even the herd of buffalo two ridges beyond this one. How sad to be so unconnected with the land.

The warrior guard sang out as they rode on to the

height. He sang a Kit Fox welcome song, for that was
the soldier society that Storm Arriving and Big Nose
called their own.

Ho! Listen!
Come! Feast!
You Kit Fox! Be merry!
Gather at the Dawn!

Then they reached the height and slowed to a stop.
One Who Flies spoke in a low moan. Storm Arriving heard his meaning. Oh, Great Spirit, the *vé'ho'e*
was saying. Look at how many there are!

Storm Arriving turned with pride to view the gathering of the People.

The hillside sloped away and down to Cherry Stone
Creek which ran northwest to the Red Paint River
and the sacred mountains. Beyond the creek lay a
broad vale of land a mile deep and more than a mile
wide along the creek and river. Upon this black dish
of land the lodges of the People had been arranged
according to the old ways. They glowed like yellow
lamps, and sparks rose from the smokeholes like stars
rising to Séáno.

Each lodge was a circle, covered with a cone of
buffalo skin, the door facing the rising sun. They were
like the nest of a whistler or a songbird, and within
the circle lived the family. Near each family's lodge
were lodges of other family members—other-mothers,
married sisters—and the lodges of all these formed a
circle, with an opening toward the morning light.

Beyond the family circle were the lodges of the
band, the clan tied together by the bloodlines of the
women. The Closed Windpipe band, the Hair Rope
band, the Tree People band, the Suhtai; the camp of
each band was arranged in yet another circle, also with
an opening in the east. Nests within nests. And the
ten bands, when they gathered together as they did
now, arranged their camps in a circle around the
lodges of the Council and the sacred artifacts. Between

the camps of the first band and the tenth, there was
an opening to the east, toward the morning sun, and
the beginning of everything.

With four or five lodges to a family, and hundreds
of families to a band, the men on the ridge looked
down on a plain where more than ten thousand
hearths glowed with the warmth and strength of home.
The camp of the People filled the whole vale.

Around the southern and western rim of the camp
stood dark flocks of whistlers. Uncorralled and free to
roam, they were kept close by hobbling a few of the
flock matriarchs.

In the center of the camp were the sacred lodges,
the lodges of the soldier societies, and the Great
Council lodge. Each was a tall cone twice the height
of a family's lodge, but the fires within them were dim
or dark. There were no meetings or dances that night.

That will change, Storm Arriving thought, when we
bring One Who Flies to them.

"Nóheto," he said, and they took off down the
slope.

They came upon the second line of guardians at the
bottom of the slope. Storm Arriving recognized one
of them as a member of his soldier society. They were
allowed to pass, but not without a challenge.

"Who is that with you?" the warrior asked. "His
face is not known to me."

"He is a *vé'ho'e,* and he is my captive."

"He fell from the clouds," Big Nose added with
enthusiasm.

Storm Arriving shushed him, but the damage had
been done.

"Fell from the clouds? Is he the one?"

Big Nose kept silent this time and they rode on.

"Is he the one she told of?" the guard called after
them.

Storm Arriving complained of Big Nose to the spirits. "Why did he have to speak? Word of this will
spread faster than fire across the dry grass."

"Would you hide this from the People?" Big Nose

asked in self-defense. "They will all know tomorrow when you speak with the Council."

Storm Arriving humphed. "You are right," he said reluctantly. "But I do not think we shall have much sleep tonight."

They circled around to the left toward the camp's east-facing sun-road. Laughs like a Woman continued onward around the rim toward his own lodge. As the three remaining riders entered the circle of the camp, Storm Arriving spoke to Big Nose. "They will know that he may be the one from the vision, but you must not tell that he is the son of Long Hair. Laughs like a Woman does not know this and cannot tell it, but you and I both heard him say it. If the People learn of that, there are some who will surely kill him before morning. The Council must decide what to do with him."

"And if they decide he should be killed?"

"Then he dies beneath tomorrow's sun. Not before."

Big Nose agreed.

"Then I shall see you at the Council Lodge. He will be no trouble?"

"No. He will be big trouble. But I will deal with it."

Big Nose chuckled through a wry smile. Then he spoke to his mount and rode ahead toward the western edge of camp where his wife and family waited. Storm Arriving rode on, One Who Flies behind him.

The vale was alive with the familiar sounds of home. He heard the lively chatter of gambling songs from women playing the seed game. He heard robust voices of soldiers of the Elkhorn Scraper society singing camp songs. To one side, he heard the slower, serious songs of a medicine man tending to the ailing with rattles and deliberate words. And from every point came the beat of a drum—to time the game, to count the coup, to call the ever-present gods—and it ran like a heartbeat through the camp; a thousand hearts, each pulsing at its own speed, but each a part of the whole.

From the rim of the camp he heard the conversations of whistlers, the flute song of a lonely lover, the chuff and growl of walkers, and from the ridge, the heartsick howl of a coyote as he sang to the stars and the souls in Séáno, the place of the dead. Beneath it all, like the stitching that holds the cloth together, he heard the voice of the river and the shimmer of crickets.

These were the sounds of home, the sounds of his life from his birth. A Tsétsêhéstâhese was born in song and died in song. The drum was a circle, as was life; all a sacred hoop.

But the rhythm of the camp had already begun to alter as word of the *vé'ho'e* spread.

Doorflaps opened as the news traveled from lodge to lodge, family to family, and people stood near their lodges and searched the darkness for a glimpse. Reflected firelight turned faces into dark moons of curiosity and eyes into winking stars.

"Is he the one?" someone asked.

"Did he truly fall from the clouds?" asked another.

Storm Arriving did not answer them. Their questions disturbed him, for they were questions he himself had been avoiding.

One Who Flies was the one foretold by the vision given to Speaks While Leaving twelve winters past? Did he *really* fall from the clouds, carried to earth by the thunder beings? He looked at the *vé'ho'e* who rode silently, eyes taking in all. He searched for evidence of a silken thread that tied him to the Horse Nations. He saw none, but the blue wool of the coat he wore represented a different kind of thread that bound him, perhaps more firmly, than any single thread ever could.

"Is something wrong?" One Who Flies asked, aware of being scrutinized.

Storm Arriving shook his head. "Stay close," was all he said. Could this scrawny bluecoat really be the key to the People's future? Speaks While Leaving's visions had never proved wrong, seen through the fullness of time, but this man seemed an unlikely hero.

He decided that Big Nose had been right. It was something for the Council to decide. He had been wrong to want to kill him at the cloud-that-fell.

They passed through the camp of the Hair Rope band and into the lodges of his own band, the Tree People. People who had come out to welcome him home stood silently, staring guardedly at the stranger he had brought into their midst.

Finally, he spied his family's lodge. Like the others, it was alight with a welcoming glow, but his lodge was a bit larger and was decorated on one side with blue stars and a white moon, and on the other with dark handprints over hail and bolts of lightning.

They stopped before it.

"This man is called One Who Flies," he said to his family and the gathered neighbors. "He was found trespassing on our land near where the White Water meets the Big Greasy. He has told me that he fell from the clouds. I did not see this happen, but he says that it is so. Tomorrow I will take him before the Great Council of Chiefs. That is all I have to say about it until then. *Hámêstoo'e.*"

The four whistlers crouched to the ground at his command. He stepped off and greeted his mother. Then he turned to his sisters. "Blue Shell Woman. I am glad to find you here." His eldest sister blushed and his younger sister smiled at his half-teasing. Storm Arriving hesitated. He wished for a quieter welcome, but the man who had ridden in with him denied him that. Looking at the solemn faces all around him, Storm Arriving felt that the world had changed while he had blinked his eyes.

"There is food," his mother said. "Are you hungry?"

He smiled. *That,* at least, had not changed. "Yes, Mother. Some food would be very good."

"Come," the tall Indian said. "Come with me."

George slid off his whistler. The three women—kin to Storm Arriving, it seemed—went through the oval door in the side of the skin lodge. Storm Arriving motioned for George to follow. With a backward glance at the crowd of stern faces, he complied.

The lodge seemed larger on the inside than the outside would allow. The large oval floor was perhaps fifteen feet across the width, nearly twenty front to back. A score of bark-stripped saplings supported the skin sides of the lodge, rising from the edge up through the central smokehole. Additional skins, pale and supple, lined the inside of the walls from the floor to the height of a man. In the middle had been dug a rectangular firepit in which a low fire burned. It was warm, cozy, and filled with the comforting scents of dressed hides and fragrant wood.

The women settled in on the left side of the lodge. George moved to follow but a strong hand pulled him back and pushed him toward the right.

"Sit there," Storm Arriving said. The right-hand side of the tent was relatively empty. The ground near the lodgepoles was covered with dry grass and hides. There were a few packets and bundles arranged neatly in the low corners near the edge, but absent was any sort of furnishings such as filled the left of the hearthpit.

"There," Storm Arriving said, pointing to the empty area. "Sit." George did so.

The eldest of the women moved to the fire. She picked up several rocks from the rim of the hearth and set them within the coals. The youngest girl brought an armful of sticks to feed the flames.

The left side of the lodge was obviously the living and sleeping area. Atop the grass-and-hide flooring lay willow twig screens, mats filled with rushes from the river, and more hides. Storm Arriving sat on the bed farthest from the door. Behind him was a backrest made of woven willow twigs and covered with another pelt. It creaked as he leaned back against it. The Indian sighed. He and the older woman spoke quietly as the girls brought a piece of leather and a waterskin to the hearth. They fashioned a bowl in the dirt and ashes and lined it with the leather. They filled it with water and, using two sticks as tongs, picked up the rocks that the older woman had placed in the coals. Gently, they lowered the rocks into the bowl where they made the water hiss and steam. The water was quickly heated and George's stomach grumbled as they then added dark pieces of dried meat and slices from a round, white tuber. The girls said nothing, but their eyes were eloquent with surreptitious looks at him and anxious glances exchanged with one another.

The younger of the two was perhaps thirteen or fourteen years old, very pretty, with the raven-black hair of her kind, and the eyes of a week-old fawn. The older girl was in the last of her teens Her face was broad of brow and cheek, yet with a narrow chin. Her eyes, when she stole a look at George, seemed like abyssal depths of darkness. Her skin was like burnished wood; too fine to be living flesh, she seemed instead to have been carved by a master artisan—a wooden Galatea come to life. From her ears hung several pairs of earrings made of shells and feathers and porcupine quills, and bands of gold and silver metal adorned her wrists and fingers.

The girls worked with modest grace. When they sat, it was not cross-legged as George and Storm Arriving sat, but always with knees together and feet to their left. When they stood or moved about the lodge fetching implements or supplies, it was with a silent fluidity and poise that George had rarely seen in the young women of society, much less in girls on the Frontier.

Storm Arriving sat forward as the aromas of the stewing food crept beyond the firepit. He, too, was a fine-looking creature, and George noticed a strong resemblance between him and the older girl.

"This is your sister?" George asked, opening the conversation with the safest of many possible assumptions.

"Yes. She is called Blue Shell Woman. This woman is my mother, called Picking Bones Woman. And this one—" He poked the young girl in the side with a teasing finger. She twisted and smiled but neither laughed aloud nor spoke. "This one is called Mouse Road. She is my youngest sister."

"Mouse Road? What does that mean?"

"Mouse Road? It means . . . the road a mouse travels. The tiny tunnels through the ground and grass."

George nodded. "You have no wife?"

"No," Storm Arriving said. "Not yet."

"Still, it is a fine family."

The mother spoke to them. From within another of the tall wicker backrests she produced a pair of shallow wooden bowls and a horn spoon. She lifted a small slice of meat from the pot. It was still dark, but now was plump from its stewing. She handed the spoon with its morsel of food to Storm Arriving. The tall man took it and, from his position near the fire, held out the spoon to each of the four directions in turn, then upward to the rising smoke. Finally he lay the strip of meat close to the edge of the fire and handed the spoon back to his mother. She then ladled meat and slices of boiled white root into the bowls. The aroma was overwhelming but George did not immediately fall upon the meal when it was handed to him. Life as the son of a man of politics had taught him the art of diplomacy. His stomach, however, had never taken to the many lessons at long banquet tables, and it let out a long, feral squeal. Mortification set fire to his cheeks. The girls hid their smiles, adding fuel to his embarrassment.

"Your tapeworm is talking to you," Storm Arriving said. "You should feed him."

Put at ease by their gentle humor, George took his host's suggestion.

The meat was thick, flavorful, and easy to eat. The tubers lent a mild spice of their own to the stew and helped to fill his squeaking belly.

While the two men ate, Blue Shell Woman and her mother prepared the sleeping areas. They laid out heavy buffalo pelts and blankets in the three areas between the wicker backrests. Blue Shell Woman brought another pelt and blanket and made a sleeping pad for George. He watched her as she did these things, fascinated by her every move.

Her hair was done up in two braids that, though pinned up behind her head in long loops, still fell to her waist. Her dress, like the one her mother and sister wore, was made of two panels of supple hide— front and back—that were tied together at the sides. Elbow-length sleeves were attached also, with ties rather than stitches. Her blouse-front was decorated with the kind of blue shells George had often seen on the sandy Missouri beaches. The wide neckline was tied closed at the right shoulder, but the left side of the neckline was held by only a loose strap. The top seam of the left sleeve had been left unfinished, leaving it to fall open at her side, revealing the curve of her collarbone, the swell of her shoulder, and the bare length of her arm.

Belted at the waist with a thick leather sash with brass disks sewn to it, the dress fell past her knees; longer on the right than on the left. Beneath her dress she wore fringed leggings and, on her feet, moccasins of leather and hide.

George had known only two types of women. The women of society whose garments covered every inch of their forms from neck to wrist and toe, and the tawdry women of the frontier saloons who left little to a man's imagination. This young woman, however, was an extraordinary combination.

She moved with the confidence and grace of a well-bred dilettante. She was modestly clothed in all ways except for the bareness of her bow arm, a nakedness that served only to accentuate that which was hidden.

He tried to view her as a primitive, as a barbaric heathen, and to feel the pity and revulsion that should come from proximity to such a creature, but he could not. Her quiet manner forbade it, as did her steady regard of him. The shape of her neck and the curve of her shoulder—instead of instilling repugnance or lust—set within him a fierce appreciation of her beauty.

The bed laid, she retreated around the far side of the fire, never crossing between anyone and its light. She settled with her sister on the bed they would share near the door.

George noticed that Storm Arriving and his mother were both looking at him with no little interest. The family sat for a time without speaking. Outside, far off in the darkness beyond the glowing skin of the lodge, George heard a flute playing in a minor key. Storm Arriving said something in his own language. Blue Shell Woman stared at her hands in her lap. She blushed, a cloudy sunset along her cheekbones.

"Do you hear the music?" Storm Arriving asked George.

"Yes. It seems a sad little tune."

"It is Standing Elk, a young warrior with a good future. He is a suitor to Blue Shell Woman."

George understood at once: his appreciation of Blue Shell Woman's beauty had been too frank. "I see," he said, and then, "I am very tired and my head begins to ache. May I lie down?"

Storm Arriving waved a hand in gruff permission. George lay down on the thick pelt, faced the wall, and put the blanket over him. The blanket was of heavy wool and carried the broad striped design of the Cabot's Bay Company.

George found that oddly ironic. The Indians allowed only a few French-speaking traders to settle in the Unorganized Territory. The French traded with them, and with the British to the north. Thus, through this strange set of circumstances, George lay on a buffalo skin in a lodge in the middle of an uncharted land, and was kept warm by the wool of Shropshire ewes from a land a world away. He wondered for a moment how his mother and sisters were faring. It had been over a year since he had seen them, and now he might not ever again. He recoiled from that conclusion, and listened instead to the quiet whispers between Storm Arriving and his mother. Eventually, the shadow of sleep washed over him.

He woke once in the night. The fire was low but still burning with flame that waltzed across the pulsing coals. Blue Shell Woman and Mouse Road lay asleep together near the door. Picking Bones Woman slumbered noisily in the bed next to them. The place for Storm Arriving was empty. Instead, the Indian sat cross-legged near the fire, his eyes full of borrowed light, watching George.

"Sleep," George whispered. "I won't attempt anything."

Storm Arriving made no motion, said no word. George closed his eyes again and let sleep once more have its way.

In his dreams, a dark-haired woman touched his cheek with a teakwood hand.

"Today is a no-hunting day. No one may go hunting today." The deep voice of the crier lifted Storm Arriving from his half-sleep.

"Today Storm Arriving wishes to address the Council of Chiefs. Three Trees Together calls all chiefs to meet at the Council Lodge when the sun is three hands high. Council meeting at three hands high.

"Today is a no-hunting day . . ."

The crier passed close to the lodge and continued on his rounds through the encampment.

Today the *vé'ho'e* would be believed or disbelieved; one way or the other, today would mark his life. Storm Arriving appreciated the importance of the situation, for it would mark his own life as well.

The *vé'ho'e* lay curled under his blanket like a squirrel under autumn leaves. He stirred and rubbed at his eyes a moment, then came awake with a jolt. He stared about him, unsure of his whereabouts until he saw Storm Arriving.

"Good morning," One Who Flies said as if the day were like any other. "Where have the women gone?"

"For water," he replied.

"Did you sleep well?"

The simple question—so ordinary—nettled Storm Arriving. He surged to his feet. "What kind of man are you?" he asked. The *vé'ho'e* sat back and blinked. "What are you? What kind of man? Today is *not* like any other day. You are my *captive,* and in a short time I will bring the Son of Long Hair before the Council of Chiefs and they will likely say that I should kill the Son of Long Hair." He stepped closer to the man he had brought from the prairie into his home. "You will most likely die today, *vé'ho'e.* And yet you wake up and ask me how I slept. What kind of man are you that whines when captured but faces death with calm?"

One Who Flies blinked again through a puzzled expression. "I . . . was just . . . being polite."

Storm Arriving stared at the man with hair as pale as summer grass. "I do not understand you, *vé'ho'e.*"

The other straightened and looked at him with cold confidence. "Ame'haooestse," he said. "Do not call me by that other word. I do not know what it means but I can tell by the way you say it that it is not a good word. To you, my name is Ame'haooestse."

The doorflap opened and Picking Bones Woman looked in. "What is it?" she asked. "Hiding Antelope said he heard loud voices."

Storm Arriving clenched his teeth and took a deep breath. "It is nothing, Mother," he said. "He just makes no sense."

His mother laughed and entered the lodge. She carried several water skins in a variety of sizes. "Who can make sense of the men of the Horse Nations?" She hung the smaller skins on pegs and lay the large ones on the ground. "They have forgotten Grandmother Earth. They do not know *Nevé-stanevóo'o.* How can you expect them to make sense to a sane person?"

Storm Arriving sighed again. "You are right, my mother. I expect too much of him." The girls entered the lodge carrying the rest of the day's water. He caught Blue Shell Woman stealing a bold glance at One Who Flies. He scowled at her and she scurried over to her mother's side.

"I hope the Council knows what to do with him," he said to his mother. "I do not want him here another night."

His mother gave Blue Shell Woman a long, meaningful glare. "I agree with you," she said. "But he is your responsibility, and you must watch over him until the Council decides otherwise."

The sun seemed to rise slowly through the morning sky. Storm Arriving checked on it several times, and each time, though his mind told him a hand should have passed, it had not moved more than a finger's breadth. His patience—usually a strength—was tight and worn thin like an old drumhead, and he felt it likely to crack beneath the slightest pressure. He was able to last through the early morning only through occupation.

By the time the crier's call for the Council meeting began to drift across the camp, Storm Arriving had cut and sharpened four arrowheads out of sheet iron traded from the Snake People of the southern deserts. The *vé'ho'e* had sat nearby as he worked; not speaking, only watching, always watching, his pale eyes taking in everything, his brow beneath the angry slash of his wound furrowing whenever Storm Arriving slipped and cut his finger or scraped his knuckle.

"The chiefs are meeting," the deep voice sang out. "The Great Council meets."

Storm Arriving took his arrowheads, his honing stone, his carving knife, and his small piece of flat iron and rolled them up in a flap of thick leather. He gave the bundle to Mouse Road to put inside with his other arrow-making tools. Then he stood, arranged his hair and his earrings, and set his long knife in the wide belt that cinched his pale buckskin tunic about his waist. He motioned for One Who Flies to get up.

The *vé'ho'e* stood and raked his white hair back

behind his ears. He brushed the dust from his seat and buttoned the front of his blue coat.

"Are you stupid?" Storm Arriving asked, not unkindly. "Is it that you do not understand that you may die today?"

One Who Flies looked at him with eyes suddenly sad. "No. I am not stupid," he said. "I understand the danger, but I am an officer in the Army of the United States of America. I must behave with a certain level of dignity. I have failed at this in the past, but today I will not."

Storm Arriving took a deep breath and let it out slowly. "I think that I have misjudged you," he said. "You are still a crazy *vé'ho'e,* but perhaps you are not the whining coward I once thought you were."

One Who Flies looked out toward the center of camp, his features melancholy. "I do not wish to die," he said in a confidential tone. "I do not think that any man truly wants to die."

Storm Arriving thought of his father in his final days; a once proud and powerful man struck down by the spirits, unable to speak, unable to use his right arm, unable even to hold his own water. He had watched his father hobble off through the snow-shouldered trees to ask the sacred persons to finish the job they had started.

"You are wrong about that," he told One Who Flies. "There are times when a man may truly wish to die. But wished for or not, it is always better to die bravely.

"Come. We must go."

Custer could hear the arguments before he entered the meeting. He stood outside the open door of the rough-sided building that Colonel McCormack used for staff meetings. It was a small, one-room cabin that was large enough for the command staff at The Whit, but it was too small by far to hold some of the personalities now inside.

"It's foolhardy," said one of the generals. "Premature and foolhardy."

"But we must do something," said another, turning palms up on the polished table.

"I agree," said Custer from the doorway. The assembled officers rose.

"Mister President," they said in loose unison.

Custer moved to the empty chair at the head of the table. Samuel, his aide, followed in behind, and the two special service guards took up their posts by the door.

The generals were shoulder to shoulder and there was a fair amount of shifting of chairs and *sotto voce* muttering as they retook their seats.

On the long table lay maps of the frontier territory. Custer noted with irritation that a great deal of the paper was blank.

He remained standing as the others settled in. As he prepared to speak, he leaned forward on the table to confer his earnestness and trust.

"Thank you for joining me this morning. To reiterate sentiments already spoken in this room, we must do something. We cannot continue to treat this 'Indian Problem' as if it were going to somehow resolve itself and disappear because frankly, gentlemen, it will not. Samuel?"

Samuel stepped forward with several sheets of paper. The pages were covered with rumpled lines in his tiny script, accompanied by glyphs and sketches so cryptic that no one else could ever guess their meaning. The thin aide shuffled the sheet and, after settling his glasses on his narrow nose, began in an unsteady tenor.

"Gentlemen, the president has asked me to provide you—as far as is possible given the limited resources of Fort Whitley—with an historic perspective on this situation, so that you might better appreciate the true scope of the Indian Problem." He swallowed and launched into the body of his report.

"It has been over four score years since this land was acquired from France. Since that time, the United

States have been unable to successfully establish a presence in the territories." He squinted as he leafed through the papers until he found the one he sought. He pushed his spectacles farther up on his nose and continued.

"The Army's victories in warfare and successes in relocation and civilization of tribes such as the Osage and Pawnee—actions many of which were led by President Custer himself—have not been repeatable against the Cheyenne and their allies; the Arapaho, the Lakota, and others. In the past twenty years there has been an escalation of aggression along the Kansa, Yankton, and Santee borders. What started with acts of vandalism and theft has grown into arson, assault, and murder; all are now frequent occurrences along the frontier. More recently, we have seen increased attacks against our patrols and forts. Skirmishes, ambushes, and raids on supply transports have all become commonplace. In the estimation of many—including some of the great strategists in this very room—the possibility of large force contact is inevitable."

The officers mumbled among themselves. Custer smiled grimly. He knew that last statement would cause a stir. Admittedly, he was probably the *only* man present who felt that such a dire statement was true. The statement had succeeded, however, in starting the minds of his all-too-complacent commanders down the path he wanted them to travel.

Samuel went on, chronicling the attacks and losses of the past five years. The list was long and thorough; Custer had kept close watch on all efforts to advance into the frontier. The generals, however, had failed to adopt new, bolder actions, as fear of even greater failure weakened their devotion to duty.

Samuel delivered his list in a dispassionate monotone, placing the evidence before them. The officers began to fidget as their own failures and losses were read out loud. The old man's reedy voice laid down the names of the dead like sheaves of wheat. Dates and facts buzzed about the room; carrion flies, lazy and bloated, each one droning closer than the last.

"And just this week, the Alliance attacked and downed the *Abraham Lincoln.* Value of the craft is estimated at $250,000. Wounded: Private Louis J. Lescault. Killed: . . ." He paused a moment as Custer had instructed him. The news had come only hours before.

"Killed: Lieutenant Elisha H. Reed. Missing and presumed captured: Captain George A. Custer, Jr." Samuel organized his papers and sat down.

"Are you sure?" asked Meriwether. At forty-five years of age, he was the youngest general in the room. A solid Methodist from Carolina, he had a son of his own in the Army; a young man near the age of young George.

To answer Meriwether's question, the president leaned back in his chair and reached into his vest pocket. He pulled out a chain to which a gold watch was attached. It had been a fine piece of workmanship, but its case was dirty and dented, almost obscuring the ornately etched "R" on its cover. He pulled the cover open, revealing the broken crystal and the hands forever still at 1:58. Custer laid the bent and broken timepiece on the table.

"This came to me a few hours ago. Kiowa natives, working on behalf of U.S. forces, traveled deep into the Unorganized Territory and, utilizing information provided by Private Lescault, discovered the wreck of the *Lincoln.* A shallow grave had been opened by local wildlife. They found this watch near the body. It belonged to Lieutenant Reed." He let the watch lie on the table as a tangible reminder of the sacrifices made trying to tame the Frontier.

"What we have done up to this point," he told them, "has not worked. We move ahead only to be beaten back, burned out, starved off, or killed trying to hold our land.

"*Our* land!" The watch danced as his fist hit the table. He stood and began to pace the narrow width of the room.

"Three generations ago we *bought* that land. It is *ours*. Yet, for the past eighty years we have done nothing with it, nothing except send men into it to die. And I tell you now that it must stop."

He returned to the head of the table. "Today, I call an end to this ridiculous practice of encroachment and retreat. The enemy does not treat this as a series of unrelated incidents. They treat it as a war, and so should we.

"I leave for Washington within the hour. There I will address the Congress, and I will not leave those marbled halls until we have declared war on the Cheyenne Alliance."

The assembly rose with a shout of denial. They all spoke at once, each drowning the objections of the other until Meriwether raised a hand for silence and got it.

"You would send us into another war over this? Haven't we laid down enough dead in these territories?"

"And how many more men will you consign to their deaths with *current* methods?" Custer forcibly reined in on his own anger. "Gentlemen, we *must* take this logical next step. I refuse to waste good men in futile efforts. If young men are to die for the Frontier, I say let them die with the hope of victory in their hearts."

"But, Mr. President . . . war?"

"What else can we do, John?" Custer pointed to the watch on the table. "I will have no more of that," he said. "So, what else? Shall we give it up? Those savages have held that land for eighty years, gentlemen. Eighty *years*. Shall we wait eighty more? Shall we leave it to the British colonies in Canada? To New Spain in the south? Shall we let the *French* take it back? Shall we simply walk away from it and say to our neighbors 'Go ahead. Be our guests. Take it if you can'?"

The officers responded with quiet denials; some shook their heads, and a few sat down looking bewildered.

"I do not relish the prospect, gentlemen, but war

has become necessary to our safety as a people, and to our prestige as a nation."

"But how can we?" Meriwether asked. "The Cheyenne are not a recognized nation. We can't declare war on a group of renegades. They're not even citizens."

Tibbings spoke. "We did it during the War Between the States. As far as we were concerned, you and yours were nothing more than a group of renegades. Citizens or not."

"We had rights. The states had *rights*." Others rallied to old sides until Stant raised two fists and slammed them down upon the table.

"Quiet! All of you!"

The others froze and looked.

Stant was an older man, gray of hair and whiskers, but still as strong and vigorous as a man in this thirties. A veteran of several wars and countless battles, he had served with Custer during the Kansa campaign.

"The question of whether or not the United States can declare war on the Cheyenne Alliance is irrelevant." The others took their seats as Stant spoke. "Our commander-in-chief has given us our orders, and whether they are a nation, whether they are citizens, it makes not a whit of difference. They are an enemy force within our borders, and it is high time we rid ourselves of them. Now just settle down, the lot of you, and take your orders like soldiers."

Custer viewed the faces before him. He saw pain in their eyes: pain, sadness, worry, fear, but he also saw, in every gesture and every glance, the resignation he needed.

Sway them with logic, drive them with discipline, he had often said. He only hoped that it would work half as well with the Congress. Civilians were so unpredictable.

He picked up Reed's battered watch, put it back in his pocket, and walked over to the side of the table. Leaning in between Colonel McCormack and General Stant, he put his finger on the border that separated

Yankton and Santee from the guesswork that lay beyond them.

"This is our biggest problem," he began. "The Missouri and Santee rivers. Once we get beyond them, we have to be able to stay there."

After the meeting, as his luggage was being loaded onto the coach that would take him through the fifty miles of draining muck and to the rail spur at Candide, Custer turned and looked to the northwest.

He saw the walls of the fort, the low, rising land beyond them, and the faint haze that hung forever above the Gulf of Narváez. The air from off the inland sea was cool and smelled of low tide. It calmed him somewhat, breathing the fresh air and feeling the forenoon sun on his back, but his knowledge of actions now in motion tightened his gut and made his throat dry.

At that very moment, messengers rode to the north and east with orders. Within hours, squads of heavily armed reconnaissance teams would ford the great rivers of the frontier, their objectives to see, to report, and not to die. Within days, troops from every region of the Union would begin to move, to gather, to prepare for what every American had hoped would never come again: another war.

The last war had been long and vicious. A field in Maryland still lay fallow, poisoned with the outpourings of the twenty thousand men who died there. Farmers in Kentukee and Virginia plowed their furrows and watched as the bright curving blades turned up white bones and black cannonshot. Men still limped for want of a leg that lay under the grass in Georgia or Penn's Sylvania. Custer had fought in battles from the Atlantic to the Gulfs. He had led the campaign that had swept clean the Missouri Territory. He had seen a thousand men die in the drawing of a breath and had risen from lieutenant to the brevet rank of brigadier general in three short years, standing all the while ankle-deep in the blood of men. The War Between the States had defined him. His subsequent commands in the Kiowa and Kansa campaigns had established him, had made him a national hero, and had paved the way for his rise to the Presidency.

Even so, even though it had made him who he was and made possible all the good things he now enjoyed, he hated war. He hated the death, the waste, and the excess that was war. He felt in his pocket for Lieutenant Reed's battered watch. He held it in his hand, feeling its scars with his callused fingertips, and tried to see beyond the veil of haze that hung across the Gulf. He wished he could see, by an application of will, through it to his only son, just to see if his dearest boy still lived. But the lands did not open up before him, the distances kept their secrets, and when Samuel came to tell him the carriage was ready, he turned away knowing no more than he had in hours prior.

CHAPTER 5

Hatchling Moon, Waxing
Fifty-Three Years After the Star Fell
Along the Red Paint River

Two Cuts still ran like a wild whistler, keeping low to the ground and blending his color as they passed through brush and tall grass. Without a rope saddle to steady her, Speaks While Leaving had to lie close along his back and guide him with her feet and her calm commands. The People were encamped nearby—she could taste the smoke in the wind—but she did not realize how close she was until she came upon the first guard. She passed by the outer guard before he could stand. He shouted a whoop of warning and Two Cuts whistled in alarm.

"He'kotoo'êstse," she said to him and *"Nóxa'e,"* Be quiet. Wait. But he did neither. They approached the last rise and three more guards stood up from their posts. The smell of the camp, of woodsmoke, and the sudden appearance of men drove Two Cuts into a panic. He trumpeted dire warning, the three-tone call resonating loudly from his hollow crest.

He turned to flee and Speaks While Leaving, rather than fight with a frenzied mount, slid from his back and tumbled to the ground. She watched him go, head high to watch for pursuit, her thin rope trailing in the wind of his flight. He had done what she had asked, and she would ask no more of him today. He would make his way to the main whistler flocks to the west of camp. Tomorrow she could find him again. She thanked the whistler and the spirits for their help and lay down in the grass, exhausted.

The three guards ran up to her. *"Népévomóhtâhehe?"* one of them asked. Are you all right? Her dress torn and bloodied, her legs bare; they were right to ask.

"Héehe'e," she told them. Yes, I am fine.

"You should hurry then. Storm Arriving is before the Council with a man that fell from the clouds, just as your vision foretold."

She stood and swayed. *"Ne-a'éše,"* she said. Thank you. Then, sleep dogging at her heels, she ran down the slope.

There was a large crowd around the opening of the Council Lodge. Men and women stood shoulder to shoulder. The three men near the doorway listened closely and turned periodically to report in barely audible whisperings the important points of the proceedings to those nearby. Those people in turn passed the observations onward—word for word, so as not to distort the words of the chiefs. The process was repeated with rapidity and accuracy. As Speaks While Leaving came near, she could see the information from the lodge move outward with the nodding and turning of heads. Whispers spread like the ripples from a stone cast into still water. She arrived just as the latest ripple reached the limit of the crowd.

"Red Wolf speaks," a large man from the Ridge People band told them. " 'You cannot believe a man like this. He says he is the son of Long Hair. He says he fell from the clouds. If you believe the first thing, then he is a liar because Long Hair is a liar. The second thing he says must then be not true. If you believe the second thing instead, then you cannot believe the first, because the thunder beings would not send us the son of a great enemy. I do not believe either of the things he says.' " The people nearby signed their agreement with Red Wolf's words. The speaker noticed her, his brows growing close in concern.

"Eestseohtse'e," he said, recognizing her. The others nearby turned to see her. "Are you all right?"

"Héehe'e," she told them, "but I must speak to the Council about this man."

The man before her did not hesitate. He turned and applied his bulk to the crowd.

"Eestseohtse'e is here," he said in a loud voice. "Speaks While Leaving must address the Council."

A path appeared, lined with reverent faces. She heard her whispered name precede her like wind through tall grass, surrounding her but never coming near.

Eestseohtse'e, the wind sighed. It is Eestseohtse'e.

She began to follow her escort but tripped and stumbled to her knees. The wind held its breath. Her days without food or rest fell upon her and made the world dim. Friendly hands lifted her to her feet. She thought of thanking them but in concentrating on her goal the thought evaporated.

The Council Lodge was very tall. It stood before her, imposing, its top so very far away. The lodgepoles stuck out of the smokehole like a bristle of quills, and from their tips hung over-the-smokes—decorations made of long tufts of buffalo hair and small silver bells that talked to one another in the lazy breeze.

She stopped at the door to the lodge and looked at the faces behind her. She saw those she knew and those she did not. She saw faces of those she had healed or whose children she had healed. She saw the relations of those who had been beyond her aid. She saw warriors and wives, grandfathers and grandmothers. And in them all she saw herself reflected. She saw clearly the hope her vision had brought, the hope of a world where Ma'heo'o protected the People, and where battle was only a matter of honor, not of survival.

But she also saw the name of Tsêhe'êsta'ehe—Long Hair. The name brought confusion and pain at the

memory of those lost in the battle and fires along the
Big Salty. Many of the People had died attempting to
defend that land. Their names were still sung in lonely
moments. She saw the pain of past loss cloud the vision of future peace and she knew that only she could
cleanse their hearts, if indeed anyone could.

She turned from them and faced the dark interior
of the Council Lodge. All was silent, within and without, her only companion the drum of her own heartbeat.

One of the young chiefs who guarded the door
beckoned with two fingers. She swallowed with a
mouth suddenly dry and stepped from the past—from
the vision and the dance—into the darkness and its
reality.

For a moment she was blind, but soon the lodgeskin
above her became pale and the dark shapes on the
ground became stern-faced men seated around a
small, ceremonial fire. Smoldering sagebrush created
a smoky spiral that spun as it ascended into the sunlight. It gave the scent of holiness to an air already
heavy with tension. The sixty-men—the forty-four
chiefs of the People plus the sixteen from the allied
tribes; the Inviters, the Little Star People, the Sage
People, and the Earth Lodge Builders—sat cross-
legged in a double circle, the youngest of them closest
to the door and the eldest and most respected toward
the back. In the *vá'ôhtáma*—the place of honor farthest from the door—sat the four principal chiefs. Eldest among them was Three Trees Together, a
venerable and most respected man of the People
whose father had fought the iron-shirt-*vé'hó'e* of the
south.

"Nenáasêstse," he said. "Come here so I can see
you." He patted the ground beside him.

No one spoke as she walked around the outside of
the circle of chiefs. She passed behind One Who Flies
and Storm Arriving, who sat near the wall. She passed
behind her father, One Bear, who sat with the younger
chiefs. When she reached the back of the lodge, Three

Trees Together patted the ground again. She knelt at his side.

He touched the rip in her sleeve, touched the dried blood on her arm. She felt his gaze searching her face. "You have had a hard ride, Daughter."

"Yes," she said.

"And you have something you wish us to hear."

"Yes. About One Who Flies."

He lifted a hand that had seen a hundred summers. "Tell us," he invited her. "We will listen." And then he smiled, softly, gently. It filled her heart, his smile, and made her breath come easier.

As she faced the circle of chiefs, she saw much hatred there, especially in the chiefs from the Inviters, who had suffered the most and lost the most at the hands of the father of One Who Flies. She needed something extra to give her words greater weight.

She went to the fire and took up four sprigs of grandfather-sage from the bundle that lay near the firepit. She touched the leaves to the coals. They crackled and snapped and curled up like a living thing. When they began to smoke, she took them from the fire and placed them on the floor before her. The pungent smoke rose in a thick coil. She passed first one hand, then the other, through the cleansing smoke. Then she pulled the smoke down each leg and down each arm saying a silent prayer each time. Finally, with both hands she pulled the smoke over her head, completing the ritual. The smoke purified her. The chiefs would know now that when she spoke, she spoke the truth.

"I have heard some of the words you have said about this man," she said, pointing to One Who Flies. "They are wise words. They are cautious words. But I have seen something that you have not, and it is something you must know before you decide about this man."

She stood so that all could see her; and pointed at One Who Flies. "That man fell from the sky. I saw a thing that was like a cloud, but not a cloud. It was white and it was big and it floated high up in the sky and it rumbled with thunder. I saw lightning flash upon it, too, but unlike any cloud it fell and after it fell I found him. One Who Flies. And when I saw his face, I knew that I had met him once before. This is the man from my vision, the one who will help us turn back the bluecoats of the Horse Nations.

"He is the one I foretold." The chiefs were disturbed by her words and looked at one another for answers. "But there is more you must know," she continued. "After the cloud fell and the patrol came and left with One Who Flies, I saw another bluecoat; a survivor. He was wounded but alive and able to walk. He had hidden in the woods as I had. I tried to kill him but all I had was a stick and he had a pistol. He killed my whistler and I fled, thinking it better to tell you than end up dead with the Council not knowing."

She stepped back away from the firepit. "That is all I have to say." The chiefs were silent as she made her way around the perimeter toward the door.

Three Trees Together spoke.

"Nóxa'e," he said. "Stay with us a little while."

She agreed, unable to refuse the invitation, and seated herself outside the circle of the Council.

All remained in quiet thought, considering Speaks While Leaving's words. Then Two Roads, warrior chief of the Kit Fox soldiers, rose to speak. He was a brave warrior of many years and his arms and chest bore the scars of many battles. "Speaks While Leaving was right to tell this to the Great Council and I do not doubt her story." Heads around the circle signaled their agreement. "There is one thing I do not understand, however. If you knew that One Who Flies was the man from your vision, why did you leave him alone on the prairie?"

Two Roads sat, indicating that he was done. Speaks While Leaving stood. "I knew Storm Arriving was on patrol in the area. I knew he would see the smoke and would come and find One Who Flies." She sat.

Two Roads stood again. "But why did you leave?"

Speaks While Leaving had known this question would come. She could only give one answer. "That is between Storm Arriving and me," she said, and put it to rest. No one would pry further, at least not publicly. Queries would be made, quietly, one-to-one, and the truth would be known if it was not already—there were no secrets among the People—but Storm Arriving would not be shamed, as he might were she to bring their private matters into the Council lodge.

One Bear stood. Though the youngest of the chiefs of the Closed Windpipe band, he was highly respected. His chest and arms bore scars, some the jagged lines earned in battle, but most the methodical stripes and patches of a skin sacrifice. Eight finger-long lines on each arm, and two rectangular patches on his chest spoke of his devotion to the People. Speaks While Leaving listened with pride as her father spoke.

"I, too, believe the words of Speaks While Leaving," he said, "but not because she is my daughter. Her visions have always come true, given time, and when we danced her vision of the cloud-that-fell, we all felt the power of it.

"I believe the claims of One Who Flies as well. It makes sense to me. We could not ask for a better tool than the son of an enemy's greatest chief. As an ally, this man could tell us much. As a hostage, we could make Long Hair suffer and fear for his son's life. And as a corpse, he is one less enemy to fight.

"But this news of another bluecoat makes trouble for us. If he survived, Long Hair will learn of it. He will surely come after his son and he may come soon. We must be very careful in what we decide to do."

Dark Eagle rose before One Bear had retaken his seat—a rudeness that brought scowls of disapproval from the others.

"We have been careful too long," the young chief said heatedly. "It is time we dealt with this like the thing it is: a war. Until we beat them, the *vé'hó'e* will continue to come into our land. I say that Ma'heo'o has brought us the son of Long Hair so that Long

Hair *will* come to us. He *will* come, and we will attack
him and kill him and feed him to our walkers. Then
the *vé'hó'e* will leave us alone."

The impetuous chief sat down, and despite his disrespect to One Bear, everyone gave his words silent
regard. At last, Three Trees Together spoke from his
place in the *vá'ôhtáma.*

"We have heard much today, and we must decide
what to do. What shall we do with the *vé'ho'e* called
One Who Flies, and what will that mean for our future? We must not decide this now. We must go and
think and hear the wisdom of the People. We will
meet again tonight, when the crickets are singing.
Then we will decide."

The chiefs all rose from their places and filed out
of the lodge. Outside, the crowd began to spread out
with the news. Word would radiate quickly, ideas
would be discussed over chores or a pipe of tobacco,
and opinions would form and be shared. By evening,
the chiefs would have heard from their clans and societies and they would reconvene to create a consensus.
It took time, but long history had proven that the
method was sound.

Speaks While Leaving waited as the chiefs left the
lodge. Then Storm Arriving rose and walked to the
door, One Who Flies behind him. Speaks While Leaving lowered her gaze as the tall warrior approached.
He stopped as he passed her and took a breath to
speak, but the breath caught in his throat.

She reached out for him before she could think. She
froze with her hand suspended in midair, so close to
his arm that she could feel the heat from his skin.
They stood there for a moment in that way—nearly
touching, nearly speaking—until he took another step
and was gone from the lodge. One Who Flies followed him.

She was alone then. The shaft of sunlight through
the smokehole made the shadows dark and solid. She
saw nothing in the darkness but her hand, hanging
there where it had come so close to touching him. So

close. She heard again his breath, the word almost spoken, the word that would free them both from their pride and their stubbornness. She ached to hear it, to hear his voice.

Tears welled, hot and sharp. She did not fight them. She let them overtake her vision. They made the shadows writhe and ripple. They spilled from her eyes and fell into extinction against the hard, dry ground.

George rushed to catch up with Storm Arriving. "What was that about?" he asked.

The Indian wore a scowl that spoke of death and mayhem. "The Council is considering. They will meet again tonight and decide your fate."

"No, that much was obvious. I meant the woman. What did she—"

"That was Speaks While Leaving, daughter to One Bear, a chief of the Closed Windpipe band. She told the Council that she saw your cloud as it fell from the sky."

George shook his head. "I mean between her and you. What just happened between her and—"

Storm Arriving had stopped and George felt the Indian's scowl turn upon him. His words became dust in his mouth.

"I apologize," he said. "She just seemed . . . I just meant . . . nothing. I meant nothing. I apologize."

They resumed their walk back toward the lodge, though at a much reduced pace.

"How many wives do you have, One Who Flies?"

The question took George off-guard and he laughed in surprise. The glare returned and he held up his hands. "I'm sorry. It's just that in my country we never have more than one wife."

Storm Arriving agreed. "That is the usual way among the People, as well," he said. "Do you have one?"

"No."

They walked a bit more. George was not sure, but they seemed to be taking a more roundabout path to their destination than the one they had traveled that morning.

"Do you have a paramour?" the Indian asked. The word seemed odd coming from such a man, but George made no comment and simply answered the question.

"No, I do not," he said.

It was bright as they walked past the lodges at the limits of the encampment and out toward the river. The dust that had dogged their footsteps did not follow them into the rough prairie grass. Sunlight reflected from stalks that bent in the ever-present breeze. From the river, the squeals of children at play could be heard. From the woods to the west George could see women returning with bundles of sticks for the evening fires, walking in a line as they came down from the hills; a hundred dark-clad figures singing an eerie tune as they marched toward camp all a-bristle with branches and twigs.

Like Great Birnham Wood on the move toward Dunsinane, George thought.

"Then you know nothing of women?" came the question.

He shrugged. "I would not say that. I just haven't found the right one to marry."

Storm Arriving picked up a stone and threw it out over the prairie. "I have."

"Speaks While Leaving?"

The Indian shrugged. "Except she will not have me."

George ventured his opinion carefully. "Back at the Council lodge, she seemed to have some feelings for you," he said. "But she would not look you in the eye."

They stopped walking. They gazed out to the east where the valley opened onto the plain. Clouds with towering white crowns slid across the land on blue-gray bellies. Columns of light slanted down from heaven to touch the earth.

"I forbade her," Storm Arriving said as they re-

garded the epic view. "In the third year of our courtship we had an argument. She said she could never
be the wife of a man who thought as I did. She told
me not to speak to her until I changed my mind. Out
of spite I told her not to look at me until I did."

"How long ago was that?"

Storm Arriving squatted and picked up another
stone, a round green stone the size of a hen's egg. He
took two long powerful steps and threw it. It disappeared from sight while still in the air and George did
not hear it hit the ground.

"It has been four years."

George picked up a similar stone and felt its weight
in his hand. He stepped up alongside Storm Arriving
and threw it with all his might. It remained in sight
and landed with an audible thud.

"There is such a thing as too much pride," he said.

The Indian smiled as he looked out across the
world. "If I am too proud, then she is too stubborn."

"Is there a difference?" George asked.

Storm Arriving laughed out loud, a sudden, almost
bitter sound. "No," he said. "I suppose there is no
difference."

They turned and began to walk back toward the
camp.

"By the way," George said. "What was the argument about?"

Storm Arriving's smile lingered.

"You," he said. "The argument was about you, and
about what we should do when you came."

George walked alongside his tall companion, putting
the pieces of conversation together. "Wait. Do you
mean to say that four years ago you knew that I
was coming?"

Storm Arriving cocked his head to one side. "Not
you exactly, but someone like you. And we did not
expect you to be the son of a hated enemy."

George ignored for the moment the comment about
his father. "And you knew this . . . someone . . . would
come? Four years ago you knew this?"

"No. Not four. Twelve. We have known you would come for twelve years."

George continued walking, mouth agape. "How?"

The Indian's smile had finally faded, replaced by features of a solemn mien. The two men were walking—aimlessly, it seemed to George—but Storm Arriving had made a point of listening to every word George had spoken. Now, the Indian took a moment to phrase his statements with great care.

"Speaks While Leaving is a woman of great power. Ma'heo'o and the *ma'heono* have sent her visions on several occasions. They have always come true. Her first vision came when she was very young. It was in the Ball Game Moon, and she was given the vision of a great snow that would come upon the camp. No one believed her except her father. He brought all his whistlers' eggs into his lodges. During the night the snow fell and the air became bitter cold. Many families lost many eggs that night. They believed in the truth of her visions after that.

"Then, twelve years ago she was given a very powerful vision. She saw a great conflict between the *vé'hó'e* and the People. She saw a cloud fall from the sky and a man upon it, brought to earth by the thunder beings. With his help, she saw the People make an end to the conflict."

They were walking through the camp once more. The families were spread out—a group of lodges here, another group thirty or so yards away. Women sat in the sun and worked at hides or sewing or grinding meal on flat stones. Men sat in groups making arrows or shields or talking and smoking their pipes. They all looked up as the odd pair walked past, but they neither spoke nor made signs of greeting to Storm Arriving. It did not seem to concern him, so George gave it no mind.

"Four years ago, I asked Speak While Leaving what she thought the vision meant and how she thought it would come to pass. She told me she thought that you would be—*qu'est-ce ĉ'est—un homme philosophique*?

She said that you would be like an advocate for the People; that you would help us make the *vé'hó'e* understand."

"And what did *you* say?" George asked.

Storm Arriving smiled again, but ruefully. "I laughed at her. I told her she was stupid to think such a thing. *Eya.* I was the one who was stupid, to treat her with such disrespect. I told her that when you came you would be a great warrior. I said that you would help us and that we would make a big war against the *vé'hó'e* and drive them from our lands forever."

George chuckled. "You were both wrong. I am neither a philosopher nor a great warrior. A soldier, perhaps, but not a warrior."

"No," Storm Arriving said and turned. He put a hand on George's shoulder and looked at him with eyes as black as the space between the stars in the sky. George felt a great intensity in the Indian's gaze. "No, you are not a philosopher. You are not a warrior. You are neither of those things. But you are *here,* and that is very important."

"What do you mean? What do you expect *me* to do?"

"I do not know what you will do, but you *will* help us keep our land."

"But this land isn't your land. It belongs to the government, to the United States government. I can't help you keep it. It isn't even yours."

"Not ours?" Storm Arriving looked down on George from his full height. "Who lives in it? Who keeps it?" He took George by the shoulders and pointed him to the north.

"There. That river. I played in that river as a boy. So did my father, and his father. And his." He turned to the south. "There, on that ridge. See that tall dead tree, the one that looks like two bony fingers pointing to the sky? When that tree was young and green, my grandfather stood beneath its branches and asked my grandmother if she would be his wife." He pointed to the east. "And in that valley my grandfather's grandfather's grandfather fell defending this camp from the Wolf People. And there," he said turning to the hills to the west. "Up there are the sacred hills and the Teaching Mountain where the People were given our most sacred objects, where we have sought guidance from Ma'heo'o and the sacred persons for all time."

He took a step back and spread his arms wide. "We have lived and traveled from the Big Greasy to the Big Salty to Grandmother's Land and to the mountains of the bighorn sheep. For ten years times ten years times ten years we have done this. We were created in this land. We *are* this land. We and the Inviters and the Cloud People and the Little Star People and even the Earth Lodge Builders. This is *our* land. Whose else would it be? Yours? Because one *vé'ho'e* writes it on a piece of paper? Because the chief of the Horse Nations gives some of the yellow *vé'hó'e*-metal to the chief of the Trader Nation, that makes it yours? Did the chief of the Trader Nation ever live here? Are the bones of *his* father in that valley? Do the spirit powers of *his* people live in that mountain?"

He leaned close and put a fingertip on George's chest.

"You cannot sell what is not yours. You know this. In your heart you know this. You cannot sell what is not yours."

George stood there, fuming at the affront. "This land belongs to the Union," he rasped. "To the United States of America. We have paid for it, in *blood* as well as in gold. Fighting the French, the Spanish, the English—"

"Fighting *vé'hó'e!* Fighting each other over something you do not own!"

"We *do* own it! We bought it from the French."

Storm Arriving laughed and suddenly George felt like he was falling.

"You cannot buy the land," he said. "You cannot buy it any more than you can buy your own mother."

George threw up his hands in exasperation. "If it

can't be owned, then how can you say that it is yours
and not ours?"

"Because this land is *my* mother, not yours,
vé'ho'e."

George straightened, stung by the term. "I told you
not to call me that."

"When you deserve your Tsétsêhéstâhese name, I
will use it. Right now you are talking like a crazy
vé'ho'e."

George trembled with anger. He wanted to lash out,
to strike, to destroy this man's every hope. "I will
never betray my country. Not to help you. Not to help
your people."

Storm Arriving was calm once more, his passion
tempered by confidence. "Yes, you will, *vé'ho'e.* You
will help us. You know that what they are doing is
wrong. And you know that this is my nation and not
yours."

"I know no such thing."

"Yes. You do," Storm Arriving told him. "Your
heart knows. Your head just hasn't stopped talking
long enough to hear it."

George hit him with a fisted blow to the jaw that
sent the Indian stumbling backward. Then he turned
and walked away, shaking stinging fingers.

"Where are you going, *vé'ho'e?*"

"Away from you," he shouted over his shoulder.

"Listen to your heart along the way," came the
reply. "Listen to it."

George walked. He felt the stares of onlookers like
goads. He walked faster. Eventually he ran. He ran
until his rage and his frustration were tamped down
by fatigue and trembling muscles. When he stopped,
he found himself far to the south of the encampment.
The only sounds that reached his ears were the whisper of the wind in the grass, the flutings of distant
whistlers, and the pounding of his own heart.

Listen to your heart.

The words taunted him and rekindled his anger.

What arrogance! Why, that savage did everything

but call us thieves. Thieves! Us! When everyone knows that they are the ones that . . .

The thought died in his mind, unable to complete itself. The land around him had taken on a different aspect. It was no longer mute; no longer a vast, wild country that lay between him and the horizon like a dumb beast of the frontier—beautiful but untamable, visible but unknowable. Now, it had a voice, and it spoke of love and of war, of youth and of old age. Storm Arriving's stories stood up from the roots of the trees and from the banks of the waters.

Frustration clouded his vision with tears. He wiped them away and fought back the ones that threatened to fill the gap.

"I will *never* betray the Union," he said, and though no one was there to hear him, he felt stronger for having spoken the words.

He sat for a long time on the hillside as the sun began its slow fall down toward evening. George watched the activities of the camp. Patrols came and went with regularity. The trails between the camp and the river were never empty as children went back and forth. There was a quiet, small-town atmosphere that seemed to George to be out of place in this rough manner of living.

At length he lay back and watched the lazy transformations of clouds so white they made him squint.

Should I run? They are not watching me. I could just walk away. And walk and walk and walk.

The sun—warm—and the breeze—cool—doused his thoughts and lulled him into a slumber.

"To'êstse."

He awoke with a start and sat up. He was in shadow, and the sky had darkened to evening. He heard a footstep in the grass and turned.

And froze.

The walker chuffed twice, two harsh coughing calls that echoed across the bowl of the encampment. In a small calm corner of his mind he knew the beast was half-again the size of a whistler: at least ten feet tall and over twenty feet long. At the moment, however, the greater part of his mind was concerned with only one thing: its head.

More specifically, its mouth.

It straightened its neck and chuffed again and George smelled carrion. It cocked its head and peered down at George with a large dark eye. The head was long and narrow, like a bird's, but no bird had ever had a mouth like this.

The walker's mouth was not beaked like a whistler's; it was a long, lipless gash lined end-to-end with pointed, interlocking teeth the size of a man's finger. This monster was no grazer, no browser. This was a predator of incredible proportions and ferocity. George had seen what they could do and the memory nearly paralyzed him.

"Ame'haooestse," someone said. Only then did George notice the girth rope around the walker's keel and the two legs kneeling astride the huge beast's back. A rider sat, perched atop the nightmare.

"Ame'haooestse," the Indian said. *"Nenáasêstse."* He pointed downslope. *"Nóheto."*

George looked to where the man pointed. Way down at the foot of the hill stood a woman, Speaks While Leaving. She raised a hand in greeting. George waved back.

"Nóheto," the rider repeated, followed by a long string of words that George had no hope of comprehending. His gestures were enough, however, and George stood—albeit slowly and with unsteady knees—in the shadow of the walker's terrible maw. When offered a hand to mount behind the rider, George stepped back reflexively with emphatic motions of denial.

The Indian laughed. He pointed again to Speaks While Leaving and told him with signs that she wanted to talk to him. George nodded. *"Héehe'e,"* he said. Yes, I will go.

The rider said something more, only one word of which George recognized: *vé'ho'e.* He then turned his great beast with the touch of two fingers. Its tail cracked in the air over George's head and then it was gone, loping off in ten-foot strides.

It was a full minute before George reacquired the ability to walk. He descended the hillside with everything a-tremble. It seemed a longer trip down than it had been going up.

"Come," Speaks While Leaving said when he came near. "You must eat something before the Council reconvenes."

"Thank you," he said, though the thought of eating was inconceivable to him at the moment. They began to make their way through the camp.

"How is your wound?" she asked, touching her forehead.

"Oh," he said. "Just a bad bump."

"You were insensible for quite some time. I think you make light of it."

"Perhaps," he said. "But I feel fine now. Thank you . . . for your help."

"It was my pleasure. I have a great interest in your survival."

He did not want to speak of visions and prophecies, so he changed the subject. "You speak French very well," he said, which was true despite her flat Quebecoise accent.

"I thank you," she said. "My stories and my talents at healing have made me welcome in many homes, even among those of the Trader Nation. I have spent many evenings with them in the years I have traveled our lands in hopes of finding you."

And again it came back to signs and portents. He sighed, exasperated.

"You do not believe in the truth of the vision," she said, a statement of fact. "That is understandable."

He tried to put his feelings in words. "I just don't know what you people expect me to do. I am an officer in the Army of the United States. How can I possibly help you?"

"Before you were an army officer," she said, "you

were a man. It is the man who will help us, not the officer."

"But don't you see? This confidence of yours—this faith in me—it's unreasonable. I am the sworn servant of the United States of America. I took an oath. I will not betray that trust."

Her smile was kindly and her manner was full of patience as they continued to walk. "Our confidence is not in you, One Who Flies. Our faith is not in you. It is in Ma'heo'o and in the *ma'heono,* the sacred powers. It is through them that I saw the vision, and it was with their help that we were able to dance the vision and bring it from their world into ours. Our faith is in the spirits and in the vision. You, whether you accept it or not, are simply the vision made manifest. Or to put it in words of your religion, you are an 'instrument of God.' "

George shrugged. "There is no point in arguing against such faith. I can only say that I will not turn against my own people."

She laughed then and shook her head. "You see things in such terms of this or that, all dark and all light. Very well, let me put it another way.

"If your neighbor had an ailment—a fever perhaps—and you knew that a tea made from the bark of a red willow tree was good against such fevers, would you give your neighbor some of that tea?"

"Yes," George answered tentatively.

"Even if you knew that the tea was very bitter and might even give him stomach pain for a while afterward?"

"I suppose so, yes."

"Then you might do something unpleasant to someone if it would do them an ultimate good?"

"I see what you are trying to say with this, but it will not persuade me to—"

"I am not trying to persuade you, One Who Flies. The time for persuasion is long past. We have tried to persuade your people to see their errors for two hundred years, but like a willful child, you will not listen. We Tsétsêhéstâhese do not punish our children. In the case of your nation, however, we may have made an error."

George stopped and laughed. She turned, puzzled.

"Children?" he said. "Us? Do you truly see *us* as children? How can you possibly, when we are so much stronger, so much more civilized than you? We have won every war we have faced. We have the weaponry, the industry, and the manpower to wipe you off the map if we put our resources to it." He stopped laughing and looked at her with somber sincerity. "And we will. Soon, if you don't cooperate with us. My country is running out of patience with your Alliance. We will come. And in greater numbers than you can imagine."

She signaled her agreement and began to walk again. "You are the stronger one, that is true; but being strong does not make you wise. Nor does it make you right. That is for Ma'heo'o to decide."

She continued to speak softly as she walked. "I had a dream several nights ago—not a vision, just a dream. I saw white men playing with my father's bones. They kept his bones in a box, and the box was in a chest, and the chest was in a room, which was in a stone lodge, in a city. He seemed so far from his land that I was sad, and waited for his spirit to cry out. But then I saw that the city was in the middle of the prairie, in a place I know along the Unexpected River, and I realized that his spirit had long since cried all it could."

She faced him squarely and he felt suddenly uneasy beneath her inspection.

"If you come, you will have to kill us all, and that will be a shame. But we will not be the first people you have erased, nor will we be the last. But I ask you to think about this: you are a brave man; it took great courage to fly the cloud into our lands. It also takes great courage to stand up to a great wrong. Do you know what it is to destroy an entire people? Do you know what it is to kill the last song of the last man? I remember the stories about the Sweet Water people that used to live on the far side of the Big Water. They are gone now, killed to the last one. This is a great wrong, One who Flies."

He could think of no suitable reply. She regarded him with frank honestly. No guile, no hidden purposes. He could see that she meant every word that she said in all earnestness, but meant *only* what she said. Even her judgments—judgments he felt were harsh and false—were given without cruelty. Somehow, that made the impression all the deeper.

"But I apologize," she said. "We have talked too long and I have upset you. In answer to your question, I do not know what you will do, only that you will do something, and that it will help us. Let that be enough for now and we will speak of other things, yes?"

"Yes," he agreed. "Please."

And so she turned their words to more mundane topics. They spoke of the weather—which they both agreed was not unusual—and of her journey back from the wreck of the *Abraham Lincoln*—which he thought remarkable and she found merely tiresome. But throughout their long walk and the quiet meal eaten under the silent stares of her father and mother, he could not forget her earlier words, nor those of Storm Arriving. All of their talk of everyday things served only to fill in the empty pieces in his puzzled view of these people. Every common scene, every detail made them all the more real, and just that much less alien. Finally, when the crickets were in full voice and the call came to reconvene the Council, he walked with her in silence. He entered the lodge and walked behind all the others as he had been told one should. He sat down next to Storm Arriving without a word, and through the whole of the long evening, as the chiefs stood and spoke and politely listened, he did not wonder what they were saying. He heard only his own incessant thoughts, and the questions that refused his ready answers.

* * *

Storm Arriving listened to the arguments, most of which now tended toward keeping One Who Flies as a hostage or, hopefully, as an ally. During the day he had helped to inform the People of the morning's occurrences, had talked to them as they considered their options, and had heard them speak to their elders, their chiefs, and the leaders of their societies. Their opinions had gelled during the day, and came back in favor of Speaks While Leaving and One Who Flies. Even most of the chiefs from the four allied tribes spoke in favor of the more prudent course of action.

A few groups—the Suhtai band, the Elkhorn Scrapers, and the chiefs of the Little Star People—recounted their heavy losses against Long Hair in the war along the Big Salty and called for rightful revenge. The chiefs all spoke and listened respectfully, but stolidly held their ground. Unless someone changed their position, the deliberations would likely continue into the morning's light.

For a while Storm Arriving watched One Who Flies out of the corner of the eye. The *vé'ho'e* sat without looking or listening, and acted much differently than he had that morning.

"Do you want to know what they are saying?" he asked him.

One Who Flies shook his head, his eye fixed on an invisible spot.

"No," he said.

Storm Arriving left him alone then, and waited patiently as the chiefs crept toward consensus.

CHAPTER 6

Thursday, May 13, A.D. 1886
Washington, District of Columbia

"It is, therefore, much more than your right to do so." Custer's voice echoed in the still House Chamber. It was a closed session. The doors were all shut and the gallery above hung vacant. He raised the sheet of paper he held and showed to all as he spoke. "In the face of these facts, and this solemn list of youth that now lays dead beneath the soil of the Unorganized Frontier, it becomes more than your right. It becomes your duty—your *sworn* duty—to declare immediately and without equivocation that a state of war has arisen within our territories. By any man's definition, this is so."

He put the list down on the lectern and stepped back. He hooked his thumbs in his vest pockets and looked at the worn carpeting at his feet.

"It is not an easy thing I ask you gentlemen to do. War is an ugly business, and even at its most glorious, it is still painful and bitter as bile." He looked up then, and never before had he seen a group of men graver than the senators and representatives before him. "I trust you, though. I have faith in you. I have faith in your courage and I have faith in the wisdom of the framers of our Constitution who reserved for this august body the power to declare war. I leave it to you, then, to help us overcome this terrible situation.

"Thank you, gentlemen. I await your response."

He folded his papers lengthwise and put them in his coat pocket.

The assembled houses of Congress rose as Custer stepped away from the lectern. There was none of the pomp, none of the cheers and approbation that always accompanied his State of the Union addresses. He turned and shook the hand of Speaker Carlisle, and of Vice President Hayes.

"You know what needs to be done," he said to his second-in-command.

"I'll see to it," the elder statesman said.

There were a few more handshakes and words of support as he made his way down the broad aisle, but not many. The senators and representatives had already begun talking among themselves.

Samuel met him at the door.

"The speech went well, don't you think?" his aide asked.

"Yes," Custer replied. "The *speech* went well. Its reception, however, is another matter entirely."

The Speaker rapped his gavel repeatedly as the doors to the House Chamber were closed. Custer and his aide walked through the Statuary Hall and down the newly marbled corridors of the Capitol Building. The flames of the gas lamps made reflections that fluttered within the polished stone. Custer said nothing, his mind consumed by the magnitude of his actions. He gave thanks that Samuel was not one of those men who felt it necessary to fill an awkward lull with insubstantial prattling. They let the silence wreathe them. As they walked, as their footfalls echoed down ahead of them, the silence lost its awkwardness and became a thing of comfort. They shared it easily, and Custer felt his burdens lighten.

The noonday sun bounced up from the new white stone steps like a thrown ball. The men squinted, emerging from the Capitol's dark halls into the brilliant day. Carriages rattled along the dusty streetstones, and touring visitors gawked as their president approached the curb where his own conveyance waited.

"Is Libbie home?" he asked as they climbed in.

"Mrs. Custer? Yes, sir, I believe so. At least there was nothing on her schedule for this afternoon." The carriage shifted as the two presidential guards stepped up on the rear and then it lurched off on its short trip up Penn's Sylvania Avenue. The whole contraption swayed and vibrated as it shuddered over the cobbles.

"I haven't told her yet," he said. "I can't wait any longer, though. The newspapers will learn of this soon enough."

They fell silent again as the carriage bumped across Eighth Street. Custer thought for the thousandth time how much he hated carriages. He would have much rather ridden horseback or even walked the short distance between the Capitol Building and his current domicile. He didn't bother his aide with his opinions, however. The old man had suffered them often enough.

He wondered how Libbie would take the news. The girls would be frantic, but they were at the age when melodrama permeated their every fiber. He consoled himself with the fact that their histrionics could hardly be worse than the tantrums the whole household had endured when Maria spilled tea on her new gown and had to go to a ball in an old dress, or when Lydia had been forbidden to go to the theater to see Miss Bernhardt perform. They would cry and wail, to be sure, but Custer could withstand that.

But Libbie . . . Libbie was a different matter altogether.

Throughout their married life, Elizabeth Custer had always been the epitome of the officer's wife. Always resilient, always resourceful, she had never complained of their post or their quarters or the roughness of their existence. She had suffered through years of frontier living among rough men. She had run the household with inadequate and incompetent servants. Custer knew he had not furnished her with the life a judge's daughter expected or deserved, and yet she had accepted it all with sweetness and strength and had given him in return three wonderful children; three gifts far in excess of his talents at providing. And now he must tell her that one of those gifts was in danger.

As they turned up onto the curving drive that led to the White House, he hoped that she would be able to forgive him should he fail to recover their lost son.

An hour later he and Libbie were sitting near the hearth in the Yellow Drawing Room. Her left hand covered her trembling right, a quail held to by a trapper's net. On the floor a cup and saucer from the rose-patterned tea service—a gift from the Earl of Norfolk—lay shattered in a pool of cooling tea. Janie, the colored serving maid, knelt at Libbie's feet sopping up the spill and collecting the pieces of damask china. The room was made cavernous by the silence of his wife's shock. The tiny sounds as Janie placed shard on shard were amplified into a tooth-grating cacophony that threatened to drive Custer mad. He bore it, however, with patient fortitude, taking it as a form of penance.

Finally, with exaggerated care, Janie finished and retreated to the hallway. The butler entered with another cup and saucer, which he set on the tray next to the teapot.

"Leave it," Libbie said as he began to pour. Her voice was heavy, thick: an anguished contralto. Her eyes were looking at the tea service, but she was seeing other things.

"Thank you, Douglas. That will be all for now." The aged Negro bowed slowly from the waist but his gaze never dropped. In the man's eyes Custer saw sorrow and the consolation of one father to another. He smiled sadly in response, and Douglas exited, closing the door behind him.

"How long has he been missing?"

"A week, give or take."

"Give or take?"

"We are doing all we can. I have mobilized the army and I just asked Congress to use their War Power to make it official. We're going to use everything we have to get him back."

Libbie stood quickly. The flounce of her dress pushed at the table leg. The tea set rattled like sun-bleached bones. "As if it were not bad enough that my only son is kidnapped by savages, now you are going to put him in the middle of a war?"

Custer stood, too, hands open and placating. "No, dear. It's not like that."

"Is it not?" she asked, suddenly imperious. "Tell me how it is not."

"But Libbie. Dear. He's not going to be in the middle of it. We intend to draw him away."

Her bravura cracked and tears spilled into the breach. "Oh, Autie. You can be so stupid at times." And she fled the room, leaving Custer to beetle his brow in an attempt to fathom this woman he loved so dearly and thought he knew so well. After a few minutes without success, he set it aside in favor of things he understood far better, and could do something about.

It was hot. The sky, clear for days, held nothing but the white dish of the sun in its blue vastness. George lay on a rock on the top of a ridge. The sun pressed down and he wished he had left his wool coat back at camp.

He had been staying as a guest with Storm Arriving's family since coming to the camp. He had been treated well and with open trust since the return of Speaks While Leaving and the decision of the Great Council of chiefs. He was of course pleased that they had let him live, regardless their reasoning, but the implication that he would somehow act against the United States made him nervous. How long would they wait for him to help? What would they do to him when he refused to act? He could not imagine that they would keep him alive after that so, while the

Council had decided to let him live, George saw it as only a stay of execution.

His thoughts turned once more to the idea of escape. Previous days had been without opportunity, but today! Today everything was different.

Today was a hunting day.

The crier had come early that morning, passing through the bands, giving the orders of the day. It was an earlier call than had been given on other mornings and George asked Storm Arriving why.

"Fire Bear says that today is a hunting day. Everyone should make ready for the hunt. He says that the Kit Fox soldiers will be in charge of it. That is my society, so I will help in leading the hunt."

"Is there anything I can do?" George asked, genuinely interested.

Storm Arriving signaled no with his hand. "It is a dangerous business. You would only be in our way."

"I have read how you hunt but I have never seen it. Is there some way I could watch?"

Storm Arriving pondered the request then spoke to his mother, who was rekindling the fire for morning. She replied with open hands and a few words. At that point Blue Shell Woman sat up from her bed and broke her customary silence, speaking to her brother and indicating herself as a willing guide. Storm Arriving said no—that much would have been obvious even if George had not already learned a few of the most basic phrases of their intricate language—but the young woman persevered.

From the look on Storm Arriving's face, it was clear that he was not pleased with the prospect. He spoke once more to his mother. The old woman pointed to Mouse Road, the youngest daughter. Storm Arriving brightened, and by the same margin, Blue Shell Woman's level of excitement was diminished.

"All the men will be involved in the hunt, but my sisters will take you to a ridge overlooking the path of the herd. You must make a promise to me, though. You must guard them and keep them out of danger."

"Agreed," George said.

"Good. But we must hurry. There is barely time to bathe before the walkers must start."

The Indians bathed every day. Usually the women bathed first as they went out early to retrieve the day's water. The men went down later, after the crier had come. Initially, George had refused to participate, his more cumbersome clothing and his modesty prohibiting such an exposure of his person. On the fifth day of his captivity, however, Storm Arriving had made a comment about meat left in the sun. It was obvious George had to overcome his reservations in favor of hygiene. There was a good deal of snickering and not a few stares at the paleness of his skin, but as he was the first white man many of them had seen and certainly the first naked one, he did not mind too much.

That day, two days ago, as he had worked on laundering his clothes, a few of the boys came close. They approached him as they would a wild animal, with sidelong steps and wary eyes. He smiled at them but it did not ease their anxiety. Finally, one of the older boys—perhaps nine or ten years of age—came near at the urging of his fellows. He reached out toward George's arm with one experimental finger. He touched his skin and leapt back. The boys conferred in their language and the same youth advanced again. This time he touched the pale skin of George's arm with his whole hand. Surprise swept across the boy's features and he spoke to the others. They all touched George in turn and, curiosity satisfied, ran off to play at mock battles along the riverbank, leaving him to finish his laundry no wiser as to their purpose.

Today, however, while the dawn had lain like a dream beneath the eastern rim of the world, George and Storm Arriving were scrubbing themselves with river sand when the boys had returned. This time they brought others. Ten or twelve young Indian boys came up to George, and after he signaled his acquiescence, they each took their turn touching the pale flesh of his upper arm. Bemused, George turned to Storm Arriving.

"What is it they want?"

"Your skin is white, like the clouds that brought you to earth, but warm to the touch. This is a surprise to them. They thought it would be cold, like the clouds overhead."

"Ah," said George with a laugh. "Tell them that the clouds are always in the sunlight. It's only cold beneath them."

Storm Arriving related this to the boys, who suddenly grew fearful and ran for camp.

"What?" George asked. "What happened?"

Storm Arriving shrugged. "I only told them what you said. That, and that when you break wind, lightning bolts shoot from your rear end."

George gaped, then recalled the look of terror on the boys' faces and broke into laughter. The laughter convulsed him and he sat down in the river. Storm Arriving was laughing, too. As the moment faded and George was wiping tears from his eyes, he felt purer. Sitting there, naked, with the live water swirling around his body and the breath of dawn paling the crystal sky above him, he felt a freedom in his soul. Then that, too, faded. The world returned, and he was once more a lone man adrift upon the unknown deep.

A short time after that, George had stood with Big Nose as the hunt began to organize. Big Nose explained the events occurring around them, translating each command as it was issued.

Storm Arriving stood with the other Kit Foxes at the lead of the gathering hunters. Almost all the walkers were in place and ready to go. The riders of whistlers were only just beginning to congregate, their mounts skittish, at a respectful distance from the monstrous walkers.

Two Kit Foxes arrived on their walkers. Storm Arriving immediately directed them to the front. "These two men," Big Nose explained, "White Feather and Has No Blanket, they will set the center. All others

will spread out in a line to either side. Those four . . ."
He pointed to a group of Kit Foxes at the end of the
column. "They will be the ends. They will split into
pairs and be the ends of the line." Storm Arriving
addressed the others and Big Nose continued to translate. "The rest will watch these men, he says. They
are in charge of the line. Do not attack until they do.
He tells the young ones to be patient, and to learn
from the experience of their elders."

The walkers were agitated. Big Nose pointed to one
of them. "These are not grazers like whistlers. They
do not crop at the grass every day to fill their bellies.
These are hunters. They eat a great deal, but not
often. They have not eaten for a week and they know
a hunt means food for their empty bellies."

Other soldiers were organizing the whistler riders,
keeping them in check until the walkers were clear and
it was time for them to take up their own positions.

"Walkers!" Storm Arriving shouted. *"Nóheto!"*

The riders whooped once and then toed their mounts
into action. The huge beasts pushed off toward the
south with long, ground-shaking strides. In moments
they were gone, lost in the mist that hung low against
the ground, their chuffs echoing from the black hills
in the predawn air.

George felt a tug at his sleeve. He turned to find
Blue Shell Woman and Mouse Road with two whistlers standing nearby to take them all to their vantage
point. The girls mounted, Mouse Road tucked up behind her sister and hanging on to her waist. George
climbed aboard the other whistler, and they took off,
heading northeast out of the camp, away from the
direction taken by the walkers.

They traveled quickly, and though George had
come to trust the lizard-like beasts and their abilities,
his stomach still lurched as they leapt across unseen
rills and swerved around shadowy obstacles. They traveled back over the ridge George had crossed on his way
into camp, down to its foot, and then turned southeast
along its base. Blue Shell Woman squealed and slapped

at Mouse Road's hand. Mouse Road giggled and George could see the flash of her grin through the gloom.

The air was fresh and moist, but the sky was cloudless, promising a day both hot and humid. Miles passed beneath them.

They circled back around to the south, then turned to climb a slope to their right. They reined in near the top, and Blue Shell Woman tied their mounts to the bough of a nearby alder. She and Mouse Road motioned for George to follow, and they led him in stealthy approach to the crest.

George and his two guides crept through the dew-wet grass until they reached a flat boulder that leaned out toward the plain. They climbed upon it and peeked over the edge. Beyond, the prairie lay like a frozen sea, becalmed in geologic time. It rolled away from the world in motionless swells until all details were lost in the morning mist and the purpled distance of the south. Blue Shell Woman was on his left and Mouse Road was on his right. They talked to one another, barely audible, whispers in a whispered language. Mouse Road began to shiver. She snuggled up close to George, continuing to talk through chattering teeth. Blue Shell Woman came close to him on the other side. She was shivering as well. There, keeping one another warm, they waited.

An hour passed before the sun shot its first rays over the eastern horizon. Mouse Road tugged on George's sleeve and pointed. Down on the flat, the horizontal light accentuated every irregularity in the nearly featureless plain. With her help, however, he was able to study the scene and soon discerned several odd shadows forming a long curved line stretching out away from them like a string of dark pearls in the green grass. The nearest was at the base of the hillside, a quarter mile away; the farthest was two or so miles distant. George concentrated on the nearest and saw the hint of movement. It was a walker, prone in the grass, its body flattened down in a shallow trench of its own digging, its head lowered so only its eyes were above the level of the knee-high grass. Beside it he spied its rider, crouched down as well, his hand on the first rope.

George looked at the other lumps in the long line, each a walker lying in wait. He had neither seen nor heard them arrive, but nevertheless, there they were. The sun ticked higher and the long shadows shrunk to nothing. Even though he knew of their presence, he could no longer spy them in the grass. They were virtually invisible now, an incredible feat for a group of beasts so large. Only the nearest one could he still see, and that one only through an application of determination and focused attention.

Now, the chill was long gone. The sun was approaching the top of the sky and the day had grown hot as they kept their vigil on the rock. Blue Shell Woman lay beside him, sleeping on her back in the sunlight. Mouse Road sat at the base of the stone, braiding grass stems into intricate plaits. He looked back down toward their whistlers cropping at the abundant grass. All he had to do was run over there and grab one of them. He could be mounted and gone in moments. Pursuit, if it came, would be miles behind him.

Mouse Road just then motioned for him to get back down out of sight as she crept back up onto the rock. She pointed to the eastern limit of their view. There, coming from the southeast, was the long dark line of the expected herd.

The ragged edge of the herd approached slowly but inexorably as the buffalo ambled along the traditional route toward their northern pastures. First came a handful of bulls, one- and two-year-olds, still too young to go out on their own. They plodded through the grass, stopping now and again for a mouthful before continuing on in advance of the main body of the herd. Their complaints and grumblings filled the air with a sound like groaning trees.

As the bulls came within a mile of the line of hidden

walkers, George could see the rest of the herd. These were mature beasts, huge creatures with high, humped shoulders taller than a man, a ton or more of danger on the hoof. Nearly all of them were females, but a few ancient bulls paced along on the fringes of the herd. Amid the cows were all of the season's calves, small spindly creatures dwarfed by the size of their relations. More bulls, younger ones again, straggled behind. The bulls of mating age did not travel with the main body, he knew, but would arrive later in the year, in rutting season.

The bison progressed in this loose formation, eating as they strolled through the landscape. Their winter coats hung on them like tattered clothes that had been torn through, worn out, and patched in a hundred places. Strips of hair dangled from their flanks and shoulders, swinging with their slow steps like moth-eaten scarves.

The young bulls approached the hidden line of hunters, walking calmly ahead across the plain. George, concentrating on the nearest hunter, was sure that the lead bulls had walked right past. In that moment, the hunter struck.

On strong rear legs the walker lunged up from its shallow lair. Reaching the nearest bull in one great stride, it seized him just behind the massive head. It jerked its prey twice and George heard the bull's cry of panic cut short. All along the line the hunters struck, riders hanging on to their ropes, and four-score buffalo went down. The rest of the herd stood stunned for a heartbeat, then started to run.

The rider shot a marking arrow into the fallen buffalo, and at his command, the walker dropped its kill and ran after another. The others did the same.

The air was filled with the cries of startled bison and the thunder of hooves. Then another sound shimmered through the air. A multitude of voices rose from the northeast.

Mouse Road stood up, pointing and shouting with excitement. From around the rise on which George and the girls had rested rode hundreds of riders on whistler-back, and from the far side of the herd came hundreds more. The herd was flanked and cut off. The whistlers began to circle. The bison created circles of their own, calves in the center surrounded by a ring of massive adults. The riders charged the defensive groups. When they drew a defender into chasing them, then the riders turned and shot. Arrows hit their marks with unbelievable accuracy. George saw a huge cow dropped by a single shot from a hundred yards. Rifle shots snapped in the air above the plain, but they were few, as most hunters rejected these imported weapons in favor of their own short, but powerful and accurate bows.

The riders harried them, the walkers stormed them. Soon the herd abandoned all defense and simply fled. Then the hunt began in earnest.

Riders used lances and arrows to drop their quarry. Fleeing bulls turned to charge their attackers. Most failed but a few succeeded and whistlers and riders went down under rampaging hooves.

The two girls stood arm in arm, pointing and shouting, all need for stealth long gone. The scene was brutal for both man and beast, but neither the carnage nor the injuries on the field dampened their exuberance. They cheered and waved and clapped their hands. Blue Shell Woman beckoned to George. She pointed into the dusty fray and, in thickly accented French, said, "My brother."

George followed her pointing hand and finally spied the tall Indian with the shorn right temple and the white feather in his hair.

Storm Arriving was in the thick of it. Dust filled his nose and the taste of metal filled his mouth. He crouched over his whistler's back, his heels pressed in close to his mount's spine and his knees pressing outward beneath the first rope to keep it tight. He fitted another arrow to his bow and guided his course with a dig of his left toe. The bull was big but with the speed of youth. It galloped away and to the left wanting distance from its pursuer but not from the herd.

"*Nóheto*," he shouted, and his mount put on more speed to overtake the bull. Storm Arriving moved them even with their target, but not close.

The bull saw the threat approaching along his right flank. He put his head down.

That was the move that Storm Arriving had been awaiting. He aimed as the bull turned to charge and let fly. The arrow struck, but high—a wound but not a kill. He dug in with his left foot and they turned sharply inside the arc of the bull's attack. The move took them past the bull, and they turned to pursue once more. They came up on his left side this time. Storm Arriving took out another arrow and sang a song to the spirits, asking for this arrow to strike true. He pulled and aimed. The bull halted just as the arrow flew and the shot went wide and pierced his hump above the shoulder. Then the buffalo headed into the thick of the herd.

Storm Arriving followed, weaving between riders and buffalo alike. The bull carried two of his arrows. The wounds, while not mortal, would weaken him and make him easy prey to wolves should he escape this hunt.

Please, he prayed to the bull as he put another arrow to his bow. Please.

They rode through the herd and beyond it, back out into the open. The bull's tongue hung down as he panted for breath. The whistler fluted, sensing the beast's fatigue. Storm Arriving gave a nudge to his mount and they sped to challenge the bull again, but the bull halted just as they came close, forcing them to turn away to avoid the thrust of his powerful head and sharp, black-tipped horns.

When Storm Arriving came around for another pass, he saw that the bull had stopped. He stood, facing them, his breath coming on hard. One arrow stuck out of his hump, and the other was buried to the feathers in his side. He pulled at the grass and shook his huge frame. Dust lifted from him in a cloud.

Storm Arriving knew that this was the moment, the moment when the bull had to decide.

"My friend," Storm Arriving said to the buffalo. The bull looked at him, his brown eyes steady and clear. "I know that you feel the pain in your side where my arrows have hit you. I know you feel the blood running down your side. I know, too, that you still feel the power of life within you and the desire to run forever on the plain. You have run well and fought bravely, my friend, and I ask you to give me your life, so that I might feed my family."

The bull blinked and shifted his feet. Then he shook himself again and turned his side toward Storm Arriving.

Storm Arriving raised his bow and pulled back on the string.

"Thank you, my brother," he said.

The arrow flashed between them, flying from hunter to hunted like a thought. It struck the bull in the side, just behind the foreleg and under the slope of his shoulder. It drove deep and punctured his heart. The bull crumpled, his legs suddenly dead, and fell heavily onto the grass.

Storm Arriving sang the song of thanks to the spirit of the buffalo, for it was a great gift the bull had given. Then he turned and rode back toward the herd.

He worked hard, but quickly, and took two more kills. Within three hands of time it was over and he sat on his panting whistler, the scent of blood in his nose, and the sunlight pressing the sweat from his skin.

The hunters had taken what they needed from the huge herd and hundreds of carcasses littered the landscape. The rest of the herd, ten times ten thousand strong, had veered to the south and could still be seen like a dark stain on the green and gold of the plain. A few riders—the inexperienced and the unlucky—still harried the trailing edge of the herd. Most of the tribe, however, was now gathering at the site of the hunt.

Families gathered around their kills and sang their thanks to the departing spirits for their sacrifices.

Here and there across the field of the hunt, walkers took their prizes, finally allowed by their riders to feast on one of their kills. They ate with violence, holding the body down with a taloned foot and ripping off joints and strips of flesh to be swallowed whole. Bones and all.

From up on the ridge he heard his sisters' voices. Blue Shell Woman and Mouse Road ran down the slope toward him. Behind the girls came One Who Flies, leading the whistlers. Picking Bones Woman rode in from the west, bringing two other whistlers with travoise.

They were all smiles as One Who Flies approached.

"Three!" Storm Arriving said, jubilant. "Did you see?"

One Who Flies nodded. "It was very impressive," he said. "I have never seen such a hunt."

"Ah, the spirits favored me today." He turned as others came to congratulate him. Men old and young, themselves fresh from their own kills, clasped his wrist and greeted him with joy. Big Nose and Laughs like a Woman stood nearby. Laughs like a Woman came up to him, a frown on his face. He looked Storm Arriving up and down, made a sound of disgust, and walked off. The gathered men laughed and began a new round of congratulation. They were all speaking at once until Big Nose began to sing. Then they all joined, singing the high-pitched tune through grins that did not pause for breath.

Brothers:
When we fight,
We all
Must stay together.
No Kit Fox
Will run away!

Storm Arriving's brother soldiers heaped him with praise. No one had taken three in a day in many years.

"It is a good sign," Big Nose said. "First we find One Who Flies, and now this. These are good signs for the People."

Storm Arriving's gratitude over his good fortune spilled out in grins and laughter. "I believe so, too," he said, and then spoke to all the friends and fellow Kit Foxes that had gathered.

"I have had great fortune today, and I intend to share it with the People. One of my kills I give to Antelope Leaping Woman, who lost her husband last winter, and to Trees Under Snow, for he is old and has no family to provide for him. A second one I give, this one to those of you, my brother Kit Foxes, who made no kill today. Your families shall eat tonight of my good fortune."

The men around him grinned and congratulated him on his luck and generosity.

"You give too much," his mother said with a poke to his ribs. "One would have been plenty. You have three mouths to feed, you remember?"

"Would my father have given only one?"

Picking Bones Woman waved a hand. "He gave away too much as well. I think he did it just to annoy me. The both of you, you would starve us with your generosity."

He chuckled at her crabbing. "Don't worry, Mother. We won't starve. Besides, we may soon have one more provider in our family." He pointed to Blue Shell Woman.

Standing Elk was very close to her, speaking softly but very quickly. He had done well in the hunt and had brought down a bull of his own. Blue Shell Woman was silent. She stared at her toes and showed no interest as he spoke, but her lips played tug-the-rope with a smile. She glanced up and caught sight of her mother and brother. The blood rushed to her cheeks like a fire through grass in late summer.

"Perhaps," Picking Bones Woman said. "As long as you do not put him off again."

"I won't. This last year has made a great change in Standing Elk. He has seen battle twice and has killed one of the Crow People. He has learned much and now is more man than boy. No, if he comes, I will not dissuade him."

"And One Who Flies?" the old woman asked. Their guest stood nearby, listening to Big Nose weave the tale of his first buffalo hunt.

"I do not worry about him anymore. Blue Shell Woman is fascinated with him and takes any excuse to be near him, but One Who Flies has always treated her as an other-father would. Besides, One Who Flies does not make her blush." He waved at his sister and she spun to hide the fire in her cheeks. Standing Elk glanced their way and grinned, a little embarrassed himself at having been caught courting.

Storm Arriving clapped his hands and motioned to his sisters. "Come. The day is waning. Time to work. Blue Shell Woman, you will help your mother. Mouse Road, I want you to go prepare the racks and fetch the water we will need." He turned to One Who Flies and, in the Trader's tongue, told him, "I need you to take Mouse Road back to camp. She will make things ready. We will be along shortly with the first of the day's kill."

"As you wish," the *vé'ho'e* said.

Mouse Road sat behind and held on to George's waist as they rode the whistler back to camp. He had taken off his coat and tucked it under the first rope. Now the wind of their passage billowed his shirt with a welcome coolness. Behind him, Mouse Road kept up a steady stream of one-sided conversation.

"Ota'tavehexovona'e, náhéméhotâtse. Xaomemehe'e, náhevése'enôtse. Náháéána. Námésêhétáno. Néháéána?"

It did not seem to matter that he did not understand her. Mouse Road was about the same age as Maria, his youngest sister, and she was just as talkative. It comforted him to interact with her, even in this unintelligible manner. He had not seen his own sisters in over a year due to his duties for the military, and Mouse Road was a consoling stand-in.

She continued talking and he felt sure that she would have kept on even without his participation, but he did not want her to feel ignored. Every now and again he would say "I see," or give an "Ah" of comprehension. When her voice rose in a question he gave a noncommittal shrug. He could respond to the peaks and valleys of her intonation and, at the same time, plan his escape.

They rode into camp from the south. There were no guards. The place was nearly deserted. Here and there women and children worked in front of their lodges erecting poles and racks for drying the meat that would soon come. From the river came the sounds of play and high spirits. George let Mouse Road toe the whistler through the maze of bands and lodges to her home.

There they dismounted. Mouse Road ran inside while he tied the whistler to the tying post in front. She came out with several empty waterskins. She said something in her language—of which George could only pick out *Thank you* and *water*—and then she was off toward the river.

As soon as she was out of sight, George dashed inside the lodge. He had seen where Storm Arriving kept his arrow-making tools. Among them was the short, heavy-bladed knife he used for trimming the shafts and splitting feathers. He unwrapped the thick piece of hide, took the weapon, and replaced the bundle in its spot behind Storm Arriving's willow-branch backrest. It felt good to have a weapon in his hand again, even if it was little more than a simple utility tool. It bolstered his confidence and his sense of purpose.

He tucked the knife into his belt behind his back. Outside, he put on his coat and mounted the waiting whistler.

"Nóheto," he told it, and with a touch to its withers, he steered quickly to the northern edge of camp. Then, pointing the whistler toward the open east, he crouched down as he had seen others do. He grabbed on to the first rope and once again gave the command.

"Nóheto!"

The acceleration was fierce, and the velocity was frightening, but they were heading east across open land and all George wanted was distance between himself and the camp.

A gentle touch turned them northeast, up the ridge he had descended when he'd first arrived. The whistler did not slow its pace as it took on the slope.

He heard a shout and looked back. Guards! There were pickets on the eastern approaches. He swore. Another guard appeared ahead of him. George veered away. The man sprinted to block him, waving his lance. The whistler shied and sped up to go around. The guard was shouting and waving for George to stop, but George had no intention of relinquishing this opportunity. He sped past the guard and over the crest of the ridge—and into the path of a returning patrol.

Whistlers trumpeted and men cried out in alarm. Seven or eight riders were right in front of him in close formation. With nowhere to turn and no time to stop, they collided. George saw feathers and surprised faces. He saw a flash of brass on navy blue and then he saw the sky and the ground as he was thrown from his mount. He hit with a shock that forced the air from his lungs. A moment later, as he lay on the ground blinking and gulping empty breaths, a pain seeped into his side. He reached back to grab the knife as the Indians ran over to him. He found the handle but could not find the blade as it was embedded deep within his side.

"Aw, Hell," he said as he at last regained his breath. "Aw, Hell."

The Indians of the patrol helped him to his feet, speaking frenetically and all at once. He hissed in pain. One of them lifted the back of his coat. The sight of blood and the handle of the knife protruding from his side cut short all argument. A second of silence ensued—eight men holding their collective breath—and then they were all talking once more.

They lifted him up.

"I can walk," he protested and took a step. Pain shot from his knee up into his thigh and his leg crumpled beneath him. The men caught him before he fell and George saw the rip in his pant leg and the dark stain of blood that reached from knee to boot top and made the fabric cling to his leg like dead skin.

"Aw, Hell," he said again. "Hellfire and damnation!" He did not think it was broken but it was cut for sure and deeply, too.

The Indians supported him as he limped his way back to the whistlers. Several more men stood with the mounts. Through his squinted pain, he once more thought he saw the wink of brass within their midst. As he got closer, the group parted and George found himself face to face with an officer of the U.S. Army, at attention and saluting.

"Captain Custer, sir! Corporal Hollings from Fort Whitley, reporting with a message from command staff, sir!"

George looked at the young man before him. He recognized him as one of the several new recruits that had arrived back in March, though the man's freshly sunburnt brow marked him as such. He was still fairly fresh-faced, despite the miles of travel and the healthy helping of terror that made his eyes wide and his hand tremble at the brim of his hat.

"Sir. What are your orders, sir?"

George took a moment to concentrate on breathing, a task that had become difficult, as each respiration caused the knife blade to grate against his rib.

"Corporal," George rasped. "What are you doing here?"

The youth straightened even more—a feat George would have thought impossible. "Sir! I am here to ascertain your whereabouts and condition, and if I find

you here, I am to deliver an invitation of parley to
the chiefs of the force holding you hostage."

"Oh, for the . . ." George grimaced, regretting the
outburst for several reasons. More calmly, he continued. "Corporal, your timing is miserable. Had you
come ten minutes later, I would have been healthy
and on my way to Fort Whitley. As it is, however . . .
Aw, Hell!" He motioned to the men who held him
upright. *"Nóheto,"* he said, and to the corporal, "Follow, if they let you."

Carefully they placed him atop a whistler and then
led it back down the embankment toward camp. George
clenched his teeth and swore with each rolling step.

Speaks While Leaving had just arrived with the
wounded from the day's hunt when they brought One
Who Flies to her. She shooed the men back outside
her father's lodge, not wanting their clumsy help and
incessant questions. Mouse Road had met them on
her way back from the river, and she sat near, ready
to assist.

"Bite down on this." Speaks While Leaving said
and placed a thick fold of parfleche in the bluecoat's
mouth. He lay curled on his side on the floor. Sweat
beaded his brow but he did not cry out. She wished
that Storm Arriving was there so that he might see
the fortitude of One Who Flies, but he was still out
on the hunting ground. It would fall to Mouse Road
to testify as to his bravery in the face of pain. Of
course this was nothing compared to a skin sacrifice
or the Sun Dance, but for a *vé'ho'e,* it was a fair test.

"Will he die?" the little girl asked. "My sister will
be crazy angry if he dies."

"Your sister?" Speaks While Leaving inquired as
she prepared her tools and wrappings. "Why will she
be angry?"

"Blue Shell Woman is crazy in love with One Who
Flies. Crazy in love. She hides it well, so my mother
and my brother do not know of it, but she has told
me. Crazy in love."

"Truly? What about Standing Elk?"

"She says no one can compare to a man who rides the clouds."

"And what do you think?"

"I think she is silly. One Who Flies is nice; I like him, but he will not be here very long. Standing Elk has courted her for three years. He is strong and he is brave and he loves her. I think she should pick Standing Elk."

"Blue Shell Woman would do well to heed the advice of her younger sister." She handed her helpmate a cloth. "Wet this down and be ready to clean away the blood when I ask."

The girl did so as Speaks While Leaving picked up her small tin box. Opening it, she searched until she found her heavy needle. From a length of buffalo sinew she separated out one thin strand. This she threaded through the eye of the needle.

"Are you ready?" she asked One Who Flies, using the Trader's tongue. The pale man—paler than ever now—nodded and hugged the bundled robe she had given him. "Try not to move," she said.

She pulled back his shirt. The wound was crusted with dirt and bits of grass. Blood seeped out with every breath taken. The knife was in deep; she could see the outline of the finger-long blade beneath his flesh.

"You were lucky today."

He spoke from around the dried hide. "Luck like this I do not want," he managed to say.

"Better I suppose if the blade had not been turned by your ribs? You would have sung your death song by now. Hold your breath—"

He held. She pulled.

The knife slid out. He growled and bit down on the parfleche. The wound poured fresh blood down his side but that was a good sign. She favored Mouse Road with a glance. The girl sat close, moist cloth at the ready, unfazed by the jeweled flow.

"Wipe now," she told her. "Clean it with smooth strokes."

The girl did as instructed as Speaks While Leaving poured water on the injury. One Who Flies growled again through with less energy now. His gaze had gone vacant and slack. She splashed water on his face. He spluttered and gave her a vicious glare.

"Stay awake," she told him. Then to the girl, "That's good. You're a fine helper. Now put your hands like this and hold the wound closed while I sew it up. Good girl."

She stitched quickly, tying each one off individually the way the holy man of the Trader folk had taught her years before. Her needles were her most prized possessions. They were a rare enough commodity among the Trader folk, but the People used only awls and hooks in their sewing, which made the needles rarer still. They had been worth the price, and repaid their cost tenfold at moments such as this.

"Done," she said. "I seem to do nothing but patch you up." One Who Flies dropped the hide from his mouth and let out a long-held breath. She washed the wound again and dressed it with a pack of powdered quince and red river-berries mixed with a few other herbs. She covered it with a thick pad of blanched hanging-moss, sat him up and wrapped his ribs with strips of deerskin, tying them tightly to keep the dressing in place. Then she turned her attention to his knee.

"What were you doing out there?" she asked.

He hesitated as if considering his response.

"I do not think you would believe me if I said I was heading back to the hunt to lend a hand." He snarled as she cleaned the laceration on his knee.

"No. Not with you heading in the wrong direction with a useless blade tucked in your belt."

"Useless? It was good enough to skewer me."

"But on the field after a hunt it would be too small to do anyone any good." She looked up from her work. His face was sweaty and dusty and a week's worth of red beard stubbled his chin and jaw. Still, she found him not unhandsome—for a *vé'ho'e*. She wrapped the knee with cloth and sat back on her heels.

"So, since I would not believe your first tale, what will you tell me instead?"

He studied her; she could see it in his eyes.

"I was trying to escape," he said.

She made no overt reaction other than to nod and say, "Now that I *do* believe."

She stood. He moved to follow but she sat him down. "You will stay here tonight. I want to watch that wound." She held out her hand to Mouse Road. "Come, Little One. Your mother is probably back by now and wondering where her youngest girl is."

They stepped out of the lodge and into the crowd that had formed when they carried in the wounded One Who Flies. There was a handful of grandfathers sitting in a patient circle, three men from those who guarded the camp squatting nearby, and a curiously quiet group of boys—too young to participate in the hunt—who stood as if made of wood, awaiting her report.

"He will be fine," she said.

The boys ran off without a word. The men walked off in their separate ways. The grandfathers halted their conversation for a moment, then continued.

Just as the area was clearing out, Blue Shell Woman came running in from around a neighboring lodge.

"I just heard," she said, breathless. "Is he all right?"

Speaks While Leaving stopped the young woman from entering her home. "He is fine," she said. "He will be fine. It was not bad."

"I will sit with him while he mends." She moved to step past, but Speaks While Leaving stopped her again.

"No," she said. "You will not. Instead, you will take this"—she handed her the knife—"and this"—she gave her Mouse Road's hand. "And you will go back to your brother's lodge and help with the butchering. Your sister tells me he had a very good day."

"Y-yes," the young woman said as she was turned bodily and firmly propelled homeward. "He did."

"I also heard that Standing Elk took down one of his own."

"Yes," Blue Shell Woman said with an unfriendly glare. "That is true, too."

"He is such a fine young man," Speaks While Leaving said. "Thank you for your help, Mouse Road."

Blue Shell Woman protested. "But I want to—"

"Thank you. My greetings to your mother."

Mouse Road grinned and waved. Speaks While Leaving watched as the youngest sister confidently led her elder off by the hand. She saw Blue Shell Woman look back over her shoulder and mutter to herself until she was lost to sight among the lodges.

As Speaks While Leaving turned to reenter her father's lodge, one of the old men in the story circle caught her attention.

"There is trouble there, I think."

She glanced back toward the departed but probably still-complaining Blue Shell Woman.

"Perhaps," she said with a smile. "But for whom?"

Custer sat in the private library on the second floor of the White House. He sighed and turned another page in Lincoln's memoir. He had not read the last page, but felt that he had stared at it long enough and wanted to stare at a new one. He had read the book before and knew most of it by heart. The chapter he was staring at now recounted the beginnings of the great civil war that had nearly sundered the nation.

Lincoln's words concerning that time, written with the clarity that comes from outliving a crisis by a decade and more, echoed the sentiments in Custer's own heart. With effort, he focused on the paragraph in the middle of the page.

I did not, in the course of my response to the matter in April, 1861, consider within the limits of credibility that these heretofore stalwart men—many of whom were well-known to me—could be anything but misguided or deceived by the machinations of others. I did not and could not conceive of the authors of such actions as reasoning, civilized members of an otherwise flourishing country. It was, therefore, a much altered response that was formed and given up than might otherwise have been crafted. Had it been foremost in my mind that these were not demons, not a handful of simple minds waving the banner of zealotry, but that they were men—intelligent men, well-intentioned men, good men—whom we faced across the bloody waters of war, then I would have allowed none of the half-hearted actions nor felt any of the confidence that so infused my spirit. Had I known these men to be of reasonable and sober character, then I would have responded at once with a force assured to bring them low. There is, however, a malady that walks with war and that affects everything that its more sanguine partner might touch. This sickness infects the mind and causes the disorganization of thought. That such a pestilence had already swept the South was clear; what was less so was that, unbeknownst to us, it had also seized the North. We, the men responsible for the care of the Union, had already been affected. *We were already prevented by our own prejudices from treating the enemy as the enemy and, as a result, I believe—to my most profound sorrow—that many good men died who might otherwise have lived. The only one among us at that time who seemed immune to this "illness" as I have called it—though it is in truth a set of the mind—was Sherman. He saw at once, though he could not, for years could not convince us, that the enemy was, in dire fact, the enemy, and was thus entitled to our complete and total attention.*

Custer closed the book. He felt its weight in his hands, felt the pebbled surface of its leather cover beneath his fingertips. Lincoln's words bolstered his resolve and his faith in his own decision. The nation had ignored the Alliance long enough. It was time for Sherman's solution: total war.

There was a knock at the door. Samuel entered, a folded and sealed letter in his hand. He crossed the room and without a word he handed it to the president.

As Samuel turned to leave, Custer said, "No. Stay. You worked diligently on this. You deserve to know the results of your work."

He cracked the wax seal on the back and unfolded the heavy paper. "It's from Carlisle," he said. "It will take a few days for them to formulate the language of the declaration, but the votes are there, though barely so."

"Congratulations," Samuel said. "Your wish has been granted. The war you wanted."

Custer was surprised by his aide's tone. "You are wrong. I never wanted this."

"Really?" Samuel asked in an uncharacteristic show of impertinence. "With all due respect, Mr. President, you've hated the Indian ever since Kansa Bay; perhaps even before. Is there really no thirst for vengeance within you?"

Custer felt his pride pricked by the accusation. He stood and walked the length of the room. "No, it has nothing to do with vengeance, Samuel. You should know me better than that."

"All I know, Mr. President, is that I've spent my recent days and nights amassing a set of lists, the only purpose of which was to justify the use of the War Power against the Indian."

"It shows them to be the *enemy,* and the enemy must be dealt with *as* an enemy."

"Sir, they're just *Indians.* How much trouble can they be?"

Custer bit down and ground his teeth. "Samuel, if I learned nothing else at Kansa Bay, it was to respect the Indian in battle. They are not 'just Indians.' They are talented and innovative soldiers who whipped the tar out of three of my regiments before we put them down. I did *not* want this war, Samuel, but I believe that it is necessary. It is time to protect ourselves and assert our territorial rights. Don't underestimate them, Samuel. It is a grave mistake that I made once and will not make again."

Samuel faced his employer with a grimness of mouth and a stability of eye that Custer had never before seen in him. He did not, however, press the issue.

"Yes, Mr. President," was all he said and, with a curt bow, turned and left the room.

The President of the United States stood alone. He looked out the window, then at his book. He opened the cover and touched the narrow loops and shaky lines of the author's inscription.

> *Though battle sees the best in men,*
> *War knows but the worst.*
>   *A. Lincoln*

He closed the book and held it close to his chest beneath folded arms. He took a deep breath. It came out in a shudder.

"It's not revenge," he said as he sank down into an upholstered chair. "It's not."

He shut his eyes tightly, but the memories were too strong; Kansa Bay knew all his weak places. The sounds of long ago filled his mind. The smells of battle invaded him.

Gunsmoke. The tang of the sun on the tidal mud-flats. The pain of the arrow through his thigh and the choking heat. The screams of men and horses from the field just quitted, being rent limb from limb by monstrous lizards, eaten while still alive. The heralds of the Indian whistlers signifying another charge of the cavalry's position. The shrills of panicked horses as they faced that charge. The staccato of rifle volleys, the shouts of orders given too late to too few. The light that beat down on the brassy blades of late summer grass, only to bounce back up from them as from a mirror, blinding all. The breeze that cooled the sweat on his back. The surge of blood as hope returned with an idea. The crack of his own voice, breaking with exhaustion as he issued his commands. The urgent sound of breaking lantern glass. The pungency of kerosene. The rattle of a matchbox in a nervous hand. More shouts. More screams. The acrid smoke and the heat, more heat than he ever knew possible, so much heat that he thought the sky would melt. And then the awful, terrifying quiet as the world lay dead and charred around him and his surviving men.

Custer hugged himself as the memories drained away, leaving him—as they always did—trembling and sick. He sat in the chair, his ragged breath loud in the empty room, the long summer evening fading into night outside the window. He sat and he rocked back and forth, ever so slightly, as he mastered his emotions and his body. He prayed, but for neither strength nor forgiveness. He prayed for the safety of his son, trapped as he now was before the onrushing powers of war.

George limped toward the Council Lodge. Speaks While Leaving pressed through the gathered crowd before him and held the doorflap open for him. He grunted as he bent both knee and torso to enter. The Army, showing its ignorance in such matters, had sent out messengers who did not speak French, and George was therefore required to act as a link in a chain, translating English to French. Speaks While Leaving would take it from him and translate into Tsétsêhéstâhese.

Most of the chiefs were already present and seated. The place of honor at the back of the lodge was unoccupied. Speaks While Leaving led him to a place near the empty spot. She sat. George noticed several of the chiefs watching him. He lowered himself to the ground, and though he was slower than his companion, he did manage to neither groan nor wince. He could not, however, sit cross-legged as the other men were and it took him some time and several positions before he finally found one that was bearable for both his knee and his side. He settled in, holding one leg flexed up near his chest while leaving his injured leg outstretched.

More chiefs entered and filled the empty spots around the cold firepit. The air began to grow heavy with the press of men and the slanting sunlight that still lit the western side of the lodge. Several men rose and went outside. There was movement around the perimeter of the lodge, and then the bottom of the lodgeskin was raised. The men tied the skin to the poles, and a welcome breeze moved through the large room.

Finally, the eldest chiefs arrived: Three Trees Together and the other three whose names George did not know. Behind them were two young warriors who held by the arms the young Corporal Hollings.

Hollings looked scared. His skin was pallid and beaded with sweat. His eyes looked here, then there, like a nervous dog who has disobeyed but is unsure of the coming punishment. The warriors escorted him roughly behind the seated chiefs.

"Hámêstoo'êstse," one of them told him. He looked to George.

"Sit down," George said. Hollings nodded and sat down. The two guards sat down behind him.

Three Trees Together settled himself in the place of honor. As he did so, the rest of the assembly quieted. The old man, with eyes bright and youthful in a face weathered by time and untold years, looked at George and spoke.

Speaks While Leaving translated in a quiet whisper. "Three Trees Together says: 'In the three and fifty years since the star fell, I have known of only four *vé'hó'e* who did not come to take from the People.

" 'Two were holy men who came to tell us of the god who was killed and lived again. One gave up on us after a while and left. The other stayed longer, but it made no difference. The third man was a trader who asked our permission to travel our lands. He lived among us for several years, but was killed by the Crow

People one winter after an argument over a blanket. The fourth one was a man we called Talks to Spirits. He came to us when I was first asked to be a chief. He was an odd man, but his heart was good. We accepted him among us and he lived as one of the People. He took a wife, and lived many years. He was killed by Long Hair in the great fires along the Big Salty, fighting for the People.

" 'All the other *vé'hó'e* who come to the People come to take from us. Settlers, hunters, soldiers, they all come to take something that is ours—our lands, our buffalo, or our lives—and so we drive them off. For ten years times ten years and more we have driven them off. Thousands of *vé'hó'e* we have either killed or driven away.

" 'In all that time, only four men. And now, you come, One Who Flies, and this man next to you comes. Are you like the four, or like the thousands? It is not hard to guess.' "

He settled back against his backrest. The woven willow twigs creaked.

" 'Speak to the man beside you,' " he continued via Speaks While Leaving's translation. " 'Tell him that we would hear what he has to say, and then speak for him so that we might know his message.' "

George relayed the chief's words to Hollings. "And don't speak too fast," he added. "My French is still rusty and you'll get too far ahead of me if you charge ahead without a breath."

"Yes, sir," the corporal said. He cleared his throat and sat up straighter, his hands on his knees.

"I am here on behalf of General Stant of the United States Army, with a message from the President of the United States." He paused for George to catch up. "It is the request of the president that you and your selected delegates meet with him and his advisors to open discussions on the subject of a treaty between the United States and the Cheyenne Alliance. The meeting is to take place twelve days hence, on the twenty-fifth of May, at the place where the Missouri River meets the White River."

Speaks While Leaving stumbled at the river names. "Where the cloud fell," George told her. He motioned for Hollings to continue.

"It is the president's request that you grant free passage to his party and his security detachment, so that they might travel to the meeting place without incident. It is also the president's request that Captain Custer, his son and your captive, accompany your chiefs to the meeting place."

The message passed through the translators to the chiefs. George could discern no emotion or reaction in any of them. They sat, impassive and silent. George had learned enough of these people and their open nature to know that this was a show. Like any good poker player, they were not giving their opponent any more information than necessary.

Three Trees Together spoke, and the words were passed back up the chain.

" 'We will consider this request. You will have our decision in the morning. Until then, you will stay at the lodge of One Bear and his daughter, Speaks While Leaving. We will call for you when we need you.' "

It was as abrupt a dismissal as George had heard from any general. He stood with the help of Speaks While Leaving and the use of his uninjured leg. Hollings rose, too. George directed the corporal to walk behind the seated chiefs, along the lodge wall. They exited into the whispers of the crowd and the last of the day's light. The sky was a pure dome of dark blue that was blushed with rose and lit with orange along its western rim. The sun, a beacon of fire, slipped down behind the already dark hills beyond the river. A cricket played a few notes from a nearby hiding place. The smoke from a thousand cookfires added their scent to the air.

The crowd dispersed before them, carrying the news to friends and families. George walked beside Speaks While Leaving, Hollings a few steps behind. Speaks

While Leaving was pensive, her hands clasped before her, her gaze downcast, her step slow and measured.

"How do you think they'll respond, sir?" Hollings asked. "I couldn't tell from their faces."

"Nor were you meant to," he replied.

"No," Hollings admitted. "I suppose I wasn't. They are a stone-faced lot, that's for sure. But you've been here for a while. I thought you might have a better idea of what they'll answer."

George glanced back and motioned toward the Council Lodge. Hollings looked back to find all the chiefs casually making their way back to their homes.

"Where are they going?" he wanted to know. "Aren't they going to even consider the president's request?"

"That's just what they're going to do," George said. "Every Indian here will have his say in the matter, if he wishes it. By morning, you'll have your answer, but as to which way they'll respond, I haven't the vaguest of ideas. They are suspicious of us—and with reason. It could go either way."

The evening meal was perfunctory: fresh buffalo meat roasted over the fire. Despite the meat's inviting aroma and warm, velvety texture, George ate little as his discomfort sapped his appetite. Hollings ate reluctantly, his hunger barely winning out over his distaste of the roughly prepared food and the carcass just outside the door.

One Bear—an intense man of perhaps forty years whose lean, athletic physique was defaced by ritual scars—ate quickly and left, presumably to discuss the president's request with his fellow tribesmen. Speaks While Leaving, her mother Magpie Woman, and her "other-mother" Diving Lizard Woman—her maternal aunt, if George had understood the relationships correctly—all left as soon as their guests were finished eating. There was still much work to be done on the large female bison One Bear had brought down during the hunt.

"The meat must all be removed, stripped, and hung

to dry," Speaks While Leaving said as the women excused themselves. "The bones must be scraped, the innards brought to the river to be cleaned, not to mention the work required to dress the hide and preserve the sinews, though that can wait until tomorrow. Please, though, be seated and be comfortable. We will be just outside if you require anything."

George and Hollings remained then, alone in the lodge. The fire cracked and fussed and lit the room with its lively light.

Outside, the camp was busy. Families chatted and called to one another as they worked on their kills. All around, George heard the beat of drums and the eerie melodies favored by the Cheyenne as the evening's feasts got underway. Beyond the doorway, Speaks While Leaving and her relations talked and laughed as they skinned and butchered the buffalo. He heard Speaks While Leaving begin a quiet song, heard the others join in. The song rose and fell; its rhythm was happy and light. The song dissolved into laughter and embarrassed giggles. He wondered what the words meant that they might so amuse.

"I pity you, sir," Hollings said as he picked at his teeth with his thumbnail. "Being out here with these savages. I wish there was a way I could take you back when I go. I imagine it must have been awful for you here. I don't know how you managed."

George found himself wishing the corporal would disappear. "It hasn't been all that bad," he said. "They've treated me quite well. No worse than a fortnight at Whitley, actually."

"Oh, come now, sir. You don't have to play the brave officer for me. We're both from well-bred families. We were both raised to the life of a gentleman. This must have been a trial of the harshest sort."

The corporal's accent and turn of phrase reminded him of Elisha, who now lay dead beneath a landscape as different from his home district as could be imagined.

"Where are you from, Hollings? Boston?"

"Yes, sir. Is it that obvious?"

"Not really," George said. "It's just that my navigator was from Boston. Did you know Lieutenant Reed?"

"Certainly I did, sir. We were related, don't you know. He was my cousin."

"My condolences, then. He was a fine officer and a good friend. I miss him."

"Thank you, sir. I'll pass your words along, but please don't worry on my account. He was only a distant cousin. Just a name on the family chart until I was posted to The Whit, sir."

"Ah," said George. "Then you missed knowing a remarkable man."

"Yes, sir. So I understand."

Hollings grew quiet and George was glad to have him so. His side jabbed at him malevolently and the deerskin dressing pulled with every breath. If he could only lay down, just for a moment.

"How did he die, sir?"

George's head jerked up, having nodded as he touched the edge of sleep. "What?"

"If you would, sir. Elisha was a favorite of my great-aunt. I'd like to bring word to her of how he died."

George sighed inwardly, unable to refuse such a request but wanting only to sleep. He lay down on his bed of pelts and blankets and looked up into the cone of the lodge. The lodgepoles, sapling trees stripped of twigs and bark, were pale in the firelight and their scent was sharp and fruity. The smoke rose through their nexus. Beyond them, up in the sky, George could see the bright prairie stars.

"He died bravely, Corporal, and did not suffer much. Put another branch on the fire and I'll tell you how it happened."

His story and Hollings's questions lasted until the women completed their work for the evening. At that point Speaks While Leaving told George he should sleep and he was more than willing to comply.

When morning came, it was too early. He awoke to find Speaks While Leaving and Magpie Woman still asleep. Hollings lay on his back, snoring to the rafters. One Bear was not in bed.

George lay there, wondering what the Council would decide to do. He looked up through the smokehole and could see the stars fading in a sky aging from night to day. Hollings rolled on his side and in the silence that followed he heard the quiet steps of early risers on their way to get water—or to make water. Whistlers fluted their songs of morning welcome as young sons searched the wristbands for their family's pattern. From the hills came a chorus of howls as wolves sung to the fingernail moon.

He looked across the firepit and saw Speaks While Leaving watching him, her eyes shining in the gloaming.

"Bonjour," she whispered. *"Comment ça va?"*

"Ça va," he replied, and her smile calmed his troubled heart.

Voices came from outside. Footsteps approached, heavy and forceful. The doorflap opened with violence, jolting the remaining sleepers awake. One Bear stepped inside, the scowl on his faced so fierce that George became afraid. The chief glared at the bleary Hollings with open hatred before he clenched his fists and controlled his emotions.

"To'e," he said. Wake up. With harsh gestures and rough words he gave orders to Speaks While Leaving, pointed toward Hollings and George, then spun and walked out. Speaks While Leaving and her mother shared a glance and a sigh of dismay. Then they rose from their beds and got to work.

Magpie Woman set about collecting the many buffalo robes and animal pelts from the beddings. Speaks While Leaving came over to the two confused men.

"What is it?" George asked.

"We are leaving."

"What? All of us?"

"Yes. The camp is moving."

"Him, too?" George asked, afraid Hollings was now captive as well.

"No," she said. "The Corporal will be taken back to his country and will deliver the Council's reply."

"And what is their reply?"

She lifted one hand and cocked her head in a gesture that George could not interpret.

"They will meet."

CHAPTER 7

Thursday, May 22, A.D. 1886
Somewhere in the Unorganized Territory

Having spent nearly his entire life living with or in the military, George had seen his share of parades. He had seen streets filled storefront to storefront with ranks of men in freshly brushed wools, their polished buttons glinting in the noonday sun. He had seen endless waves of cavalry riding in formation down a rutted country road. He had seen the ragged procession of a hundred wagons returning from the Sand Hills of Kansa Bay with their burden of ten thousand dead. Yet in his experience, of all the displays of military might that had passed before him, never had there been a sight to compare with the one now before him.

For seven days the camp had been on the move. The logistical organization of such an undertaking would have daunted even the most experienced of commanders.

Today had been typical of the week gone by. George had been traveling with Speaks While Leaving and her family, ostensibly due to his recent injury but also, he thought, to keep him away from Blue Shell Woman. He had learned from Speaks While Leaving what he had already suspected: that the girl had developed an infatuation. With her brother so often gone on patrol or advance duty, it seemed prudent to stay a fair distance from her. Traveling with the family of One Bear gave him that distance, both physically and emotionally.

It was before dawn when George had awakened beneath blushing clouds—lodges were not raised while the camp was in transit. Larksong carried through the empty day and the calls of the criers had begun. The men moved through camp delivering the day's orders. Under the dying stars, Speaks While Leaving translated for him.

"One Green Eye says that movement will begin after the sun is two fingers above the horizon. The Red Shield soldiers are in charge of the march today, and the Kit Fox men will ride in advance to secure this evening's site. We will make permanent camp tonight near the bones of Red Squirrel Woman along Fishing Lizard Creek."

"Permanent? No more moving?"

"No," she said. "Not for at least a moon. The hatchlings need time to grow."

George looked to the horizon and guessed that they had less than an hour before the sun would have risen to a height of two finger-widths above the horizon. In a week on the open prairie he had learned—at least in basic terms—how to judge the span of time in hands. Three hands from the horizon, one hand past the top of the sky, two hands and two fingers before sunset . . . it was a surprisingly accurate system that could be applied to either the sun, the moon, or the morning and evening stars. It did, however, require an intimate familiarity with the land, the seasons, and the lunar phases that George lacked. As a result, his guesses were sometimes off by several hours. Speaks While Leaving had tried to show him how the sun and the moon traveled different paths across the sky but the subtlety escaped him. For her part, Speaks While Leaving was unable to understand his inability to comprehend something so obvious, and quickly she gave up on teaching him.

This morning, however, the guessing was easy. The glow of the ready sun was distinct and two fingers on the horizon translated to half an hour or so. George was quite aware that his guess of less than an hour was more common sense than expert knowledge.

Once the criers had delivered the day's instructions, the routine that followed had been well established by six days on the march: gather the whistlers, load them up, and head out.

It was a household of ten—Speaks While Leaving, her parents, two aunts, two uncles, two cousins, and Healing Rock Woman, their incredibly ancient matriarch. The whole of it included five lodges with poles and coverings, twelve beds, robes, clothing, tools, weapons, furnishings, cooking utensils, food both fresh and preserved, extra hides, pelts, skins, and one three-month-old puppy named Barks like Thunder, which the youngest cousin carried slung over her shoulder like some prized sack of salt. Everything, with the sole exception of Barks like Thunder, was either loaded onto a travois or piled on whistler-back. Healing Rock Woman was given a travois of her own, while everyone else took a whistler from the family's ample flock. In all, it took over thirty whistlers to move One Bear's extended family. The hatchlings—already the size of large geese—prowled near the feet of their parents.

The packing went quickly, as it always did. Past attempts had shown that George only got in the way of the women's practiced movements, so he contented himself with appreciating the efficiency and precision of their operation. Everything had a place, and the place for most everything was one of the ubiquitous parfleches that every family had in abundance. They were large pieces of rawhide, folded like an envelope and filled near-to-bursting. Each parfleche, tied closed, was easily stacked with the others. There were small ones for personal items, medium ones for food stores, and large ones like stiff leather chests that held just about anything, and most of them were painted or beaded with geometric patterns and bright colors. They were briskly filled, and in no time the travois was stacked high.

It was so not only with the household of One Bear, but all over the prairie people made ready for the day's travels. Families were not set up as close here in this informal camp as they had been at Cherry Stone Creek, and there was even more of a distance between bands as between families. As a result, George looked across the gentle land and saw it dotted for miles with small groups, small flocks, and here and there the standing bulk of a waiting walker or the smoky trail of a dying campfire. He judged it a full three miles or more between him and the farthest camp to the south and perhaps another mile to the northernmost.

By the time the sun had broached the horizon by the width of two fingers, its orange light wrought long shadows from a people on the move. George shook his head as he mounted his whistler. Within an hour's time, a four-mile-wide camp of ten thousand families had packed up and was en route. It wasn't the trim formation of a parade or even the loose organization of a march. It was a picture of the absence of military order and discipline. Some families lagged behind. Some rode ahead. There were walkers and whistlers and dogs and even a few chickens—all pacing along at their own gait and not a few of one group belea- guering those of another. Children squealed and laughed, chased one another, or stood pouting. Men gave orders to women. Women returned the favor. Soldiers rode between the families bent on duty and heedless of the havoc around them. Whistlers yodeled. Hatchlings stayed close to their flocks, peeping like monstrous chickens. Young mothers sang to their babes. Nearby, three boys with bows stalked a fourth. Walkers chuffed their impatience. It was pandemo- nium, and yet the task had been done. George could not help but compare it to the effort required to get U.S. Army soldiers on their feet in the morning. The contrast only made this daily performance all the more impressive.

To accommodate the frailness of their matriarch, One Bear's family traveled slowly, as did most other families. She rode in silence amid the parcels and bundles, her back straight, her eyes focused on the west and the sacred mountains that grew ever dimmer in the distance.

George rode his whistler in a solitude enforced by his clumsiness with the Cheyenne language. He would try a phrase or two with a family member or a nearby traveler, but no matter how attentively he listened, if they didn't respond with a "yes," "no," or "I don't know," he became utterly lost in the conversation. Speaks While Leaving was the only one in her family who could speak French fluently, so he rode onward, as quiet as the grandmother, his eyes and hopes on the horizon opposite the one the old mother watched.

Along the amorphous perimeter of the march there were constant comings and goings. A patrol of five men on whistlers rode in at high speed and spoke to the chiefs of the Kit Fox soldiers who traveled with the families. Within moments, another patrol rode out. It was an activity that would continue throughout the day, and George, by noting the men who went out and how long it was until they returned, calculated that at least twenty such patrols were out in advance of the main body. How far they ranged, he had no idea.

When the sun was nearing noon, two familiar faces appeared. Blue Shell Woman rode up on a whistler, Mouse Road behind her. The younger girl waved, standing up on the beast's rump to get a better view. Blue Shell Woman, in contrast, seemed solemn. She guided her mount up next to George and instead of speaking to Speaks While Leaving, she spoke to him directly.

"Bonjour," she said, taking great care to pronounce the alien words correctly. *"Comment allez-vous?"*

Mouse Road mocked her big sister with silent moues and exaggerated gestures. George, however, could not help but be flattered by the elder sister's efforts and did his best to keep a straight face.

"*Ne-a'éše*," he said in his pidgin Tsétsêhéstâhese. Thank you. "*Nápévomóhtahe. Nahe'pe, émomóhtóhta.*" I am feeling good. My rib, he got well.

Now it was the young woman's turn to hide a smile, though she was far less successful than George had been, and Mouse Road was seized with a fit of giggles that nearly knocked her off the whistler.

"*Éénomóhtahe,*" Speaks While Leaving said as she rode up beside him. "Not *émomóhtóhta.*"

"Ah. *Ne-a'éše,*" he said, and switched back to French. "What did I say?"

"You told her your rib has diarrhea."

The blood rushed to his cheeks and the girls renewed their laughter.

There was a sudden uproar about a mile ahead. Voices cried out in great yips and whoops. George saw many riders take off to the north. Other riders appeared in the distance—a dozen or so, riding toward the main group.

"What is happening?" he asked. "Is it an attack?"

"No," Speaks While Leaving said, smiling. "It is more of the Inviters, our neighbors to the north. They have heard of this meeting and will join us. I expect to see some of the Sage People from the south as well."

He looked to the north and saw them. They rode, now hidden, now visible as they crossed over the shallow folds of the terrain. He saw them, hundreds, perhaps a thousand or more riding in on whistlers and walkers to swell the ranks of this army. George had a sudden, sinking feeling.

"Why so many? Why are you all traveling to the meeting place, and not just the chiefs to parley?"

Speaks While Leaving looked at George with an enigmatic expression. "Why does your father want to meet with us when for years he has only wanted to kill us?"

"You're going to ambush him?"

"No," she said, and with contempt. "But neither

will we let our leaders walk into a trap. They will be well defended."

George's feeling of dread only increased.

Storm Arriving knelt astride his whistler and looked out over the site of the evening's camp. Beside him, Laughs like a Woman let his own whistler crop at the fragrant grass.

"I hate this place," the Contrary said.

"Yes," Storm Arriving said. "I love it here, too."

The land was rumpled, like a kicked-off robe. The two men, out in advance of the People, were the first of their patrol to arrive. They had stopped to rest their mounts on the last fold of land before the campsite. The low ridge stretched around this, the southern side of the site, like a protecting arm. Within its embrace lay a large sloping plain of short grass. Along the northern perimeter curled another, taller ridge with steep cliffs along its inner course. At the base of these cliffs ran Fishing Lizard Creek, and even from this distance the men could hear the water as it tumbled from the deep fishing pond down onto the slick smoothness of the rocky streambed. They could also hear the peeps and chitters of the fishing lizards that lived in burrows and crevices in the stone cliff faces.

Beyond the ridge, the western and northern approaches were open. From the top of the cliffs, a guard could see for miles. To the east the cliffs softened and ended while the creek ran ahead into a dense wood of white-bark and shaking-leaf trees that would provide the People with wood, fruits, fish, and small game.

It was a beautiful spot, a favorite among the People.

Storm Arriving smiled and pointed to the place where the stone of the cliff leaned out over the fishing pond like a nosy neighbor.

"Do you remember?" he asked his companion. "Your uncle? And that big woman from the Sage People?"

"No," the Contrary said firmly.

"And you went out on the ledge to get a better look?"

"No!" Laughs like a Woman bit his lip.

"And then you slipped and . . ." He could barely contain himself at the memory.

"I do not remember." His friend's face twitched and there were tears in his eyes from fighting his laughter.

"Ah," Storm Arriving said, wiping his eyes. "He was so angry with us."

"I do not think it was very funny."

"Yes," Storm Arriving agreed. "It was. Those were fine days. I miss those days."

"I do not think they will ever come again."

Storm Arriving sighed. "Oh, I hope you are right," he said, understanding perfectly the Contrary's reversed words.

They turned as the rest of the patrol came into sight with whoops and shouts. Six men with bows and lances rode up on whistlers. Storm Arriving greeted them. Laughs like a Woman ignored them.

"We saw one of the Greasy Wood People."

"Here?" Storm Arriving asked, alarmed.

The soldier pointed southeast, grinning. "Not far," he said. From his belt hung a bloody braid. "He will not see his lodge again."

Storm Arriving agreed, satisfied. "It is good," he said. "Was he working for the bluecoats?"

"We think so." The soldier turned and untied a bundle from his war-whistler's riding pad. "We found these things on him," he said as he flipped the bundle open.

In the leather bundle were some chunks of salty-fat, a leather pouch of cut smokeweed, and a bottle of water-that-burns-the-throat.

Storm Arriving picked up the bottle. "Do you remember what the Council says about this?" He uncorked the bottle and poured the contents out. He watched the faces of his patrol as the brown liquid gurgled onto the ground. Only the young soldier who had taken the scalp was upset. He fumed through flared nostrils.

"This angers you?" Storm Arriving asked. "Why?"

"I am angry because you think that I was going to keep it. I only brought it back to show you. I left it full so you would know we did not drink any of it."

"And what if the bottle you found was empty? How would you prove yourself then?"

"I . . . I would ask those who were with me to vouch for what they saw."

"And if you were alone?"

The soldier was flustered and angry, a dangerous combination in a young man. He spoke through clenched teeth. "I would have only my word of honor."

Despite the breeze, the evil water filled the air with a smell that bit at the nose. The whistlers sounded their anxiety and began to shift their feet. Storm Arriving shook the empty bottle twice, and corked it.

"The Great Council of chiefs has barred any of the People from possessing this water that makes *vé'hó'e* crazy. There is no excuse for having it." He tossed the empty bottle back to the angry young soldier. "Next time, trust your honor first."

Laughs like a Woman tapped Storm Arriving on the shoulder. "There are no more of them out there," he said.

"He is right," Storm Arriving said to the group. "Where there is one scout, there will be others. We must ensure the safety of the camp."

He sent them all riding off in pairs to search the surrounding lands. He and Laughs like a Woman rode to search the wood.

The air quivered with the sounds of rushing water and fluttering leaves. It turned from warm and heavy to cool and light as the two men moved from the grass-clad meadow in among the quiet boles. They separated; Storm Arriving took the creekward path and the Contrary stayed upslope.

They progressed slowly, halting their mounts more often than allowing them to walk. They listened to the forest, the creek, the dappled leaves above them, listening for something out of place and letting their whistlers taste the air for any sign of an enemy.

Storm Arriving found it difficult to concentrate on his tasks, though. His mind kept wandering. He did not like this move of the summer camp to a place so far east and south. It was against tradition, against time-honored paths laid down in the Grandmother Earth by the *ma'heono*. The buffalo did not come this way at this time of year, and for the People to come here now was against the very way of things. And why, he asked himself? Why come here? Because Long Hair wants to talk with the Council? When has Long Hair ever wanted to *talk* to the People?

His thoughts bounced around in his head and gave him neither peace nor answer. They just rattled up there like seeds in a dried gourd, making no sense, but refusing to leave him alone. They kept at him, like—

The birds, he thought. They do not sing.

The brush behind him hissed. He ducked but the arrow caught him, drawing a hot line up his back. He shouted as he grabbed his war club from his belt.

"Nóheto!"

His whistler leapt to the order and he let it slip from beneath him. It ran on and Storm Arriving slid off and crouched in the brush. The ferns before him tore apart as his attacker came out of hiding and pulled back his bow to fire again. Storm Arriving swung before the bowstring sang and the man went down with a howl. He hit him again and something cracked—not the club. With a quick move he had his knee on the man's chest and his knife at his heart. Four hands clasped together on the hilt of the blade as the men struggled. The tip broke the skin of the man's chest and his eyes widened.

Storm Arriving spoke with effort and force. "No puppies from. The Greasy Wood People. Will spy on us. For the bluecoats."

The man's strength began to fail. The knife inched downward. Four arms trembled, two with fear, two with anger. The blade continued. The man pushed the air from his lungs to avoid it. To breathe would only bring his chest closer to the knife. His position was desperate, for to breathe was to live, but to live was to die. Storm Arriving looked down into his enemy's eyes. They were dark, the brown nearly swallowed by pupils made wide by the nearness of death. The man's face grew red and turgid with pounding blood as he fought the need for air.

They struggled, quivering, nearly motionless, until the man's body overrode his fear. His body chose life, and with that breath, that gasping breath, it brought his chest up onto the knife.

Storm Arriving felt the man's heart pop under the blade, felt the arms go slack, saw the life go out of those all-black eyes, and heard his final treacherous breath run out again in a phlegmy wheeze that played with the spittle on his lips.

Storm Arriving stood. He felt every dose of life within him, each made precious by the struggle. He shouted up to the rustling branches and the sky beyond, a barking Kit Fox call to the spirits.

"Ai! Aioo! I am Storm Arriving, soldier of the People! Aioo!"

He grabbed the dead man by the hair and took his trophy from him. The body fell back to the bracken and Storm Arriving cried his victory once more.

Laughs like a Woman rode up, Storm Arriving's errant whistler in tow.

"Any others?" Storm Arriving asked.

"Yes," the Contrary said, meaning no.

"Good." He took a buffalo-hair rope from his whistler's back and looped it around the feet of the Greasy Wood man. The other end in hand, he climbed atop his mount. The blood that ran down his back had already started to dry.

"I will not have him here to foul the air or water. I will take him out to the plain and leave him there as a warning to others." He turned his mount toward the forest edge. "I do not want any company."

Laughs like a Woman remained mute. They rode off together, dragging the bloody corpse.

By the time Speaks While Leaving and her family arrived at Fishing Lizard Creek, many of the People had already established their camps. More lodges went up as they approached. The air buzzed with voices and whistler calls and the songs of lodge raising. Barks like Thunder did his best to live up to his name. He barked and squirmed until his young captor was forced to let him out of her grasp. The puppy yipped and growled and charged everything they passed until his quarry turned to challenge him in return, at which point he retreated to hide amid the whistlers with their hatchlings.

One Who Flies rode close by, silent now as he generally was during the second half of the day. Once the sun passed the top of the sky, fatigue descended upon him like a stone eagle. He roused a little at the puppy's noisemaking and looked around at the scene.

"I think I slept," he said.

His skin was very pale and the light seemed to penetrate him as if he were made of tallow. She nudged Two Cuts closer, hoping he was only suffering from too much sun. His wrist and cheek were hot to the touch. From the look in his eye, he knew what was wrong.

"It has gone sour, yes?"

She signed agreement.

He sighed and shook his head. "I can't seem to do anything right . . . even heal."

"Do not despair of it," she told him. "With a wound like this, it would have been unusual if it had *not* gone sour."

He looked at her from beneath a furrowed brow. "I must be well for the meeting."

"We will see," she said.

"No. I *must* go to the meeting. It is my only hope of going home."

"Then you will either be sick or well when you go.

Now calm yourself and stay quiet. We will look at the wound as soon as the lodges are raised."

The Closed Windpipe band gathered in its traditional spot, immediately south of the east-facing sun road that welcomed the light of morning and creation into the heart of camp. One Bear led his family to an open spot near the center of the area, for as a chief he wished to be accessible to all in his band. Once there, he pointed down to the ground. There they would raise the family's main lodge—the big seventeen-skin lodge—and all around it, in a circle like the circle of the lodge itself, would be the family's other lodges; those for Speaks While Leaving's other-mothers, and the women's lodge where the women would spend their moon-time. The circle of the lodge, the circle of the family, the circle of the band, and the circle of the People. Raising the lodges was like rebuilding the family and the band all over again, each time better than the last, and the gathering of the bands in the summer months meant a time of plenty, of stories, and of friendships renewed after the separation of the winter moons. This was Speaks While Leaving's favorite time. She took a long look around before she dismounted. A hundred-hundred people, all joined together in a circle—a family around a cookfire, birds in a nest, petals on a flower—now here to share and meet, soon to disperse with the promise of reunion in the next year.

"Little Dreamer," her mother said, calling her by an old nickname. "Will you be helping us today?"

She hid her smile behind her hand. "Yes, my mother," she said and bid Two Cuts to crouch.

She directed One Who Flies to sit down next to her grandmother and then she lent a hand with the lodgepoles. Her mother lashed the three main poles together. Each pole was nearly three times the height of a man. They raised them and set their bases wide to form the tripod that would support the rest. The end of the rope that bound them was staked to the ground.

Speaks While Leaving began a song as the rest of the poles were laid in the arms of the first three. She sang of a young girl and her fears for her departing lover. Her mothers and aunt joined in.

Where are you going?
Why do you ride, beloved?
Are you going to the Ree River?
Do you go there to marry?

The rope was woven in and around them all and staked again. They tied the lodgeskin to the final pole, and when it went up, it flapped in the wind like the skin on the sailing canoe Speaks While Leaving had seen once on a visit to the Big Salty. The rope went around again and was staked in its final place, inside the lodge and to the left of the door. Then the skin was pinned together and staked to the ground.

It was hot work, but the breeze cooled the sweat on her neck and face, and the song and the many hands made the labor a pleasure. In two hands of time they had raised all of the family lodges, and each woman set about unpacking her own household.

Already the creek was filled with children swimming and splashing. Already the flocks of whistlers had been driven to the western edge of camp. Already the poles for the Council Lodge were raised, and the red and black skins of the two sacred lodges were being pinned and staked. It had not taken long for the camp to take shape and establish itself. Speaks While Leaving took a deep breath and set to preparing the guest lodge for One Who Flies.

George lay on his stomach and grunted as Speaks While Leaving and her grandmother pulled at his shirt. The seepage from his wound had dried in a crust that plastered the cloth to the dressing. Speaks While Leaving tugged again and the shirt peeled away with the sound of crinkling paper. Healing Rock Woman clucked her tongue—a universal sound of disapproval, George had learned.

Amid the pain, he felt a warmness spread down his side. His head swam and his entire body shivered with a chill that raced through his soul. A stink rose as Speaks While Leaving cut the ties on the dressing and pulled it away. George had smelled that smell many times before—sour and sickly sweet—growing up in forts and encampments along the frontier. In this situation, he was afraid of what it foretold.

He glanced down at the wound and wished he hadn't. It was swollen, puckered by the restraining stitches. The skin was livid all around the edges and purple and green toward the gash. It stank of rot and corruption. He bit his lip.

Speaks While Leaving and her grandmother spoke in conspiratorial tones as they conferred about his condition.

"You don't have to whisper," he said. "I can't understand you."

The ancient crone asked a question. Speaks While Leaving answered and the old grandmother cackled and patted his shoulder. The two women conversed a short time longer—without whispering—and then Healing Rock Woman rose and toddled out of the lodge.

"My grandmother goes to gather some remedies," Speaks While Leaving told him. "She has the easy task. You and I must stay and clean this out." She reached for her leather bag and began rummaging through it. She produced a knife, a bottle, and some cloth. George looked away, resting his head on his arm.

"Who was the woman you spoke of this morning?" he asked, taking the conversation far away from the subject at hand.

"What woman?"

"Red Squirrel Woman. The woman whose bones lay nearby." He took the offered piece of heavy leather and bit down on it as Speaks While Leaving began her work and her tale.

"Red Squirrel Woman lived among the People very long ago, many years before the star fell, how many I am not sure. She was of the Broken Jaw band and was in love with a young warrior named Red Hawk who was of the Ridge People band." George muffled a cry as his side erupted in pain. More warmth flowed and Speaks While Leaving daubed at it with the cloth.

"But Red Squirrel Woman's father, Standing Bull, did not like Red Hawk. I should say, he did not like Red Hawk's father, for many years before he had shamed Standing Bull in his face. So, when Red Hawk sent a hand of whistlers and a quilled robe in payment for Red Squirrel Woman as wife, Standing Bull sent them back the very same night."

George felt her tug at the wound. He looked back and saw her pulling at the stitches and cutting them free. The swelling was visibly lessened. She shooed his curiosity away. He resumed his previous position and she picked up the thread of her story.

"Red Squirrel Woman was heartbroken, but the worst was ahead. Another man, an older man who was a friend of Standing Bull and who also hated Red Hawk's father, sent over only three whistlers and no blankets or robes for Red Squirrel Woman's hand. Standing Bull accepted them."

The light from the doorway darkened as Healing Rock Woman returned. She carried a wooden bowl filled with water. Speaks While Leaving had removed all of the stitches and the wound, though swollen and discolored, remained closed. George's entire torso throbbed, but the feeling of impending rupture was gone. He removed the piece of leather from between his teeth and put it aside.

From within the bowl Speaks While Leaving pulled out what looked like a thin, finger-long slice of fresh liver. Dripping, dark, and shiny, she held it carefully between thumb and forefinger. When it convulsed—a slow, twisting ripple that ran the length of its body—George recognized it as a leech. He turned away, not wanting to see more, but when he felt the cold thing on his skin, felt it move of its own accord, he shuddered in revulsion. Speaks While Leaving reached into the water once more.

"Red Squirrel Woman refused the match, but Standing Bull insisted and kept her close so that she would not elope with Red Hawk during the night. The next day, once it was clear to the camp that Standing Bull would not return the marriage gift, the match was sealed. Red Squirrel Woman was desolated.

"She cried for three days and begged her new husband to strike the drum and throw her away, but he would not. He held her close so that she would not run off with Red Hawk, and he took her without her consent and beat her when she fought."

Speaks While Leaving laid a damp cloth over the wound and the leeches that she had planted there. She patted his shoulder in a manner most maternal to calm him as she finished the tale.

"The next morning, she was gone. Her husband went to Standing Bull, shouting that his wife had run off with Red Hawk and that he wanted his three whistlers back and two more besides for the dishonor. It was then that Red Hawk came upon them with many soldiers behind him.

"Red Hawk spoke: 'I did not run off with your wife, though it were better if I had. She is there, hiding in the woods, sent there by her father's vengeance and her husband's evil ways.'

"Standing Bull went to the forest to bring his daughter back to her husband. When he returned, she was not with him.

"Standing Bull spoke: 'Red Squirrel Woman is dead. She has hung herself from a red willow tree.'"

Speaks While Leaving took a breath. "Normally, to meet death at your own hand is considered the murder of one's self, but in this case the Council decided that Standing Bull was guilty of murder by driving his daughter to kill herself. He was banished from the people, according to the law, and the sacred arrows were renewed to remove the blood of the People from them. He went to live with the Little Star People. He lived among them for many years before he was allowed to return to the People.

"For his part in the tragedy, the husband was beaten, also according to the law. Red Squirrel Woman's body was placed up on the high bluff, overlooking the camp, so that we all would remember her when we come to this place."

George did not say anything for a few moments. "That is a sad story," he said.

"Yes, but it is the only sadness that lives here," she said.

The grandmother said something to Speaks While Leaving. Then she placed her hand on George's injury and began to sing softly.

"What is she doing?" George whispered.

"She is asking the spirits to help you," Speaks While Leaving told him. "She asks them to make the leeches hungry so they will drink all of the bad blood. You must rest now, and let them do their work."

"Which?" George asked. "The leeches or the spirits?"

"Both," she said, and he heard the smile in her voice.

The chant was soothing, starting on a high note and tumbling down gently like water over riverstones. Healing Rock Woman sang it four times, once to each direction of the compass. She sang it a fifth time with a hand raised to the sky, and then she touched the ground and sang it a sixth and final time.

"Rest," Speaks While Leaving said. "We will be back in a hand or two to refresh them."

George shivered, suddenly cold. Speaks While Leaving put a hand to his brow. She unfolded a nearby blanket and tucked it in around him.

"Rest," she said again, and the two women left.

George lay there, shivering as the fever poured ice into his belly. He hummed to himself the tune of the chant Healing Rock Woman had made over him.

I do not believe in their spirits, he told himself. It is merely a pleasant tune. That is all.

Still, he hummed the chant six times before he allowed himself to drift off to sleep.

Custer stood his post in the reception line, greeting the guests and dignitaries as they filed into the Diplomatic Reception Hall on the southern side of the White House. It was to be a small gathering—twenty-eight guests, if he remembered correctly—in honor of a visit from the Archbishop Corrigan from New York.

The room was awash with black coats, white gloves, and starched collars. The handful of ladies present did their best to add a splash of color to the somberly dressed gathering, but neither their pastel satins, their winking jewels, nor the deep red of the velvet carpets could compete with so much sobriety. It was not simply the clothing of the clergy and gentry that was so black. It was the mood. Word of the formal declaration of war had finally wormed its way beyond the walls of the Capitol and into the ear of the public. The city was afire with rumors and speculation, and the word of war marched across the banners of the press in black letters half a hand high.

More black, Custer thought. *The town is draped with it. And my mood is no help, either.*

The War Department had sent orders out to Stant that morning, but Stant had not yet wired back his confirmation. Custer had approved the choice of Stant as commander of the operation, but doubts had been dogging him all afternoon.

At his side, he felt Libbie's nudging reminder. He returned from his private thoughts to see the archbishop approaching along the curved carpetway, a covey of cassocked priests in his wake. Conversation in the large, oval hall suddenly became muffled, as if a cloak had been thrown over it. All of the guests watched, anticipating the meeting of the host and his guest of honor.

"Your Excellency," Custer said. "Welcome."

"Mr. President," Archbishop Corrigan said as he took Custer's hand in a grip designed to crush. He stood tall and straight and looked directly into his host's eyes. Custer could smell the cigar his guest had left outside.

Neither man inclined toward the other—Corrigan was just as determined to be unimpressed by their meeting as was Custer.

"The Church is very distressed by the recent news," the archbishop said.

Well, Custer thought. The first shot has been fired before we even made it up the stairs.

"It is a distressing situation, Your Excellency," he replied, hoping to avoid a direct confrontation here in the foyer of his home. "In fact, I'd like to ask your advice on a few points concerning the public understanding of the situation. Perhaps after dinner?"

Corrigan raised a bushy gray eyebrow. "I know when I'm being put off, Mr. President." Next to Custer, Libbie cleared her throat. "But you are correct. This is not the place for such a discussion. We will take it up at a more appropriate moment. And this lovely creature must be the famed Elizabeth Custer. I've read a great deal of your work up North, madam. Your descriptions of frontier life are especially popular with the children."

Thank you, Lord, for Libbie, Custer thought and turned to the next guest in line.

Two callow clergymen and one tipsy senator later, he caught sight of Samuel standing at the foot of the east staircase. The old man tugged at his ear: a request for his presence. Custer raised a hand to him as he might to any other new arrival, only his gesture was a signal; three fingers raised and thumb and pinky tucked close to the palm: a request of three minutes' time to make a graceful exit. Samuel responded with a shake of his head and another tug at his earlobe. No, he meant. Urgent. Now. He turned and left the room through a side door.

Custer turned to his wife. "I'm sorry, dear," he began.

"Oh, I saw him. Go on, if you must. Abandon me

here to the onslaught." She smiled but under her breath she added, "I sometimes wonder just who it is that runs this country."

He bowed out of the line and followed his aide's route of retreat. Samuel was waiting in the conference room beyond with Jacob Greene, the Secretary of War. The secretary was quite agitated.

"If this is one of your pranks, Autie, it isn't funny."

"What are you talking about?"

"Stant has telegraphed." Greene waggled a pudgy hand that held a sheet of paper with block letters hastily written upon it. Custer took the message and read:

ORDERS RECEIVED VIA COURIER
CANNOT LEGALLY PROCEED
REQUIRE CONFIRMATION HIGHEST LEVEL
STANT

"The old warhorse balked," Greene said. He pulled at his mustaches and paced across the room like a rotund cat. "What the Devil can he mean, 'Cannot legally proceed'?" He pointed at Custer with an accusatory digit. "You told me he had what we needed. You told me he would lead the others in this action."

"No, Jacob. I said he was the only man who *could* lead them. It is still up to us to convince him."

"Could, would, should. It doesn't matter now. He's balked at the fence and won't jump over. 'Cannot legally proceed.' What rubbish!"

"Don't worry," Custer said, walking over and putting a hand on his friend's shoulder. "I know just what to say to him. Samuel, take a message upstairs to the telegraph and have it sent to our General Stant." Samuel sat down at the desk and took out a piece of stationery. Custer dictated his message. "Reference Lincoln's General Orders Number 100, Section V, Articles 101 and 102 Stop. Orders confirmed Stop. Proceed with action Stop. Sign it 'Autie.' "

Samuel scribbled the words and left the room through the rear door. Greene watched him go.

"Refresh my memory," he said.

"Article 101," Custer recited. "Deception in war is consistent with honorable warfare. Article 102: The law of war makes no difference on account of sexes."

Greene turned and plopped himself down into a wing-backed chair. He took out his handkerchief and pressed it to his brow. "Do you think that will be enough to move him?"

Custer hooked his thumbs beneath his vest and walked to the front window. The lamps, with their satellite moths, lit the curved steps of the South Entryway, but no farther. Lightning bugs drew lazy lines in the gloom beyond.

"I don't know," he said. "For Stant to question an order, no matter how distasteful . . . it took a bit to bring him to that point. I don't want to insult him with a direct order, but I'll give him one if I must. We've got to be ruthless in this." He turned back toward his Secretary of War.

"Come along, Jacob. There is nothing we can do at this point except hope he overcomes his reservations on the matter. Let's get back to the party. Samuel will inform us of any further developments."

Greene scowled up at his president.

"Come on," Custer urged him. "Libbie's waiting. She hasn't had a chance to talk to you in weeks."

The secretary sighed. The leather chair groaned as he stood. "Very well," he said, resigned. "I suppose you're right. But if that old warhorse of yours comes back with anything other than a smart salute and a 'Yes, sir, Mr. President,' he'll get more than a direct order as *my* response."

Custer nodded and put his hand to the door that led back to the reception hall. "Let us hope it doesn't come to that," he said. Then he put on his best company smile. "Ready?"

Greene straightened his waistcoat and brushed back his whiskers. "Onward, General."

Custer opened the door and the sounds of a dozen conversations floated past them. He saw the archbishop look up from across the room. The prelate extricated himself from his conversation and began his path toward his host. Custer cleared his throat.

"Onward, into the fray," he said, and strode into the room.

CHAPTER 8

Hatchling Moon, Past Full
Fifty-Three Years After the Star Fell
Fishing Lizard Creek,
Near the White Water

Standing in Water leaned back to throw, his gangly limbs all knees and elbows. Speaks While Leaving watched as he kicked out and hurled the small, brown ball. The boy with the bat swung. His teammates cheered and whooped as he ran toward the first bag.

"Hová'âháne!" One Who Flies shouted. *"Nóxa'e, nóxa'e!"* He turned to her. "Tell him he has to hit the ball before he can run, not just swing at it."

She translated and the boys groaned and complained. "They think you are making up the rules," she told him.

"Making them up?" He laughed. "I suppose it must seem that way to someone who has never played the game before. I grew up with baseball. I never had to learn it." He scratched his head and squinted into the sun that had come out from behind the clouds. "I never realized how complicated it was until now." He shrugged and lay back with an exaggerated sigh. "Tell them to decide which rules to keep and which to ignore. As long as they have fun, I guess."

Speaks While Leaving passed his words along to the boys and girls on the field. A whoop went up from both sides.

One Who Flies grunted as he stood up. She questioned him with a look but he waved away her concern.

"Don't worry, my Lady Surgeon. It is mostly habit by now. I'll be ready to ride to the meeting tomorrow."

"I think you would say that no matter how you felt."

He barked a short laugh and stretched his arms over his head. "I have never lied to you," he said, "and I am not going to start now. I'll be fine." He slapped his healing knee. "I am still in no condition to run away, but I can ride, after a fashion. I'd give a great deal for a horse and saddle, though. A great deal."

She thought of the meeting scheduled for the next day, and wanted to tell him that she would be sad to see him leave the People, but she stopped. Storm Arriving was walking toward them. She looked down at the ground, her heart suddenly beating like a sparrow's.

The tall warrior came toward them with purposeful steps. With each stride, dust puffed from his leggings and the silver of his earrings jingled. He stopped before One Who Flies.

"The Council wishes to speak to you," he said. "Come, and ask the daughter of One Bear to come as well." His errand complete, he turned to go.

"Why do you not ask her yourself?" One Who Flies asked him. "She's right here." Speaks While Leaving felt the blood rush to her cheeks and she turned to hide her embarrassment.

She heard Storm Arriving stop mid-stride. "I have asked you to relay the Council's request," he said. "Is that task too difficult for you?" There was an edge to his voice that she knew meant danger. She hoped One Who Flies heard it, too.

"Oh, no," One Who Flies said cheerfully. "Not at all. I was only surprised that it seemed beyond *your* abilities."

She heard the warrior's long intake of breath. She spoke quickly, eyes still fixed on the ground at her feet. "Do not worry, One Who Flies. I have heard the Council's request and will accompany you to the Council Lodge."

One Who Flies snapped at her. "You are no better

than he." She looked up, surprised by the anger in his voice. "The two of you are incredible. I swear it. He won't speak to you, and you won't even *look* at him. My God, but you make a ridiculous pair. I don't know whether to laugh or to cry. How long are you going to continue in this stupid contest? Until love dies?" One Who Flies threw his hands in the air and cursed. "Go ahead," he told them. "Play your game. Ignore each other. Die alone. Idiots." He limped off toward the center of camp. "And don't follow me," he said, stopping them both. "I'll have Red Whistler translate instead."

She stood there, frozen by shock and abashment. She had not thought of love as something that could die, and the words of One Who Flies set her heart racing even faster than it had been beating before.

One of us, she thought as she looked back down at the ground. One of us will have to give in. One of us will have to lose. One of us will have to disobey the other's edict, or it will be as One Who Flies has said.

She looked up. It was not difficult. The habituated years of averting her eyes did not drag at her gaze. She simply thought it, and then she did it.

He stood four paces from her—tall, lean, his earrings glinting in the sun and his hanging feather turning in the light wind from the distant mountains. He was looking away, staring at the back of One Who Flies with an expression that sent arrows into the bluecoat's heart. But even in his anger, he was beautiful, just as she remembered him, only . . . She noticed that the stubble of hair on his shorn right temple was dusted with gray, and several hairs from the crown of his head were bright silver against the shining black.

That gray had not been there when last she had looked upon him. How much time has passed, she asked the spirits. How much time have we lost?

Grief burned her eyes. She wiped at them, and when her sight was clear, he was gone, walking with anger after One Who Flies.

Following him was impossible. Her courage was gone,

spent all on one bold glance upward. Now she was empty, unable to walk after him, unable to call out; she could not ford that river again today.

But tomorrow, she promised herself. Tomorrow we will speak.

Behind her, the pitcher caught the ball and ran after the batter, trying to tag him with the ball. The batter took off in the direction of the river and the chase was on. Both teams evaporated, the air was filled with shouts and laughter, and in three breaths Speaks While Leaving was alone with the dust and the streaming sunlight.

Storm Arriving stooped and entered the Council lodge. One Who Flies sat in the front near the cold firepit. Red Whistler was beside him, translating as the chiefs listened attentively.

"He speaks, saying that he does not know the plans of Long Hair, nor would he tell us if he did. Would one of us tell our enemy of our war plans if we were captured? He says we would not, and that until there is peace between our two peoples, neither will he."

There was a good bit of grumbling at this statement, but Three Trees Together raised a hand and silence returned.

"One Who Flies is right in this. If one of us was captured by the Crow People, we would not tell them of our plans. If we caught one of the Cradle People after a raid, we would not expect him to speak to us."

He pointed at One Who Flies, who leaned to the side to hear Red Whistler's words. "This man is a likable fellow, but he is a *vé'ho'e* and the People have often walked the path of war against his kind."

One Who Flies stiffened. The translation lagged far behind the chief's words, but One Who Flies knew the word *vé'ho'e,* and he did not like it.

Two Roads, warrior chief of the Kit Fox soldiers, stood.

"One Who Flies does not know the thoughts of Long Hair. He cannot know, for he has been with the

People since the Hatchling Moon was new. He does not know this, but it is not what I wanted to know. What I ask is this: Why do my brother Kit Foxes return with reports of *vé'hó'e* soldiers all up and down the Big Greasy? The meeting is at the place where the White Water meets the Big Greasy, not south at the Tallow River, or the Unexpected River, or at the River of Big Round Rocks up in the north. Why are there bluecoats for a day's ride in either direction? Is this the way *vé'hó'e* abuse our promise of safe passage?" He sat, and Storm Arriving saw many others commend Two Road's analysis and question.

One Who Flies listened to the slow translation and then responded.

"Perhaps it is because the soldiers of Long Hair do not know if they can trust the word of the Council. The extra patrols across your lands may be to protect their leader from war parties or any others intent on killing Long Hair. It is not hard to imagine a young warrior who goes out on his own, determined to count coup on my father's head."

Those who spoke the Trader's tongue laughed at this. The others laughed, too, when Red Whistler translated the words.

Dark Eagle, who had acted so rudely to One Bear the day that One Who Flies came to the People, stood to address the Council. Since his discourtesy, the other chiefs had treated Dark Eagle with stony silence. He had learned from this, and now his manner was quieter and more restrained, as befits a chief. The older chiefs gave their approval with their silent attention.

"It is true," he said. "Any man would be proud to carry the locks of Long Hair on his belt, but to do so would not help the People. I would say at this time that One Who Flies does not help us. I think that Speaks While Leaving may have been wrong about him." When Red Whistler translated, One Who Flies looked at the faces of those around him, searching for support. He found none.

Three Trees Together knit his brow and gazed at his hands. The other chiefs brooded on the thought.

"It has been," said one of the four chiefs of the Sage People, who were part of the great alliance, "more than half a moon since this bluecoat came to us. He has not helped in all that time."

"And when will he?" Dark Eagle asked in turn. "When will he if not now, when armed bluecoats walk freely and Long Hair rides again in our lands?"

The assembly grew more anxious by the moment. Storm Arriving could see that One Who Flies felt the change in the wind. The chiefs spoke from their seats, against all propriety and tradition, the words of one walking over those of another. Red Whistler could not keep up, and One Who Flies could not interject a word.

"Speaks While Leaving has never been wrong," said Iron Shirt.

"For everything there is a first time," said Bull's Hump.

"If he refuses to help us, then he should be driven away from us."

"More than that—"

"Yes, more than that—"

Amid the building confusion, it came to Storm Arriving that they all might be wrong, that they might all have misunderstood the vision. He stood, and even though not a chief himself, the others subsided and allowed decorum to return.

"I apologize for interrupting," he said once it was quiet. "I know that I am here only by your invitation." Red Whistler spoke quietly into the ear of One Who Flies. The look on his face was still touched with fear.

"You say that One Who Flies has not helped us. You say that he tells us nothing, that he does nothing. This is true, but that does not mean he is not helping us."

He took a moment to gather his thoughts, for the idea was still new in his mind, its edges still vague and forming. The chiefs waited.

"In the vision . . . when we danced it . . . there were ten warriors, one from each band, who attacked the great Spider-Trickster, Vé'ho'e. The man who fell from the clouds did not fight. He only opened the way. Do you remember?"

He struggled with the words as pieces of his past fell into perspective. "Many years ago I argued with Speaks While Leaving. She thought the man from the cloud would be a great thinker. I thought he would be a great warrior. We thought only of what he would *do* for us, and not of what he could *cause*.

"We did not think of the thread that bound him. Perhaps that thread was the most important part, for it was tied at *both* ends. A rope can tie a man to a place, but it can be pulled both ways."

Three Trees Together understood. "He pulls Long Hair to us?"

Storm Arriving sighed, grateful that his poor words had made their point. He saw the worry on the face of One Who Flies blow away, leaving behind a calmer puzzlement as the statements came to him from Red Whistler. Storm Arriving sat down once more.

Three Trees Together spoke to Red Whistler. "Please take One Who Flies outside."

The young warrior rose, as did One Who Flies, and all were silent as the two left the lodge.

When they were gone, Three Trees Together continued. "A rope pulls both ways, but only as long as we keep hold of our end. If we give One Who Flies back to Long Hair and the other bluecoats, we lose our grip on the rope. We meet with Long Hair tomorrow, but I do not think we can give Long Hair back his son. What does the Council think?"

The night had dragged along, and through most of it George had been alone in One Bear's guest lodge. Throughout the camp, people were occupied in festivity or prayer, but in neither of those was there room for a paradox such as himself. He was part of their world, but he was not of it, and as he had lain there, waiting for sleep to find him, he had felt many things. What he had felt the most, however, was alone.

Now, as the camp began to quiet, as the only music was the flute of a lonely lover and the distant howl of a hungry coyote, he gave up on sleep and put another stick on the coals. The sweet smell of burning wood was welcome after a week of using buffalo chips for fuel. Outside, the crickets in the grass sang to the frogs along the creekside. He heard a step near the door.

"Ame'haooestse? Are you awake?"

"Héehe'e. Né'éstséhnêstse." Yes. Come in.

Speaks While Leaving pulled the doorflap open and stepped over the threshold. She did not close the flap behind her.

She stepped to the guest side of the fire, opposite George. Her hair was done up in two braids, and each braid was doubled up into two loops that had been tied behind each ear with small quilled disks of leather. Intertwined in the braids were sprigs of sage, and the ends of each braid were tied off with rolls of fringed deerskin. Bracelets of iron and brass sounded as she sat, her knees together and feet to the left in the manner of all women from the Closed Windpipe band.

She sat for a long moment, not speaking, just looking into the heat that rippled across the coals. George did not interrupt the silence. He had learned that quiet moments were not wasted moments to the Cheyenne. He picked up another stick with its sweater of lichen and laid it delicately next to the first. Smoke twisted up from between the pieces of wood. It rose, twining, thickening, until with a soundless flare the wood caught and the flames took over the work.

"I wanted to thank you," she said, though so softly that the hiss and spit of the tiny fire nearly drowned out her words. "For your honesty today before you went to speak to the Council."

George looked into the fire, embarrassed. "I was harsh and rude," he said. "It was not my business to say."

"No," she said and looked at him earnestly. "It is a friend's business, if his friend is eating rocks, to say that it is stupid to eat rocks. A friend will do that, and I wanted to thank you and to say that I have decided to stop eating rocks."

"I am glad to hear it," he said. "And I hope that Storm Arriving will stop in his stubbornness as well."

Silence sat with them again for a time, and they watched the two sticks turn from wood to coals.

"I should let you sleep," she said finally.

"I will not sleep tonight," he told her.

"Do you wish to be alone?"

He shook his head. "I would not mind company."

"What were you thinking about when I came in? What is it that keeps you awake?"

He thought back to the moment he sat up and put the first stick on the fire. "Home," he said. "I was thinking of my home."

She reached out and took another branch from the stack and placed it in the flames.

"Tell me about your home," she said.

CHAPTER 9

Tuesday, May 25, A.D. 1886
Washington, District of Columbia

Even in late spring the mornings were chill and damp. The White House, cold and drafty on even the most clement of days, magnified the morning's chill into a veritable frost. Custer's numb fingers fumbled with the buttons on his vest and he cursed the house and its designer.

"Autie," his wife exclaimed at his profanity. She came in from her dressing room, all lace and silk. She took over the chore of buttoning, and her touch, her genteel smile, and the heady scent of tuberoses melted away his chill.

"You're up especially early," she said. "Do you have a busy day ahead of you?"

"Yes," he said. "Very busy." He did not want to concern her with the details of the day. He was worried enough himself over the situation. "I will most likely be kept late."

"Oh?" she said and paused at his top button. "Really?"

He'd said too much. Libbie was smart and quick and could deduce his hidden thoughts from the most innocuous of statements. He could not pass it off now. Instead, he feigned annoyance.

"Yes. Samuel says I'm booked through the whole day, and when he says that, we always run late."

She looked up at him from beneath a suspicious eyebrow. "You're hiding something, my Golden Cavalier. I can tell."

"Really, Libbie. I don't know what—"

"Never mind," she said, interrupting. "If you can't say, then you can't say." She finished buttoning his vest and smoothed it out across his chest.

Custer took her hands in his. Her fingers had been knobbed by years of military life, but they were still long and supple. He brought them to his lips and kissed their soft skin.

"You are my finest prize," he said, and she blushed as if the years had melted away and they were back at a church dance in Monroe. "Besides," he said. "You and the girls will be busy tonight."

"Busy? With what?"

There was a perfunctory knock on the door just as the bedchamber door flew open in a tumble of chiffon-covered limbs and rag-tied curls. The girls—Lydia and Maria—were impossibly breathless and simultaneously full of excited chatter. There was no sense to be made of them as they heaped hugs and pecks upon their father and peppered their mother with interrogatives.

Custer smiled as Libbie called for order. Beneath her stern gaze the girls managed to rein in their exuberance to mere effervescence.

"Isn't it di*vine*?" Lydia said, and "I can't *believe* it," said the younger Maria.

"Believe what?" Libbie said with a sidelong glance at her husband.

"Hasn't he told you?"

"I can't *believe* it!"

"We're going to the theater—"

"Tonight—"

"To the *National* Theater—"

"To see Sarah *Bernhardt* "

"In *La Dame aux Camélias*," they swooned in chorus.

"Isn't it di*vine*?"

"I can't *believe* it!"

"General . . ."

Libbie said the word in the same tone she used when she found Tuck or Cardigan Two with their dirty paws on the furniture. The girls ceased bubbling and their jaws froze mid-word as their dream of a night at the National with The Divine Sarah was suddenly cast in jeopardy.

"You know how I feel about the girls staying out so late," Libbie said.

"I thought it would be a nice diversion," Custer said. "Besides, it's just down the street. You can have them back and in their beds ten minutes after the curtain rings down."

The girls' attention alternated between parents as the battle waged. Libbie renewed her suspicious glare. Custer tried boyish charm. Libbie intensified the accusation in her look. He countered with a shrug of honest intents gone athwart of a greater power. Her gaze softened with the return of good humor. He encouraged it with a smile and open arms. Libbie conceded defeat and embraced him, chuckling.

"I knew you were hiding something," she said, and the girls squealed.

"Isn't it di*vine*?"

"I just can't *believe* it!"

Big Nose crept through the ferns and underbrush that lined the banks of the White Water and came up alongside Storm Arriving. "Have you seen him?" Big Nose asked.

"No," Storm Arriving answered. "I have seen plenty of bluecoat soldiers and one of their warchiefs, but no sight of Long Hair."

"Perhaps he stays in that lodge."

Storm Arriving looked at the scene that had changed little since before dawn.

The bluecoats had arrived after sunrise with four wagons and hundreds of men on the domesticated elk the *vé'hó'e* called "horses." They had spent the first two hands of daylight inspecting the bones of the cloud-that-fell and shouting at once another like deaf men in a story circle. When they came to inspect the trees along the riverbank, it was as easy to stay hidden from them as to hide from a child. The bluecoats made so much noise of their own—crunching through the brush and shouting to one another—that they could not hear the river's voice, much less the breath of the men who lay beneath the ferns at their feet.

The rest of the morning had been taken up with raising the strange lodge. It was a clumsy thing, with poles meant to stand straight and alone instead of leaning in on one another for support. It required ropes at every point to keep it from falling down and they had set it up with its door to the west so with every breath of the prairie wind the lodge billowed and pulled at its ropes.

The lodge was flanked on both sides by a cloth-covered wagon. The curving tops of the wagons reminded Storm Arriving of the cloud-ribs that still stood so eerie and bare against the rain-heavy sky.

Since then there had been a great deal of activity, but little purpose as far as he could tell.

"There," he said, pointing. "That man at the door of the lodge. He seems to be one of their chiefs. See how the others come up to him with questions and walk away with answers? He seems to be the leader of this group of *vé'hó'e*."

"Yes," Big Nose said, "but he is not Long Hair. The bluecoat messenger said we were to meet with Long Hair."

"I do not think he is here. That warchief is the only one who has gone in or out of the lodge in three hands." He rolled over on his back and looked up through the canopy of waving greenery. "The sun is two hands from the top-of-the-sky."

"We must hurry," Big Nose said.

The two men gathered their weapons and crept down to the river's edge. From there they ran along the banks until they came to their whistlers and thence they rode against the building wind, back to the Council.

The gathering of chiefs waited at the brow of a low rise, in a line along its length. The wind was at their backs, and the deer tails, fox tails, feathers, and fringes that decorated their clothing and weaponry danced and fluttered. In their midst was One Who Flies, an island of dark blue amid the bright colors of the host.

Like the *vé'ho'e* warchief, the chiefs of the Council, too, had brought their warriors. Storm Arriving saw several hundred men on whistlers and over a hundred walkers at the Council's back. The faces of the men and the haunches and tails of their mounts had been painted with the stark patterns of war.

"It looks like all of the rifles are here," Big Nose said.

Storm Arriving looked again and saw that, indeed, many of the warriors held rifles across their legs instead of bows.

They rode up to the Kit Fox chief, Two Roads, and the rest of the Council.

"Any more to come?" Storm Arriving asked him.

"No," Two Roads said. "You are the last ones to return. What did you see?"

Storm Arriving and Big Nose related the layout of the force and the numbers they contained. "The horses are corralled directly east of the meeting place," Big Nose said. "That is a bad choice. With this wind, they will smell our walkers before they can see them. The bluecoats will have their hands full just keeping them quiet."

"Did you see Long Hair?" Two Roads asked.

"No," the two men said in unison.

"I do not believe he is there," Storm Arriving said. "I would like to ask One Who Flies what this might mean."

Two Roads conferred with the chiefs and agreement was quickly met. Storm Arriving spoke the Trader's tongue to One Who Flies.

"I have been to see the meeting place," he said. "Your father is not there. Why?"

One Who Flies was genuinely surprised. "Not there? Are you sure?"

Storm Arriving described what he had seen and asked his question once more. "Why is he not there?"

There was fear in the eyes of One Who Flies as he searched for an answer. "He . . . he might have been delayed—he is always late—or maybe he couldn't make the trip. He is very busy, you know."

"Too busy to save his own son?" Storm Arriving asked.

One Who Flies did not respond to that. After a moment, he asked, "What are you going to do?"

Storm Arriving pointed to the chiefs. "It is up to them." He turned back to Two Roads and the others. "He does not know. It seems that the son is not as important to the father as we thought."

In the presidential offices, the mood was much more severe than it had been in the family quarters.

Samuel and Jacob Greene waited near the door while General Meriwether and his attaché stood behind the desk, near the window. A large table had been brought in, leaving an aisle along the bookcases. Custer used it now, pacing slowly and methodically.

The table—a heavy, pillar-legged oak affair left by one of the house's Federalist tenants—was covered by all manner of paper. Around the limits of its surface were notes in Custer's hasty scrawl, sheets lined with his aide's minuscule notation, and block-lettered telegraph messages. Small stacks of books rested near the corners: military tactics, the memoirs of Lincoln and the perfunctory musings of Sherman, the writings of Cicero, Plutarch, and Caesar. The weight of their words, assisted by four teacups, held down the large yellowed map that took up the center of the dark surface.

Thin brown lines meandered across the age-stained paper like ant trails. Custer studied them as he paced off the length of the Frontier. On the map, inked lines paired up to form the Red River of the North, also called the Santee after the natives who used to live there; the wide Missouri, which they called the Big Greasy or the Fatfoam River; the Niobrara, known as the Unexpected River to the Cheyenne; and—the crux of Custer's attention—the one river that carried the same name for both races: the White.

On the table, on the map as it was out on the Frontier, three groups of figures had gathered. On the table they were small painted blocks of wood: blue, with various strips. On the Frontier, they were phalanxes of might: men, horses, guns, and artillery. Three groups, all beyond the Mississippi, beyond the Red, and now, beyond the Missouri.

"Mr. President," said Jacob, opting for formality in the tense atmosphere. "It will be some hours before we hear anything."

Custer scowled but did not look away from the tokens on the map. "Permit me to worry, Jacob. There's a little more at stake here than I'm used to."

"Yes, Mr. President."

He stopped at the corner and picked up the stack of telegraph messages. "You told him about the sabers?" he asked, paging through the sheets. "You told him to ride in without sabers?"

"As per your request, sir." Meriwether came to his side and lifted out the sheet that had been used to send the information.

"Good," he said, and resumed his pacing. "They make an awful racket, you know. You couldn't sneak up on a deaf banshee riding in with sabers."

"He knows," Meriwether assured him. "He learned it from you."

Custer pulled out his watch and checked the time. Noon. An hour yet at least before the meeting would take place, nearly a thousand miles distant. His boy was approaching the nexus, the fulcrum point of power. His survival—along with the future of the Frontier—depended on how well his father had guessed.

* * *

There was no other way for George to put it: he was frightened. While the Council had sat down in the waves of green grass to discuss their next action, he had tried to rename his feelings as anxiety, worry, nervousness, even as excitement. Each time, however, the lies scattered like dead leaves and he was left with only the cold, bare truth.

He was afraid.

They rode in three groups: the Council chiefs with their whistler escorts, and two squadrons of walkers loping along to either side. At the news that his father was not present at the meeting place, most of the warriors were sent off in another direction. Of the remaining delegation, the attitude had transformed. Before, they had been serious, with few words exchanged and a strong sense of purpose among them. Now, however, they were all completely silent, and every eye was grim. Rifles—and there were many—were held on hip, unraised but ready. Quivers had been laced to first ropes. The sense of purpose had been honed and focused down to a point, and that point was now aimed due east.

George jumped as Two Roads shouted a command. The two squads of walkers moved ahead and away from the group of Council chiefs. When they were a hundred yards to either side and perhaps a quarter mile in the lead, he heard another shout.

The men atop the walkers began to sing a pounding, angry chant. The rhythm pulsed and one by one the walkers fell in with it. Their long strides matched it, their feet coming down in heavy concert, and George could feel and hear the very ground around them reverberate like a huge, monstrous drum. The warriors around him joined in the song. Only the chiefs remained silent. No one would meet George's gaze; each man was set only on the goal that lay ahead. He felt as if caught up in one of the twisting winds of the Frontier, surrounded by danger and power, helpless to alter anything.

The wind swept across their backs and ran before

them. Gray clouds piled up behind them and George heard the distant cannonshots of thunder.

The men sang. The walkers pounded the earth. The land rang and the heavens rumbled. They crested a rise and George saw the spars and beams of the ruined *A. Lincoln*. Toward the river were a tent and wagons, their fabric luffing in the wind. Beyond that, he could see soldiers running to help.

"Nóxa'e!" came the order and the Indians halted an eighth of a mile distant. At the meeting place, soldiers took up ceremonial positions at attention with rifles at right shoulder arms.

The arriving Indians surveyed the scene from their three-pronged vantage, and then, as one, the warriors shouted and the walkers sounded, issuing forth a terrifying mix of sound like a ten-story locomotive and the scream of a monstrous eagle.

Down at the meeting place horses reared and soldiers lost their footing with knees turned to water. Many horses broke free, adding their own screams to the cacophony. The bellowing continued for some seconds and then the walkers stepped forward, advancing at a menacingly slow pace and blasting their challenge with each breath. It was terrifying. George felt his own heart thudding in his breast. He could not imagine the fear of the soldiers ahead as fifty giant, toothsome, taloned lizards approached them, maws open and howling for blood.

More horses broke free and ran. Chaos bred within the heart of the army position. The walkers advanced to within two hundred yards, halted, and fell silent. Only the clouds above continued with their ominous thunder.

Three Trees Together motioned to Two Roads. The chief of the Kit Fox soldiers beckoned to Big Nose and Storm Arriving. Storm Arriving looked in turn at George.

"Nóheto."

The quartet headed out from the group of chiefs, riding up to within a stone's throw of the nearest soldiers. Even from this distance George could see their eyes glancing back and forth, from whistlers to walkers, and his own fear was somehow drowned out by the terror of the others before him.

From within the tent came a gray-bearded officer flanked by two others. The older man walked slowly, almost leisurely, to meet the emissaries. As they came closer, George saw the man was a general with steel-gray hair to match his beard and eyes the color of soot. He recognized him from long-ago days along the shores of the Gulf of Narváez. At his side were a captain and a lieutenant, both unfamiliar to George.

"Good afternoon, honorable guests," said General Stant. The lieutenant translated his words to French, and Storm Arriving took the words onward into the language of the Cheyenne.

"My name is Stant, and I am here as the representative of the President of the United States. I would like to welcome you—"

Two Roads spoke loudly. "Where is Long Hair?" he asked.

Storm Arriving translated. The lieutenant glanced at his superior, puzzled at the question, but he relayed the words. Stant, a longtime comrade of The General's, knew the Cheyenne's name for his commander-in-chief.

"Long Hair is not here, and sends his apologies. I have been authorized to speak to you on his behalf."

The words came back, and before Stant could finish, Two Roads had turned and started back to the group of chiefs. Storm Arriving grabbed George's mount by the halter and began to lead him away.

"George!" Stant shouted. "Run!"

George slid off his mount, but not before Storm Arriving grabbed him by the sleeve. They both tumbled to the ground. George cried out as his side flared in pain, and whistlers shrilled the alarm.

Two Roads and Big Nose stopped. George looked up. Storm Arriving had him by the collar. His knife was in his hand and death was on his face.

"Do not move," Stant ordered, and the sound of rifle bolts chattered in the air. George glanced over toward the general.

Soldiers went down on one knee and now aimed at the Indians. The covers of the wagons had been thrown back and the multiple barrels of two Gatling guns gleamed in the gray light.

"If you harm him," Stant said, "you will die. You will all die."

Storm Arriving stood unmoving, his knife still raised to strike. George saw the blackness of his eyes and heard the sound of impassioned breath through flared nostrils. The general's words were translated and the corner of the Indian's mouth crept upward.

"You are outmatched," Stant continued, "and harming the son of Long Hair will only earn you his eternal hatred. We can end this day in peace, if you return to us the son of Long Hair."

George saw the smile above him broaden, as Big Nose passed the general's words along. When the translation was complete, Two Roads spoke.

"You are wrong, bluecoat Stant. You are the one who is outmatched."

From the woods along the river came a chilling ululation. The brush and ferns moved, and a long line of whistlers dropped their forest colors for angry patterns of red and white. In a heartbeat Stant's position had fallen from one of even numbers and superior firepower to being outflanked and outnumbered three to one.

The general's face twisted with frustration as he took in his change of fate. Arrows were ready to fly at front and rear. A walker chuffed its impatience. Others joined in, underlining their own threat. George could see the calculations that roiled in Stant's head—first volley, initial wounded, second volley, distance to target, travel time, cavalry versus infantry. His lips pulled back and his teeth showed white beneath bristling gray whiskers. His neck was corded and his every muscle tensed as he gave the order.

"Stand down."

"But sir—"

"Stand *down!*" he shouted. "There has been enough carnage today. I won't add your lives to it. Stand down!"

Rifles retreated, pointing to the heavens, and the gunners relaxed from the brink of turning the firing crank. Lightning flickered between the clouds. George felt the shy touch of a first raindrop as thunder rolled across the sky.

Two Roads spoke to the general in a strong, steady voice carried by the rising wind.

"We came to speak to Long Hair," he said, "but he is not here, so we will leave. We came to give Long Hair back his son, but he is not here, so the son will stay with the People. We gave Long Hair permission to cross our lands, but he is not here, so you must leave. You have until the sun has set to leave our lands and cross the Big Greasy. When the sun rises again, if you are still in our lands, *you* will die." He turned before the translation was complete. Storm Arriving yanked George up by the collar. He commanded the whistlers to crouch and they mounted, though he kept hold of the halter to George's beast.

George twisted in his seat and saluted as best he could. Stant returned it, and called out.

"Forgive me, George. May both you and God forgive me."

The clouds released their rain like a long-held breath. George watched Stant dwindle and fade away behind the sheets of rain. The general remained where he was, arms held wide, embracing the storm's violence as a penance. Thunder was his only answer.

George turned away from the sight, struggling against hopelessness and wrestling with suspicions. His military education and his knowledge of Stant clashed with the events of the past few minutes. Stant had come ready for a fight, but without the men to carry it off. He was outmaneuvered too easily, and had been unwilling to add the lives of his men to . . .

To what?

"Something is wrong," he said to Storm Arriving.

Some of George's concern penetrated the Indian's disdain. "What?"

"I'm not sure, but something back there was wrong. That man never gets into a fight that he isn't sure he can win."

"He made a mistake. It can happen to the best of men."

"No, you are forgetting who *his* chief is. My father. Long Hair. *He* put Stant in this position, a situation where he might not be able to win."

"But why?" Worry creased the Indian's brow.

George reached for the sense of it. "Victory here must have been a secondary goal." He shook his head, trying to remember. "Why was it Stant said? 'There's been enough carnage today'? What was he talking about? No one was killed here today . . . Oh, God—"

"What is it?"

George turned to Storm Arriving, suddenly agitated. "My father is famous in war for two things, correct?"

Storm Arriving agreed. "Stealth and surprise."

"Two Roads said that there were Army patrols all up and down the Big Greasy. I thought they were to protect the president, but he is not here." He grabbed Storm Arriving by the sleeve. "And neither are the patrols. We are not the primary goal!"

Storm Arriving saw it at the same moment.

"The camp."

Storm Arriving shouted to Two Roads and the Council stopped to hear the news. He pointed to George several times during his narration and George saw the same light dawn in their eyes. It was an angry light.

"Nóheto!"

They were off at a reckless pace that turned the heavy raindrops into cloud-born bullets. The whistlers were pushed to their limit and the walkers were unable to keep the pace. Orders were given and the walkers peeled off from the main body. Grimly, George watched as the huge beasts regrouped and headed back toward the meeting place, urged on by the whoops of their riders. He tried not to think of the men who would die because of his own words. He tried not to think of how they would die. Between the Gatling guns and the jaws of a walker, there was little to recommend one choice over another.

As they rode against the wind, it occurred to him that he was more concerned about the camp of the Cheyenne than the soldiers of his own nation. But then he thought of Speaks While Leaving, of Blue Shell Woman and Mouse Road, of the people and families he had come to know, and he ceased to worry about the appropriateness of his feelings. He simply crouched down over the neck of his speeding whistler and squinted into the pelting rain.

Speaks While Leaving ran back into the lodge.

"Bluecoats," she said to her mothers and grandmother. "Many of them. Get my grandmother to safety."

"What will you do?" her mother asked.

In answer, she went to her father's backrest and threw off the pelt that covered it. From within the wicker frame she took his old bow and a quiver of arrows. "They attack from the south," she told them. "Go to the woods and hide there."

The older women and their matriarch took up what weapons they could and made for the door. Speaks While Leaving poked her head outside. It was raining but the attackers were still outside the camp. Shouts and gunfire told her it would not be safe for long. She urged her mothers along and then turned to face the enemy.

From the west came the panicked shrieks of whistlers amid the organized crackle of rifle shots. She could imagine the bullets ripping into the flocks as the bluecoats tried to disperse them. Other volleys sounded to the south and she ducked in reflex as bullets slashed through the skin of the lodge before her.

Soldiers cried out—in pain and in fury—as the blue-coats came onward.

She tore the two deerskin strips that tied the top of her left sleeve. It fell open at her side, baring her bow arm. She fumbled an arrow from quiver to string with hands out of practice to the task. Then she stepped around the lodge and sighted on the first bluecoat she saw.

He was young, with hair like shiny chestnuts. He was struggling with the lever of his rifle as he walked toward the camp. He saw her and stopped, pulled again at the lever. She sighted down the arrow. A limpid raindrop hung from the barb on the iron head, trembling. Beyond it, the soldier raised his rifle.

His aim sagged. He let the rifle fall and touched with disbelieving fingers the fletching that now pro-truded from his chest.

Speaks While Leaving stared as the man fell. She had never killed before, and she wondered if she had even now. She did not remember loosing the arrow, though it was gone from her bow. She had held it back, and then it had killed him. She had not even seen it fly between them. The bluecoat went down heavily to his knees, and then fell over on his side.

Shouts broke her fascination. Men joined her, using the nearby lodges as protection and firing at the ad-vancing line of bluecoats. She sent many arrows flying into that line.

She heard hoofbeats and two horsemen rode down on them. A heavy chain was suspended between them, and as they rode, the long chain pulled over lodges two and three at a time.

The bluecoats opened fire into the empty space, aiming at anything that moved. Men and women went down before the volley, combatant and innocent alike. Speaks While Leaving felt her heart cry out in torment but her body did not. Her body was busy putting arrows to the string and sending them into the enemy.

"Come on," shouted White Cloud. He grabbed her by the arm. "We must fall back. The riders need more time." He pulled her and they ran toward the center of camp.

She heard the screams of children from beneath one of the fallen lodges.

"Come on," the warrior urged her.

"No!"

She broke from him and ran to the sound. She lifted up the heavy skin and long poles, rummaging underneath them until she found the two children.

"To the woods," she told the eldest, a boy of perhaps seven summers. "Take her."

He grabbed his infant sister and ran for the north.

Another volley of shots sent bullets whizzing through the camp. Speaks While Leaving snatched her weapons and turned to run.

The boy lay facedown in the trampled grass. The baby girl lay two strides in front of him. The bullet had caught them both, and they lay silent amid the chaos.

Her heart found a voice and she shrieked in fierce anguish.

A bugle sounded to the east.

"They come again," someone shouted.

The horsemen with their chain passed through the camp again. Behind her there was a thick line of bluecoats that stretched far to either side. They had knives on the ends of their rifles and they began to run toward the camp.

Toward her.

She reached for the quiver. One arrow was left. She sent it and couldn't help but hit one of them, so near to one another were they. Then she turned and ran.

She helped several who had been knocked down by the riders' chain, but for every one she helped, another had to be left. Finally, she reached the center of the camp. Many had stopped at the lodge of the sacred arrows to try and slow down the bluecoats. Quivers were passed so every bow was ready. With the other men and women she set her back foot and waited for the enemy.

They came around the center line of lodges like the surge down a storm-swollen creek. Both sides fired. Speaks While Leaving heard a bullet snap by her ear and people went down on both sides. In the time it took the bluecoats to work their rifle levers, the People got off two more volleys of arrows. Then a whoop was heard in the west. The bluecoats turned toward the sound and the People shouted as a hundred whistlers and riders poured into the heart of the camp. The bluecoats stood against them and the collision of forces was vicious as beak and lance met bullet and bayonet.

After that, all order was lost and it was a melee. Speaks While Leaving wiped the drenching rain from her face and tried to help one of the nearby wounded. The dazed man was unrecognizable through the blood and mud and pain that covered his face. His head had been grazed by a bullet. She cut away a section of his leggings and pressed the folded hide against the wound.

"Hold that. Press hard." He did. She turned to help another. The man shouted warning and she turned back. A bluecoat swung his rifle butt and hit her across the face. She went down with a cry of shock. Her hands found the wounded warrior's hatchet in the mud. In one move she stood, spun, and struck the *vé'ho'e* in the neck. The light in his eyes went out at once and he fell across the wounded man's legs.

She looked down at the dead man. The hatchet had gone halfway through his spine just below his jaw. The sight of it did not sicken her as she had thought it would; it fulfilled her, and when the wounded warrior offered her his knife, she took it and she used it. Her own blood blinded her in one eye and her efforts were clumsy, but she completed the task and handed back the knife.

"You are part of a very exclusive society," the warrior said and she recognized him by his voice. He was Fire Bear, crier for the Tree People band. "There are few women who have counted any coup at all, and fewer still who have done what you have done today."

The battle had carried away from them and most of the gunfire now came from the east. She extended her arm to Fire Bear. He kicked off the dead *vé'ho'e*, took her hand, and stood.

"We are not done today," she said as she checked his wound. "The bleeding has slowed. A patch of deerskin will stick to it like a bandage." The reports from rifles sounded nearer.

"Come," he said. "We must gather arrows from the fallen."

The land swept toward and beneath them in slow undulations. They ran their whistlers over rise after rise. The rain had lessened but still stung on cheeks and brow. Storm Arriving had been hoping as they rode, hoping that One Who Flies was wrong, that there was no second force attacking the camp of the People, but as the bluff above Fishing Lizard Creek came into view, hope vanished.

To the south in a hollow of the land and hidden from the sight of the guards on the bluff stood hundreds of horses gently cropping the sweet grass. Their heads came up and their ears swiveled as the soldiers cried out and changed course to charge the herd.

The several bluecoats with the horses fired shots into the onrushing pack, but none were hit. The oncoming soldiers shouted again with whistlers joining in, unsettling horses and bluecoats alike. Horses reared and pulled up the stakes that tethered them. Storm Arriving heard One Who Flies yelling as they bore down upon the herd, a short phrase he repeated ceaselessly—something like "Ogad, ogad, ogad"—and louder as the distance closed.

A few of the bluecoats got off another shot, but that was all. The warriors rode them down and rode on, piercing the herd like a knife. The horses scattered like shellcatchers on the shores of the Big Salty, fleeing in all directions. Three men pulled up to return and finish the job while the others raced on ahead.

They came up out of the hollow and saw the camp. The field was thick with smoke from gunfire and burning lodges. Clear swaths crisscrossed the encampment where lodges had been pulled down. Bodies littered the spaces between, and combatants from both sides ran among them.

To the west Storm Arriving saw the empty area where the flocks had been. Throughout the camp there were no more than two hundred riders.

A bugle sang out and the bluecoats began to run together.

"They are falling back," One Who Flies shouted. "That's the call for retreat."

He was right. The bluecoats—hundreds strong—began to run back toward the horses. One group stopped and fired while the rest ran on. Then another group took up the defense while the first retreated. But there was no answering attack from the camp. The riders were outnumbered and the enemy was fleeing. That was enough for many of them.

It was not enough for Storm Arriving, however, nor for the rest of the Kit Foxes.

"After them," he shouted, but Two Roads countermanded him.

"No," he shouted. "They will be some time collecting their horses. We must first see to the safety of the camp and the Council."

Storm Arriving saw the wisdom of this, but his rage pulled at him.

"Think of your families," Two Roads said, and there was no more argument.

They rode with all speed into the camp.

It was a disaster.

Lodges were down throughout the camp and many of them burned where the skins had been dragged aside and the poles or furniture knocked into the firepits. The sounds of agony filled the air, and the flutings of frightened whistlers echoed off the stone cliffs. Storm Arriving heard a woman singing her death song as she lay in her husband's arms. Her voice was strong, the words clear.

Nothing lives long,
Only the earth and the mountains.

He heard a man shout and saw him point at One Who Flies. There was danger for him here. He grabbed the other mount's halter and steered away from the angry man.

They crossed the center of camp, where many lay wounded near the lodge of the sacred arrows. West, in the camp of the Tree People band, many lodges were down and the fighting had been fierce. He led them through the devastation until at last he saw the handprints and hailstones that decorated his lodge. His heart lifted at the sight. He urged his mount around a neighbor's lodge and pulled up short.

"No," he said as he saw his mother kneeling at the door to the lodge. "No."

She held a young woman in her arms.

"No!"

The blue shells on her breast were stained bright red with blood that darkened her dress from neck to waist.

"No!" He leapt down and ran, slipping on the slick grass and crying out the whole way, *"No!"*

His mother was weeping. She held Blue Shell Woman in her arms as she might a sleeping child, only her daughter's dark eyes were not closed. They stared blindly up into the sky and did not blink as the raindrops pattered on her face.

"Little Rabbit," her mother sang. *"See the fox. Run and hide."*

"Mother," Storm Arriving said.

She looked up at him from far away. "My little rabbit."

"Where is Mouse Road?" he asked, fearing the answer.

"Little Rabbit," she sang again. *"See the fox. Run and hide."*

Storm Arriving could barely see for the rain and his tears. His breath burned in his breast like hot smoke. He reached out and took his sister's hand in his. It was still warm. The blood that blackened her sleeve dripped onto the ground to pool beneath her and thin in the puddling rain.

Slowly, he became aware of laughter. Someone was laughing. How, he thought, can anyone laugh at this sight? All his hate and rage incandesced within him. He roared and surged to his feet, turning to face—to kill the man who laughed at the death of Blue Shell Woman.

Laughs like a Woman stood there, the rain streaming through the blood that covered his chest, his arms, and his legs. His hair was matted with gore and his thunder bow was sodden and red. He stood there, and he laughed. He leaned back and laughed his high-pitched woman's laugh to the clouds above. He laughed to the sky, and Storm Arriving could not stand it.

He strode over to him and would have struck him except for the look in his eyes. The Contrary's eyes were tortured, filled with pain; desolate. Tears ran down his cheeks and he bared his teeth in a smile that was not a smile. And he laughed.

Storm Arriving embraced him, and they held one another, laughing or crying as their responsibilities allowed.

The rain intensified and lightning seared the sky. Thunder shook the ground, but the Contrary did not flinch. Storm Arriving held his friend at arm's length and looked again into his face.

The laughter was gone, and only the tears remained. Laughs Like a Woman looked up into the sky as another glassy bolt lit the gloom overhead. The thunder rained down upon him and he showed no fear.

"The thunder beings have released you," Storm Arriving said.

Laughs like a Woman signed agreement. "I am free," he said.

Storm Arriving embraced his friend again.

"I have . . . seen Mouse Road."

"You have? Where? Is she safe?"

"She is . . . safe," Laughs like a Woman said. He spoke slowly, fighting the years of a Contrary's habits. "I saw her." He pointed toward the center of camp.

"My thanks," Storm Arriving said. "Mother, did you hear?" But his mother had not heard, nor could she. She was still lost in her grief. He turned back to Laughs like a Woman. "Will you watch over her?"

"No," the other said, and then realized his mistake. "I mean, yes, I will watch over her."

Storm Arriving started off toward the center of camp. He stopped when he saw One Who Flies. The *vé'ho'e* stared at the tragedy before him. Angry words came quickly to Storm Arriving, but he could not use them in the face of the bluecoat's sadness. Even though all this was the work of the *vé'hó'e,* Storm Arriving knew it was not the work of this one *vé'ho'e.*

"One Who Flies," he said. "Please take my sister's body into the lodge."

He nodded, and Storm Arriving left him.

There was much confusion in the center of the camp as healers tended to the wounded and mourners tended to the dead. In the clear space before the Council lodge three men kicked a bluecoat soldier. If the *vé'ho'e* was not dead now, he would be soon.

"Mouse Road," Storm Arriving shouted over the noise. "Mouse Road!"

A young voice answered. "I am here."

"Mouse Road." He walked toward the sound of the voice, weaving through the moans and wails.

"Here. I am here."

She ran toward him, thin and frail in her rain-soaked dress. She ran to him and he held her tight. Her arms and her legs were bloody.

"Where are you hurt?"

"I am not hurt," she said. Her voice quavered like a dying leaf. "I was helping."

"Helping? Who were you helping?"

She pointed.

Speaks While Leaving stood among the wounded. She was covered head to toe in blood. Her dress was torn and her hair was loose and her face was swollen and bruised along the left side. She stood there, looking at him, and he saw her eyes for perhaps the first time in four years. She gazed upon him, bold and unafraid. There was pain in her eyes, but something else, too. A pleading. A prayer.

"Speaks While Leaving," he said in answer, but his emotions swept forth to close his throat and he could say no more. She had heard him, though, and her breath came out in a sound that was half-laugh, half-sob. She covered her mouth with her hands in an attempt to still her weeping.

Without another word, Storm Arriving walked over to her. He reached out with his free arm. Mouse Road did likewise, and together they enfolded her.

Speaks While Leaving wept against his chest. Storm Arriving felt years of pain build up in him as he held her and thought of the many times he had wanted to hold her thus, only to have refused himself. He tried to speak, tried to find a way to express the regret of lost years. No words came, but two.

"Forgive me," he said, and felt her arms reach out around him. She squeezed and held on tightly to him, and wept all the more.

George walked slowly over to where Picking Bones Woman sat holding her daughter's body. The woman was nearly catatonic with grief, but as he knelt down, her eyes snapped back to awareness. She screamed at him and flailed at his chest. She beat him until Laughs like a Woman came and hid her face in his arms. She melted against the soldier, her wails calming and growing weaker until they finally subsided into tattered sobs.

George exchanged a look with Laughs like a Woman and it was clear that the Contrary had undergone some sort of transformation. His gaze was softer, and George did not sense the feral danger that had surrounded him. There was more of the human in him now, and much less of the wild.

The Contrary stroked the old woman's wet hair. He pointed to George's chest and then pantomimed taking off a garment. George looked at his chest.

Navy blue wool. Brass buttons. Gold trim. The uniform of her daughter's killers.

He took off the heavy jacket. Laughs like a Woman made another gesture, a tossing motion. George stood and threw the jacket over the incline of the lodge. It landed with a wet splat, out of sight.

Laughs like a Woman unfolded his sheltering arms. Picking Bones Woman did not scream as George put his arms beneath the dead girl. He lifted her. The hot knife of pain jabbed him in the side, but it was of little matter to him. As he looked into the girl's staring eyes, he wished for a great deal of pain, enough to burn away the massive guilt that gripped his soul.

Laughs like a Woman led the girl's mother inside the lodge. He picked up a buffalo robe and laid it down near the hearth. George put Blue Shell Woman down upon it. He set her hands upon her belly, then reached up and closed her eyes.

Outside, a wail separated from the general noise and drew nearer. It was a child crying, and soon it was at the door. Storm Arriving stepped inside, Mouse Road at his side. The girl hid her face in her brother's chest and wept out loud. The tall man said something to his young sister and she shook her head in refusal. He exhorted her and with reluctance she turned to look upon her sister's body.

The crying stopped and Storm Arriving released her. She knelt near the body. She touched the dead hand and recoiled, then reached out to touch it again. She held it for a breath or two, then turned and flung herself into her mother's arms.

Picking Bones Woman awoke from her grief. She blinked and looked down at Mouse Road, then wrapped the girl in her arms.

Storm Arriving knelt beside his mother and one by one they began to sing.

Laughs like a Woman motioned to George. They both stood and left the family to mourn their loss.

The rain had let up and the westering sun poked holes through the billowed clouds. In the center of camp, riders gathered and, with a whoop, headed off toward the retreating Army soldiers. George shivered in the slanted light. His shirt—wet, bloodstained, and muddy—clung to him like an unwanted skin. He held himself against the wind's chill.

Laughs like a Woman stepped around the side of the lodge. He returned a moment later, the army jacket in hand. He offered it; against the cold, he gestured.

George looked at the destruction around him. He looked in the doorway at the family singing for their lost one and thought of the hundreds of others around the camp who did likewise. He thought of Stant and his guilt for defiling the flag of truce and attacking a civilian population. He looked at the offered jacket, its brass stained with the results of the crime.

"Hová'âháne," he said. *"Ne-a'éše."* No, thank you. He did not know the Cheyenne words and so used French instead. "It is yours. A gift. A present."

Laughs like a Woman seemed to take his meaning but gave silent inquiry once more to be sure.

"Yes," George told him. "Take it. I shall never wear it again."

Custer finished reading the message.

"Dear Lord."

The paper trembled in his hand. The block letters shouted at him, accused him, berated him.

CPT CUSTER STILL CAPTIVE
ENEMY POSITION DECIMATED
HEAVY LOSSES AMONG CIVIL POPULATION

*SUBSTANTIAL LOSSES AMONG ATTACK
FORCE*
MUST REGROUP
STANT

"Dear Lord," he said again, and crumpled the message in his hand.

Samuel had retreated toward the door after delivering the message. The others—who had been so eager when word had finally come—now stared in gaping disbelief.

Meriwether scowled. "What the devil could have happened?"

"At least he's still alive," offered Jacob Greene.

Custer threw the wadded paper at his Secretary of War. "Still alive? And how long do you think *that* will last once they return to their camp? Dear God, he's probably dead already."

"Do you intend on operating under that assumption?" Meriwether asked.

"*What?* Why, you cold, son of a—"

"I'm sorry, sir, but it is a valid question. Do you wish us to proceed under the assumption that your son has been executed by the enemy?"

Custer stared at the general. He was mad enough to spit in Meriwether's Carolina eye, but his training came to his service and stopped him. He took a deep breath, closed his eyes, and let the air drain from him like blood. The anger bled out with it, and Custer rolled the question around in his mind. Should the forces in the field assume that George was dead?

"It *is* a valid question," he said, squaring his shoulders. "And no, I do not want us to assume that he is dead. I'm sure that if he is, the Cheyenne will want to offer us proof. We may have misjudged them, but I at least know them well enough for this: If they kill him, they'll want to rub my nose in it. They'll want me to suffer. My apologies, General."

"None needed, sir. Entirely understandable."

Custer placed his hands on his desk between plates

and cups and papers. He leaned on the desk and felt every year and every wound he had ever endured.

"Gentlemen, we are in a bad situation. In order to make anything of it, we need to know what happened and where we are now. Find out. We will reconvene in an hour. Have Cook brew up some coffee. It's going to be a long night."

He walked out of the room and closed the door gently behind him. The hallway that crossed the breadth of the White House was empty and the gas lights had been turned low. The house was quiet. Libbie and the girls were still at the theater.

Libbie.

He lit a taper from the hall sconce and took it with him into the family library.

The large room resisted the intrusion of the candle's light. Shadows lingered at either hand and the curved windows were dark.

Custer walked in and sat, placing the candle on the side table. He sat there in the stillness and gloom and stared out through the mullioned panes into the blackness.

Beyond the balustrade and the dark void of the south grounds, the lights of the city shone like wan fairies. A carriage made its way up Hamilton Place, its lamp jumping and swinging through the night.

He sat there and watched its progress, and suddenly he felt a pang of grief for lost things. He thought back to '68, when he had traveled down to Kentuckee to survey a horse farm he was considering for purchase. He and Libbie and three-year-old George had arrived by carriage when the sun was just preparing to crest the mountaintops. The pine-thick slopes created a cascading tide of mist that tumbled down to settle in the meadowed vale. It set the distances apart with gradients of clarity so that the nearest tree stood crisp and cool against the gunmetal sky while the fence, the barn, the house, and the nearby hills were obscured by veils of progressive density until, at last, the fog-

shrouded mountains themselves were made nearly indistinguishable from the roof of clouds.

Horses walked leisurely across the pastureland, cropping sweet grass and flicking an ear or a tail at the
occasional blue-bottle fly.

Custer strolled through the bucolic landscape, Libbie at his side, his son toddling nearby. His lungs were
full of the clear air and his chest was filled with the
excitement that comes from seeing a lifelong dream
about to come true.

They stayed on at the farm, the guests of Joshua
and Elisheba Hawthorne, an aged couple who owned
the place. The two of them had been married for more
than sixty years and looked as if they were made of
the dirt beneath their feet.

"The good Lord blessed us with three lovely boys,"
the tiny Elisheba told them as she served the dinner
meal. "But they were taken by the War. We have a
daughter in Memphis, but she's nearly city folk now.
Poor Joshua, he's getting on and just can't . . ."

Joshua sat at the head of the table, the scowl of Job
on his face. He was a man made of sticks and cord.
His fringe of white hair hovered around his head as
if held there by static electricity, and his deep-set, dark
brown eyes were hooded with a private pain.

Elisheba never finished her sentence; not then, perhaps not ever. The old man's look said it all, and in
it Custer saw his own dreams die.

The next morning, with much apology, Elisheba saw
them off.

"A change of heart," she told them. "He just doesn't
want to sell it no more, is all. He never thought it would
happen, I guess, until you folks came and, well . . ."

Another sentence left undone. She apologized to
them all the way to their waiting carriage. Custer had
stopped listening to her, though; he was looking at the
old man.

Joshua stood a little bit off the path that meandered
the distance from the creaky planks of the rundown
porch to the gate in the post-and-rail fence. He did

not look at his departing guests; he had not looked at them through the whole of their visit. Instead, he stared off toward the pastures. A pair of bay geldings ran across the lea.

Custer knew the real reason behind Joshua's change of heart and he could not blame the old man. He stepped up into the open carriage, tipped his hat to Mrs. Hawthorne, adjusted his gloves, and brushed a stray hair from the breast of his military longcoat.

The coat, the braid, the uniform, and most especially the name; these things had changed old Joshua's heart. In his eyes Custer had seen the death of three sons, a family's hope thrice slain. That sight had killed Custer's own hopes, for nowhere in Kentuckee or Tennessee or anyplace in the South would his name be welcome. Not in his lifetime, anyway, and he had no desire to raise a family beneath that kind of onus.

They returned to Monroe and the lingering cold of the Michigan winter. In the spring, Custer and his brother Nevin bought a hundred-sixteen acres north of town and that made an end to the dream.

He was generally not the sort of man to dwell on past regrets, but tonight they all came home to him and thundered on the bastions of his mind.

The carriage swung from Hamilton Place onto the long curving drive to the White House. Custer pulled out his watch and checked the time by the candle's light. The theater was letting out. He did not know whether he should give Libbie the news when she arrived or wait until morning. Her mood, he decided, would tell. If she was happy from the night out, he would let her stay that way until morning.

No harm in that.

CHAPTER 10

Wednesday, May 26, A.D. 1886
Cheyenne Alliance Camp at Fishing
Lizard Creek
Unorganized Territory

When Speaks While Leaving came out of her family's lodge, George was waiting for her. Her dress still bore the stains of yesterday's violence. She carried four empty waterskins, and blinked in surprise when she saw him.

"One Who Flies," she said. "You are up with the women."

She looked tired, but he did not remark upon it. "I waited for you last night," he said. "I wanted to talk to you, but you were very late coming home."

She stifled a yawn. "There were many who needed my help. My help, and the help of others. I would have liked to talk, but your fire was out when I came back. I did not want to wake you for my own sake."

Speaks While Leaving's mother came out of the lodge.

"Ame'haooestse," she said with the barest of nods. Her tone was icy.

"Mo'e'haeva'e," he said, greeting her by name in return. He did not know the words that might thaw her heart, so he bowed. It was a gesture that meant nothing to the Cheyenne, but the intent was understood. Her expression wavered. She challenged his gaze, then looked at him with openness, then avoided looking at him altogether and went on about her chores.

He had seen that look a dozen times and more since the Army's butchery. The ties that bound him to these people were near to breaking. That he would die if they snapped was unquestioned in his mind, but there was something else that meant more to him even than that.

"Your mother tries not to hate me," he said to Speaks While Leaving. "I can see it in her face when she looks at me. I see it in others, too. That they who have such reason should even try . . . I just wish I could tell them all how much it means."

"You will find a way," she said. "You look cold. Where is your soldier's coat?"

"I threw it away."

She smiled. "In the language of the People, that phrase means much more. In Tsétsêhéstâhese, to throw something away means to discard it completely, to divorce yourself from it."

He thought about it, and then said, "That is what I did."

Her demeanor turned serious and she questioned him without words.

"It is what I wanted to talk to you about." He fought for the right words, for to think a thing and to say a thing were suddenly two very different propositions.

"I want to help," he said.

It was not what he really meant and Speaks While Leaving knew it. "What are you trying to say?" she asked him.

"I want to help. For Blue Shell Woman. For all the others. I . . . cannot be part of what was done here yesterday. I want to do something so it won't happen again." He shrugged. "I want to help."

She smiled again and he saw her eyes were bright. "I must tell my father," she said and was gone, back into the lodge. Her empty waterskins lay on the ground, forgotten.

They had left in the night so as to be ready when the day appeared. Storm Arriving rode in the lead,

Mouse Road in front of him. On one side rode his mother, and on the other, Standing Elk kept pace.

Behind them, two whistlers dragged travoises. One carried the poles and hides and other supplies they would need. The other carried the shrouded body of Blue Shell Woman.

They had traveled from Fishing Lizard Creek to the Sand Hills in quiet. The miles of grass passed silently beneath their whistlers' feet. Now, as the morning star rose in the east and the breeze brushed their faces with the taste of salt, the blanket of prairie grass pulled back to reveal the tufts of sedge and sawgrass and creeping sage that favored the lands around the Big Salty.

As they made their way up the final rise, Storm Arriving could hear the skrees of diving lizards out on the rocks. The whistlers called out to their airborne cousins. They reached the top of the bluff and halted.

The Big Salty lay before them, a huge watery road that began at their feet and stretched on to the end of the world. The thinning moon touched each wave with brilliance, glints of silver atop the brooding darkness. Fern trees lined the limit in a thick band that rustled and swayed in the wind. The whistlers called again to their ancestral home. It answered them with echoes, and from far off, they heard the long hoot of a swimmer-that-kills-from-below.

They dismounted and staked the whistlers. The horizon was infused with green.

"We do not have much time," Storm Arriving said.

Picking Bones Woman took Mouse Road downhill to gather items from the shore. Storm Arriving and Standing Elk set to digging the holes for the posts. The soil was loose and easy, but they had to dig deep so the poles would not shift. Soon, the four posts were in place and the two men worked to form the crossbeams and lash them to the supports.

They spoke only by gestures and looks. For Storm Arriving, words were not needed. The tasks were clear and simple. Dig the hole. Cut the pole. Tie the beam.

Silence was a friend that worked alongside him, and any words he might use to try to dull the edge of grief would be a dishonor to the memory of his sister.

Picking Bones Woman and Mouse Road returned just as the eastern sky began to burn. The men finished weaving the lattice of leather straps that would be Blue Shell Woman's final bed. Storm Arriving looked up. Already they had been seen. He showed his mother, pointing skyward. She looked and saw the gathering of angular wings: diving lizards, the large soaring creatures called Little Teeth by the Sage People. These graceful fliers lived only here on the cliffs around Big Salty. They soared on the rising warmth and dove down or skimmed the waters to catch their silvered prey.

The lizards hung overhead on the wind that rose from the bluff. Their leathery wings, each as long as a man's arm, were translucent in the growing dawn. They hovered, waiting for the family to leave. There were two tens or more already, with more swooping in from the misty cliffs every moment.

His mother smiled. "She will go quickly to Séáno," she said.

Storm Arriving lifted the body up onto the platform. Higher than a man could stretch his hand, it would keep his sister out of the reach of four-leggeds and leave her to the winged ones.

He untied her shroud and bared her face to the sky. She was still beautiful, even in the ashen pallor of death. He laid a buffalo robe atop her and tucked it in, swaddling her in its richness. His mother had sewn designs upon it with quills and bones and the blue shells his sister had loved so much. Standing Elk climbed up the stick ladder. He and Storm Arriving shared a long look over the body of the woman they both loved. The wind tugged at the young man's braid. He reached within his shirt and pulled out a long reed, his courting flute.

"I made this myself," he said. "To sing to her from the hills. She should have it now, that she can sing to me from the sky." He placed it with her, and both men descended.

They tied white feathers and blue shells and strips of copper to the frame. Storm Arriving lifted up his youngest sister and let her add the decorations she had made: woven ropes of grass and prairie flowers.

As the sun rose, Picking Bones Woman took out her drumskin and began to sing a farewell song. The first rays of day caught the Little Teeth that soared overhead. The light was so strong that it turned them into insubstantial spirits against the fading night. Their skrees and mews added shrill descant to the song, for they knew that, with the drum, their feast was near.

Storm Arriving sang with his mother. Standing Elk and Mouse Road burned white grandfather-sage and juniper. When the song was done, they packed up their few tools, dropped the travois poles, and headed back toward the People. Before the bluff was lost to the course of the land, Storm Arriving looked back over his shoulder, then pulled up to watch the spectacle.

The Little Teeth had already descended and the platform was a mass of flapping wings and scrabbling talons. They would rip open the shroud and rip open his sister's body, freeing her spirit for its journey to Séáno. The sight filled him with peace.

"I am glad that she did not die in winter like my father did."

"Yes," his mother said. "My daughter goes to Séáno this very day. It will be more pleasant for her."

They turned and tapped their mounts into step. Home was several hands away and there was much work there to be done.

The table was littered with scraps of paper and the air was rank with the stale smoke of too many cigars. Dawn touched the curtains and around the room men sat in poses of dejection.

"We're getting nowhere," Custer growled. "We have to get better information as to their losses."

"I'm not disagreeing with you, sir," said Meriwether. He rubbed eyes red from too little sleep and too much smoke. "But we have no way of getting the information. Stant says his troops are still being harried by the enemy and his Indian scouts have all been scared away. He cannot spare enough men to mount an expedition just to find out if the field officers' reports were accurate."

"You're missing the point," Custer said. "We've got to keep an eye on them. They are together in one place and we know where that is. When has that ever happened before?"

"Stant will surely be able to find new scouts in a day or two—"

"They could be halfway to New Spain in two days. They could scatter and disappear into a million square miles of territory."

"Then *let* them." The general's vehemence caught all by surprise. He threw his sheaf of papers onto the table and slapped the map's empty territory. "Let them disappear, for God's sake. And let *us* forget about them."

Custer felt his heart pound and his hands begin to shake with a rage that threatened to burn out of control. "What . . . are you saying, General?"

Meriwether slapped the map again. "Have you looked at this? Have you really looked at it? Do you realize what you're fighting for? It's a handful of land. It's nothing." He traced lines with his finger.

"They're hemmed in on three sides by the greatest powers on Earth. To the west, Spain. Britain, to the north. To their east, us, and nothing but water to the south."

"And if we don't take the land—" Custer started.

"Then what? Britain will take it? Or Spain? Don't you think they've tried? The Cheyenne Alliance has kept us all out—Spanish, British, French, and American— for hundreds of years. We've squeezed and chipped away but we've all gone as far as we can go. Our artillery is superior, but it's useless in the open country. It only makes us immobile and that's the one thing we cannot be. They are waging a running war against us, the kind of which we've never seen, and we are unable to win it."

"Really, Meriwether," said the Secretary of War. "Let us not lose our perspective. After all, they're just savages."

Meriwether slammed his fist on the table. "Those savages just cut our strike force down by a third, Mister Secretary. Three hundred men. Three *hundred*. And those 'savages' were unprepared and at half strength." He turned back to Custer. "This isn't worth a war, sir."

"It is our land," Custer said.

"And you've taken most of it." The general pointed to each conquest on the map. "Missouri, Kansa, Yankton, Santee. You've taken most of it. You, personally, are responsible for a great deal of these territories. But now, sir, it is time to stop."

"You expect me to just give up? What kind of president do you think I am?"

Meriwether looked him right in the eye. "The worst kind, Mister President. You have forgotten that you are a president and not a general. You have forgotten that life is better than land. And you have forgotten that diplomacy can win wars more easily than armies."

The two men stared at each other. Custer felt his rage winning the fight against his will. He felt his fingernails pressing into his own palms, he heard the trembling of the muscles in his jaw, and he tasted blood.

"Get out," he said. "All of you."

They did not argue. They left. Meriwether matched his stare until the last, then turned and left the room.

When they were gone and he heard their footsteps descend the stairs, he gave in to it. He cleared the table with a straight-armed sweep that sent maps, tokens, books, and cups flying. China shattered against the wainscoting. His anger spewed forth in a roar. Words, even curses, were beyond his capacity. He strode the length of the room, wading through papers and kick-

ing books into the corners. He kicked at the chairs until
he missed and barked his shin on the table's heavy,
claw-footed leg. He roared again with frustration and
hopelessness and then the strength left him. He thud-
ded to his knees and stretched his arms and chest
across the table. His breath seethed in and out between teeth clenched and bared. He stared at the grain
in the oak, but saw nothing but his own fate.

"Autie!"

He recoiled. He had never allowed himself to be
seen in such a state. He tried to collect his legs beneath him but only fell back against the bookcases.

"Autie!"

Footsteps ran toward him. He held up his hands to
hide his weakness and distress. Libbie knelt and held
him, submerging him in silk and the fragrance of orange blossoms. She was so fine and the concern in her
eyes was so genuine, he could not bear it. He hugged
her, held her, and the words came out.

"It's all coming apart," he said. "I can feel it. And
I don't know what to do. We've come so far; I wanted
you to have everything. We've come so far but now
it just makes the fall that much longer. I thought we
could do both." He waved at the strewn clutter of
maps and messages. "I thought we could get him back
and strike a decisive blow at the same time. I should
have known better, but damn me . . . you always say
I try to do too much at once. I'm sorry, Libbie. I'm
sorry. I'm sorry."

He let the tears come and held her tightly, but
rather than words of comfort, she was silent. Her body
was taut beneath his hand, and her gentle caresses
ceased. Her hands left him.

"What has happened," she asked him, voice even
and calm.

Custer leaned back against the shelves. He could
not look her in the eye; he knew what disapproval he
would find there, so he looked at her hands that lay
still and lifeless in her lap.

"Our son is still in enemy hands," he said. "Still captive, only we have attacked them as well, and attacked them in such a way as to do great damage and create much anger. I fear that they will kill him in retaliation. I fear it may already have been done, and we have simply not heard of it. I have failed us all, miserably. But I need you, Libbie. I need you to forgive me. My generals are insubordinate, and the public is ready to pull it all down. Even Samuel—faithful Prendergast— even he questions my motives. I need you, Libbie. Please. Don't you abandon me, too." He looked up into her eyes just as she struck him across the face.

She glared at him, naked anguish disfiguring her smooth features. Her lips moved soundlessly, a whispered question of one word. "Why? Why?"

"Libbie. Please—"

She slapped him again, then collected her skirts and stalked away.

"Libbie—" he said, following her.

"No!" She whirled on him with a fist held high. "Not this time. Not for our son. I have forgiven you everything before this day. The years of deprivation. The rush into politics. I've forgiven everything, but not this. I will not absolve you of this."

Tears spilled from her eyes and she fled, ushered out by the whisperings of silk and organdy.

"No," Two Roads said. "We must attack. To flee will teach the *vé'hó'e* nothing. There must be retribution for their cowardly attack."

Speaks While Leaving did not like the chief's words. One Who Flies sat beside her, cross-legged and respectfully silent, waiting for her to translate. He leaned close as she gave him the words of Two Roads. When she finished, he nodded that he understood.

The debate had gone back and forth for four hands of time and no progress had been made. The Council was split, the sides just as far apart now as they had been when they walked in the lodge. The four soldier societies, the Broken Jaw band, the Hair Rope band, and the Suhtai had all stood and called for an attack on the *vé'hó'e*. The Closed Windpipe band, the Tree People band, the Eaters, the Flexed-Leg band, and the Scabby band held that moving the People to safety was the primary concern. Even the allied tribes were divided on the issue, with the Cloud People and the Sage People calling for attack, while the Inviters and the Little Star People advised removal of the camp. The rest of the bands were undecided, but the arguments of other chiefs had not swayed them in either direction.

Two Roads continued in his statement.

"The Kit Fox lost many soldiers to the *vé'hó'e*, but many of the enemy were killed in return. We must finish the task and engage their forces. We must go to the bluecoat forts and burn each one of them until the sky is black with smoke." The chief of the Kit Foxes sat down.

Before another chief could rise to speak, Three Trees Together held up his hand. The old man conferred in whispered tones first with Stands Tall in Timber—the keeper of Maahótse, the Sacred Arrows of the People—and then with the two other principal chiefs who sat to either side. Then he spoke.

"Do any of the chiefs have anything to say that another has not already said?" He scanned the room, but no man rose. "Good. We have heard all the arguments. Now it is time to hear from a new voice.

"One Who Flies, you have said that now you wish to help the People. Tell us then. How do you think we should proceed?"

Speaks While Leaving translated the words. Now, she prayed, now will come an end to the slaughters.

One Who Flies stood. He looked around the lodge at the chiefs, and every one of them looked to him with hope.

"You must flee," he said. Speaks While Leaving felt her heart strike hard in her breast with joy for his words. There was reaction from the chiefs who understood his simple words in the Trader's Tongue. There was no need for translation.

"And," One Who Flies continued, "you must attack."

Again those who understood him told those who did not. Chiefs stood to refute him.

"We cannot do both."

"He is a crazy *vé'ho'e*."

"We must protect the People."

"We cannot divide our forces."

"This is not help."

One Who Flies held out his hands for silence. The chiefs realized their rudeness and quickly subsided. The pale-haired man looked to Three Trees Together. The old chief waved a withered hand, permission to proceed.

"You must flee, because your greatest strength— one which has caused my father many sleepless nights—is your mobility. You can move quickly and without the need for roads. You must do this now, for as long as they know where you are, you are at risk, and I do not wish to see repeated the kind of horror I saw here yesterday." One Who Flies waited for her translation to catch up with him.

"At the same time," he continued, "you must take the offensive."

Speaks While Leaving balked at translating this. "No, you cannot mean it," she said, pleading with him. "Has there not been enough blood?"

"What is it?" Three Trees Together asked.

It was wrong of her to interrupt One Who Flies. She knew it. She was not here as a chief or a speaker, but she just could not believe what he was saying.

"My daughter," Three Trees Together said. "Why do you stop?"

"Because what he is saying is wrong," she told him. "It is wrong, One Who Flies is wrong. We and the *vé'hó'e* have been killing and warring since long before the star fell, and it has brought us nothing. To fight them now is wrong. There *must* be another way." Passion tightened her throat and made her words come out in a harsh whisper. "My vision does not lead only to more killing. This is not what I foresaw."

The old chief leaned forward. "You question your own vision?"

"No," she said, desperate now. "I question what is happening. But if it means more lifetimes of death, then yes, I question my own vision."

Three Trees Together sat back and listened to the words of the three other chiefs next to him. "We agree that whatever path we choose, it should meet the approval of the vision. In this I believe we all agree." Chiefs around the circle signaled their concurrence.

Speaks While Leaving felt a wave of relief. "Thank you," she said. "An attack is the last thing—"

"But see now," Three Trees Together said. "One Who Flies still stands. We have been rude, my daughter, and have not let him finish. How can we know how poorly his words fit the vision if we have not heard them all?"

Gentle laughter rolled around the room and she felt her cheeks burn at the admonishment. She bowed her head and turned to One Who Flies. "My apologies," she said to him. "Please. Continue. I will give them your words."

"Thank you," he said in the language of the People. Then he returned to the Trader's tongue.

"But just as you send your families to safety, you must also strike a blow against the . . . the *vé'hó'e*." His use of the word took her by surprise, but he urged her on with a look.

"This blow you must strike—it cannot be the kind of blow you are accustomed to. There are more *vé'hó'e* than you can imagine. If you try to kill them, they will overrun you a thousand to one. Speaks While Leaving has told me of other peoples who you knew and who are no more, all because of the *vé'hó'e*. If you try to kill them, this will happen to you as well."

He spoke at length, and Speaks While Leaving passed his words along. With each phrase, with each words, she felt her faith restored. He did not speak of death or of war. He spoke of power and presence and of something every chief of the Council understood: honor and coup.

When he had finished, he sat, abruptly and without ceremony. Speaks While Leaving completed her translation and looked at Three Trees Together.

"Does this still go against the vision?" he asked her.

"No," she said and smiled, for she felt in her heart how true it was. "No, it is precisely what I saw."

When Storm Arriving and his family returned to camp, everyone was talking and working. The People were buzzing with plans for another move, and when he rode up to his family lodge, there was a new lodge being raised. People stood in a long line that wound in between the existing lodges. One by one each person took a turn walking across the new lodgeskin—an old tradition to drive sickness out of the new home.

"Storm Arriving!"

Laughs Like a Woman stepped out of the crowd and ran toward his friend. "Storm Arriving, come. You must walk over my new lodgeskins. I am back among the Tree People today, though it seems only for a night."

Storm Arriving slipped down off his whistler and handed the halter rope to his sister.

There was much laughter as people from the band trod across the pale skins. White Buffalo Woman stood nearby and sang a song of protection. Young boys held on to one another's shoulders and hopped across the skins in a large, giggling group. Kills in the Morning stopped in the middle and counted his many coup, striking the skins with a stick for each man he had killed.

"Quickly," Laughs Like a Woman said. "We are wanted after this. All the soldier societies are gathering near the Lodge of the Sacred Arrows."

Storm Arriving was ushered to the edge of the skins. He stepped onto the supple hide and strode across the length of them.

"Good. Thank you," Laughs like a Woman said. "Now, we must go."

A huge crowd had already gathered around the large red and black Lodge of the Sacred Arrows, the Maahótse. A thousand men sat in silence on the short grass as the bundle with the sacred arrows was brought out. Stands Tall in Timber, keeper of the Maahótse, held the bundle out to the east, the south, the west, and the north. The scars of his keeper's skin sacrifice shone like roads along his arms and down his legs. The scars on his chest—sun with crescent moon above—stood out against his dark skin. He held the bundle up to the sky, and down toward the earth. Then he held it close to his chest and faced the gathered soldiers. He spoke, and his voice carried across them all.

"When Sweet Medicine brought the Maahótse down from the Teaching Mountain, he told us to be wary of the *vé'hó'e*. He warned us away from them, and we heeded the warning. Because of that, we have kept our lands where other peoples have lost. Many of those who did not join with us are gone now: the Cut-Hair People, the Wolf People, and most of the Greasy Wood People.

"We, however, have survived against the Iron Shirts, the Traders, and the men of the Horse Nations, but now we are at a place that Sweet Medicine did not foresee. Now, it is not enough to defend ourselves and our land. Neither is it enough to attack a fort over here, or a group of wagons over there. We must do more."

The chief motioned someone forward. From within the group behind him stepped One Who Flies.

"What is he doing here?" Storm Arriving said aloud.

Laughs like a Woman smiled. "He helps us now. He has thrown away his blue coat."

Storm Arriving gaped. "Truly?"

His friend signed agreement.

"This man," the keeper of the Maahótse went on, "is known to you. He is One Who Flies, and he fell from the clouds, as was foretold. Now, he has offered us a plan to help us against the Horse Nations. The plan is according to the vision of Speaks While Leaving, and has been accepted by the Council. Now, we need you.

"From each band we will choose three times ten men. These will be joined by three times ten men from each of the allied peoples. All societies will be represented—the task before us is too great for only Kit Foxes, or Red Shield Men, or Elkhorn Scrapers. All are needed.

"One chief from each band will join, as well, to make a war party of four hundred. This is a sacred number, and in keeping with the vision.

"Those not chosen to go are chosen to protect the People as we move them to safety. This place is no longer safe for us. This duty, too, is an honorable task, for we will be moving deep within our lands, away from the bluecoats, but all that much nearer to the Crow People and the Cradle People.

"Now go. Return to your lodges and prepare."

All the warriors stood and quickly made their way home.

"What is this plan?" Storm Arriving asked.

Laughs like a Woman shrugged. "No one has said, but I do not remember a war party of this size since my grandfather's time."

Storm Arriving agreed. "Neither do I. This must be a very important war."

At his home he found Mouse Road crouched outside, hugging her knees, while inside his mother was weeping as she wrapped up the belongings of Blue Shell Woman. Storm Arriving knelt by his mother's side and helped her roll up the robe and bedding mat that had been his sister's. Her dress, her comb, her old deerskin doll, and all her other things were put in a bundle and tucked in a folded parfleche. Picking Bones Woman handed the bundle to him.

"Take it to Good Robe Woman. Her daughter needs some new things. No, wait." She opened the flap and took out the little doll. It was worn. Its painted face was faded, and the buffalo hair stuffing poked out from where one of its arms used to be. She closed the flap and patted the blue sign of *Nevé-stanevóo'o* that decorated it.

"Give the doll to Mouse Road," she told him. Then she turned and continued in her work.

He took the bundle and the doll outside. Mouse Road still sat by the doorway, rocking back and forth and staring at her toes.

"Here, Little Chipmunk," he said. "My mother says this is for you."

She looked up at him and the doll he held out to her. She took it and tucked it in between her legs and her chest. Then she looked back down at her toes. Storm Arriving stroked her shiny hair and turned to go.

"Storm Arriving." It was Red Tailfeather, one of the four chiefs of the Tree People band. "I have a question for you," he said. "We have decided to ask you to be a part of the war party. Do you wish to represent our band in this?"

"Yes," he said without hesitation. "I was hoping to be asked."

"Good. Tomorrow we will see the camp safely on its way and prepare ourselves for our own journey. We leave the morning after tomorrow."

"I will be ready," he said. They shook hands and Red Tailfeather went on to make his next call. Storm Arriving watched him and smiled when he saw him going to the new lodge of Laughs like a Woman.

"It will be just like old times," he said to himself. Then he set out quickly, for now there was another errand he needed to run. He needed to speak to One Bear before nightfall.

CHAPTER 11

Hatchling Moon, Waning
Fifty-Three Years After the Star Fell
Fishing Lizard Creek,
Near the White Water

"Don't cry, Mother." Storm Arriving put down the long leather bundle that held his father's pipe and hugged his mother tightly. She seemed older than she had a few days before; frailer, as though she might disappear in the wind. He touched her chin and tilted her gaze upward. "Mother," he said. "Please?"

She sniffed a runny nose and agreed.

"Good," he said. "And you, Mouse Road. You must be a help. Agreed?" The young girl consented.

"My mother, I have asked Standing Elk to help you as well. He will look in on you every day. If you need something, ask him and he will do it."

"He is a good boy," she said.

"Yes. He is."

Families around them started on their way. His own family's whistlers trilled and paled their colors. His mother's riding mount stamped its foot in impatience.

"They are anxious," he said. "The others are leaving. They do not want to be left behind. You should be going now. 'An early start—'"

"'—means an easy ride,'" she finished along with him. A tired smile touched her lips and he was glad to see it. He coaxed her whistler down and helped her onto it.

The sky was clear, but the morning wind held a chill

that seemed to come from the heart of winter. He put a heavy buffalo robe about her shoulders.

"Keep this on until the sun is a hand high," he asked of her.

"I am not a child," she told him.

"Do you want me to worry?"

She smiled and pushed him away. "You sound like me," she chided him. *"Nóheto."*

The whistler rose and started off. Storm Arriving went over to kiss his sister. Mouse Road grabbed him around the neck and squeezed. "Don't die," she whispered into his ear.

He kissed her cheek. "I won't," he said.

They started on their way. He pushed the rest of their meager flock into motion after them. The travoises scraped and bumped their way across the hard ground. The two drakes he kept for his own purposes called to their departing mates. Storm Arriving felt the hens' answers in his chest: the low rattle that they used only in moments of great insecurity. The three hatchlings looked back, but kept close to their mothers' haunches.

This war plan is odd, he thought. It has always been the men who left and the women that stayed. Everything about this is backward. He chuckled despite his concern. "Just like a *vé'ho'e,*" he said. But he had another thing to do, before the war party set out.

He heard a step and turned. Laughs like a Woman stood near the whistlers, their halters in hand. "Do you still want to do this thing? Didn't One Bear tell you what it was like?"

"Yes, he did," Storm Arriving assured him. "But there is something important you do not know. Two nights ago, before the bluecoat attack, I had a dream."

"Oh, yes? What was it?"

He hesitated, for the dream had been strong, and strong dreams were an important thing among the People. He had never had a strong dream before, and it frightened him.

"One Who Flies was in the dream. We stood in a

place where the ground was white and hard and men floated in the sky above our heads. Bluecoats ran at us, their rifles ready. One Who Flies tried to stop them but I held him back. They fired and thunder filled my head. I looked at my chest and saw that I had been struck twice." He touched the spots and frowned at the memory. "As I watched, the wounds turned into fresh scars—like the ones of One Bear. I know if I do not do this, One Who Flies will die and we will fall." He laughed at the serious look on his friend's face. "It can't be worse than what you have endured for the last eight years."

Laughs like a Woman smiled. "No," he said. "It is an honorable thing you do. As long as you are sure."

"I am," Storm Arriving said. He picked up the pipe bundle that lay at his feet. "I must go. I will be back before the moon sets."

The whistlers shied as Laughs like a Woman raised his hand. "Do it well," he said.

"I will see you," Storm Arriving said, and left.

He jogged across the emptying campground, weaving in between the lines of families as they headed west. The sun was still a few fingers below the horizon and the day promised to be warm. As he made his way toward the southeast and the grounds of the Closed Windpipe band, he wondered if it would be worse because it was a warm day. He imagined that warmth would make it much more of a trial than if it was cool, but one never knew.

All across the plain, other warriors sent their kindred westward. They stood, hands on hips, their lips in stern lines, and watched their women and children go off without them.

The people of the Closed Windpipe band had almost all departed. One Bear's family was just now mounting up. Storm Arriving shouted and ran. Speaks While Leaving heard him. She slipped down off her whistler, and he stopped before her, momentarily confused.

"I do not know how to greet you," he said. "Are we courting again? Or are we friends?"

She laughed and the sound of it made him happy. "My love," she said, "we have been courting all along. We just had a quarrel, is all."

"A quarrel? It lasted four years."

She touched his shoulder. "But it was only one quarrel. Would you throw away a courtship because of a single quarrel?"

He laughed and shook his head. "No. But I will never quarrel with you again. Who knows how long the next one might last?"

"So kiss me," she said. "Quickly, before my father sees."

"You make me feel my youth," he said, and kissed her—a quick, gentle touch of his lips to hers—and the scent of her, the thrill of her stole his breath and left him speechless. He stepped away from her just as One Bear came around the waiting whistlers.

"Daughter," he said. "It is time to go."

"Yes, Father." She climbed back aboard her mount and tucked her knees under the first rope.

"Nóheto!" One Bear shouted, and the whistlers moved out. The two men stood and watched as their women headed out. Last in line was the travois that carried Healing Rock Woman. The old grandmother waved when she saw Storm Arriving.

"Hello, Son of Yellow Hawk. Have you finally come to marry my granddaughter?"

"Soon," Storm Arriving said to her and raised his hand in farewell.

"Make sure it is," she said. "And welcome back. I have missed you."

One Bear put a hand on Storm Arriving's shoulder. "Are you ready?" he asked.

Storm Arriving took a large chestful of air and sighed. "Yes."

"Then take those," he said, pointing to a rope and a lodgepole that lay nearby. "We will do this up by the bones of Red Squirrel Woman."

The thin rope was made of buffalo hair, woven and braided tightly. It was quite long and each end was divided into two loops. Storm Arriving slung the coil over the shoulder that carried his father's pipe. The pole he balanced on his shoulder as well.

For his part, One Bear carried only a small leather bundle which he tucked into his shirt, above his belt.

They walked briskly to the stream and forded it below the pond. Then they took the path that went through the woods and eventually led to the narrow, crook-back trail that would take them to the top of the bluff.

The lodgepole was not heavy, but its length made it cumbersome among the rocks and switchbacks. To deal with it, Storm Arriving tried shifting it from shoulder to shoulder. He tried carrying it in one hand but almost lost it down the hillside when its far end hit a rock. He tried carrying it like a bluecoat rifle, but that made the long end too heavy and it threatened to tumble him down the slope as well. Eventually, he returned it to his shoulder and resolved to endure its recalcitrance.

When he got to the top, One Bear was already striking sparks into tinder for a fire. Storm Arriving set down the pole and the rope and turned to take in the vantage the bluff provided. He could see the People, already far to the west, a scattering of small dark shapes drawing a long, slow line of trampled grass across the prairie. Down in the camp, warriors gathered around open fires or bathed in the pond below the bluff's cliffside. Whistlers stood or crouched near their riders. Those who rode walkers were already out hunting with their mounts. The walkers would feed this morning and laze the rest of the day, showing their swollen bellies to the sun. They would slow the war party a little on the first day, but it was better than having a few whistlers disappear in the night. Feed them today, and they would be sated for a week.

"Come here," One Bear said. "The sun is rising."

Sticks snapped and wheezed in the flames of the small fire. "Sit," he instructed.

The two men sat down next to one another, facing the fire and the rising sun. One Bear held out a small pouch of tobacco. Storm Arriving took his father's pipe out of its bag of fringed deerskin. His mother had decorated the bag with quills and shells, and on it were painted pictures of grasshoppers and spirit men.

The pipe itself was decorated, too. The carved bowl was painted blue and white. The pipe stem, longer than a man's forearm, was also carved and painted with angles and shapes along its length. The two halves of the stem were tied together with sinew and wrapped at top and bottom by leather strips. Two eagle feathers were bound with red Trader's cloth to the ends of the stem.

Storm Arriving filled the pipe from One Bear's pouch. The chief gave him a sumac leaf to add to the bowl. Storm Arriving lit the pipe with a twig from the fire. He puffed it to life, but before drawing the smoke for himself, to turned the pipe around and offered it to the sky and to the earth, and to the east, south, west, and north in turn, so that all the spirits could partake before him. Then, holding the pipe by bowl and mouthpiece, he drew a long puff of smoke. He closed his eyes and breathed the smoke in slowly, smelling its sharpness, tasting its tang, feeling its warmth on his face and in his lungs. He let the smoke caress him and soothe him. He let it prepare him for the ordeal he was about to undertake.

He put the bowl on the ground between himself and One Bear and offered the stem to the chief. One Bear took the pipe and drew from it, letting the smoke waft upward to coil in his hair and around his head.

They smoked in silence, and kept their movements slow and deliberate as befitted the ritual. Storm Arriving rarely smoked—most young men did not, as it tended to make them short-winded—but it was something one always did with solemnity. As he and One Bear traded the pipe back and forth, their actions took

on a rhythm—a long, slow seiche that fluctuated between them like the rise and ebb of a spiritual tide.
To Storm Arriving, it seemed like the heartbeat of the
earth was moving him: take the pipe, draw the smoke,
breathe it in, let it out, pass the pipe, and rest. He
sensed his own connection to the world. He felt it
around him, and he felt it within him. He loved it, and
he wanted to give something of himself, to sacrifice
something of his body to prove that love, to make him
one with the spirit of the world. When the bowl was
smoked out, it was emptied and placed reverently on
its leather bag.

One Bear pointed to a spot away from the fire.
Storm Arriving took off his belt and shirt, and his
leggings and moccasins. He sat there facing the east
wearing only his breechclout. The sun was a hand
above the horizon and it shone upon him with a full
white light. He closed his eyes and took in the warmth
it offered him while One Bear tied the rope to the
lodgepole and rammed the pole deep into the ground.
Storm Arriving could hear the chirrs of quarreling
chickadees in the trees and the buzz of honeybees as
they visited the small yellow flowers that dotted the
northern slope of the bluff. He heard the whistle of a
dove's wings as it flew overhead, and then he heard
the step of One Bear. Storm Arriving opened his eyes.

One Bear knelt on one knee in front of him. The
pole was a few paces to the east. The rope's middle
was tied near the top and the ends trailed onto the
ground. The chief took the bundle out from within his
shirt and laid it on the ground.

"Are you ready?"

Storm Arriving agreed.

One Bear unrolled the little bundle. Within it were
two straight, finger-long sticks of cherrywood and a
long, thin knife. He reached for Storm Arriving's chest
and pinched at the skin a hand-width above his right
nipple. He pushed and squeezed the skin until it
bunched up between his finger and thumb. Then he

took the knife and pierced the ridge of skin, side to side.

Storm Arriving bared his teeth and held his breath so he would not cry out. The pain was sharp and hot and it made his loins pull up against his body. He blinked his eyes to clear the sudden tears.

One Bear pulled out the knife and ran one of the cherrywood sticks through the wound. A third of the stick on either side was exposed while the center was encased in flesh. As quickly as he had done the first, One Bear made a second cut on the left side, inserting the second stick there.

Storm Arriving felt light-headed. The pain suffused his chest. He was queasy, and could not feel his legs. One Bear stood and retrieved the ends of the rope. There were two eyelets woven into each end and he slipped the eyelets over the exposed ends of the sticks. Then he stepped behind Storm Arriving and lifted him to his feet.

Storm Arriving shook his head to clear it, then managed to stand. The chief led him backward. The ropes grew taut and the pain that was sharp agony became a pillar of light that blazed within him. It burst from him in a shout. He clamped down upon it.

"Do not fight the pain," One Bear counseled him. "Embrace it. It is part of your gift."

Storm Arriving tried. He took a breath and held it. He planted his feet and locked his knees. He leaned back, the ropes pulled, and Storm Arriving shouted to the sky and the sun that shone upon his face. The skewers in his chest pulled his skin away from his body and the pain shot out of every finger, every toe. It shot out of the top of his head and he shouted again, giving his pain to the world along with his flesh.

He felt One Bear's hands leave him. He stood by himself, leaning back, suspended by his own skin.

One Bear picked up the pipe and handed it to him. Storm Arriving took it with weak fingers.

"Offer the pipe to the south and return here."

Slowly, Storm Arriving sidestepped the quarter circle to the right. Keeping the rope taut, he tried to kneel. His knees buckled, but One Bear was there and caught him. Together they laid the pipe down, south of the pole. Storm Arriving rose on his own and traversed the distance back to his original spot, facing the east.

One Bear signaled approval. "Now there is only the waiting," he said.

Storm Arriving leaned back against the ropes and into the excoriating pain. He forced his arms to hang loose and his fingers to release their clenched grip upon the insubstantial air. The sun hit him now full in the face and he knew then that it did not matter whether the day would be warm or cold, for warm or cold, the sun would not climb higher into the sky nor rush more quickly in its path down toward the west. The sun would move as the sun always moved, and Storm Arriving would simply have to wait—and endure—until it was ready to set.

When the sun was high overhead, George walked to the pond. He sat down at the base of a tree in the armchair formed by two buttressing roots and gazed at the rippled mirror before him. The pond was long— a bowed ellipse beneath the bluff's sudden side—and for the moment, it was empty. The men had all bathed earlier, shortly after the camp had been struck, and since then they had all been occupied with their own preparations for the days ahead. Even here near the pond's gurgling outflow, the drumbeat pulsed through. George could hear the warriors' eerie songs bounce between the cliffs and the water.

He looked up to the overhang and saw one of the cliff-dwelling lizards leap off the rocky face. It dove down, guided by flaps of skin and webbed toes, then furled all at the last moment and hit the water with a sound like tearing cloth. A moment later it surfaced, a small fish in its jaws. The fish wriggled, the silver ribbon of its body flashing in the noonday sun.

George shivered with a chill born of old memories.

He remembered the first time he had seen a walker—
the only time, until he had come to be with the Cheyenne. It had happened many years before, when he
was only a child. The rain had been biblical and he
rode with his mother in a carriage as they traveled to
The General's newest frontier command. It was an
ancient brougham that transported them, unsuited to
both the uneven road and the unseasonable weather.
The hood was up, but still the rain poured in the open
front, soaking the hems of his mother's skirts. He was
spared such a watering, as he was still quite young
and his feet did not reach the floor. He and his mother
huddled together beneath blankets and oilskins, making—as they were often forced to do—the most of a
miserable situation.

The driver had no such protection as did they. He
sat up on the hard side-seat, hunched over, the noisy
springs beneath him shrieking with each hole and
stone. His collar was up and his brim was down, and
streams of water sluiced off his shoulders and down
his back.

The sky was gray with clouds and the ground was
brown with mud and the grass of late summer.
George's childish mind imagined that they rode on a
silken ribbon on a tawny blanket, and that their weight
made in it a depression that moved along with them
so that the muck and water coursed along beneath
them and that the featureless plain never showed them
anything beyond the rim of the shallow bowl of their
traveling. The grass was hip-high and he could see the
heads of grain bow to the wind along the sides of the
road, but beyond the limits of the muddy ruts it became an ocean, a thing whole unto itself, and the indi-
vidual stalks were lost in it as a drop was lost in the
sea.

His mother held him close, surrounding him with
her arms, her warmth, and her perfume of sunny
flowers. She sang to him of gingham and calico and a
cat and a dog, and though he did not know what gingham or calico was, he did know of cats and dogs and

of how they fought, and so he listened to her quiet song. They giggled when the bumps in the road came out in her words, and he felt safe and sound and the chill air was not as cold as it had been.

The driver shouted. George saw him reach for the Spenser rifle next to the seat, but a cloud eclipsed the sun—only there was no sun, and it was no cloud. It was a head, a monstrous head, and it reached in from the side and grabbed the driver by the body. The man screamed and George heard a crunch like kindling and then the man made only short, strangled sounds as he was lifted out of his seat.

The horses bolted at once and only the ruts and the high grass kept them on course. George's mother scrambled forward to grab the loose reins while George looked back out the brougham's rear window of sewn-in glass.

He saw the walker standing in the center of the road. The driver was crosswise in that terrible mouth. He twisted and squirmed and kicked his legs in futile attempts, and while that image was horror enough, what George had always remembered and what had haunted his childhood nights was the sight of the beast as it tossed its prey into the air and caught the man head-first. As the brougham was brought under control, George watched the walker jerk its head forward in lunging gulps until the man disappeared—shoulders, torso, legs, and feet—into that fearful gullet.

The fishing lizard paddled along the surface of the pond. It swallowed the fish and George sat in the shade of the pine tree and wished for the sun. The memory had always chilled his blood. Now fate had turned him around and he found himself leading a squadron of the monsters in an attack on his own country.

He longed for someone to talk to. With Speaks While Leaving gone and Storm Arriving off on some clandestine errand, there was no one left with whom to converse. Red Whistler and the wounded Big Nose had both gone off with the main body of the tribe, so

George was essentially alone. It was a place he had never liked. The military life had kept it at bay—one was never alone in the military—but here there was no escape. He was alone among strangers, and it was as plain as that. His thoughts wandered back to the Army's attack on the Cheyenne encampment. For that, he could blame no one but himself. If he had not been there, it would not have happened. He had tried to blame his father and had tried to blame Stant, but he could not fault them for being as they were. Only a short time ago he, too, had felt as they did, equating the Cheyenne's primitive existence with unabated savagery. But he had discovered instead a people with history, religion, government, and law. Their lives were violent at times and their technology was crude, but their ideas were not, and it was the ideas, he discovered, that defined a people.

Would we have been so proud, he wondered, had we lost our Revolution? Do we really judge ourselves not by the successes of our generals, but by the loftiness of our ideas?

No, he thought. We see only the vanquished and the victor. Ideas are a casuality of war and the commodity of historians.

He threw a pebble out into the pond. The lizard dove beneath the jade waters and the sun winked from atop the slowly spreading ripples.

The sun had scorched his face, baked his head, and burned his back. Now, Storm Arriving felt the evening rise in the songs of the frogs in the trees and the swallows in the air. He sensed the world cooling, the wind rising, the light fading. Dusk approached.

The day had been a haze to him. He remembered only the creak of the rope and the songs One Bear sang as he sat vigil by the little fire. His thoughts had drifted very little. He had thought of his sister once at midday and of how he would miss her. He had thought a few times of Speaks While Leaving and of the power of her smile. But those thoughts had not stayed with him long. They had been ushered out by the pain just as the night now escorted the day to the edge of the world.

One Bear left the fire and walked up behind him. "You have done well," he said. "Are you ready?"

Storm Arriving blinked slowly and signaled his consent. He had no strength to spare for speech. The skin on his chest had been pulled by the rope and sticks until it was stretched out thin like a piece of blood-smeared hide. One Bear put his arm around Storm Arriving, then took his knife and sliced away the skin behind the sticks. Storm Arriving snarled. He felt himself falling but he did not hit the ground. Instead he seemed to float and he realized that One Bear was carrying him over to the fire. The sensation of lightness remained after he was laid on the grass and his vision took on a clarity he had not known before.

Three stars were visible in the twilight sky. They shone like minute beacons in the purpled shell above. The flames of the fire danced with a rhythm that bordered on comprehension. He felt them reach out to warm his bones, while on the other side night stole the heat from his body. He felt the blood on his chest as it oozed and began to clot and dry, and he felt each blade of grass that touched him with its rough edge. He smelled the greenery, the smoke, and the metal of his own blood. He heard the crickets begin their nightly chants, and heard One Bear sing the final song.

Storm Arriving turned his head to the side and watched as the father of his beloved picked up the flaps of sacrificed skin. The chief showed them to the four quarters of the world and placed them at the base of the pole as he sang the sacred words. Storm Arriving heard the power in the words. It welled up from the ground like spring water; it bathed him and it refreshed him, and when he saw the image of his sister standing at his feet, he was not surprised.

She smiled down upon him and he smiled, too, happy that she was at peace in her new home.

We thank you, Blue Shell Woman said, though her

lips did not move. *Your love is strong and your sacrifice has been great. The People are renewed.*

Her form wavered and she became a white buffalo.

Our blessings are upon you, she said and loped away into the darkness.

He had never had a vision before—not a true one. Only dreams.

"This is interesting," he said and heard the gravel in his own voice. He sat up, slowly but without much pain. He looked at his chest and saw the raw spots where the skin had been cut away. They glistened in the fading light. There was some blood, but not much.

"How do you feel?" One Bear asked him.

"I am well," he said. "Sleepy, but much better than I had expected to be." He did not speak of the vision of his sister and the white buffalo. It did not seem proper to mention it.

"Shall we return?"

Storm Arriving acquiesced. He put his leggings back on, tying them as best he could. His shirt he would carry, along with his belt and the pipe bundle. They made their way slowly down the hill and walked back toward the nearly empty camp just as the horned moon touched the horizon.

He heard a shout, and Laughs like a Woman came running up to greet his friend. The two men said nothing to one another: they just exchanged smiles; one of satisfaction for one of pride.

"Will you eat at my fire tonight?" Laughs like a Woman asked.

"No," Storm Arriving said slowly, then laughed at his friend's look of dismay. "It is only that I am not hungry, but it would please me if I might sleep by your fire, for I am very tired."

Laughs like a Woman smiled again, his large white teeth gleaming in the last of the moonlight. "That is best, for even after eight years, I am no cook. Come."

"A moment." Storm Arriving turned to the man who had seen him through the day. "My thanks, One Bear."

The chief bowed his head in acknowledgment. Then he reached within his shirt and took out the bundle with the sticks and knife. He held it out for Storm Arriving.

"For when someone asks your help to do the same."

Storm Arriving took the bundle, and shook the chief's hand. "I will see you in the morning," he said. Then he let Laughs like a Woman lead him away.

George gasped as Laughs like a Woman brought Storm Arriving into the light of the fire. The tall Indian looked a grisly fright. His body was covered with dried gore and fresh blood wept from two wounds on his chest.

"Are you all right? What happened?"

Storm Arriving smiled with genuine good humor. "Do not worry. I am fine." He yawned, his movements slow and lethargic. George had never seen him in such a state.

Laughs like a Woman pointed to a buffalo robe and bade George roll it out. He did so and Storm Arriving lay down upon it. He looked up at them both. "It is good, my friends," he said in the language of his people. And then he was asleep.

George looked at the wounds as Storm Arriving breathed in and out in peaceful slumber. They were not like wounds had in battle; they were too regular. Then he remembered and knew that they were the same shape and placement as the old scars borne by One Bear. A ritual, then; and his civilized sensibilities recoiled.

Why, it is nothing less than self-mutilation, he thought to himself.

Then he stopped. He knew this man, knew him to be intelligent, thoughtful, stubborn, and passionate. He was not a mindless savage. He did not revel in blood-letting or the slaughter of babies to a dark unseen god. Then why?

George turned to Laughs like a Woman, pointed to the wounds, and asked him. "Why?"

Laughs like a Woman did not have much French nor did George know much of the Cheyenne tongue, but between the two they worked the meaning out.

"From him," George attempted to summarize. "To the spirits—*Nevé-stanevóo'o.* To the People, for strength?"

Laughs like a Woman agreed and pointed. "Strength, to he. Strength, to me. Strength, to all." He smiled and pointed to George. "And to you. Strength, and . . . *bon chance.*"

"Well," said George. "We could certainly use it. *Néá'eše.*" Thank you.

The camp had quieted and fires burned low as the war party began to bed down. Men slept next to their mounts in groups of three or four. The crickets laid down their tapestry of song while from above, just beyond the limits of the firelight, George heard the chitter and flap of a bat in search of a nighttime meal.

He prepared for sleep. The morning would come quickly—too quickly, he thought. He found no joy in the course he had laid out for them. It was long, it was dangerous, and it would throw them all into the path of the most dangerous man he knew.

The moon had set. It was, he guessed, close to midnight; even later than that at home. He thought of his mother and of his sisters and regretted the strife and shame they would suffer on his account, but then he thought of Blue Shell Woman and her quiet adoration. That death—that one and the hundreds of others—required answer.

Custer sat in the big chair in the upstairs library. It was dark. His taper had guttered out an hour before. The house was silent, sleeping, as quiet as death.

It's been a house of mourning, Custer thought. A house of death. We're all dead.

The girls had been crying all day and Libbie had not said a word to him since she had fled the war room. She had never shut him out like this, not in all their twenty-three years of marriage.

He is dead, Custer thought. We are all acting like it, even I.

There was a knock at the door, a polite double-rap.

"Don't you ever sleep, Douglas?"

The door opened and the house butler came into the darkened room carrying a tray and a candle. Custer heard the rattle of china and smelled the bitter sweetness of Cook's hot cocoa.

"Nossir," the butler said. "Not while any of the family are awake." He put the tray down on the table next to Custer's big chair. Along with the cocoa were cookies and quarters of dry toasted bread. "It's nearly morning, sir. The paper's just come. Do you want to see it?"

Custer nodded, and from a slot in the base of the tray, Douglas pulled out the corner of the morning's news. Custer took it from the slot. The headlines were black and bold.

"I don't think I've ever asked you, Douglas. Can you read?"

"Yes, sir," the aged Negro said. "My mama taught me on the Bible when I was a boy."

"Quite commendable of her," Custer said. "So what do you think of these headlines?" he asked.

"Oh, I never read the newspapers, sir. Never anything good in the newspapers."

Custer chuckled ruefully. "That is true enough today, at any rate. Thank you, Douglas. And thank Cook, too."

"Yes, sir. Thank you, sir."

The old man headed out the door.

"Oh, Douglas."

"Sir?"

"How did you know I wasn't asleep?"

"Sir? You snore, sir."

He chuckled again. "Of course," he said. "Thank you. And Douglas, please throw out the rest of the papers. Mrs. Custer is upset enough as it is. Will you do that for me?"

"Yes, Mr. President. Right away, sir."

He left and Custer sipped at the cocoa. Cook added a dollop of sweet butter and always kept it on the bittersweet side of the fence. It was gently sweet, rich, woody, and went down as smooth as satin. He set down the cup and once again perused the headline:

CUSTER'S WAR LOSES FIRST BATTLE

And beneath that, in smaller print:

HUNDREDS LOST IN ROUT OF ARMY FORCES

Most disturbing to him, however, was the picture beneath the headlines. It was a likeness of young George—the pose was copied from the photograph taken to commemorate his graduation from West Point. The caption read, "Young Cpt. G. A. Custer, Jr., believed lost in the battle."

Custer turned the paper over. Below the fold was a cartoon. It showed Custer, distorted and inflated into an immense, gluttonous man surround by pie plates. Most of the plates were empty and had been labeled with the names of the territories; Missouri, Kansa, Yankton, Santee. One pie plate was uneaten. It was labeled "Unorganized Territory," and the balloon of words that hung above Custer read, "I'll eat them all if it's the last thing I do."

He cursed and folded the paper once, then twice, then gripped it like a chicken's neck and wrung it like the hated enemy it was. When it was a tight spindle, he held the end of it to the candle's flame. The end caught and the flame slowly started to eat its way upward. Custer stood and walked to the hearth. He threw the paper into the bed of ashes.

"What do you want me to do?" he asked of it. "What do you expect me to do?" The paper began to unfurl as the flames embraced it. It unrolled just enough so that he could see the picture of George in his Academy uniform, all solemn for the occasion, the

Custer chin held up and his eyes leveled at the camera's lens.

That day had been difficult. George had graduated from his father's *alma mater* with all the honors that Custer himself had never been able to achieve.

"I never knew how to talk to you," he said to the picture of his boy. "You were always different from me. More like your mother's people: quiet, bookish. I never knew what to say." He frowned as his eyes swelled with tears, but he forced himself to continue, compelled to confession by the picture's sober regard and the feeling that time was running out.

"The truth of it is," he said as the heat began to curl the front page, "that I've always been afraid of you. You and that intellect of yours. Afraid . . . afraid of the day when you realized that you were smarter than your old man. Afraid that you would be ashamed of me. Ashamed of your own father." A sob broke through his façade. He bit it off. The picture curled, darkened, and disappeared in the flames.

CHAPTER 12
Friday, May 28, A.D. 1886
Washington, District of Columbia

The still-groggy corporal sat down in the hard-backed chair in the little office set aside for the telegraph equipment.

"But sir," he said, rubbing his eyes. "Do you know what time it is?"

Custer gestured to the unshuttered window. The sunlight outside fired the clouds with reds and pinks and cast long dark shadows across the lawns.

"I am not an idiot, Soldier. I know quite well how early the hour is, and I know, too, that it is even earlier out in Kansa. Now fire up this contraption and send a message. Get the old warhorse out of bed if you have to. He and I are going to have a conversation. Do I make myself clear?"

The corporal was awake now. "Clear, sir." He turned, flipped three switches, and began to rock the telegraph key back and forth, sending his rapid clicks on down the wires.

Morse's code came back as the corporal began to navigate the web of exchanges and dispatches that rested along the wires like gems on a fragile necklace. Custer heard the *dits* and *dahs* from ever more distant points return as another gem was added to the chain.

It took ten minutes to maneuver out of Virginia, ten more to cross beyond the Allegheny Mountains;

but after that the lines were fewer and most were military. That combination brought the message across Kentuckee and the Missouri Territory in five more minutes. Soon, Custer heard the response from Candide, at the edge of the Frontier, deep in Kansa Territory, and finally from Fort Whitly, where it had all begun only three and a half weeks before. Seventeen men and over fifteen hundred miles of wire relayed the wish of a president to get an old man out of bed.

For several minutes nothing happened. The telegraph operators sent a single *dit* that bounced slowly between the White House and Fort Whitly, a *dit* to ensure the lines were still open and functioning.

The tinny speaker began to stammer. Code came through. Stant was there.

"Good. Tell the good general that my boy is still out there. I want him to be found. Send men. Send scouts. And send them now."

The weak dawn offered no warmth. George shivered and pulled the heavy buffalo skin closer around his shoulders.

"After today," he said, "we will have to do most of our traveling by night."

The war chiefs listened to the quiet translation that Storm Arriving offered them. Storm Arriving looked peaked but otherwise hale. He had washed away the crusted blood during his morning bath. The two wounds had formed scabs overnight; cracked, angry-looking seals on his otherwise smooth and unmarked flesh.

"It is very important," George continued, "that we remain hidden as long as possible. It will be difficult for us to travel all that distance without being seen, but we must avoid it for as long as we can. I will guide the party away from towns and we will travel along the gravel beds of the railways. We will bivouac in woods or cornfields. This will help us stay hidden longer. Stealth is the key."

One of the chiefs—an ugly, pockmarked man with

a deep, velvety voice—said something the others found humorous.

"Not Quite a Bear speaks: the son uses the father's tools."

The comment hurt, but he knew that such was not the chief's intent. "That is so," he said. "It is a good tool. But there is one thing we must do that my father never did." He waited for the words to pass along before he continued; he wanted their complete attention.

"We must not kill *anyone*. If we do, we will bring down the anger of the entire country and lose any advantage we may have gained. As soon as the first *vé'ho'e* is killed, we lose. I cannot stress enough how important this is. Our goal is not killing. Our goal is power."

"But what of honor?" asked one of the chiefs. "To travel into the enemy's land and not count a coup?"

"And what if we are attacked?" another asked. "We must be able to defend ourselves."

"Agreed. If attacked, you must defend yourselves, but we must avoid confrontation if we can," George said. "And as for honor, I believe there will be plenty of coup to count by the time we are done."

The ten chiefs took a silent vote with looks and small gestures. When they spoke to Storm Arriving, their agreement was clear.

"It shall be done as you suggest," Storm Arriving told him. "How long will it take to reach the big fort you described?"

George pursed his lips and made some mental calculations. "From what I've seen of the whistlers—their speed, their stamina—we can cover the distance in less than half the time it would take conventional cavalry. I don't know about the walkers, though. How much will they slow us down?"

Storm Arriving conferred with the chief of the Red Shield soldiers. They discussed the issue at some length, and the chief that represented the Little Bowstring soldiers added his own comments. George understood none of it.

"As far as a whistler can run in two days, a walker can travel in three."

"That still beats out the horse by a good measure. If we push, we can make it in . . . four days. You get me across the Santee, and I'll get you the rest of the way."

The chiefs seemed pleased by his answer. He thanked them as they rose to distribute their orders. Two Roads held back, a frown of concern across his sharp features.

"One Who Flies," he said through Storm Arriving. "This plan you have laid out for us sounds easy to accomplish. Why is it so easy?"

A few of the other chiefs hesitated, waiting to hear the answer.

"My apologies, Two Roads, and to the other chiefs as well, if I have made this sound as if it will be an easy thing. It will not. It will be very dangerous, and I fear that many of us will die. We will need a great deal of luck to succeed."

"Ah," the chief said. "That is good. Such an important thing should be hard-won. I was afraid that it was going to be easy."

George smiled grimly. "Do not worry. It won't be."

The quiet of dawn was broken by whoops and whistles as the war party began to form up for departure.

There were more than three hundred men that rode whistlers and each man had a riding mount and a war mount. Some gathered in groups around their chiefs, listening to final words of instruction. Others ran their beasts in long figure eights across the plain of the empty camp, to loosen their whistlers' legs or just to burn off their own exuberance in simple activity.

To one side stood the party's contingent of walkers. They were all of the Red Shield and Little Bowstring soldiers—the two groups that George considered the most militaristic of the six soldier societies. The men sat on their walkers, nearly one hundred strong all arranged in rank and file, and heard the words of their war chiefs.

The bellies of their walkers were large and round. In a moment of gruesome curiosity, George wondered if the beasts had all fed on buffalo or if some of that roundness was due to the limbs and bodies of American soldiers. When the chiefs were done, men and beasts alike shouted their war cry, a sound that sent a shiver down George's back.

He worried about them. The walkers were predators, and as such were an unknown to his education in military tactics and strategy. He shook his head in wonder.

Not even Hannibal rode in on man-eaters, he fretted.

With their battle cry still echoing off the stone cliffs, the Red Shields and the Little Bowstrings turned and slapped their mounts into a long-legged lope. The Elkhorn Scrapers and Wolf soldiers rode out, too, along with the riders from the allied tribes. George hurried over to where Storm Arriving and Laughs like a Woman waited with the Kit Fox and Crazy Dog soldiers. He climbed up on his riding whistler and tied the halter for his war mount—both a loan from Two Roads—to his first rope.

"Well," he said to Storm Arriving. "I guess I am ready."

Laughs like a Woman rode up beside him. Over his shoulder hung the strap that held his knife. He took the strap off his shoulder, wrapped it around the knife and sheath, and offered the bundle to George.

"Laughs like a Woman does not think you should travel into battle without a weapon," Storm Arriving explained. "We all agree."

George looked around and saw that all the Kit Foxes were nearby, watching to see the outcome of the offer.

"I remember the first time he offered me this knife. Does he?"

Storm Arriving relayed the question. Laughs like a Woman giggled and replied.

"Laughs like a Woman says things are very different now. Now you are a friend of the People and a friend of Laughs like a Woman as well."

The knife was offered again, and George saw the hopefulness in the eyes of the former Contrary.

With a bow of his head, he took the knife. He unrolled the strap and put it over his shoulder, just as Laughs like a Woman had carried it. He took the knife out of its sheath. The blade was longer than his hand and well-honed. The sheath was made of tough, heavy hide, sewn with circlets of silver and tied with strips of leather. Long, white feathers hung from the bottom, and on the strap were circles sewn with quills and white eagle's down, tied to the strap with leather and red cloth. It was an impressive weapon and one that clearly carried importance for Laughs like a Woman.

"Ne-a'éše," he said with solemnity. "I am honored."

The riders yelled their ululating cry, and whistlers called out in huge hoots that swept from their keel-like bodies up through their curved bone crests. Two Roads raised his lance and enscribed a circle in the air.

"Nóheto!" he shouted. They were underway.

George was prepared. Hand on the first rope, he held on as his whistler leapt to keep pace with the others. All of the whistlers stayed close together as they ran—George could reach out and touch those nearest to him. They moved as a flock, all the whistlers together, and when they changed direction to avoid a shoulder of stone or take an easier fording across a rill, they shifted not one after another as in a line, but all at the same moment like a school of fish or a flight of birds.

Spirits were high and soon the men began to sing. There was no need for stealth, here in Alliance lands, so George did not worry about it. Each soldier society sang its own song and the competition for the loudest group was on. George did not understand the words, but he helped as he could by joining in with the melody. All competition was over, however, when the two groups on walkers began. They sang the same percussive song they had sung on the way to the treacherous meeting with Stant. The great beasts stomped their feet and pounded the earth, chuffing in rhythm—a huge *haoh-haoh* that nearly drowned out the singers.

In response, the other soldiers joined in on a single song, one that ran to the rhythm of the walkers' beat, and with a melody that played descant to the other song's deep ostinato. They sang the two songs that were one, and to George's amazement, he heard whistlers adding their voices to the choir.

The sun was ahead of them as they headed east to cross the first of many rivers that lay across their path. This one would, George feared, be the easiest of the lot.

"Nóxa'e!"

The whistler stopped and Speaks While Leaving gripped the first rope.

"What is it?" her mother asked.

From the travois at the rear her grandmother spoke. "Be careful. They are upon her."

Her mother spoke to her again—a question, she thought it was—but the world around her had already folded in and stopped up her ears. She saw only white, and heard only the wind through the prairie grass.

Then, as from a distance, a voice separated itself from the susurrus. A voice. Many voices. Singing.

The prairie appeared below her, the sun sparkling on the morning dewdrops. She floated above it, looking down as from a low cloud. The song grew in her head, words accentuated by the chuffs of walkers.

I am going (haoh-haoh)
To search for a man (haoh-haoh)
If I find him (haoh-haoh)
There will be fighting (haoh-haoh)
Perhaps he will kill me (haoh-haoh)
Perhaps he will kill me (haoh-haoh-ha!)

And in her sight they passed beneath her, one after another, men filled with song and excitement and the joy of camaraderie. She saw her father with the other chiefs near the end of the group and, in their midst, she saw One Who Flies. On his one side rode Laughs like a Woman, favored of the thunder beings, and on his other side rode Storm Arriving. She gasped at the wounds of the skin sacrifice that marred his chest and she felt her pride choke her throat and fill her unseeing eyes with hot tears. Her vision eyes saw clearly, and she turned as the last of the huge war party rode past.

"They are on their way," she made herself say, and the vision flared back to blinding white.

When she could see again, there were worried women all around her: family, friends, and neighbors.

"They are on their way," she said again. "The vision is coming true." Her words did not console them, and they turned back to their march without comment.

"Don't worry, Little Dreamer." Her grandmother rode by on her whistler-borne travois. "It will make no difference to them, vision come true or vision prove false. No amount of faith in you will keep them from worrying about their men."

Speaks While Leaving bowed her head. She knew the truth of her grandmother's wisdom, for it was her own wisdom; she believed in it more than anyone could, and yet still the pit of her own stomach was black and tight as she thought of Storm Arriving and the road before him.

Storm Arriving knew this land. He had traveled it as a boy and had patrolled it as a man. It was the land of the Inviters, who controlled the lands north of the People, but it was a border land to the Santee—land now lost to the Horse Nations—and so it required more patrolling than the Inviters alone could adequately provide. Thus, he had worked these lands along the river of the Santee from the Big Greasy up to Big Stone and on up to the Red River, helping to protect the lands of the Alliance.

The land here was pleasant and abundant with trees and small game. The strength of summer was still a moon away and everything was green and flowers were sprinkled across the knolls and vales like stars in the night sky. He heard the *mag-mag* of a magpie scolding from a tree, and higher he spotted a hawk soaring beneath a tumbling cloud.

The river pooled up here and grew wide and sedate. Up ahead, where the land gradually lifted itself up into rolling hills, it was narrower and filled with the strength of its youth. It was also shallower, and soon Storm Arriving and the rest reached the sandy place above Crazy Woman Creek, and for the first time in his life—for the first time in the lives of nearly every man present—they turned to the east and forded the River of the Santee, crossing into the lands of the Horse Nations.

There were no more songs and no more games among the men. They were now on enemy soil and Storm Arriving saw the serious heart of every man reflected in their faces.

They passed over the land at a moderate pace, slowed only by the walkers and their swaying bellies. As the sun turned from the top of the sky toward evening, the war party turned south along the river. Storm Arriving watched as scouts went out and came back with easy regularity. There was no danger here. The land lay much the same as it did in his homelands: green, rolling prairie, gentle on the eye and no trouble to cross. It seemed to go on forever, but that notion felt wrong. This was the frontier of his world.

"How long does the land continue like this?" he asked One Who Flies.

The former bluecoat scrunched his face and gazed up at the sun. "The land? It will be much the same for today and most of tomorrow. After that we leave the prairies and the land becomes very different. Before that, however . . ." He did not finish his thought.

"What?" Storm Arriving asked. "What will happen?"

"We are traveling toward the heart of my country. We . . . we *vé'hó'e* . . . we do not live with the land as you do. You live in a place for a short time—a week, a month or two. You accept what the land offers, and ask no more. When you leave, it is as if you were never there.

"*My* people, on the other hand, we are more like the Lodge Builders. We stay in one place, and we change the land to suit our needs." He sighed. "It is what makes us strong, but I think it has also made us cruel. We take from the land, we try to control it, and we think we can do the same with men."

Storm Arriving was confused. "I do not see how this affects us. What is it that will happen?"

One Who Flies sighed, distracted. "Long before the lay of the land changes, you will see other changes— our changes, changes we made to it. Roads, buildings, quarries, mines, railroads—especially railroads."

"With the great iron beasts?"

"Yes," One Who Flies said. "And they are very important to our plan. There will be many of the great iron beasts in the next few days. We will be following in their footsteps."

Storm Arriving smiled. "You have changed since I first met you."

"Have I?"

"Yes," he said. "You talk more like one of the People. I understand you much more now than I did before."

One Who Flies laughed. "The same is true for me," he said. "Now, when I hear you speak of the spirits of the earth or the sky, I feel as though I almost understand." He pointed to Storm Arriving's chest and the fresh scars left by the skin sacrifice. "I even think I might someday understand that. Someday."

"But not today," Storm Arriving said.

"No," George said with a sad smile. "Not today."

The scouts led them away from the River of the

Santee and across a driftless plain. The horizon evened out as they traveled, as if honed flat. Within a few hands of time, they began to cross the occasional creek. Gradually, the land achieved a slope and a contour. Ahead, Storm Arriving could see the broad, shallow depression of a river as it meandered through the plain. At the same time he saw a smudge in the blue of the horizon. The scouts returned and reported to the chiefs.

"Bluecoats," one man said, pointing toward the stain of smoke. "A large camp on the other side of the river."

Storm Arriving translated to One Who Flies.

"We must keep out of sight," he said.

The chiefs agreed, and the party kept far to the west of the camp. The whistlers altered their skins to a mottled green and formed a screen of camouflage for the walkers, who could not change the color of their brown flanks and blue wattles.

The sun was nearing its evening bed when the scouts returned again with words of warning. One Who Flies listened to the translation with great interest.

"That will be Washita," he said. "It is on the east bank of the river. We'll stay on this side and ford further downstream, after it is dark. Tell the scouts to be very careful. There will be homesteads on this side from here on."

The sun set and they continued onward without catching sight of the city on the prairie.

Storm Arriving sighed.

"What's the matter?" his friend asked.

"It is nothing."

"No. Tell me what it is that bothers you."

Storm Arriving sighed again. "It is just that I have heard many stories about the cities of the *vé'hó'e*. I was looking forward to seeing such a place."

"You have heard of our cities? From where?"

He shrugged. "Here and there. A Trader man in

Santee country told me many stories of your cities, about how you live in caves and—"

"Caves?"

Storm Arriving blinked. "Caves. Is that not the right word?"

"Caves? He told you we live in caves?"

"Yes," he said, slightly indignant. "Caves. He said that you lived in holes in mountains made of stone. He seemed to think it a marvelous thing. I did not have the heart to tell him otherwise."

One Who Flies laughed out loud. "I see! I see. Of course." He smiled and shrugged his shoulders. "They are caves of a sort, I suppose, except we build the mountains ourselves, out of stone we cut from the earth and bring to the city. Don't worry. Before we are done, you will have your fill of our stone mountains."

They forded the river in the twilight at a shallow place that Sings Good—the older chief of the Crazy Dog soldiers—called Oskaloosa. He said it was the site of a great battle during the years before the star fell, a battle between the Sauk and the Fox peoples, both of whom fell when the *vé'hó'e* came. He knew it only from his own grandfather's telling, however, and that told Storm Arriving that they truly were at the end of the world. Beyond this place, only One Who Flies could guide them. He looked at the thin, pale-haired man who led them on this warpath against his own kind. He was a *vé'ho'e,* but he understood the People. He was the man from the vision given to Speaks While Leaving twelve years ago and thus was a man who carried with him the hope of a nation. The former bluecoat's shoulders did not seem broad enough to bear such a weight, but Storm Arriving knew from past experience that a man's strength was not necessarily proportionate to his size.

The waning moon led the sun beyond the rim of the world, and soon there was no light other than what the stars dropped upon them. Along the edges of the land, other stars twinkled. Yellow stars. Firelight stars.

Homesteads separated by miles of empty land. Eventually they found a collection of them in their path.

This place, too, they avoided, and beyond it they found the fabled *chemin de fer.* The warriors stared at it as it gleamed in the starlight. None of them had seen anything like it and every man dismounted to touch the long bars of iron that stretched out into the night's embrace.

The rails were cold and smooth on top.

"You can hear the approach of the iron beasts through them," One Who Flies said. Laughs like a Woman giggled at the idea. Many men laughed at the notion, but most knelt and pressed an ear to the metal. They heard nothing.

"I wish you had not told them that," Storm Arriving said.

"Why not? It is true. There just are not any trains coming."

"They heard nothing. That is all they know. They do not trust you as I do."

One Who Flies considered the statement and nodded. "You are right. I will be more careful."

They all mounted their beasts and headed down the iron path.

It was late. George was not sure how late, but it was late, probably close to midnight. No lights were lit and the gridwork of the Davenport–Rock Island rail bridge hung like dark filigree above the star-shot waters of the Mississippi.

There were two parts to the bridge. The long section with its cantilevered swing section that would open for heavy river traffic sat atop its concrete pillars in the deeper channel that ran between the near bank and the island. Past it was the short trestled length that ran from the island to the Illinois side. It was the oldest rail bridge across the Mississippi and, George knew, was their only choice for crossing. The great river was far too wide and deep for such a large number to ford without traveling for days to its northern sources. No, he thought. It's here or nowhere.

They had crept around the north of town, slipping along the riverbank, sometimes wading, sometimes walking through the mud. They now lay in the shadow of a large warehouse that stood on the river road on the Davenport side. Across the river lay Illinois, and Davenport's sister town: Rock Island.

"Tell the men not to be afraid of any sounds or noises from the bridge or any machinery," he told the chiefs. "Our only fear is being seen by the townsfolk. It is late, and they all should be in their beds, but we must still be cautious." He pointed to the nearer span. "There is a walkway that lies beneath the iron road. We will use it to cross. Once across, we will head upstream and pass by the millworks. Does everyone understand?"

The translation was passed onward and gestures of affirmation were returned.

"Then let's go."

They made their way up to the roadway, the men leading their mounts. The whistlers went first, four abreast and stepping softly on the bridge planking. There was quite a bit of snuffling and scraping as they were led under the heavy beams that supported the trains. When the walkers were led onto the narrow pathway, they had to duck their heads to pass.

George heard the planks creak and threaten to crack beneath the unaccustomed weight of the heavy war mounts. The lower pathway was designed for foot traffic, but not this kind.

"Spread them out," he rasped. "More space between the walkers. Single file."

The instructions were passed on, and while the groans of the straining wood continued, they were much less severe.

Then the first span was behind them and they crossed the narrow island to the second span. George caught Storm Arriving gawking at the stone bulk of the island's freight station with its square tower and dark windows.

"You have never been to a *vé'ho'e* town, have you?"

"No," Storm Arriving said. "Only trading posts."

"Not quite like caves," George said.

"No," Storm Arriving said. "Not quite."

The second span had no pedestrian level below the railway and they were forced to walk along the ties. The whistlers balked at this and George heard their calls of distress as the first ones were led onto the span.

"Cover their eyes," he said. "Cover their eyes with a robe or blanket. Lead them slowly."

It was painstaking work, and every sound became magnified as the blinkered whistlers were led across, sometimes one at a time. George looked at the sky and wished he could tell how much time they had before dawn. The night had already been endless, and he was sure the sun would start to color the sky at any moment. Morning would bring the early dock and rail workers from their homes, and that could only end in slaughter of one side or the other.

He jumped as a dog barked from along the far bank. It barked and yipped in alarm. George saw it, a dark shadow amid darker shadows below the last trestle, darting to and fro in front of a small cabin at the water's edge; back and forth at the limits of its lead.

"Aw, Hell," George cursed in a whisper. Then he heard a sound like a snake's hiss and the dog fell silent. From the murkiness at the foot of a trestle a warrior appeared. He ran to the dog, retrieved his arrow, and returned to the group.

They made it to the far side without another occasion for worry. The town of Rock Island lay on the downstream side of the bank, so George led them upstream, past the mill and riverfront warehouses. There, in the quiet pastures north of town, they climbed atop their beasts and cut a wide circle around the town, heading south.

They met the railroad again and followed it through the night.

"How do you know this land?" Storm Arriving asked him. "Was this your home before you came to us?"

"No," George said ruefully. "I did not have a real home when I was young. I guess I was more like you— an always-moving-people."

"A nomad."

"Yes. A nomad. My father went where the Army needed him. We only stayed for a year or two in any one place. Longer than your people stay in one camp, perhaps, but not long enough for me to call it home."

"So how did you learn this land well enough to guide us?"

"I remember some of it from our travels," George told him, "but mostly I learned of it from books."

Storm Arriving was incredulous. He leaned closer and his voice dropped to a harsh whisper. "Do you mean to say that you have never seen this land?"

"No," George said. "Not all of it. Not firsthand. But I have seen some of it, and have studied the other areas in depth."

"*He'kotoo'êstse.* Not so loudly." Storm Arriving looked around at the others riding nearby, but none took notice of their now-whispered conversation. "We have assembled four hundreds of our men for this. Do not tell me that you have never seen this land!"

George could not afford to lose this man's trust, so he endeavored to explain. "Listen to me," he said. "Twenty-five years ago my countrymen fought a great war: a civil war with one half fighting against the other. It was fought all across the land, and it became an important part of our history."

Storm Arriving signed his understanding. "So have the tales of our battles with the Crow People and the Cradle People been passed along from father to son. They tell the path of the People."

"Precisely," George said. "And so when I studied

to become a soldier, I studied all of the great battles to learn from the generals that came before me."

"Like your father."

George shrugged. "He *was* a crafty tactician."

Storm Arriving grunted. "But he had no honor."

George continued past the insult. "I have learned of this land through those battles. I have studied the maps and read the memoirs of every officer on both sides of the war. Just as I know that the sun will rise in the morning, so do I know that this iron road will turn to the southwest at the next town—a little place called Avon—and from there we must take a path east to find the next iron road, called the Great Western Line. We will pass close to where one of our greatest presidents lived and worked. That railroad will take us on our way across the river called the Wabash."

Even in the blue light of the stars the Indian's sidelong glance was apparent. His companion was still not convinced.

"Wait," George said. "In an hour or so, you will see that I am right."

Storm Arriving sighed. "I will wait. Even if you *are* right, you must never let the others know what you have told me. They would not give you the chance to explain."

In a short time they came to a small town. From the crest of a gentle rise they saw it, dark and somnolent in the deep night.

The town of Avon was much like any town on the Frontier—a few streets that ran parallel to the rail line, a few storefronts along the main street, a few rutted roads leading out into the surrounding farmlands. It was a small, peaceful town, and at this hour, it was quiet and dark.

The silver rails ran past the buildings and onward, curving to the southwest as they left the town behind them. From the heart of the town a road emerged, heading due east in a line that did not waver.

"We take the road from here to Springfield,"

George said in his most confident manner. "From there, we take the Great Western Line to Decatur and the Illiniwek Central across the Kaskaskia River and on to Sandoval. Then, the Ohio and Mississippi Line crosses the Wabash into Indiana, where we turn south with the Evansville-Crawfordsville line that crosses the Ohio River."

Storm Arriving looked up at the eastern stars and measured the sky with his hands. "How far can we go in five hands of time?" There was no longer any doubt in his voice.

Inwardly, George sighed, pleased that he had kept this, his most important ally.

"The Kaskaskia. We can make it to the woods along the Kaskaskia River."

Custer was awakened by a knock on the door. Cardigan Two lifted his shaggy head from his paws and whined. Old Tuck slept on.

"Yes," Custer said. He sat up and swung his feet off the guest room bed. "What is it?"

The door opened. It was Douglas.

Custer squinted at him. "I thought you said you only stayed awake while the family was up." He yawned. "I was dead asleep."

"You're awake now, aren't you, sir?" He held out a small platter. On it was a folded piece of paper. "This just came."

The president took the note and read it.

"Get Samuel here. Jacob too. That will be enough to start." He looked at Douglas. "We've been invaded."

CHAPTER 13

Saturday, May 29, A.D. 1886
Near the Kaskaskia River, Illinois

Before dawn, they had found a large wood with a creek and settled down within its concealment to rest themselves and their mounts and wait out the daylight hours. It was a bucolic setting, one in which George would gladly have stayed for some time. He yawned and stretched and felt the dappled sun upon his skin.

Overhead, branches swayed in an unfelt breeze, their broad leaves layered every imaginable shade of green between him and the blue sky. He could smell the fertile earth beneath him and the spice of the whistler against which he reclined.

Nearby, several warriors talked quietly in their whispered tongue. They played a guessing game called "Hands," passing the time until evening came.

The others found places to rest. Some leaned back against their whistlers and slept—as did Storm Arriving and Laughs like a Woman, now George's steady comrades—or told stories, or just sat quietly and listened to the wood around them. The walkers were all bedded down in the densest part of the wood. There was little movement, for movement meant noise and noise meant risk and risk was something they already had in abundance. The stream that had slaked their thirst and washed the dust off their bodies flowed through the woods with a friendly exuberance. It

plished and splashed between rounded boulders
rubbed clean by its constant attentions. It flowed, leading the forest along with it, until less than a half mile
away, it met its goal: the Kaskaskia, a meandering
tributary of the stately Mississippi. If George listened
very carefully, he could hear the thrum of a pad-
dlewheel barge as it carried its cargo against the river's current.

The final two miles of last night's journey had
brought them within earshot of four homesteads, and
there would be more the farther George led them.
Even the woods in which they now bivouacked were
within sight of a farmer's house and barn. Their proximity had concerned George greatly until he learned
that the Red Shield soldiers had been charged with
picket duty. Just as they would give warning should
anyone from the homestead come toward their position, they would also keep any member of the war
party from exploring beyond the perimeter.

George looked to the west, and far beyond the
shrubs and ferns and trees that hid them from the
world—beyond, too, most likely the great rivers they
had crossed the previous night—he saw the white tops
of thunderheads blazing in the sunlight. They stood
like some colossal, Antaean trees, their dark slate blue
trunks shaded by their own overhanging branches.

Laughs like a Woman rolled over and stretched, his
muscles bunched and tight along his limbs and across
his bare chest. He sat up and sniffed the air which, to
George's perceptions, barely moved down here on the
forest floor. The still-yawning Indian back-handed the
shoulder of Storm Arriving, who woke with a start
and a squint-eyed glare.

Laughs like a Woman spoke between his yawns.
Storm Arriving flopped back onto his bed of fronds
and grass.

"He says it is going to rain."

George looked at the bloom of thunderheads to the
west. "I think I knew that."

Storm Arriving rubbed his face with his hands. "He

says the thunder beings are pushing the clouds to us. They will be here after the sun sets." Laughs like a Woman said something else and Storm Arriving translated. "Six hands. The rain will be here in six hands. With lots of thunder."

George could not help but doubt the precise prediction and it must have shown on his face for Laughs like a Woman spoke up again.

"He says you say we must trust you to guide us across this land you have never seen. In return, you must trust us in what we know."

George nodded. "It is a shame it wasn't coming a few hours earlier. We could use a few more hours of darkness."

Storm Arriving relayed the words and listened to the reply.

"He says he will see what he can do."

The music of Mozart and the quiet conversation of his dinner guests were pushed from the room as Custer gently closed the door behind him. He took off his white gloves and threw them onto a chair.

"What do you mean he's lost them?"

Jacob shrugged and held out empty hands.

"They're using the railroads, Autie. It's impossible to track them across the ties and gravel, and Stant simply cannot keep pace with them. He lost them in that maze of rail lines in Illinois."

Custer shook his head. "Well, now, that's just fine. Just fine. Does he have any idea of how large a force it is?"

"I asked him about that." Jacob's round cheeks were flushed and his brow was pale. "He said it was hard to say but thought it might be anywhere from several hundred to as many as a thousand."

"A thousand! Do you mean to stand there and tell me that my senior general on the Frontier can't find a thousand savages traipsing through his own cornfields? Hell, Jacob, a blind three-legged mule could find them."

"You know it isn't as easy as that."

"*Hell* if it isn't!"

"Autie, keep it down."

"I will not." He felt his blood surging in his temples. "This is inexcusable. We're talking about a thousand giant lizards running loose through the state of Illinois and a forty-year veteran who says he can't find them. I tell you he doesn't *want* to find them. I should have listened to you in the first place. So tell me, Jacob. Has he at least found the eight or nine thousand Indians that headed the other way?"

Jacob winced. "He says his scouts are overdue."

"He hasn't found them either."

"No. He hasn't found them either."

Custer stood there, hands on hips and his toe tapping the hardwood floor. He considered his next action carefully. "That's it, then," he said finally. "Stant is relieved."

"*Autie—*"

"He. Is. *Relieved,*" Custer said, jabbing each word home with a pointed finger.

The two men faced one another, aware of the censure that would accompany such an action. No general had been relieved of active command since McClellan. Custer clenched and reclenched his jaw, while Jacob— at a loss and unable to form his thoughts into words— simply stood there, his face devoid of any emotion but befuddlement.

"It will crush him," Jacob said at last.

"I don't care," Custer said, but he did. He simply knew of no other course. "He's either unwilling or unable to make the quick progress that we require. I cannot afford another slaughter of our men."

"Who shall replace him?"

"I don't care," Custer said, meaning it this time. "Just get me results." He picked up his gloves. "Now, if you'll excuse me, I have guests."

He opened the door and the strains of Beethoven entered the room, fierce and brooding. Custer did not bother to close the door behind him.

*   *   *

"Speaks While Leaving," said a voice.

She heard it and fought her way back from the vision world.

"Speaks While Leaving."

She felt her cold limbs and felt the rough touch of the Trader's wool blanket. She smelled the smoke of the fire and the luscious aroma of stewing meat. She heard the hiss of the heated rocks as they were put into the water to boil it.

"Speaks While Leaving, come back. You need to eat."

"I am here," she said. "Food sounds good."

Her sight returned—always the last—and between the shell-pink clouds she saw the bowl of heaven, a deepening blue the color of spring irises. Night was coming.

She propped herself up on her elbows. Her mother was tending the fire while her grandmother cooked. The other families were spread out on the blanket of the plain, taking a well-earned rest after two and a half days of constant marching. The chiefs were taking no chances and had not stopped for rest until the People were deep within Alliance lands.

"Where are they?" said a young voice.

Speaks While Leaving turned to see who it was who spoke. It was Mouse Road. She sat a whistler-length away, poking the ground with a stick. Under her arm was an old doll.

"She has been waiting for you to return," Healing Rock Woman said. "She has been very patient."

Speaks While Leaving beckoned and patted the ground at her side. The young girl came over and sat down. Her sadness and grief had changed her. To Speaks While Leaving, she seemed no longer a girl, but a young woman. Speaks While Leaving held her hand.

"I do not know the place," she said, "but it is very beautiful. It is nearly night now, though, and a storm is upon them."

"The same one that we had yesterday?" There was hope in her question, hope at the possibility of even so tenuous a connection with her brother.

"Yes," she told her. "The very same storm that rained on us yesterday will rain on him tonight. See? He is not so far away."

Mouse Road sighed and closed her eyes. "Thank you," she said. "I must go help my mother now. Thank you." She ran off toward the north to where the Tree People band had camped. The three women watched her go.

Magpie Woman ladled some stew into a shallow horn bowl. "Eat, Daughter. The *ma'heono* will come back upon you soon. Eat while you can."

She took the bowl with a nod of thanks. She took a piece of meat out of the stew and laid it at the edge of the fire, an offering to the spirits that were with her so much of late. Then she sipped at the hot broth. It was strong with meat and the flavor of lily root. It was good going down, and helped to melt the ice that lingered within her. The visitations by the spirit powers were tiring. The stew, and the spirit of the buffalo it held, restored her strength.

She and her mother and grandmother sat like a triumvirate before the fire. The buffalo chips burned with orange and red flames. Overhead, the clouds did the same, ignited by the setting sun.

"He is all right?" her mother asked.

"Yes," she said. "My father is well." Sometime during the past two days, Magpie Woman had ceased to question her daughter's persistent visions.

"What are they doing?"

Speaks While Leaving laughed. "Complaining about the rain," she said. "And giving thanks for it."

It was a veil—no, George thought—a curtain of rain that fell upon them. Not only had Laughs like a Woman worked to bring the storm to them early, but it had unleashed such a downpour that no sane person would have been caught out in it.

"Which says something about us," George muttered to himself. "We've got to pick up our pace," he said to Storm Arriving.

"It is early yet," the Indian said. "We have all night."

"We won't have this rain for cover all night. Look." He pointed to the sky behind them.

Along the horizon, the clouded heavens had separated themselves from the earth and a fine line of starry darkness showed between the two.

"For the next two hundred miles we will be dodging villages and towns every step of the way. The rain and thunder will help to hide us. I'd like to stay beneath this storm, hopefully until we reach the backroads of Kentuckee."

Storm Arriving signaled his agreement. "I will tell the chiefs what you say."

"Oh, and ask Laughs like a Woman if the thunder beings would please push this storm a little to the south."

He saw Storm Arriving's smile even through the gloom and night. "So you believe him now?"

"I see no reason not to," George said. "Until I see that he cannot, I will believe that he can."

Storm Arriving waved and fell back to talk to the chiefs.

To either side of the shiny iron rails, the small mounded hills of southeastern Illinois lifted their secret heads above the level ground to peer at the bizarre procession of men and mounts. The storm had eased, and though the rain still fell, the men did not have to shout to hear one another above its fury.

They forded the Wabash at the lonely wooden trestle bridge outside of Vincennes. Beyond it, they turned south and followed the Evansville & Crawfordsville Rail Road through the deep valleys that wound past the sharp-ridged terrain known as Little Egypt. As they approached the border and the Ohio River, the rain intensified once more. The thunder cracked above their heads, and George turned to Laughs like a

Woman. He pointed to him and then to the sky, asking: Did you do this?

Though Laughs like a Woman merely shrugged and smiled without commitment either way, he accepted the thanks just the same.

They came upon Evansville from the north. George kept them to the outskirts of town, bypassing the main rail lines and running along the Belt Line Rail Road past the cemetery and coal mines, past the stockyards and the baseball field. They crossed Pigeon Creek at the fringe of the neighborhoods and crept past the long, four-story mass of the cotton mill, then continued onward, avoiding the town entirely. At the bridge, however, it would not be easy.

One of the long bridges that crossed the Ohio at Evansville had been built downstream of the town. George and Storm Arriving and two other men left the rest of the party and went to scout the scene.

Despite the hour—which George refused to place at anything less than midnight—lantern lights still shone from the engineer's shack at the head of the bridge and, barely visible through the rain, from behind dirty windows in a long, low building on the far side. George pointed them out to Storm Arriving.

"There's no reason for anyone to be awake," he said. "They must be watching for us."

Storm Arriving scoffed. "Not everything is about you," he said. He gave orders to the other two men. "They will find out why these *vé'hó'e* do not sleep."

George watched as the two others climbed up into the girdered spans. Then he waited.

The bridge sat high atop cylindrical stone plinths that grew up out of the restless water. Their wide, heavy feet stood in the river and their sides tapered as they rose until, at their tops some fifty or sixty feet above the flow, they were just wide enough to support the iron trestles. The section over the channel was high enough to allow even the tallest-masted ships to pass beneath it, though most of the travel these days was by the faster paddlewheels and other steam-driven craft.

George began to get nervous. He squinted into the rain, trying to make out the forms of the returning scouts. Surely they should be back by now, he thought worriedly. Time ticked on, however, with no sign. He glanced at Storm Arriving and wished he had a fraction of his companion's confident equanimity.

"Where are they?" he had to ask at last.

"They will be back."

George sighed. He cupped his hands and caught the rain dripping from his nose. When his hands were overflowing, he emptied them and let them fill again. He did this twice more, waiting with little patience but a great determination not to seem impatient. More time passed. He took a breath to speak but halted as a figure detached itself from the bridge's overhanging bulk. Another man joined the first. The scouts had returned. They crouched down beside Storm Arriving and spoke quickly with words and gestures.

"There," Storm Arriving said, pointing to the engineer's shack. "One. Asleep. And there." He pointed across the river. "Five. Playing with cards. Drinking."

George smiled. "You were right. Our luck is holding. Get the others. We must cross at once. Quickly and quietly."

The scouts left to bring the others ahead from their hiding place. George chided himself.

"I apologize," he said.

"For what?"

"For worrying about them. It was silly of me to worry. After all, if something had happened to them, it would not have been terrible."

Storm Arriving looked at him like he was looking at a bug.

"What I mean is, it would not have been the *worst* thing that could have happened. That's one lesson I never seem to learn. If something is to go wrong, it will go wrong at the worst moment. It's a military fact."

Storm Arriving chuckled. "You are like a new mother, worrying at every breath and cough. Be calm. It will be fine or it will not be fine. You have done what you can to affect the outcome. The rest is up to Ma'heo'o."

The others arrived and they went to meet them.

"Have the whistlers go first," George told Storm Arriving. "I'll come across with the walkers. I want to be here in case the night guard wakes up."

The warriors began to lead their mounts across the bridgework. Just as at Rock Island and at Vincennes, they blinkered their fractious beasts with blankets or lengths of cloth. This bridge was especially treacherous, though. The rain had made the old wooden ties slick, and the swollen current swept against the pilings below with the sounds of an eternally cresting wave. The whistlers balked at the roar and the unsure footing. Fortunately, the rain and the current drowned out their quiet whistles of distress. Still, George watched and prayed as fifteen score men led their beasts over the waters.

While the others crossed, he crept up to the shack. From a short distance, he peered through the smudged glass of the small window.

Inside, a man slept in a chair that leaned back against the wall. The chair rested on its back legs and the man's hat was perched forward over his eyes. A small tin-backed lantern burned on the lone table, its wick turned low, and George could see the brown ceramic bottle that lay on its side nearby, empty. This man would provide no problems. He let out a breath that he felt he'd been holding for a week.

The walkers were all on the span now. He moved into place behind them. The huge creatures—so powerful and quick in open country—were clumsy and uncertain perched above the open waters of the Ohio. They lurched and twisted as they made their way, eyeing every plank, girder, and tie like hens on a grate.

They were near the end, and George felt the knotted rag that was his stomach begin to relent. The whis-

tlers were waiting up ahead—dark shapes massed
along the roadside. The walkers were moving off the
span quickly now as the invitation of solid ground
drew them onward.

A bloom of light shot across the darkling scene, a
swath that stretched out in a fan of illumination, catching the last of them in its glare.

"Hámêstoo'e," George rasped and they all—man
and beast alike—stooped to the squelching mud.

George heard voices; the men who were playing a
midnight hand of poker. "Just deal me outta this one
is all." The man's voice was thick and heavy with
drink. "I'll be back in a wee . . . in a wee bit."

Even with the rainfall and the sound of the nearby
river, the man's sloshing footsteps were still audible
as he tramped up toward the raised railbed. George
and four warriors hid behind their crouching beasts.
The footsteps came closer, hit brush, and then gravel.
The Indian with the walker nearest the man whispered
quiet words to keep it calm and quiet. The monster
lay perfectly still. It did not move as the man came
up to it in the dark, his breathing labored from his
walk up the slight slope. Nor did the beast move when
the man mistook its rain-slick bulk for a slab of stone,
nor as he unbuttoned his trousers and proceeded to
relieve himself along its side. But when the sky
cracked open with lightning and the man saw the head
and eye and the bone-white teeth of the monster before him, he screamed. Only then did the beast move.

It rose and turned in one swift movement. It bellowed down upon the man with a sound that overwhelmed the thunder from above. The man screamed
again and stumbled backward down the slope.

The doorway light was eclipsed by bulky men. The
walker bellowed again, its brethren joining in. The
men disappeared from the doorway and the light
returned.

"Nóheto!" George shouted, and calls went up all
along the railway line. Lightning crashed above them
and thunder rocked the earth. George grabbed an ex-

tended hand and was pulled up onto a walker's long, narrow back. He held on to the warrior in front of him as they took off. Shots were fired behind them— small and puny sounds in comparison to the walker's roar. George saw one of the warriors set arrow to bow.

"No," he shouted, and then *"Hová'âháne."* The warrior glared at him but did not shoot. From the bridge, more shots came, but none came close. Darkness and drunkenness conspired to keep them safe.

They ran on for miles at headlong speed until George felt they were past any immediate danger. There was no pursuit and no defense was required. They rested their mounts for a small time, and then continued onward.

The Ohio was behind them, the last major river save one. Back on his own familiar whistler, George guided them along the backroads of the Kentuckee countryside.

Now they were in the arenas of war that George knew so well. Madisonville, Bowling Green, Munfordsville, Logan's Cross Roads; all passed by in the distant darkness as the war party climbed up from the mint-laden fields of Pennyrile onto the slopes of the Cumberland Plateau.

But as dawn began to light the sky that showed through the trees and the steep, sharp-ridged cleft in which they stopped for their rest, George could think of one thing only.

They had been seen.

"They have been seen."

"What?" said Custer. "Where?"

Jacob smiled and waggled the sheet of paper. "Kentuckee," he said. "Meriwether sent bulletins to every rail post in five hundred miles. They were seen at the bridge between Evansville and Henderson. His forces are tracking them across the backlands now."

"Kentuckee." Custer stepped up to the table and began leafing through the maps that covered it. "Last we heard was Illinois. What are they doing in Kentuckee?" He found the map he sought. Pulling it from the pile, he laid it on top of the others. "Kentuckee." He scratched his head.

Jacob leaned over from the other side. He pointed to the western portion of the state and drew a line across it to the east. "There aren't any railroad lines that cross the state lengthwise. They'll have to use the roads if they want to move east."

"What makes you think they're heading east?"

Jacob pawed through the stacks and pulled out a large-scale map of the nation. He stepped around to the end of the table and spread it out. "Just look at the whole of it," the secretary said. He inscribed a line with his fingertip. "From deep within the territories they went into Yankton, then to Illinois, then Indiana, and now they're in Kentuckee. They're heading east."

"More south than east, it seems," Custer said.

"Autie. You're being obtuse. What is there for them in the south but what they've already passed by?"

"I'd ask you the same question. What is there in the east that they've not already seen?"

Jacob extended his line through Kentuckee and into Virginia. He stopped at the Potomac and Washington.

"You," he said. "You are in the east."

"Me?" Custer laughed but it sounded hollow, even to his own ears. He took a step back from the table. "What could they want with me?"

"What else?" Jacob said with a shrug. "Revenge."

"That's absurd."

"It's not and you know it. Why else would they invade us with such a force? Why else would they sneak through our backroads, hiding from us at every opportunity?"

"Perhaps," said a third voice, "it is because they did not care overmuch for their last meeting with us."

Custer turned in annoyance. "Don't fence, Samuel. Say what you mean."

The thin man turned from the window where he

had spent the last hours gazing out at the growing light. To Custer he seemed the owner of every bit of his sixty-odd years.

"I only mean to say that they might easily have come to expect a violent greeting from us and our kind. Avoiding direct contact with the locals would only be a prudent course of action."

"What?" Custer said with a laugh. "Do you think we are planning to shoot them on sight?"

"What else do you think the everyday corn farmer would do? What do you think Meriwether's men will do when they meet up with them?"

Custer turned to Jacob. The plump secretary seemed once more at a loss.

"They're an invading enemy force," he said. "They will deal with them accordingly."

"And open fire upon them," Samuel pressed.

"Yes."

"Regardless of their actual purpose in coming here."

"Yes. I mean no. I mean—"

Custer stepped into the argument. "Samuel, they are coming to assassinate me."

"Or to bring you back your son."

Custer felt as if the air had gone out of the room. It had not occurred to him. From the look on the face of his Secretary of War, it hadn't occurred to Jacob either. "An offering of peace?"

"To be given to you and no other," Samuel said.

"Or it could be as we thought," said Jacob. "An attempt on your life."

"Which is the more likely?"

Samuel's calm monotone irritated Custer. "Frankly," he said, "it's a hell of a lot more likely that they're out for my blood."

"I should say so," Jacob said, and then apologized with a weak smile.

"And the risk?"

Custer growled at Samuel and set to pacing the length of the table. He walked back and forth past

the ranks of maps and notations, back and forth between Jacob and Samuel, his evaluation of the situation vacillating with each turn.

Finally he stopped. "Talk to Meriwether," he said
to Jacob. "Have him rescind the attack orders."

"But they're in the field."

"They're in Kentuckee, not Tangiers, for heaven's
sake."

"But they're already in motion. We may not find
them in time."

"Then quit wasting time here. Jacob, just do this.
Rescind the attack, but find them just the same. We
can mount a defense at the Potomac if needs be. Even
a thousand Indians can't break through to me if we've
got our artillery pointed down their throats at the
bridges. They'll come in from Arlington, most likely.
That's the main rail line. But have Meriwether set up
at Georgetown as well. Now go."

Jacob, flustered, saluted out of long habit, and left
the room.

"Samuel, please take whatever precautions you wish
around the house."

"I'm sure Secretary Greene would rather you were
on a train to New York."

Custer laughed. "Perhaps, but we won't go that far.
But do see that Libbie and the girls are safe. I want
them in town if it's good news, but not in this house,
just in case it isn't."

"Yes, Mr. President," he said and walked to the
door.

"Samuel."

Custer's aide stopped, his hand still on the knob.
"Yes, Mr. President."

"Thank you, Samuel."

"Yes, Mr. President."

The door closed and he was alone. He sat down
and pulled the map of his nation close. From Kentuckee he traced a path up through the Cumberland
Gap, across the Allegheny Mountains, and past the
farms and towns of central Virginia.

"Are you with them, Son?" He tapped the twisted line of the Potomac. "Are you?"

"To'e. To'e!" George helped to wake the men. *"To'e. Nóheto."* He knew how little sleep they had had in the past three days—he was feeling the lack himself, and even the whistlers were beginning to complain. Now, however, was not the time for compassion. He stopped for a moment and listened. The rain had passed over, and now the forest was coming alive with the calls of birds. There was no sound out of the ordinary, but that did not comfort him. The scouts had said that bluecoats were coming and every moment he expected to see soldiers in Kersey blue coats appear from between the dark-boled trees.

"To'e, nóheto. Hurry up now."

Within minutes they were up and on their way. The tiny town of Cumberland Ford lay down in the valley behind them, hidden by dense spruce and rugged land. A few miles ahead was Tazewell and a quick turn through the eastern tip of Tennessee. Between the two was the famed Cumberland Gap, and George wanted little more than to see it from the other side.

They guided their beasts up the steep slopes. There was not much undergrowth beneath the heavy canopy, but the lizards were creatures of the open plains and tired more quickly in the mountainous terrain. Many of the riders of whistlers switched to their war mounts so as to rest their riding mounts. The walkers were especially affected. They found the climbing much more strenuous than coursing across the prairie, and the entire war party was slowed as the larger beasts pushed step by step up the incline.

George led them back down to the roadway with relief. On the uphill side of the gap, any Army cavalryman would have a slight edge in speed, but once headed downhill, the whistlers and walkers would own the clear advantage.

They heard the first shot when they were near the crest of the pass. George heard the bullet snap through the leaves and branches. Another shot slashed overhead and torn greenery fell from above. The chiefs called for speed and somehow the animals gave it. They passed up the final slope. George could see past it and to the lands beyond. Through the trees he could see down the Allegheny slopes and all the way across the valley that separated them from the cool distances of the Blue Ridge Mountains.

A third shot urged them on. The last rise gave way and the mass of riders flowed over the crest and down the other side like a river. When gunfire blasted out before them, George realized the magnitude of his error. Smoke belched from behind every tree along the slopes that flanked the road. Warriors and mounts fell in the neck of the gantlet, trapped in the crossfire.

Quicker than orders could have been given, the Indians abandoned the roadway. They dispersed to either side. Weapons appeared—bows, lances, clubs— and George cried out.

"No killing!"

But his words, even had they been understood, could not have stopped them. With whoops and shouts of fury they scattered into the trees and climbed up to the Army positions. The gunfire was sporadic as men now fired not to slay a foe but to save themselves.

"No killing!" he shouted again, uselessly. "Keep moving. They have no horses. We can outrun them. *Nóheto! Nóheto!*"

The woods were filled with gunshots. The Indian warriors met the danger head-on as they engaged their foe. They struck to kill, and did so with bloody efficiency. George felt his rage rise, but could not blame them for defending themselves.

The rear of the column came up behind him and he was swept forward by the current of the battle. His whistler chose the path through the forest. Limbs swung past, forcing him down along its back. Then in front of him he saw an officer, his pistol raised and aimed. The man's jaw dropped open as he saw his target clearly.

"Get out of the way, damn you!" The whistler bore down on the man. The officer stepped back against the trunk of a tree and George was past him.

"Nóheto!"

More gunfire, and more men cried out. Whistlers carved the air with their screams.

"Nóheto!"

Soldiers fell back in disarray. Warriors sped through the battleground and headed downslope. George stopped his mount on the mountain path. A warrior on walker-back commanded the roadway, shouting in defiance as bullets zipped through the trees around him. Bowmen on whistlers took aim and let fly in among the trees. George shouted and the men turned.

"Nóheto!" he shouted and waved at the melee that flourished in the woods. "We've got to leave, *now*!"

The meaning was understood. The warrior spoke to his walker. *"Ótahe! Hó'ésta!"* The beast took a breath and roared. Three long blasts from its immense lungs sent Army soldiers scurrying and brought the Indian warriors pouring from the forest.

"Let's go!"

The survivors left the field. One look back showed George the damage and loss. The road was clogged with heavy bodies. Whistlers thrashed and paled gray and green in their distress. A rogue walker stormed the forest chasing terrified soldiers, taking bullet after bullet and not stopping, and beneath the trees lay the bodies of men in buckskin and men in blue, the dead and dying left behind.

George smelled gunsmoke and tasted blood. He kicked his mount. *"Nóheto!"*

They ran down the rutted roadway. Their numbers grew with each step as warriors and loose whistlers rejoined the flock, but they had lost many. George tried to gauge their losses but could not. He looked for Storm Arriving and found him.

"How bad?" he asked.

"Bad," the Indian said. "Perhaps a fourth of our forces, and many of the bluecoats killed as well." He frowned and took a heavy breath. "I am sorry we killed them, One Who Flies. I know you did not wish it, but it did not keep them from killing us, did it?"

"No," George said. "You must believe me, though. Killing them does not make it any easier for us."

"Perhaps," Storm Arriving said. "But it is too late for that argument now."

George looked around. "Have you seen Laughs like a Woman?"

Storm Arriving's face grew even harder. "No. I have not seen him."

George disliked the answer as much as Storm Arriving. He looked around again, trying to spy the former Contrary. The war party was stretched out a quarter mile along the twisting forest path. Above them the sunset painted the bellies of the clouds.

"He is with us," George said. "Look at the sky. The thunder beings would have told us if he'd fallen."

Storm Arriving glanced upward. "Perhaps," he said. "Perhaps."

They rode down the mountainside like three hundred demons possessed of a terrible determination George hoped no one got in their way. He did not think that they would survive.

Speaks While Leaving wept.

"I do not *know*," she cried. "I do not know."

Her mother shooed away the neighbors from the door. "Go now. You heard her. She does not know."

Speaks While Leaving pressed her fists to her eyes. Tears stung with their sorrow. The memory of the vision ran once more across her mind and she was transfixed by the image of the fallen. Her mouth opened in silent anguish and her lungs refused to breathe. She could only shed her tears and gasp between each paroxysm of grief.

It was deep at night when Custer was awakened. He rubbed at raw eyes and reread the message.

Samuel said nothing, nor did he gloat. His eyes

showed only sadness, and then he turned and left the room.

Custer crumpled the paper in his hand. He bared his teeth and shut his eyes so tightly they hurt. Anger and frustration wracked him and twisted his soul. "Damn you," he said to everything, to the world at large. "Damn you to perdition and hellfire."

CHAPTER 14

Monday, May 31, A.D. 1886
Prince William County, Virginia

Laughs like a Woman caught up to them during the night along with several others from the battle. He was riding a dead man's whistler and his arm was bloody and bound. George was glad to see him, but no man's relief could match that of Storm Arriving.

They rode on through daybreak and finally stopped in a small wilderness near Bristow Station. The men needed rest, and the whistlers needed to forage before they continued on to the city.

But should we, George wondered.

"They know we are here," he said as the circle of chiefs gathered at their resting place. "And I daresay they know where we are going. After all, they may be *vé'hó'e*, but they are not idiots." He sighed. "So the question is this: Should we continue?"

Storm Arriving passed along his words, and the chiefs discussed the issue.

George fretted. They were such a short distance from their goal—less than fifty miles—and yet they now had arrayed before them not just the last physical obstacle, the Potomac, but also the military power of the United States Army. If the chiefs opted to continue, how would they avert that threat? After all, it wouldn't just be a thousand rifles they faced; it would be Gatling guns and artillery. It was one thing to run past such weaponry before the gunners knew the party was there, but to ride into them when they were ready and primed to fire . . . God, George thought. We'd lose everything in the first cannonade.

"One Who Flies."

George realized he had not been paying attention to the discussion he himself had begun. The chiefs waited patiently for him to rejoin the conversation.

"I'm sorry. What did you say?"

Storm Arriving started again.

"One Bear says the bluecoats may know that we are coming, but they do not know that *you* are coming."

George blinked. "That is right. They don't know."

"Would that make a difference?"

He smiled. "All the difference in the world. I've been thinking like a soldier when I should have been thinking like a hostage. We can take the guns right out of their hands."

"So One Bear now puts the question to you. Should we continue?"

"Why not?" George said. "They're going to do everything but open the door for us."

He laid his new idea out for them. They listened, and one by one he saw comprehension light their faces. When he had finished and all the details were understood, Two Roads called for his pipe.

The chief of the Kit Fox soldiers filled his pipe, struck fire to tinder, and lit the tobacco in the bowl. Then, after the proper offerings to the spirits that were with them always, the pipe was passed from man to man. George took his turn when it came to him, and enjoyed the tang of the thick smoke. He passed it on to Storm Arriving, and saw in his friend's eyes a different regard. There was no name that George could put to it—the steadiness of his look, the set of his jaw, perhaps—but there was a difference. As he looked around the silent circle, he saw that many of the others, too, viewed him differently. He felt a sense of approbation in their consideration. It made him feel . . . respected.

When the pipe returned to Two Roads and was put away, they all rose and went on toward their duties and tasks, as well as some needed rest. George, however, had other things to do.

"I want you with me," he said to Storm Arriving. "But I want us to make an impression. Can we go in on walkers?"

"There are a few that lost their riders. We can use two of them. Be careful, though. Walker-back is different."

"We won't be going far."

They checked in on Laughs like a Woman before they left. When they found him, he was swinging a cavalry saber he had picked up off the battleground. He flailed it at a stout tree limb and George winced at the mistreatment of such a fine weapon.

Storm Arriving talked to him of his wound and how he felt. The bullet had pierced the meat of his right biceps. Though it was not his strong arm, it did keep him from holding his bow. It did not keep him from punishing the sword, however.

"How is his arm?" George asked Storm Arriving.

"He says it is swollen and sore, but the bleeding has stopped."

"Good. Please tell him that if he wants, I will show him how I was taught to use such a sword."

Storm Arriving relayed his words. "He says it is not difficult." George sighed but smiled and left the friends to talk some more.

While he waited, he saw a man leading two of the great lizards toward them. They followed him like two docile plow mares, their bodies twisting in their ungainly, two-legged walk. The man came up to George and handed him the halter ropes.

"*Hámêstoo'e,*" George bid the beasts. They lay down obediently.

They were huge. He walked between them. Their backs were as high as he was tall and even prone on the ground they looked down upon him. His fear of their species had been somewhat reduced through weeks of living among the People but still he felt his heart race at their closeness. He reached out to touch one of them. Its green-rimmed eye watched his every movement.

The beast's hide felt much like a whistler's, warm and supple, but it was a bit harder, a bit coarser, and there were fine hairs that covered it, like the silken strands on a pale woman's arm. The walker opened its mouth and George froze.

"Scratch her," Storm Arriving said, walking over.

George did so, lightly at first but then with a little more vigor. The walker craned its head back over its neck, its mouth agape, its tongue lolling out to one side. From deep within its body came a rumble that was more felt than heard.

"She is yours now, I think," Storm Arriving said with a chuckle. "She will eat any whistler you try to ride."

"Are you serious?"

Storm Arriving nodded.

"What about her former rider?"

"Walkers know death," the Indian explained. "They do not mourn for one lost if they see him dead. But for one lost outside their seeing, there is great grief. Dull Knife was her rider, and he fell from her back and she saw him dead. She has chosen a new rider now. There is no greater loyalty, but she will demand her own measure in return."

George rubbed his stubbled chin and shook his head. At last he shrugged and dropped his hands to his sides.

"Aw, Hell," he said.

They mounted their walkers—a process that involved using the beast's leg as a stepstool. The riding gear was much the same as on a whistler except that the pad of buffalo hide also had a back brace of woven wicker. When the walkers stood, George understood why. Unlike whistlers, the walker's spine was not quite level to the ground when it stood. The brace aided in keeping the rider from sliding down the long back and tail like they were a bumpy staircase banister. Otherwise, it was just the same. George slipped his feet into the trailing loops and pulled the first rope up over his knees. Then, with a gentle touch, they pivoted their mounts and headed down to the road.

It was a much higher vantage than on whistler-back, and while the beast did its best to avoid them, an occasional branch still caught George across the face.

"They are not used to the forests," Storm Arriving said as George cursed loudly for the third time.

Once on the road, it was much easier and the walkers settled into an easy, mile-eating trot.

Bristow Station was just down the line from Manassas Junction, on the banks of the Broad Run. It straddled the railroad; a bundle of houses and shops along clean-cornered streets surrounded by the vari-colored fabric of family farms. The sun shone upon the town, the light of late morning casting short, stark shadows along the flower beds and curbsides. It was Monday, and a hand or so before noon. Women strolled from store to store on weekly errands. Men made deliveries or stood before their businesses, waiting for custom to walk their way.

George straightened his white shirt, dirty and stained though it was, and slapped the dust from his army britches. He raked his fingers through his blond hair and put on his most military manner.

"Stay a little behind me," George said. "They'll be less likely to shoot if they see me first."

"Less likely," Storm Arriving said. "That is comforting."

At a quarter mile from the center of town they were noticed. George saw the people in the streets slow and stop as they squinted for a better look. At an eighth of a mile, people had come out of the shops to peer down the road and guess at the nature of the strange apparition. At three hundred yards some of the onlookers were nervous; glances were exchanged and some began to move toward the storefronts. At two hundred yards, the nervousness had grown to panic, and at one hundred, the streets were empty.

George slowed their pace as they entered the town. He rode straight-backed and with eyes front. He did not look at the pale, gawking faces that lined the windows.

A man came out of Winton's Dry Goods store with a shotgun. George's mount saw it, turned, and roared. The sound rattled the window glass and the man dropped the weapon in the dirt and fled back inside his store.

They followed the wires that swagged between the telegraph poles. They led him into the heart of town, along the railroad, and right to the station.

They stopped in front of the small building. The shakes of its roof were twisted and cracked, and its clapboard siding was the same. Through its windows he could see a desk, a chair, a counter, and one balding, middle-aged man whose fear and his spectacles teamed up to make his eyes the size of Morgan dollars.

"You, sir," George said and pointed. The man pointed to himself with a shaking hand, hoping he meant some other man.

"Yes. You, sir. Come here, please."

The man nodded and went quickly to the door. He stepped outside but came no farther.

"Hámêstoo'êstse," he said and his walker squatted down. George stepped from its back onto its knee and thence to the ground. Storm Arriving remained mounted and his beast remained standing, their gazes sweeping the deserted street, alert for more trouble. George did not think there would be any.

"I have a very important telegraph message to send," he said as he walked over to the station keeper. As he came closer, the man underwent a transformation.

Terror gave way to wonder and his stance lost its submissive crouch. He stood up straight and smiled broadly, then laughed.

"Well, I'll be," he said. "You're the one. You're young Custer." He ducked back inside the station house and returned in a moment with a newspaper. He held it out and pointed to the picture of George as a young cadet. "They've been looking high and low for you, Son. Why, we've even gone to war over it."

"At war?" George said, stunned. "With whom?" He took the paper. *Missing and presumed dead,* read the caption next to this name.

"Why, with them," the man said, his gaze slipping over to where Storm Arriving sat atop his walker.

"Listen to me," George said. "There has been a grave misunderstanding. I must get word to the president."

"Your father," the keeper said with a giggle.

"Yes, my father."

"President Custer. President George Armstrong Custer." The man was tickled by his proximity to celebrity. He waved to the storefronts around his block. "It's all right," he called. "It's Custer's boy!"

Faces peered out through cracked-open doorways.

"It is a very important message."

But the station keeper was not listening. People came out of their shops and he beckoned them over.

"Look! It's President Custer's boy. The one who's been lost all this time."

"Sir—"

"What's he want, Harold?" The people were walking toward them.

"*Sir—*"

"Says he has to send a message to his father."

"What kind of message?"

George turned to the walkers. *"Hó'ésta!"* he commanded them. He plugged his ears as the beasts took breath but still he heard their roar through his very bones. When he unplugged his ears, the street was deserted again and the station keeper was cowering on the ground. George squatted down and spoke slowly.

"I have a very important telegraph message to send."

"Yes, sir," the man said. "Right this way, sir." He

stood and scurried into the office. George turned to
Storm Arriving.

"Keep a sharp eye. Call if you need me."

The station office smelled of tobacco smoke and
mildew. The sunlight struggled to make an impression
on the windows. The station keeper produced a pen
and inkwell, then a sheaf of paper.

"You just write down what you want to say while
I set things to rights." He sat down at the telegraph
desk and started working the key.

"I'm sorry about that out there," George said.

"Don't worry about it, Captain Custer." The man
smiled sheepishly. "After all, here y'are coming to me
for help after being lost for weeks amongst the savages, and all I can think of is myself. It's me who
ought to be apologizing." The key tapped back as the
operators on the far end made ready. "Are you finished with the text, sir?"

"Almost," George said. He looked over what he
had written.

FATHER
AM ALIVE AND RIDING TOWARDS HOME
STOP SHOULD ARRIVE SOON BUT HAVE
COMPANY WITH ME STOP TELL THE
TROOPS NOT TO SHOOT STOP

It wasn't enough. He needed to be sure that his
father knew it was from him. "What's your name?"
he asked the station keeper.

"Me? Godfried, sir. Harold Godfried."

George added a final line to the message:

AUTHENTICATE MESSAGE WITH HAROLD
GODFRIED OF BRISTOW STATION.

He handed the message over. "Can you send this
and make sure it gets through to the president?"

Godfried read the message and puffed up with
pride. "Yes, *sir*," he said.

"Good work, Godfried. I won't forget this."

"Thank you, sir. Nor will I."

George left the little station house and climbed back onto his mount. Godfried followed to the door but did not come outside.

"Make sure that message gets through," George said, loudly enough for the hiding neighbors to hear. "Lives depend upon it, Mr. Godfried. Many lives." He saluted. The little station keeper stood straight and returned the honor.

"*Nóheto.*"

As they rode from town, the street filled with people. The message would be delivered. He rested easily on that score.

"Now all we have to do is get there."

"Mr. President. Mr. President!"

Custer heard someone bound up the stairs from the second floor. He turned to see Samuel run past the library's open door.

"I'm in here," he called. Samuel's frantic footsteps slid to a stop and came pummeling back down the hall. The old man skated into the door jamb. He had several papers in his hand, and a broad grin on his flushed face.

"He's . . . alive," the aide said between gulping breaths. "Young George . . . He's alive."

Custer was up and across the room. He snatched the papers and read them one by one.

"I've already confirmed it, sir. Godfried says it was definitely George. 'Saw him with my own eyes,' he said. He also said George rode in on one of those giant lizards."

Custer paged through the messages again. "Good Lord and all that's holy." He reached out to steady himself and Samuel grabbed hold. "He's alive!" His sight blurred with sudden tears and he felt himself begin to lose control. He took a deep breath and composed himself.

"Does Libbie know?"

"Not yet, sir."

"What about Meriwether and Greene?"

"They're awaiting your instructions."

"You heard from this—" He checked the messages. "This Godfried?"

"Yes, sir. Personally."

"And George wasn't forced to send this?"

"I doubt it, sir. Godfried said there was one Indian with him, but he went on to say that it looked like George was in charge of things."

Custer shook his head. "I just can't believe it." He laughed as relief swept over him. "All right, then. Tell the men to relax. No, have them line the streets from Long Bridge to here. I don't want those lizards wandering through the city. And get Speaker Carlisle and Senator Duchesnes over here—invite them politely, of course. They'll want to be here when George arrives."

"Carlisle might be able," Samuel said, "but I doubt that Duchesnes will be free. They're debating your appropriations bill on the floor today. They want to resolve the issue before the June break."

"Yes, that's right. Well, invite him anyway, as a courtesy. Now where's Libbie?"

"She and the girls are staying with the vice president's family."

"All right. Get them back over here. Go. Hurry. But get those orders issued first."

"Yes, Mr. President." He smiled and ran off down the stairs.

"I didn't know he could run that fast," Custer said to himself. "Hellfire, I didn't know the old persimmon could run at all."

He chuckled, then laughed until the tears came to his eyes. He did not wipe them away.

The vision light faded, and Speaks While Leaving floated in a cloud-studded sky. Below her the curved arm of a broad river reflected the blue and white patchwork from above. She flew, soaring in her airy home, and saw the green pastures of the land beyond the river. The land was scarred by roads that dug into the flesh of the earth. She saw a small grid of square lodges and the spirits that controlled her vision brought her down toward it.

People lined the main thoroughfare of the little village. They stood in small groups and she could hear their chatter as she sailed between the buildings. Her point of view came to rest on the high spire of a tall white structure. There was a wind that chilled her until it blew the clouds away from the sun's face. She was bathed in light and warmth and it felt good after the cold of the vision.

She heard a scream. A woman on the street below pointed down the road. All the people turned to look, and then shrank back away from the street.

Her viewpoint shifted and she saw the cause of their fear.

They filled the road from side to side for the length of a bowshot. At the front, alone atop an immense walker was One Who Flies. He sat the beast as if born to it, and the creature chuffed twice as they entered the town. Behind him were the chiefs and all the whistlers. She saw her father and Two Roads, and near the front she saw her beloved.

"I am here," she said to him, but he did not hear her. He looked so strong and fearsome, his head held high, the feathers in his hair and on his bow and on his whistler's harness all streaming in the wind.

She reminded herself that there were other women in the camp besides her and she scanned the host that trooped so regally, trying to see every face. She called out their names as she saw them, but as she did so, she saw that there were many who should be there who were not. The ambush at the mountain pass had taken a heavy toll.

At the end came the rest of the walkers. They looked lean and headstrong. They would need to eat in a few days or they would start to get obstinate.

They passed by her high vantage point and through the town and once again she was flying. Ahead, in the distance, was the river. Across it was a long bridge. White-winged gulls wheeled in the air, chasing large boats that plowed the gentle waters.

On the far bank along the river's edge lay a sward of green. Beyond that, however, it was as if everything natural had been scraped away. A mat of buildings covered the land as far as she could see. Near the river rose a spike of white stone taller than every tree in the world. To the right of it was a huge building of the same white stone. It was the biggest building she had ever seen, and the sight of it chilled her so that even the sun was helpless to warm her again.

"If they can build such things as this," she said, "what hope can we possibly have? How can we possibly overcome them?"

The war party began to sing as they approached the river. Speaks While Leaving was not sure she wanted to see what would be coming, but she felt on either side of her a presence. She looked and saw flying alongside her two black-skinned warriors with lightning bolts painted upon their arms. She recognized them from her vision so many years ago; the thunder beings who brought the cloud to earth.

Sunlight flashed off the wavelets that adorned the deep green waters. Gulls in the air below her spun and pinwheeled like children at play. Huge boats spewed black smoke and carved long V's into the river. Along the bridge and along the streets of the city, bluecoats waited.

She shut her eyes, but still she saw.

Custer stood on the south steps of his home and watched through the binoculars as the horde of hideous lizards surged onto the bridge deck. It was a disgusting sight. The beasts lurched and swaggered their way across, a herd of the misshapen, prismatic creatures in the front followed by a contingent of great toothsome monsters. There were hundreds of them, and hundreds of the Cheyenne riding them. Custer looked but could not see his son amid the crowd.

They made their way across the bridge, and even from this distance, he heard their high-pitched singing. The idea that George had been held by these people for so long . . .

What has he been through, Custer wondered. The boy is stronger than I thought if he's come through this alive and unchanged.

"They'll be coming up Fifteenth Street," Jacob said. "Meriwether is down there at the bridge terminus to guide them in."

"Let's just hope that the brutes don't cause any more trouble," Custer said. "I want this over with, and damned soon."

"Now that sentiment I can wholeheartedly support," said the Secretary of War.

Custer looked again through the binoculars. "They're at mid-span, approaching the sand bar. My Lord, but they are a motley crew. Oh, Hellfire."

"What's wrong, sir?"

"Oh, nothing. Washington's monument is in the way, is all. I can't see the end of the bridge. Oh, well." He handed the binoculars to Jacob. "Not a lot to see from this distance anyway." He looked across the gardens, beds, and lawns of the south grounds and The Ellipse. Soldiers stood at attention along the proposed route of the advancing mob.

"They'll practically fill the front law," Custer sighed. "Libbie will have a fit if they tear up her rhubarb."

Never in his life had Storm Arriving imagined that such things existed. They let their mounts walk across the railroad bridge that spanned the great river. He marveled at the rising structures on the far side. Immense square blocks of stone with openings covered by thin ice, like the ice that formed on the river edges during the Dust in the Face Moon.

How did they keep the ice cold, he wondered, in all that sunlight?

They approached the far bank of the river, singing

as they had all the way with all the air their lungs could take in. The sides of the bridge were lined with bluecoats—hundreds of them, tens of hundreds it seemed—each one standing straight and fierce, each one with a rifle. The warriors sang their song of war and bravery, but Storm Arriving could hear their hearts failing.

"There are so many of them," he said.

One Who Flies heard him but did not understand, so he said it again in the Trader's tongue.

"Look at their eyes," One Who Flies said.

Storm Arriving did. The bluecoats wore their hats low over their brows but he could still see their eyes. From beneath the shiny black brims he saw eyes that looked right and left and showed much white.

They are afraid, he realized. *They* are afraid. Suddenly he felt as if they might actually do this thing they came to do.

"Hearten, brothers," he called to his fellow warriors. "Look! Their eyes are full of fear!"

The warriors looked and saw for themselves. They yipped and whooped like boys in their renewed confidence.

The song rose up again, this time with the strength and assuredness that befitted such a procession of the People's might.

One Who Flies turned to him and the chiefs.

"See there? Up ahead? They will try to steer us to the left, up there when we leave the bridge. They want us to go to my father's house."

A bowshot ahead Storm Arriving saw bluecoats standing across the road, blocking their way. One Who Flies had told them that this would be the moment when the war party should strike.

"Here it comes," he shouted to the others. "Where the bluecoats block the road."

The word passed down through the ranks of men.

Two Roads stood on his whistler's back and shouted to the warriors.

"Today, as one, we will count the greatest coup ever known. Be ready. Be strong."

Every man raised his voice in a shout to show his fierceness. Storm Arriving saw several bluecoats shift their stance. He smiled at one of them and laughed at the man's fear.

But every bluecoat had a rifle, and every rifle had a bayonet. Many men would die today, he knew.

May we at least die well, he said to himself.

The thoughts of death ran through his mind and the turn came closer. The buildings beyond it grew larger, taller. He began to sing his death song, and three hundred men joined him.

Nothing lives long,
Only the earth
And the mountains.

They were at the turn. An officer in a blue uniform and a great deal of gold braid motioned to them with a white-gloved hand, guiding them to the left. Storm Arriving looked that way. Ahead was another turn to the left, with bluecoats all along the perimeter. They were riding into a three-sided box lined with rifles.

Give the signal, he prayed. Give it.

One Who Flies called to his walker and the beast gave voice with three rasping calls.

Haoh. Haoh. Haoh.

On the third call the men switched to their war mounts and kicked them into motion. A shout went up—a high ululation, the battle cry of the plains. The officer ahead of them stood aghast as the mounted host leapt toward him. He ducked. Others fled. Most held their ground. The riders hit the barrier of men and plowed through it like ducks through water. Storm Arriving shouted as he rode down upon a soldier. He pointed at him with his bow. The bluecoat raised his rifle and Storm Arriving saw down the length of it to the young man's cool gray eye. The distance closed. Storm Arriving shouted again and the rifle spat smoke and fire. The bullet went wide and Storm Arriving struck the man on the shoulder with his bow as he passed him by.

"Héehe'e," he cried. "That is one."

Gunfire broke out behind him, a spattering like the first raindrops of a coming storm.

"Nóheto," he shouted as they headed down the broad avenue.

They ran their beasts, a headlong press filled with the shrills of whistlers and the whoops of advancing warriors. Storm Arriving knew their goal. Even now it rose above the buildings and trees.

Horses fled before them, and people screamed in healthy panic. Wagons and carts lay overturned and abandoned in the street but the flock of whistlers simply swerved around them or leapt over them entirely.

Ahead he could see more trees and fewer buildings. One building lay directly ahead and it kept growing larger. It was a trick, he decided. They ran as fast as whistler-back allowed and still they hadn't reached it. It only grew taller, higher, larger than he thought possible. It reached so high it frightened him, but it was beautiful, too. Its dome was all white and gleaming in the sunlight. It was the lodge of white stone; the building One Who Flies called The Capitol.

More gunfire, this time from their left. Bluecoats barreled down upon them from on horseback, riding in from another broad roadway. The building was just ahead, rising from the ground like a thundercloud.

"To the right," One Who Flies yelled. "Go around and take it from the front."

Storm Arriving passed the word, though his friend's gestures and the riflemen on their left were enough by themselves.

Bullets snapped around him and he heard whistlers and men go down. He saw One Who Flies turn his walker and aim it at the bluecoats. The pale-haired son of Tsêhe'êsta'ehe shouted at the soldiers of his own country. Storm Arriving kicked his mount into a sharp turn as he took off after the man who had led them to within reach of their goal.

The walker roared and pushed toward the bluecoats with a fury born of her rider's passion. But a walker, even a driven one, was no match for a whistler pushed to its limits.

Storm Arriving swooped in on the far side of One Who Flies, forcing his walker to turn back toward the building.

"They do not care," he shouted at One Who Flies. "They do not care who you are, you crazy *vé'ho'e.*" He grabbed the walker's halter rope and pulled it back toward the rest.

More shots cracked across the open square but the cavalry horses stamped in fear of the great beasts and unsettled the aim of their riders.

Storm Arriving and One Who Flies circled back and rejoined the war party as the last of them left the road and headed around the side of the huge building.

They came around to the front and saw whistlers climbing the white stone steps to the main entrance. One bluecoat fired a pistol, but a blow with a war club sent him reeling.

One Who Flies had described this place well, but it was still hard for Storm Arriving to comprehend it. It was so alien, and to think that such a mountain of stone was hollow!

The warriors drove their mounts up the steps and through the doors. Once inside, they went right or left according to their instructions. Storm Arriving was among the last to enter, and when he did, he gasped.

It was the place of his dream. White stone paved the ground and the walls and the roof above. There was a larger room ahead. He rode into it.

It was huge and round, like a lodge but many times larger. The walls were covered with paintings of men and horses, but the walls rose to another level where many *vé'hó'e* gawked and screamed and fled. Above that were dozens of high windows. The roof curved in but did not close overhead. Through its circular opening he saw another level, and more men who leaned over and pointed down to the invaders. Beyond and above that, he saw even more windows, more walls, all so high that they seemed to enclose the sky. The roof, high above, curved over into a dome and within that vault he saw a painting of the sun and clouds and men who floated in the air like spirits. It was overwhelming and for a moment he could only gape.

The voice of One Who Flies echoed through the room. "Shut the doors!"

Storm Arriving broke from his trance. "Shut the doors," he translated.

One Who Flies and others ran to the doors and closed them. Outside, bluecoats pounded against them. One Who Flies went to each door and set blocks.

"Storm Arriving," he shouted.

"I am here!"

George ran back over to Storm Arriving. "When the Red Shield soldiers have secured all the doors, it will be time for the Kit Foxes and Crazy Dogs to start bringing all the people into the chamber."

The pounding on the doors ceased.

"They'll be back," he said. "And with more."

Two Roads rode up, still on his whistler. Storm Arriving told him of the situation and Two Roads spoke at length.

"Two Roads says we should give up the place-where-we-enter. If we fall back to the doors beyond it, anyone who comes in there will be in a three-way crossfire."

"Who is best to hold this area?" George asked.

"The Little Bowstrings."

"Good. Set them to it."

Men rode in from the hallways, ducking as their tall walkers crouched to clear the doorways. George recognized them as men from the Red Shield soldiers.

"The doors are secure," Storm Arriving translated.

"Thank them. Tell them to stack everything they

can in front of the doors. Are the two main chambers secured as well?"

Storm Arriving asked and the men gestured that they were.

"Good," George said. "Tell the Kit Foxes and Crazy Dogs to begin."

Meriwether rode up to the south steps of the White House. He took off his white gloves and threw them on the ground at Custer's feet.

"They've taken the Capitol Building."

Custer grit his teeth.

"They've blockaded every entrance," the general continued. "If we break our way through, it will be a bloodbath."

Still Custer did not speak.

"Mr. President. There are innocent people in there. The Senate was in session. For God's sake, we've got to do something. We've got to get them out."

"My son is in there, General. I won't have you riding in with guns blazing."

"*Sir,*" the general said, his face red with emotion. "With all *due* respect to you, it was your *son* who set it all in motion. He was in the vanguard, sir, and it was he who ordered the attack."

"You're daft, General."

"Sir, I saw it with my own eyes. Your son practically rode me down with that giant lizard of his. He's leading an insurrection! I've a hundred other witnesses including a dozen officers who will attest to it."

"You mean they'll attest to cover their own hides, no doubt. To cover their own inadequacies."

"I will remind the president that *all* of the entrances have been blocked. *All* of them. Main level and crypt level both; front, side, and rear. What do you think the odds are against a bunch of Indians from the territories riding in and successfully locking up one of the biggest buildings in Washington, all without the help of someone who knows the place? Your son, sir, has betrayed us. He is a traitorous—"

"Enough!"

The two men stood facing each other across implacable lines of battle.

"Just as it was between us during the last war, General, this issue we shall not resolve. Let us instead try to effect a solution that does not require us to agree."

Some of the steel went out of Meriwether's glare. "Well said, Mr. President, and good enough."

"You say they have blockaded every entrance."

"Yes."

"Well, at least that shows that murder is not their intent."

"You can't know that, sir."

"Yes, I can. An Indian never took a position unless he intended to hold it. Murder does not require a headquarters. No, they've come for another reason entirely."

"But what," the general wondered aloud.

"I don't know," Custer answered him, "but I expect it is cross to our purposes."

A soldier on horseback galloped up the drive. The horse sent gravel flying as it skidded to a stop. The soldier dismounted and saluted.

"General, sir," he said. "Major Leeds wants you to know that they've released some of the hostages."

"Thank God," Meriwether said. "How many."

"Several hundred, sir. Visitors and office staff, mostly."

"But none of the congressmen?"

"No, sir. No senators or representatives were released."

Meriwether turned to Custer. "So somehow these savages knew who was a congressman and who wasn't. Do you still believe the boy is innocent?"

Within his breast Custer felt the beginning of a deep and bitter rage.

George pounded the gavel on the desktop. He kept pounding it, trying to be heard above the din.

"I will tell you, Senator. I will tell you what the

meaning of all this is if you and your colleagues will please retake your seats." He pounded some more, but he was only adding to the bedlam, and he threw the gavel down on the desk in frustration.

The scene was surreal. They were in the grand House Chamber with its dark wood and formal red carpet and its high, soaring ceiling. Senators and representatives stood at their seats and in the aisles, every one of them shouting and railing against George and his effrontery. Meanwhile, at each of the doorways were mounted soldiers, their walkers eyeing the crowd of portly men with a hungry eye. Up in the gallery, more soldiers lined the rails, looking and pointing at the members of America's greatest legislative body like little boys pointing at the antics of monkeys at the zoo.

George picked up the gavel again and pounded some more, still to no effect. Finally he signaled to one of the mounted guards.

The walker's blast of sound cowed the statesmen in a heartbeat. George rapped the gavel a final time, for effect rather than to call for silence.

"Distinguished members of Congress, the meaning of all this is to bring to light—"

"Shame!" shouted one of the representatives. "You should be ashamed!"

Others joined in with a chant of "Shame! Shame! Shame!" George pounded the gavel yet again, and this time they quieted down on their own.

"I *am* ashamed, sir. I am heartily ashamed. I am ashamed it has come to this." He pointed to the soldiers who lined the gallery. "These men have come to you, to plead with you, to make you understand what it is you have done to them. What I have seen . . . I am ashamed of my country—"

Shouts rose from some of the men on the floor, but others called for quiet. George had engaged them with rhetoric, and they responded to it, wanting to hear the rest.

"I am ashamed of the crimes my country has visited

upon this people, crimes I have seen with my own eyes, crimes authorized by this very body."

He let them protest that statement for a short while.

"Did you not," he went on above their complaints. "Did you not vote to bring down the awful power of War upon them? Did you not? I have seen what your vote created. Women lying in the mud, slain by American soldiers. Children torn apart by Army bullets. The Army and our president invited these people to a parley for peace and then attacked their families behind their backs. I should be ashamed? By God, I *am* ashamed. What I saw, what *you* authorized, was shameful!"

He looked the congressmen in the eye as he spoke, framing his words for each of them in turn. They scowled at him as he did so, but they listened.

"In fact," he told them, "these men were attacked even on their way here, on their way to see you, to bring their case before you. We left the territories four days ago with four hundred men and on our way here we broke no law, stole no provender, and killed no man but in defense of our own lives. And what happened? The Army attacked us along the Cumberland Trail, and again here in this city, and over a hundred Cheyenne soldiers now lie dead because of it. And for what crime? For what offense were these men punished?"

The room, remarkably, was silent.

"For the crime of being Indians."

"What do you intend to do about it?" said a bespectacled man in the front row.

"Sir, I intend to do nothing." The congressmen exchanged confused glances. "My job here is nearly done. I have brought together the representatives of my nation and the representatives of the Cheyenne Alliance. Two warring factions, now face to face. From here on out, the work is yours."

One man in the middle of the assemblage stood. George recognized him as the senior majority leader, Senator Marcus Duchesnes. Tall, thin, with straight black hair and a hawk-like nose, he stared at George with a black, penetrating glare.

"Just what do you hope to achieve by this, Mr. Custer?"

"Senator," George replied. "I will lay it out for you bluntly so that there will be no misunderstanding. I hope to achieve peace."

Speaks While Leaving watched and listened as one by one the ten chiefs of the People, the ten voices of the ten bands, stood before the *vé'hó'e* leadership and spoke. She watched Storm Arriving and One Who Flies patiently relay the words through the languages, and she watched the hard faces of the *vé'hó'e* and she saw no change.

The dark-clothed men with their high, white collars sat and scowled. The chiefs spoke for a long time, and still the *vé'hó'e* were silent. The chiefs spoke of war and honor and battle and all the bad things the bluecoats had done to the People, but it made no difference to the men who only sat and listened.

Finally she saw her father step up to speak. He did not speak of war or fighting. He spoke of his family, of the People, of the spirits, and of the earth that he loved and worshiped with his every breath. It was then that something remarkable happened.

One of the *vé'hó'e* stood. The man's face was not hard and stern. It was thoughtful and a bit confused. The *vé'ho'e* asked a question.

"How long have your people lived there?"

It was not an important question, but it was a question, and as a question, it led to an answer. Another man asked another question and her father gave him an answer, too, and when her father asked the man a question in return—

"Why do you want our land?"

—suddenly it became a conversation.

She sighed, and the spirits released her.

She floated up to the ceiling and through it. The dark bulk of the building lay below her. On the ground all around it was a necklace of lights; lanterns and torches that flickered in the wind, each illuminating an armed man or two who crouched behind barricades made of overturned wagons and stacks of crates. Hundreds of soldiers, all intent on the great domed building.

At last the vision flared white, then darkened to a wavering yellow. She looked up into the cone of her firelit lodge. She felt the caress of her grandmother's hand, a hand so old that even her calluses had been worn smooth. She heard a drumbeat from a neighboring lodge and heard the blanket of song the crickets wove through the night.

"You heard?" she asked.

"Yes, my granddaughter. Your mother has gone to tell the neighbors. Sleep now."

"There's just no way to get a message in there. We even tried tying a note to a brick and throwing it through a window. The illiterate bastards threw it back, note and all." Meriwether stabbed the poker at the remnants of the evening's fire.

Jacob sat nearby on the divan and Custer sat in an overstuffed chair. All three stared into the reawakening fire.

"We're at an impasse," the general said.

Custer stood and stretched. "Only until daybreak," he said.

"Are you serious?" asked Jacob.

"Yes. We have enough of a black eye about this as it is. If we look like we're capitulating or are afraid to act, the press will eat us alive."

"But what about George?"

Custer could not help but frown at the mention of his son. "He has betrayed his country. He's shamed his uniform and his family."

"But, Autie, surely there's some reason for it."

"For collaborating with the enemy? For capturing a Federal building? For holding the entire Senate hostage?" Custer's laugh was bitter. "No reason is sufficient."

Meriwether, without looking up from the fire, asked the question that had been on Custer's mind since noon.

"What shall be done with him?"

"By all rights he should be hanged as a turncoat and spy."

"Autie!"

"Don't fret, Jacob. I don't want that to happen. It would kill his mother." He sighed: deeply, slowly. "He must be held to account, though."

"Court-martial?" Meriwether asked.

"At least," Custer agreed. "If we hand-pick the judges, he might get off with a lesser sentence. He's disgraced—"

His throat constricted at the depth of it all: the calumny that would be heaped upon his family. He wiped at tears before they could spill.

"Hellfire. Better he had died when the *Lincoln* went down." Custer cleared his throat. "Daybreak, Meriwether. At daybreak you go in there and you take back that building. Take it back and damn the cost."

The chiefs and senators talked into the night, moving from one topic to the next. The chiefs exhibited all of their usual patience as they explained what were, to them, things that required no explanation. Their spiritual bond with the land was especially hard for the congressmen to understand. George was not sure that he understood it fully himself.

Eventually, one of the representatives from Georgia stood. He spoke French, after a fashion, and stepped up to relieve George of his duty. George was glad for the break. His eyes were dry and red from lack of sleep, his voice was hoarse from shouts in battle and the hours of translating. He was only sorry that a similar relief was not available for Storm Arriving, but like many of the proud men of his nation, he showed no signs of fatigue.

He left the House Chamber by a side door and started up the stairs, intent on a seat up in the gallery where he might rest, close his eyes for a bit, but still hear the discussions from down on the floor. He stopped, though, at the sound of slow footsteps outside the staircase. Two men spoke to one another in low tones, their furtiveness confounded by the building's marble halls.

"I can't believe," said the first one, "that old man Custer would have raised such a simpleton. Does he really expect us to be swayed by a few impassioned speeches?"

George leaned into the shadows against the cold stone wall.

"He seems sincere enough," said the other. "And naïve. We can use that to our advantage."

"How so?"

"We're his prisoners here. He won't let us go until we agree to his terms."

"Ah," said the first man. "So we agree to his terms, on the surface."

"Correct. Young Captain Custer can give us the excuse to get out of this politically dangerous war before the House elections and give his father a black eye in the process. Then, next year . . ."

"We can try this all again," the first man said. "Only with our party in control of the House."

The footsteps came closer, and George saw the two congressmen pass by the entrance to the stairwell. Behind them came their Cheyenne guard, silent and uncomprehending of their cynical plans.

George squeezed shut his eyes and grit his teeth. They had not heard the words of the chiefs; they had not felt the truth or seen the evil of their actions. They had not changed nor, he realized, would they. They would smile, and wait, and plot all the while, wanting only expediency and gain and damned be the cost, human or otherwise.

Thoroughly depressed, he continued up the dark staircase, but instead of entering the gallery, he took a detour to the rotunda balcony. Two long stories below him, men with their whistlers and walkers lay dozing or resting or talking quietly on the marble floor of the large round room beneath the dome and the entryway attached to it. He had led them here and promised them a victory. They thought they had won, a great coup to count, not realizing that the battle had just been lost.

He looked up and through the tall windows above him he saw the orange blush of dawn. He wanted a better view of it and left the balcony for one of the offices along the front of the building.

In the darkened room the square office window was ablaze with glorious colors: bright orange, rose pink, and royal purple against a ceiling of steel gray. A bank of clouds stretched across the heavens, heading for the sun on a wind that tightened the flags on their standards.

Red sky at morning, he thought to himself.

Down on the plaza the army sat behind its barricades, just as it had all through the night. George looked at the sky again. It had lost most of its color in just the past few minutes as the sun rose above the level of the clouds. In the west, distant thunder rumbled.

"You're going to get soaked, boys," he said to the soldiers below. Rain began to patter down on the marble steps.

George caught sight of a knot of activity over toward the front steps. He saw one man with a cannon rod and another with a torch. The torchlight glinted along the small six-pounder's barrel.

George had enough time to run out of the office and shout before the cannon fired.

The shot slammed into the heavy front door. Fragments of wood flew, biting into the flesh of those nearby. Their barricades of furniture and bookcases blocked the brunt of the explosion.

"Get out of there!" he shouted, waving frantically. "Back, back! Get out of the way!" He ran for the stairs and leapt down them three and four at a time. On the floor of the rotunda he waved and gesticulated to the soldiers.

"To the sides! *Nóheto!*"

The second round blew through the barriers. It slapped through the torso of one soldier and took off the shoulder of a second before it exploded against the rear wall, sending shards of marble and plaster through the room. A piece struck George in the brow, sending him reeling backward. He brought his left hand to his head and saw that his little finger was gone, and only a shard of bone protruded beyond the high knuckle.

"Aw, Hell," he said and took out his kerchief. He wrapped the cloth tightly around his hand. There was no pain, not yet, but he knew it would come. He tied off the kerchief as best as he could; it would not be good for long.

Custer stood on the balcony, looking down Penn's Sylvania Avenue. The cannonfire signaled that it had begun. He had wanted to be there when it all started, but he had been overridden by several advisors. Requirements for the president's personal safety outweighed his personal wishes in this, as in all things. The wind freshened and he heard the sound of rain tapping on the steps and plants below.

He sipped his coffee and waited.

George stood in the main entryway, still a bit stunned by the blast. The entryway was open, the doors destroyed, the barrier of stacked furniture in splinters. Several Kit Fox soldiers lay dead or nearly so on the floor, their blood black in the blue light of morning. Outside, bluecoats prepared to enter the breach.

"Ame'haooestse!"

George turned as Laughs like a Woman ran up to him. The Indian grabbed George by the collar and hauled him back against the wall. Gunfire shot through the opening and the warriors took cover to either side.

"No," George shouted. "Let me go. I can stop this."

Laughs like a Woman held on to him with his good hand but George strove against his grip.

"They won't kill me," he said. "I am the son of Long Hair." He pulled back hard and the worn fabric of his shirt gave way. He ran to the opening and out into the building rainstorm.

"Hold your fire!" he shouted and held his arms open wide. "I am the son of Long Hair!"

Storm Arriving ran into the rotunda. Men lay dead and debris littered the floor. Through the blasted door he saw One Who Flies standing out in the rain, arms outstretched. Storm Arriving ran to the door but someone knocked him down. Another man stepped over him and ran outside. Thunder rumbled overhead.

Speaks While Leaving reached out from her vantage point in the clouds. Her vision was clear, unaffected by the tears that brimmed in her body's eyes. She saw One Who Flies on the steps, shouting for peace, his arms stretched out like those of his God-that-died-and-lived-again. She saw the bloody rag that wrapped his left hand and saw a man run out of the building. She saw the bluecoats and the man with the white gloves. She heard him shout. She saw the riflemen aim.

George felt the wind chill his face. Raindrops pelted his brow.

"Wait," he said again. "Hold your fire."

Beyond the barricade General Meriwether said, "Aim," and six riflemen leveled their weapons. George saw a white-gloved hand raised high, saw the general's familiar face twisted by hatred and disgust. From behind, George heard a man's voice.

"*Hová'âháne,*" the voice cried out.

No.

The white glove descended.

The riflemen squinted.
Someone stepped up beside him . . .
"Fire!"
. . . and then stepped in front of him.

She cried out in horror as Laughs like a Woman was struck.

Storm Arriving cried out again as his friend fell to the cold stone steps.
"Hová'âháne!"

Custer smiled at the sound of gunfire. "Give 'em Hell, Meriwether," he said and took another sip of coffee.

George stumbled as the former Contrary fell against his legs. He reached down for the man and rolled him onto his back.
His chest was a massive wound. His eyes stared up into the clouds. Rain beat down upon his face.
Lightning reached down from the sky and lit the steps with white light. Thunder pounded on the heads of men and shook the ground beneath their feet.
"Again!" came the command from the barricades. "Ready!"

Storm Arriving saw the bluecoats work the levers of their rifles. He ran out and down the steps. As they lifted their weapons to their shoulders, he placed himself in front of their target, just as his friend had done.

"Aim!"
George looked up as Storm Arriving stepped between him and the riflemen. He heard a man swear.
"Take them both down. Aim!"

Speaks While Leaving struggled against the vision. She had to act.

"Do something!" she screamed. She fought and turned on the thunder being that held her up. "*Do something,*" she said, but his tearful eyes told her no, he would not act.

She reached over and grabbed the skin of the thunder being's arm. Her fingers dug and she ripped from his black skin the lightning bolt that graced his arm. She turned and threw it down upon the scene below, just as the white glove came down again.

"Fire!"

Lightning sizzled through the air and stabbed the marble steps as the rifles fired. A concussion of sound and hot air slammed into everyone nearby. George caught Storm Arriving as he fell back and Army soldiers were knocked from their feet.

Thunder boomed across the plaza and through the city. It reverberated back down from the very clouds that sent it.

Storm Arriving got to this feet and extended a hand. George took it and stood. The body of Laughs like a Woman lay between them, his blood cleaned from his body by the pouring rain.

"God damn it," Meriwether yelled. "You missed them both!" He lifted the flap of his holster and pulled out his pistol. The Colt's long barrel glimmered in the gray light. "I'll shoot you myself, you traitorous bastard."

"General Meriwether, *sir.*" It was a colonel at the general's side. "Sir, he's the president's son."

"He's a traitor!"

"For God's sake, sir." The colonel's hand was reaching for the pistol. "Think of what you're doing! Please, lower your weapon."

George could see Meriwether struggling with his decision. The riflemen looked up at their commander.

"Sir," said one of them. "Don't do it, sir."

The furrow across the general's brow was washed away in the rain and he lowered the shiny Colt to his side.

"Thank you, sir," said the colonel.

Raised voices echoed in the building behind George. He turned and saw Duchesnes and several others make their way past Indian soldiers. One Bear and Two Roads were close behind the congressmen. They all stopped at the top of the steps. The chiefs stood tall, glowering down upon the scene.

"Who is in charge, here?" Duchesnes demanded. The rain drummed down upon his head and shoulders. He looked at the assembled soldiers, American and Indian both, and reiterated his request.

"Who the hell is in charge?"

Meriwether finally stepped forward. "I am, Senator."

"Thank you, General," Duchesnes said, suddenly civil again. "Would you please send up a surgeon? Several men have been wounded and need attention. Then, if you would please clear away all . . . all this." He indicated the barricades and the soldiery. "We are in the middle of an important dialogue, and I do not wish to be interrupted again. Now, gentlemen, if you would rejoin us inside?"

George realized that the senator was addressing him and Storm Arriving.

"You can wait for the surgeon inside, out of the rain. There are some topics that require further discussion and we require both your help and the help of Mr. Arriving. If you please?" He gestured toward the door with an open hand.

George looked down at the body at his feet, then up into the face of Storm Arriving.

"I am sorry," he said, meaning the body at their feet and so much more. "I am so, so sorry."

Storm Arriving closed his eyes and fought against his emotions. He knelt to pick up the body and George bent to help. Together they lifted him and carried him slowly up the steps. As they waited, Storm Arriving began to sing. Two Roads and One Bear joined and together the four of them bore the body inside.

CHAPTER 15

Hatchling Moon, Waning
Fifty-Three Years After the Star Fell
The Place Where Laughs like a Woman
Was Killed

The morning sun shone down upon them from an unbroken sky. Storm Arriving stood at the top of the steps. One Who Flies stood at his side, his wounded hand wrapped in white bandages.

On the stairs stood several *vé'hó'e* who waited to write down all that they heard and saw. The *vé'hó'e* talked among themselves but did not speak to One Who Flies or anyone else.

Standing in the plaza below were most of the soldiers who had survived the trip and the battles with the bluecoats. They stood waiting along with the whistlers and walkers that would carry them all home.

"You are quiet this morning," Storm Arriving said.

"For three days, you and I have been talking for the chiefs. Nothing but talking. I am sick of talking."

The newly repaired doors in the front of the great domed edifice opened up and the chiefs walked out into the sunlight. They walked with slow deliberation to the top of the steps and there they stopped and turned. After them came the rest of the soldiers—Kit Foxes, Crazy Dogs, and Red Shield soldiers, mostly. They carried the shrouded bodies of their fallen comrades, including the body of Laughs like a Woman. There were twenty-four bodies in all, men who had fallen here or down by the foot of the bridge. The soldiers bore them down the steps and loaded them, two-by-two, onto whistlers. It would be a long trip, but every man had agreed that all of these slain—both here and those whose bodies still lay up at the mountain pass—would return to their homeland. Leaving their bones here among these strange people and odd places was not a thing that he or anyone else would accept.

Storm Arriving thought of his family, and of Speaks While Leaving. It would be many days before he was once again among the People. He missed them, especially Speaks While Leaving. For some reason, though, he felt that she knew he was safe and about to start for home.

After the bodies had been readied, the *vé'hó'e* appeared at the doorway. They blinked and squinted as they came outside, as if the sun were an alien thing and unnatural to them. They all wore the same clothes: heavy black fabrics, long and in many layers, covering their entire bodies from their feet to the tops of their hands. They gathered in a group at the head of the stairs, next to the chiefs. Two of them came forward.

The first was the one he and the others had dubbed Dark Eyes, and who One Who Flies called Duchesnes. He was a sharp and intelligent man who had treated the chiefs with great respect. Next to him, however, was a very different creature: Long Hair himself.

Storm Arriving found it difficult even now not to reach for his knife and rush up to the man who had brought death to so many. A moon ago, he would have done it regardless of the consequences, but he had learned a great deal since finding One Who Flies in the cloud-that-fell. Part of that learning had been knowing when not to fight.

Besides, he said to himself, the man looks miserable. I can enjoy that much, and I will enjoy watching as more misery comes upon him.

Dark Eyes began to speak to the chiefs, and the *vé'hó'e* on the steps began to write. One Who Flies translated the words. Storm Arriving translated them in turn, just as he had done for the past three days.

"I would like to thank One Bear and Two Roads and the other chiefs," Dark Eyes said, "for providing us the opportunity to meet and begin the long work of understanding. We have taken the first step, and that has been to put a halt to the violence and aggression that has cost us all so much in recent weeks. This short war is now at an end, and there is peace between our two peoples."

The black-clothed *vé'hó'e* smiled without humor and clapped their hands without enthusiasm. Long Hair did neither, but only stood and stared at his son.

Dark Eyes cleared his throat and continued. "We will meet again soon, to discuss our future and to craft a solution that is agreeable to all." The men applauded his words again and Dark Eyes stepped forward, offering his hand. The chiefs shook his hand, one by one, and then One Bear spoke.

"I give thanks for our new friends and I look forward to the time when we shall meet once more. There are many things yet to be settled and understood, but much can be done when reasonable men sit down to talk. We will leave you now, but we will all sit down again when the cherries begin to ripen." He nodded in farewell and then walked down the steps before his words had passed through the veils of translation. The other chiefs followed him, and when One Who Flies finished telling the *vé'hó'e* what was said, they applauded One Bear's words as they had their own.

Storm Arriving turned to leave, but stopped when he realized that One Who Flies was not with him. His pale-haired friend was still standing at the top of the steps. He and his father faced one another. Long Hair did not look happy.

Storm Arriving had no problem with that.

*   *   *

George heard Storm Arriving call to him.

"Ame'haooestse. *Nóheto, néséne.*" One Who Flies. Let's go, my friend.

"*Héehe'e,*" he said, turning. "I will be there." He looked back at his father. The old man was mired somewhere between indignation and repulsion and didn't seem likely to free himself any time soon. "I'm sorry, Father," George said. "I just couldn't see it done any other way."

He waited for his father to speak, even to open his mouth as if to speak, but he did not. He simply stood there, ramrod stiff and just as cold. Finally, he gave up waiting.

"Tell Mother I love her. I'll miss you all." He started down the stairs.

"You've achieved nothing," his father said. George stopped without turning. "You know that, don't you?"

George nodded, the sunlight off the white steps making his head hurt. "I know," he said. "But I've bought us time. A little time."

He heard his father expel a breath of exasperation. "I can't say how disappointed I am in you," he said.

George waited to see if he would say anything more. He did not.

"Just remember, Father, that those were the last words you chose to say to me."

Then he continued on down the stairs. His walker crouched down for him and he climbed up on her back.

"She looks hungry," he said to Storm Arriving as she stood.

"Just keep her away from my whistler," he said. "I want to get home in one piece."

George laughed. "Let's go home," he said.

Custer watched as his son sat stop a lizard the size of a house and shared a joke with an Indian, just as he himself might joke with Samuel or Jacob. It rankled. More than the jeers of the press, more than his wife's silence, more than the feigned remonstrance of

Congress, watching his son so easy and friendly with one of *them* rankled him.

And saddened him.

He had never known George well enough to joke with him in such a way. Now, he was riding away, and Custer felt that every last chance was riding away with him.

The great lizard barked—a harsh, ugly sound—and the others like it did likewise. The smaller, horse-sized lizards whistled and changed color from green to white to red. Then the whole company began to move.

"George!" Custer dashed down the steps. "George!"

His son heard his call and stopped. Custer ran up to the beast that carried his son but stopped as it turned its head toward him. With a simple touch, George made the beast lie down on the ground, and Custer walked the rest of the way to speak with his son.

"Be careful," he said, and stopped, stymied and unable to think of anything else. He forced himself through it. "I . . . I just didn't want the last words I said . . . Just be careful, Son. Your mother worries so." He held out his hand.

George stepped down from the back of the lizard but did not take his hand. Instead the young man reached out and took his father in an embrace. Custer stiffened, then put his arms around his son and held him tightly. It would be, he knew—they both knew—the last time.

She was up with the morning star. It had been several days since her last vision, several days since the war party had left the city of white stone and headed for home. She wanted to get out, alone and away from the looks and unspoken questions of her family and neighbors. She wrapped a blanket about her shoulders and stepped quietly out of the lodge.

The sky was hard and clear; the air, crisp and still. The camp of the people lay spread out at the feet of the surrounding knolls and grades that sheltered the

Little Sheep River. She ran between the lodges on feet made light by anticipation, heading out toward the flocks.

The whistlers huddled close together for warmth beneath the clear night and had colored themselves a pale brown to blend in. The flock was nearly indistinguishable from the terrain, appearing in the dim starlight like a stretch of tumbled ground.

"Two Cuts," she called softly. "*Hip-ip-ip.* Two Cuts."

A crested head rose up on a long neck.

"Come to me. Come."

Two Cuts stood and stretched before he gingerly made his way out from the rest of his kin. He came up to her and she scratched him in the place-that-whistlers-love. Then he crouched and she got up on his back.

Bareback on the whistler, she nudged him into motion, supporting herself on hands and knees, guiding him with a word or a dig of her toe. He took her away from the camp and away from the river. They ran over the hilly crests—each one higher than the last—like a boat against the rising tide. They climbed up to a high place that she knew well, and there she called Two Cuts to a halt.

The hilltop was graced by an outcropping of stone and a single tamarack tree. The tree was the height of ten men and, due to its height and its solitude, had long been used as a landmark by the People. She let Two Cuts graze while she clambered up to the top of the tall pile of rock nearby.

She could see to the edge of the world. The fingernail moon was up and almost washed away by the nearly risen sun. The sky along the horizon was a pale blue-green, and growing lighter with each moment.

She frowned. It grew too light too fast, faster than was possible, faster than the world allowed.

"No," she moaned. "I am not ready." She crouched down to grip the stone to keep from falling. The vision light coursed over her, and the stone stole all of her warmth. She cried out in anguish as she was taken from her world and into the place of dreams.

There was light, as there always was, and the light lessened to reveal an open plain. At her side were her two guides, the thunder beings. They stood with her as the vision unfolded.

The land undulated like a shaken blanket, and when it settled, it was a camp by a wide river. It was the place where the People camped near Cherry Stone Creek, but it was not like any camp she had ever seen. There were many buffalo skin lodges, just like the one she had left a short time ago, but there were also among them some large earthen lodges. She looked at the people who walked and played and worked throughout the camp and saw many of the Earth Lodge Builders there: Hidatsa, Mandan, and even the shy and reclusive Arikara. Here, at Cherry Stone Creek, far from their homes on the Big Greasy, they lived and worked together with the People.

She looked further. Beyond the camp she saw plant-ings of beans and corn growing and beyond that she saw men and women of many tribes all working to plant more crops. They used tools she had never seen: they used hardbacks to pull large wedges through the earth, and they dug trenches to bring the water from the river down to the cropland.

The thunder being on her left, his arm still scarred from where she tore the lightning from his skin, pointed to one of the earthen lodges. Smoke rose up from the smokehole and the sounds of clanging metal could be heard echoing from within it. The thunder beings brought her down to the place and they walked through the walls like ghosts.

To one side, men worked at hot fires and beat hot metal on an iron stone. To the other side, men worked at melting down silver and gold and casting them into the small disks that the *vé'hó'e* prized so greatly. Then she was taken out of the lodge and back up into the sky.

She looked back over her shoulder as she was carried up toward the clouds. Behind her she saw the camp change. The lodges became buildings, the paths became roads. The land shrank below her and she saw the People move across their country, following the hunt, protecting the borders, while their camps became villages and towns. She saw machines and weaponry, and she grew afraid.

"We will become them," she said aloud.

The thunder being pointed once more and she saw dancing in the center of the town. She saw men sitting in a circle in a small room, reverently passing a finely decorated pipe between them. She saw men who now rode whistlers as they watched over and protected their herds of buffalo, and she saw the men sing to the spirit of the beast as they brought it down to provide food for their families. She saw a grandmother teaching her daughter how to make skillet-bread and showing her how to always leave a piece to the side for the spirits to enjoy.

She knew it was possible then; to change and yet to remain the same.

"My thanks," she said to the thunder beings. She looked up into the clouds and the sky turned white.

She lay on the boulder and felt the rough stone beneath her. Her sight returned and she blinked to clear it. The sun was up, streaming in from just above the horizon. The light glinted off something near her hand, a shiny spot within a crack in the boulder, a place that could be lit only by the rays of the rising sun. She reached within the crack and pulled out a stone. It was lustrous and globular. It gleamed like metal. She pushed at the stone above the crack and a piece of it came away. Within the boulder was a vein of white stone and within the white stone was another vein of yellow metal as wide as two of her fingers. She thought of the vision, and thought of the future of her People and the other tribes that lived in this land.

We will have to be careful, she thought.

Two Cuts whistled, a long and keening note. She looked up and saw him intent on something several hilltops away, far beyond the camp. She peered into the distance, and Two Cuts whistled again. There came a whistle in return, faint and nearly lost in the sound of the wind through the tamarack tree.

Then she spotted them. A long line of whistlers, tiny shadows cresting a far-off ridge. They were home.

She grabbed the piece of yellow metal and tucked it into her belt pouch, then replaced the stone to hide the boulder's secret. In a heartbeat she was up on Two Cuts' back and they were off at speed. She held on to him as tightly as she could, leaning low along his back and praying he didn't turn too sharply. At every hillcrest she stopped and made Two Cuts call until she heard the reply. When she came within sight, she saw that she was not the only one riding to welcome the returning soldiers. Dozens of others had heard the calls and were converging on the group. As they all came together, there was a great outcry of joy and song.

She saw them near the front of the column, the men who had helped her define her life: One Bear, Storm Arriving, and One Who Flies. Her father and One Who Flies waved as she rode up. Storm Arriving smiled more broadly than she had ever seen. They both leapt from their whistlers and embraced one another, standing still in the ebb and flow of the growing celebration.

"I have never been so glad to see anyone," she said into his ear. His arms were around her, enwrapping her and squeezing her. She felt his hands upon her and felt his body press against the length of her own. She reveled in it, savoring the moment.

"May I talk to your father?" he asked.

She kissed his neck and bounced on her toes as she held on to him. She beamed with happiness.

"Yes," she said. "Yes. And soon."

The walls of the Council Lodge had been rolled up to let the wind blow through the meeting place. It looked like the entire camp sat and listened from outside the circle of lodgepoles.

"You have won the first battle," George said as he stood before the Council, "but you have yet to win the war. It will take time, and you must be very careful. Do not trust them. Do not depend on their word."

"You are not very kind to your own people," Three Trees Together said. "Are you still so angry with them?"

George thought about it. "I am angry with some of them," he told the ancient chief. "But more importantly, I know them too well to ignore the danger. They still consider this land to be part of their nation. All they have agreed to do so far is not to kill you for defending your homes."

He sat down and listened as Storm Arriving translated his words. He heard the translation travel out beyond the lodge in a wave of whispers, and saw the chiefs as they considered the notion.

"I have a question," said Two Roads. "You all know that I was with the war party that went to the city-of-white-stone. I saw One Who Flies fight alongside our own soldiers. He led us to a great coup against the *vé'hó'e,* and I believe him to be a brave and passionate man. But I have seen the great strength of the Horse Nations with my own eyes. How shall we overcome such strength?"

George stood to reply. "I do not know," he said. "Ultimately, you will have to find a better way than warring with them. Sooner or later, they will win any fight through sheer numbers. There has to be a middle road that can be traveled, a way for both nations to live side by side. You must protect your lands, and you must protect your ways, but there are also some things you might learn from them. Not everything about them is bad." He shrugged. "For now, though, talk will only hold them back for so long. After that, we will need stronger weapons, *vé'hó'e* weapons, to match them strength for strength. That is the only way the king-across-the-water has held the Grandmother

Land of the north, and the same is true for the Iron Shirts to the west of us. Perhaps we can trade for them, though with whom and with what I do not know. I'm sorry, Two Roads. We'll just have to figure that part out later."

George sat down and waited for the words to be translated. After a moment of silence had passed, One Bear stood. He reached into his shirt and pulled out an object the size of a hen's egg. Even from across the lodge George could see that it was a large nugget of gold. He tossed it to George. It was heavy, bulbous, and gleamed with natural purity.

"My daughter has been given another vision," One Bear said. "I think it might hold some answers."

CHEYENNE PRONUNCIATION GUIDE AND GLOSSARY

There are only 14 letters in the Cheyenne alphabet. They are used to create small words which can be combined to create some very long words. The language is very descriptive, and often combines several smaller words to construct a longer, more complex concept. The following are simplified examples of this subtle and intricate language, but it will give you some idea of how to pronounce the words in the text.

LETTER	PRONUNCIATION
a	"a" as in "water"
e	"i" as in "omit" (short "i" sound, not a long "e")
h	"h" as in "home"
k	"k" as in "skit"
m	"m" as in "mouse"
n	"n" as in "not"
o	"o" as in "hope"
p	"p" as in "poor"
s	"s" as in "said"
š	"sh" as in "shy"
t	"t" as in "stop"
v	"v" as in "value"
x	"ch" as in "Bach" (a soft, aspirated "h")
'	glottal stop as in "Uh-oh!"

The three vowels (a, e, o) can be marked for high pitch (á, é, ó) or be voiceless (whispered), as in â, ê, ô.

Glossary

Ame'haooestse	Tsétsêhéstâhese for the name One Who Flies
Bands	Cheyenne clans or family groups. Bands always travel together, while the tribe as a whole only gathers in the summer months. Bands are familial and matrilineal; men who marry go to live with the woman and her band. The ten Cheyenne bands are:

> The Closed Windpipe People (also Closed Gullet or Closed Aorta)
> The Scabby Band
> The Hair Rope Men
> The Ridge People
> The Tree People (also Log Men or Southern Eaters)
> The Poor People
> The Broken Jaw People (also Lower Jaw Protruding People or Drifted Away Band)
> The Suhtai
> The Flexed Leg People (also Lying on the Side with Knees Drawn Up People, later absorbed into Dog Soldier society)

	The Northern Eaters
The Cloud People	Tsétsêhéstâhese phrase for the Southern Arapaho.
Contrary	One of up to four men who had an overwhelming fear of thunder; by accepting owner-

ship of a thunder bow (Hoh-nóhkavo'e) they gained some of the thunder's power, but also had to live a "contrary" life, living apart, remaining unmarried, and speaking and acting backward. Finally the Contrary won Thunder's pity, their fear was lifted, and they could return to a normal life. A Contrary was an exceedingly brave soldier.

The Cradle People — Tsétsêhéstâhese phrase for the Assiniboine.

The Crow People — Tsétsêhéstâhese phrase for the Crow.

The Cut-Hair People — Tsétsêhéstâhese phrase for the Osage.

Éénomóhtahe — He got well.

Eestseohtse'e — Tsétsêhéstâhese for the name Speaks While Leaving.

Émomóhtóhta — He has diarrhea.

The Greasy Wood People — Tsétsêhéstâhese phrase for the Kiowa.

Hámêstoo'êstse (singular), *Hámêstoo'e* (plural) — Sit!

Héehe'e — Yes.

He'kotoo'êstse (singular), *He'kotoo'e* (plural) — Be quiet!

Hó'ésta — Shout!

Hohnóhka — Tsétsêhéstâhese word for Contrary.

Hoohtsetsé-taneo'o — The Tree People band

Hová'âháne — No.

The Inviters — Tsétsêhéstâhese phrase for the Lakota.

Ke'éehe — Child's word for grandmother.

The Little Star People — Tsétsêhéstâhese phrase for the Oglala Lakota.

Maahótse — The four Sacred Arrows of the People.

Ma'heo'o	Words that can be loosely
Ma'heono	translated as "that which is sacred," referring to the basis of Cheyenne spirituality and mystery.
Mo'e'haeva'e	Tsétsêhéstâhese for the name Magpie Woman.
Náe'tótahe	I am afraid.
Náháéána	I am hungry.
Náhéméhotâtse	She loves you.
Náhevése'enôtse	She is my friend.
Námésêhétáno	I want to eat.
Nápévomóhtahe	I am feeling good.
Nahe'pe	My rib.
Ne-a'éše	Thank you.
Né'éstséhnêstse	Come in.
Néháéána	Are you hungry?
Nenáasêstse	Come here.
Népévomóhtâhehe	Are you feeling good?
Nevé-stanevóo'o	The Four Sacred Persons, created by Ma'heo'o, who guard the four corners of the world.
Nóheto	Let's go!
Néséne	My friend.
Nóxa'e	Wait!
Ótahe	Pay attention!
Ota'tavehexovona'e	Tsétsêhéstâhese for the name "Blue Shell Woman."
Séáno	The happy place for the deceased.
The Sage People	Tsétsêhéstâhese phrase for the Northern Arapaho.
Soldier Societies	The military organizations within the tribe. Membership in a society was voluntary and had no relation to the band in which one lived. The six Cheyenne soldier societies are:
	Kit Foxes (also Fox Soldiers)

Elkhorn Scrapers (also Crooked Lances)
Dog Men (or Wolf Soldiers)
Red Shields (or Buffalo Bull Soldiers)
Crazy Dogs
Little Bowstrings

The Snake People — Tsétsêhéstâhese phrase for the Comanche.

To'êstse **(singular),** *To'e* **(plural)** — Wake up!

Tsêhe'êsta'ehe — Long Hair (General G. A. Custer).

Tsétsêhéstâhese — The Cheyenne people's word for themselves.

Vá'ôhtáma — The place of honor at the back of the lodge.

Vé'ho'e **(singular),** *Vé'hó'e* **(plural)** — Lit. spider, from the word for "cocooned," and now the word for whites.

Vé'ho'e — The Tsétsêhéstâhese name for the Spider-Trickster of legend.

The Wolf People — Tsétsêhéstâhese phrase for the Pawnee.

Xaomemehe'e — Tsétsêhéstâhese for the name Skunk Smell Woman.

The Year the Star Fell — In the year 1833, the Leonid meteor shower was especially fierce. The incredible display made such an impression on the Cheyenne of the time, that it became a memorable event from which many other events were dated.